ROUGH BLOODY DIAMONDS

The diamonds are theirs for the picking but first
they must deal with the rough diamonds

Tony Waters

This book is a work of fiction. Where the story uses the names of historical characters it does so in a fictitious manner as a product of the writer's imagination. The same applies to historical events.

This is for the love of my life – yes my wife,
"Bobby"

ACKNOWLEDEMENTS

The author wishes to thank Michael Brown, English teacher, writer and friend for editing the manuscript and for his encouragement. Thanks also to James Waters (with input from Hywell Waters) for the cover design

CHAPTER ONE

The port of Beira in Mozambique lies and fries at the mouth of the Pungwe River. In 1891 it was a dreadful place of corrugated iron buildings with narrow ankle-deep sandy streets and sidewalks of black mud, top-dressed with a thin coating of sand, held in place by a balustrade of wooden stakes.

From this settlement river boats steamed up the river as far as the outpost of Fontesvilla which was thirty-five miles upstream. The remainder of the long trip to Umtali was overland, a rugged foot-slogging journey.

It was the beginning of May and fortunately the start of the few cooler months of the year. Travelling this route during the long hot Southern African summer was not to be recommended. This was when heavy rains turned normally dry river beds into raging torrents, extending the journey by many weeks.

At this time Cecil John Rhodes, the De Beers mining magnate, was in a race with President Kruger of the Transvaal to annex the land north of the Limpopo River. Meanwhile the Portuguese in Mozambique were looking to extend their territory westwards.

Both were already in dispute with the British over the territory. For this reason, Rhodes was encouraging as many of his countrymen as possible to participate in his great plan to help colonise Mashonaland or, as some called it, Zambesia.

Meanwhile the Ndebele people, a breakaway group from the Zulus, had settled several years earlier just across the Limpopo River. Their current king, Lobengula, considered himself the ruler over all the tribes between the Zambezi and Limpopo rivers; he kept the local Mashonas subservient by unleashing his warriors on regular killing raids. The recipients of these assaults literally took to the hills.

⚔

Patrick van Zyl was in his mid-thirties, of medium build with prematurely greying hair and beard. He was attractive to women, of whom he had known many, with his deep blue eyes and engaging smile. By trade he was a blacksmith/gunsmith. He was an excellent shot: back in Ladysmith, in Natal, he was known not only for his skill on the shooting range, but also for his expertise in the bedroom.

He had leased his business in Natal to investigate the possibilities of starting a similar venture in the new country of Mashonaland to the north. The fact that an attractive widow was offering to keep house for him on a permanent basis may also have had some influence on his decision to broaden his horizons. He had no set agenda for when he arrived there. He would simply play it by ear.

The skipper of the paddle-boat, the Kimberley, was Captain Dickie. He was a brawny man who had lost two fingers of his right hand as a result of blood poisoning, caused by punching a drunken passenger in the mouth.

The voyage up the Pungwe to Fontesvilla could normally be completed during the hours of daylight, but much depended on the constantly moving sandbanks and how many of these the steamer encountered. In the case of Captain Dickie's vessel, any delay was caused not so much on the degree of difficulty in re-floating, but rather on his own and his passengers' liking for Scotch whisky. It was not uncommon for him to take twenty hours to cover the distance. Mostly he made a greater profit from the bar takings than from the ticket sales.

Mr Rhodes knew of this and on the single occasion he had used the Kimberley, he first asked Captain Dickie how much liquor he had on board. He did not like the answer.

"How much for the lot? I'll buy it." he said. A price was agreed and the trip was for once completed in twelve hours.

Departure time was just before dawn and a heavy mist lay upon the water. When Patrick eventually located the steamer, a voice shouted out of the gloom, "Mr van Zyl, is it?"

"My friends call me Pat."

"We've been waiting for you, Pat. Welcome aboard the Kimberley. I trust the mosquitoes that over-populate this backwater have left sufficient blood in your veins to let you continue your travels."

"And you'll be Captain Dickie." They shook hands.

"Given time, you'll learn the necessary ratio of alcohol to blood that renders the prick of these blood-suckers impotent," the captain chuckled.

"No doubt I'll need some tutoring on the subject," grinned Pat.

"It'll be my pleasure to do so on the trip ahead. It helps to while away the hours."

Pat noticed the other three passengers already on board were seated under a canopy in the bow where it was cooler. A few minutes later the crew cast off and with two hoots and a toot on the whistle they were on their way, slowly due to the poor visibility.

It took all of Captain Dickie's experience to negotiate the many small islands that suddenly loomed ahead. It was only his deftness at the wheel that prevented them running aground.

Gradually the sun's rays dissolved the vapour and then there was a moment of disorientation. Pat was puzzled to see that the boat appeared to be moving with the current rather than against it. He mentioned this to the captain.

"Aye, you're right." Captain Dickie looked sheepish. Directly ahead and to the right was the wharf they had left an hour and a half ago. Pat saw the puzzled looks of the other passengers and shrugged, thinking what a way this was to start a voyage.

Captain Dickie seemed unperturbed as he yelled, "Turn-about!" and once more they were on their way upstream heading to Fontesvilla.

With the mist cleared Pat could see the thick green vegetation on both sides of the wide river. The mud banks were alive with basking crocodiles. Pods of hippopotami wallowed nonchalantly in the water, paying no attention to the boat motoring past them. He saw plenty of other wildlife on the banks, including elephants, buffalo and waterbuck with their rumps looking as if someone had painted a target on them. Waterfowl bobbed on the current while cranes stalked the shallows.

It became hotter as the day wore on. There was some relief for them as they wet their shirts over the side and put them back on – "D and D," explained the captain, "dunking and donning." A large canvas water-bag hung from the canopy but, despite the fact that the contents had been boiled, it still tasted foul.

At precisely 10 am Captain Dickie called out, "The bar is now open,"

This was welcomed by all except a little man named Smithers, who had opened a book as soon as it had been light enough to read and was unmoved by the announcement.

A crew member appeared with a tray of glasses and a bottle of whisky and handed it to the captain, who removed the cork with a flick of finger and thumb so it spun away into the river. No one added water to their whisky.

"Mmm," sighed Pat as he raised his glass and drank, "that kills the taste of hippo piss, doesn't it?"

"Here's to the best mosquito repellent of them all," toasted the man opposite, who had introduced himself as Brian Wood-Gush. Brian was a mountain of a man and, as he was to reveal later, came from a wealthy family of Bristol accountants. His problem was that his slide rule was out of harmony with those of his elder brother and sister; they had encouraged him to explore distant lands, the more distant the better. Pat recognised in him a kindred spirit and sensed that the trip to Fontesvilla might not be too dull after all.

The only other passenger was a stout little Englishman, a freelance photographic journalist called Colin Grieve, commissioned by The Times of London to capture the atmosphere of Mashonaland and portray it to the British public. His vast alcohol intake quickly became apparent and Brian, no slouch himself when partaking of the amber liquid, named him Grievous Bodily Harm, soon to be shortened to Grievous.

By noon the passengers, including the captain but not Smithers, had all entered into the spirit of this Pungwe adventure when Dickie introduced them to one of the boat's sporting pastimes. It was called "walking the dog". This entailed wrapping a large smelly catfish in a piece of old fishing net with only half the body enmeshed. It was then dropped overboard on the end of a long length of rope which was fed out. The idea was that a crocodile would take the bait and the net would snag on its teeth. Then the game began.

"A volunteer?" invited the skipper.

"Aye, captain." Big Brian raised his hand.

One of the crew baited the line and Captain Dickie showed him how to swing it out. He then eased the throttle to a slow trawling speed. Brian swung the catfish out into the river and passed the line once around the stern bollard. He took a tight grip on the rope and braced himself with a foot on the bollard. Five minutes elapsed before the water suddenly swirled beneath the surface about fifty feet off the stern near the bait. The rope immediately became taut and the boat shuddered as a crocodile took the bait. While the captain disengaged the paddles from the engine, letting the vessel drift back with the current, Brian hauled in the slack, closing the distance between the boat and the crocodile.

"The idea now," explained the captain, "is to let the croc tire it- self out completely. Then we bring it up alongside, keeping a tight line. Next we re-engage the paddles and continue up-river, walk- ing the doggie."

The crocodile was putting up a mighty fight, barrel-rolling and thrashing its tail. Pat moved in to help a perspiring and grunting Brian on the rope. This was a youngish reptile about six feet long with great strength and vigour. Its upper jaw was snapping up and down like some giant mechanical bellows as it tried to rid itself of the net which was snagged firmly in its teeth.

During the commotion Grievous was hopping up and down and in between gulps from his glass was hollering useless advice.

"Chuck it back, you big ox, it's too bloody small. When my sister's sausage dog was run over by a steam roller, it was bigger than that."

"Shut up," panted Pat. With those words hardly out of his mouth, they hit a sandbank. Brian and Pat had hold of the rope to steady themselves, but Grievous was grabbing wildly in the air at non-existent handholds and went over the side like a sack of coal and hit the river a few feet from the flailing reptile. The water was shallow and Grievous soon popped up like a champagne cork.

"Shit!" he cried, groping wildly in the air. "Get me out. Get me out, you buggers."

Brian waved back at him. "Want a piece of soap?

Pat chuckled. "Be sure to wash behind your ears."

Fortunately for Grievous, though he was too pre-occupied to be aware of it, the fight had finally gone out of the crocodile and its struggles, compared to a few minutes earlier, were relatively feeble. Tears of mirth rolled down the cheeks of passengers and crew alike, and even Smithers was cackling away at the spectacle of a highly agitated Grievous trying to haul his fat belly back on board, only to flop, gasping, back into the river.

"Tell you what," called Pat over his shoulder, "pay for the next two rounds and we'll have you out in a jiffy. What do you say?" As he spoke, the crocodile gave one last mighty swipe of his tail, missing Grievous by perhaps two feet. Had it connected, it would likely have decapitated him.

"D...d...damnation," stammered Grievous, almost in tears. "OK. OK! You win, but get me out now."

"Of course! We're all ready for a top-up."

With Grievous back on board and the weary crocodile released to fight another day, the sport was over. Now the skipper had the paddles in reverse while two crewmen were levering the boat off the sandbank with long thick poles. Then they were underway again. Grievous bought the next two rounds of drinks, but not without much complaining interspersed with a good deal of profanity.

They ran aground three more times, perhaps deliberately, with the longest stop being on the famed Bigamiti sandbank, giving them plenty of time to consume more whisky, which Dickie was more than willing to supply. The boat eventually arrived at its destination after dark with the passengers more than a little unsteady on their feet.

"Another successful voyage," mused Captain Dickie as he watched his disembarking passengers weave away into the darkness in search of somewhere either to continue their party or fall into a bed for the night, depending on each individual's stamina.

━⊰╂⊱━

Fontesvilla was the last post of civilisation between Beira and Chimoio, one hundred miles further west. Civilisation here consisted of a collection of corrugated iron buildings, including a church. All were on stilts so that in the wet season, when the river rose and the mangrove reclaimed the area, the inhabitants could punt between the various structures. Smithers took one look at the settlement from the steamboat's railing and promptly booked a return ticket to Beira

Pat, Brian and Grievous' staggerings eventually led them to the only hotel where they were given a room at five shillings each for the night. There were no curtains and the only furnishings were the beds without mattresses. After one last drink in the hotel bar, it mattered not to them where they slept.

The next morning, long after the sun had risen, it was not the smell of sizzling bacon and eggs that roused them but a high-pitched wailing.

"What on earth is that confounded noise?" mumbled Pat, sitting up and rubbing his eyes.

"It's a woman crying in distress," replied Brian with a yawn. "I've heard it too many times before not to recognise it."

They woke up Grievous and the three of them staggered out into a yard at the back of the hotel where a little black boy was sweeping the ground with a yard broom made of reeds. Pat asked where the ablutions were and the boy pointed to a ramshackle iron hut in a corner of the yard.

Thirty minutes later the trio emerged from the primitive facility feeling once more a part of the human race, having shaved and taken a cold shower.

The wailing persisted intermittently so they walked up the street towards it. A crowd had gathered before what seemed to be the church. A grief-stricken woman sat on a box while people fussed around her attempting to offer comfort.

"What's the problem?" Grievous asked an elderly man at the back of the gathering.

"The poor lass lost her husband to the fever last night. The body's lying in the church at the foot of the altar."

"Isn't that where dead people should lie before they are moved to their final resting place?"

"Aye," said the man. "The problem is that we can't proceed until someone gets rid of the bees." He seemed amused by the situation.

"Hell, man, are you saying that the bees are in the box with the body?"

"Exactly!" By now the man was finding it hard to control his laughter.

Pat, fanning himself with his hat against the increasing heat of the day, looked at his two companions. "It doesn't look like any of this lot is up to the job so we'll have to do something, I suppose. Agreed?"

"What do you suggest we do, go in, snatch the body and run?" asked Brian.

"No. It looks like some of these fellows have already tried that," said Pat. He pointed to several men, clearly in pain, who were pressing wet cloths against their faces and bare arms. "We need to be a little less confrontational and more subtle than that. We'll have to smoke them out. Here's what we'll do."

Fifteen minutes later they each held two string bags filled with smouldering dung. "The idea," Pat explained, "is to do a flanking attack through the side door of the building, throw in the bags, wait for the smoke to do its work unless we want an uncomfortable exit, then rush the body box out through the front door."

All went well until they entered the church to collect the box. The air was so thick with smoke that visibility was down to a few feet and they did not know the layout inside the church.

"Where's the bloody coffin?" yelled Brian.

"Watch your language," said Pat. "Remember where you are."

"That's the problem, man. I don't know where I am." Brian crashed into a chair and fell heavily. He cursed again.

"Here it is," said Grievous, coughing. "Come on, let's grab the body and get out before we asphyxiate."

"What about the bees?" asked Pat. "Are they docile yet?"

"They seem quiet enough," replied Grievous. He was standing over the coffin.

The smoke had started to rise and they could now make out their surroundings so with Grievous holding the lighter end and leading the way and with Brian and Pat at the other end, they carried the box briskly towards the double front doors.

Grievous kicked open the doors and the coughing gasping pallbearers emerged, blinking in the sunlight. A small cheer went up from the townsfolk.

"Job done, fellas," said Pat as they lowered the coffin to the ground. He was wrong. No sooner had they straightened up than the bees, equally revived by the fresh air and looking for some revenge, buzzed out from under the loose-fitting lid.

Brian howled and swatted at the bees with his hat. "Quick, someone tell us the way to the cemetery."

A man pointed and said, "It's half a mile in that direction on the right. Just follow your nose. The hole's been dug."

They picked up the coffin and moved fast towards the cemetery, but the bees were equal to the pace and formed a halo around Grievous' head, whose shouts of pain did nothing to distract them. They reached the graveyard and looked around for a mound of earth. Brian spotted it first and guided Grievous towards it.

"What now?" panted Pat when they reached the graveside.

Brian said, "Drop him in the hole and let's get out of here. The burial formalities and prayers can wait until these bloody bees have settled." So without ceremony, they lowered the coffin into the grave and took off back to the town.

The new widow was still being comforted at the church, but seemed much relieved when Pat told her that the body had been safely delivered.

"I suggest you wait half an hour and then proceed with the burial."

"Thank you, sirs." The woman sniffed. "I don't know what I would have done without you."

"Think nothing of it, madam." Brian doffed his hat. "Happy to help."

Later, when the three men were lunching in the hotel on curried corned beef, rice plus an assortment of uninvited insects, Pat raised the matter of the bees. "I wonder what attracted them to the coffin! It's not as if there were any floral wreaths."

"Maybe the poor chap had something in his pockets, we'll never know," said Brian

During the following days the townspeople had a collection for the widow and within a few days she was on her way to Beira from where she planned to catch a steamship to Cape Town.

News some weeks later reached Fontesvilla that before reaching Cape Town the grieving lady had become engaged to one of the ship's officers. As one wit quipped when he heard about it, "If her new husband snuffs it like the last one, all she has to do is toss the body over the side."

⭆⭅

Pat had been giving the immediate future much thought. It made sense to him that he and his two new-found friends pool their resources and make the next stage of the journey together, at least as far as Umtali. He called a meeting to find out what the others thought. All of them had spent time quizzing the locals and were aware of the hardships that lay before them.

"We seem to have a lot in common, so why not?" said Brian to Pat's proposal. "I for one would enjoy having company."

"I agree," said Grievous. His face was still a little puffed and rutted from the bee stings, but the pain seemed to have eased.

Apart from such items as tea, coffee, sugar and salt and their toiletry requirements, there was no need to carry much else in the way of provisions. They had heard that there was plenty of plains game and wild fowl along the route, so there would be no shortage of meat and by bartering with the locals they could obtain pumpkin, sweet potatoes and other vegetables that might be seasonal.

Coloured beads, mirrors, blankets and brightly patterned material, called *limbo*, were much in demand and it was these goods that would also be used to pay the porters they would hire.

Pat had a small tarpaulin that would provide some cover from the elements if needed. Each man had his own blankets and a palliasse rolled up in what was called a houndsfield, the standard bedding for the white man travelling in this part of Africa. Importantly, they had their hunting rifles, with Pat's choice being the envy of the others, he being the weapons expert that he was.

"Two porters each should be enough," suggested Pat.

"Perhaps we should take an extra one in case someone drops out. I'm told this happens all the time," said Brian.

"Good idea," Grievous said.

Pat stood up. "That's settled then. I'll see to it."

"When do you reckon to start, Pat?"

"The day after tomorrow, Sunday, if that suits you and Brian."

"Why not Saturday?"

"Well, I hear the biggest general dealer's store in the town is sponsoring a shooting competition tomorrow and the first prize is a case of whisky. That might come in handy to ease aching bones along the way."

"Confident, are you?" asked Grievous.

"Let's just say that I've won the odd bit of silverware in my day. I also hear that the clerk at the store is opening a book so, without wishing to appear a braggart, you fellas could do worse than put any extra cash you might have on me. I'm going to."

There were thirty entries in the competition and it was to be run on a knockout basis. The firing line was marked out across the main street, fifty paces up from the first building on the edge of town and looking down towards the river.

An elevated railway, consisting of rails borrowed from the slipway at the river, propped up by scaffolding and slightly higher on one side, was erected across the road. The actual target was an empty whisky bottle and tumbler placed on a tray in the centre of the stable door, which in turn was mounted on trolley wheels. When given a nudge, the trolley would run right to left along the rails across the road in front of the contestants. Someone's imagination had been working overtime.

A hit on the whisky bottle earned the shottist two points. Hit both and the score was five. The ten highest scorers went through to the second round, at which point the angle of the rail was increased, thus speeding up the movement of the target. A competitor could fire as many shots as he could manage before the target came to a halt.

Pat's favourite rifle was a Winchester 40-44 lever action, but one that he had customised in his workshop in Ladysmith. It had been carefully tooled and had an ivory inlaid stock and it would drop a buffalo in the right hands. He had been drawn twenty-second in the order of fire and that suited him fine.

A real carnival atmosphere prevailed. The street was decorated with bunting and fires had been lit on the river bank to later grill impala fillets and bake fish and sweet potatoes.

By the time it was Pat's turn to step up to the line, only four entrants had hit both the bottle and the tumbler, while six had hit the bottle only. Pat took his stance and took several deep breaths. He lifted his rifle to his shoulder and nodded at the range officer at his side, who dropped his flag, the signal to the trolley man to release the target. Bang, bang! Two shots came in quick succession. Pat's hand was a blur as he worked the lever. The trolley had not yet reached the halfway mark along the track. He stopped firing.

"Tumbler only, three points," reported the range officer to the recorder, who sat beside him at a table.

"Five points, I vouch, sir," smiled Pat, "the bottle and the tumbler."

"The bottle is still standing, Mr van Zyl," replied the range officer.

"What then constitutes a hit, sir?" asked Pat.

"A hit is a hit, exactly that, Mr van Zyl, and your bottle still stands." The man was clearly not pleased at having his judgement questioned.

Pat smiled pleasantly at him and said, "Shall we take a closer look, sir?" They set off down the street, followed by a crowd who wondered at the temerity of this newcomer. When they came to the target, the range officer stopped and shook his head ruefully.

"My apologies, Mr van Zyl, five points it is indeed," he said, still shaking his head in amazement. He turned and everyone followed him back to the firing line. Within seconds word spread that the bottle had indeed taken a hit; the top half of the neck was missing, taken off cleanly without shattering the bottle.

The favourite was an arrogant Portuguese named De Jesus who had won for the past two years. In his middle thirties, he was dressed like a Lisbon businessman, a complete contrast to his neighbours in this backwater. He claimed to have hunted elephants since he was twenty, but now he concentrated on buying and selling ivory and anything else that brought him a profit.

De Jesus had also shot his way into the next round with a perfect score. There were thirteen qualifiers until three were eliminated after a shoot-out. The excitement amongst the crowd increased as it became apparent that he might not have everything his own way this time. There were a few frowns too from those who had backed him heavily to win.

With the speed of the target to be increased, a practice run with the tray was arranged. De Jesus was drawn in sixth place with Pat eighth. A contestant had to score at least two points to qualify for the next round. By the time De Jesus stepped up, only two had hit the bottle but none had managed the tumbler.

Taking aim, De Jesus nodded to the starter and the target rolled down the rails like a waiter attending to an impatient customer. Two shots rang out, evenly spaced, with both scoring a hit. With a triumphant smirk on his face, De Jesus swaggered off to rejoin his group of admirers.

"Not bad," muttered Pat. The next man scored nothing and it was now his turn.

"Right, show us your stuff," whispered Grievous.

"Brian added, "Stay cool, Pat."

Pat took his place and raised his Winchester, then signalled that he was ready. Down came the tray. Pat followed its progress through his sights and then fired two shots in rapid succession, shattering both the tumbler and the bottle.

The next two contestants failed to score and there was a buzz among the spectators as they anticipated an exciting third round. Only four men had qualified. Brian and Grievous eased their tension by pouring more beer down their throats.

"Save a couple of bottles for me," chided Pat.

There was another dummy run to demonstrate the increased speed of the tray.

"You'd need a shotgun to hit that," Brian observed.

"Not easy, I'll admit," said Pat.

The two-pointers were to fire first and a coin was tossed for the leading pair. Pat won and elected to shoot last. Neither of the other two scored a point and it was finally down to De Jesus and Pat.

The crowd was silent. A hippopotamus grunted from the river as De Jesus stepped up to the mark.

Past experience suggested that anyone scoring a single hit on the target moving at such speed would win. De Jesus managed three shots and succeeded in hitting the bottle. His supporters cheered loudly.

"Good shooting," acknowledged Pat to his opponent.

Once more there was a hush as Pat prepared to shoot. His two companions lowered their beer bottles and watched breathlessly.

Since the first round, Pat had been aiming at the tumbler first, leaving the larger target for his second shot. This different tactic had been noticed by a few around him.

He went through the same breathing routine to compose himself. Then he nodded that he was ready. His first shot took the tumbler before the target had reached the centre of the street. Then something extraordinary happened. The bottle began to topple off the tray. There was a collective intake of breath from the crowd and then a second shot rang out. The bottle disintegrated before it hit the ground.

There followed a few seconds of silence while people took in this incredible exhibition of marksmanship. Then a roar of approval went up and Pat was hoisted onto a pair of broad shoulders and carried away to the hotel where the owner-sponsor was waiting to present the prize.

CHAPTER TWO

On Sunday they rose at dawn and set about organising the distribution of their equipment among the porters Pat had hired. Judas was the head porter, but despite the disadvantage of his name, he looked efficient.

"Just as well we're not superstitious," muttered Grievous, "or we might be inclined to leave him here. Makes you wonder how he got a name like that way out here in the middle of nowhere!"

From Fontesvilla they would head away from the Pungwe River on a more westerly course for seventy miles to Chimoio. From there it was a further seventy miles due west to the tiny new British South Africa Company settlement and fort at Umtali. On the way they would pass through the last Portuguese outpost of Massi-Kessi where there was a large garrison, established around 1775.

At this time of the year, the track was not difficult to follow. Being the dry season, there was no new grass covering the wheel ruts of passing wagons and no mud.

The first leg of the journey should be safe as the local tribes were peaceful people. After Chimoio it might be different. Chief

Gungunyana was a notorious bandit who sent frequent raiding parties down from his mountain kingdom north-west of Chimoio to ambush and rob travellers. Killing was rumoured to be a normal part of the process. White traders carried many goods along this route and so were prime targets. His raiders would often attack at the end of the day when the convoy was tired after a long hard day on the road. "Keep your shotguns loaded and ready from Chimoio onwards," was the advice given to Pat by a man who reported an attack only two weeks ago when one white man and several black porters had been killed and much merchantise being transported to Beira had been taken.

The other danger facing them would be wild animals, especially at night. The scavenging spotted hyena was the worst. Lions caused trouble only when mules or horses were with a party. They would boldly cause havoc during the night. However, humans were not immune from attack.

A gold prospector named Vogler had told them in the Fontesvilla hotel bar of a chilling incident that he had been involved in several months previously. He had been searching for a reef he had been told about by an old African man that was in the hills above Massi-Kessi. One day, some villagers reported to him that two white men were being besieged by lions and were barricaded in a hut not far from their village.

"I knew these men, Mac and Bob," said Vogler. "I questioned the villagers separately and found no inconsistencies in their stories. Quickly I packed a few provisions and set off on what turned out to be a four-day journey until I found the hut. A few yards from the door lay the rotting carcass of a lion. Lion spoor was all around the area indicating there had been more than one. I banged on the door and called out and someone inside removed sacks of rice that had been blockading the door and let me in.

"The scene was one of horror. Mac lay on a stretcher, apparently delirious, while Bob, who had let me in, was in a terrible state. The stench inside the hut was dreadful.

"It seems Mac had gone down with malaria and was too weak to walk. The workers had fled, as is their way, fearing this sickness.. No medical help was available so all they could do was wait and hope. One night Bob heard noises outside. He picked up his rifle and opened the door, hoping for help. Instead a lion stood not twenty paces away, staring at him in the moonlight. Bob raised his rifle, fired and killed the animal. He lowered his weapon but the danger was not yet over. Suddenly a lioness sprang at him from the side of the hut and ripped off his right hand. Bob jumped back into the hut, slammed the door shut and barricaded it as best he could with his other hand. His mauled arm was a ghastly mess with broken bones sticking out from the raw flesh below his elbow. To stop the bleeding, he melted some brown sugar in a pot and thrust his arm into it. I could see the dark crust that now covered the stump. He dared not go outside as he could no longer handle his weapon properly so they were trapped. This went on for seven days before I arrived. They lived off tins of fish, using the juices as their only source of water."

"What a story!" Pat shuddered. "What happened to them in the end?"

"Bob died two days later from gangrene. Happily Mac recovered and is still prospecting as far as I know."

After that tragedy, travellers going from Messi-Kessi and beyond made thorn bush enclosures at night for protection. Even this was no guarantee of safety from a hungry and determined predator.

⊷⊱╫⊰⊶

Barring mishaps, the Chimoio leg of the journey was expected to take about six days and then perhaps about eight more to Umtali. This section took longer because of the mountainous terrain.

Pat and his friends had become something of celebrities in Fontesvilla so many townsfolk came to see them off. Some even walked with them for a mile or two before returning home. The three were then able to increase their pace.

The land around them was flat and grassy with few trees. It was humid and they were soon sweating, especially Brian and Grievous, who carried more excess weight than Pat.

"A couple of weeks on the march will soon see you two in better shape," laughed Pat. "Perhaps you could add a few push-ups each day to speed things up."

"Full of yourself today, aren't you?" Brian grumbled. "Yesterday's performance obviously went to your head."

"Watch your tongue, my friend or I might cut down your nightly whisky ration. Don't bite the hand that feeds you."

The monotony of the march was broken by the occasional stream, where they refreshed themselves and refilled their water bottles. Late in the day Pat looked out for a small buck, guinea fowl or francolin for their evening meals. They all carried some dried salted meat, known locally as biltong, to snack on during the day.

With strips of drying meat hanging in the camp each night, hyenas became a nuisance and a waste of ammunition if they could not see them clearly.

Pat woke up on the third morning after an interrupted sleep and said, "If these damned scavengers are going to keep bothering us, we'll have to sort them out."

Just before halting that night, Pat noticed a clump of bamboo and cut a long piece as thick as his wrist at the bottom. He carried it into the camp they set up. Soon after the sun had set, the hyenas started their incessant whooping and giggling as they circled the camp.

"That's enough," cried Pat. "We'll show these brutes a thing or two."

He thrust an iron tent peg into the embers of the fire. When it was red hot, he placed it on a rock, took out a hammer and tongs from his tool kit, and forged it into a large hook.

"Going fishing, are we?" asked Grievous.

"I intend to sleep tonight."

He bound the bamboo pole to a small tree at the edge of their camp, using it as a brace. Then he hammered a foot-long peg into the ground a few feet in front of the pole. To this he attached a leather thong, called a *reimpie,* at the end of which was tied the trigger. At the narrow end of the pole, he tied another length of *reimpie,* making a sort of fishing rod and at the end of this he tied his great hook.

"Now, lads, I need your help to bend the pole towards the peg. Brian and Grievous joined him while Judas stood by with a lump of meat. They pulled the hook down until it was about five feet from the ground. Pat then told Judas how to bait the hook firmly with none of it hanging below the hook and left him to do it while he set the trigger himself.

Right," announced Pat, "all we have to do now is wait and it won't be long, I'll bet, so let's make ourselves comfortable."

Thirty minutes elapsed and then the hyenas became vaguely visible in the firelight. There were at least six of them whooping up into a frenzy on the other side of the thorn bushes. They had caught the scent of the bait.

"Come on, you noisy bastards," muttered Pat, "who's first?"

Then it happened. A hyena, perhaps the leader of the pack, was leaping at the bait, frothing at the mouth, clawing at the air, trying to reach the bait. Its third attempt saw its powerful jaws clamp down on the hanging meat. Then came a whoosh of air as the trigger tripped, sending the hyena hurtling into the air with the hook embedded in its jaw. Now the giggling became a pitiful gargle as the beast bounced about in the air like a freshly caught catfish suspended from a rod. Macabre, but as a spectacle it was hilarious and Grievous started it off, and soon they were all laughing, including the porters.

The rest of the pack took off fast, sensing that something was seriously amiss and that they would be better off somewhere else.

Pat nodded to Judas, who mercifully ended the animal's misery with a blow from his knobkerrie.

"The things one has to do in Africa to get a good night's rest," said Brian. "So, if you have no further entertainment laid on for us this evening, Pat, I think I'll turn in." They all slept well that night.

The only excitement during the next two days was provided by a herd of elephants which refused to budge from the track until several of them had emptied their bowels while others trumpeted loudly, a spectacular symphony of sound and smell.

The men and their bearers sat mesmerized as they sat waiting, unfortunately downwind, but safely to one side of the track, should they need to hastily withdraw.

The next day they stopped for a few hours at Chimoio where they were able to replenish essential items before pressing on. The countryside was changing. Where before there were great plains as far as the eye could see, now they were faced with rolling hills covered with the indigenous Msasa trees. On the horizon they could see a blue mountain range rising several thousand feet like a barrier to some mysterious undiscovered kingdom. Only the natural fauna and flora seemed to populate the land. However, they proceeded with vigilance, aware that marauding bandits could emerge at any time.

Four days out of Chimoio they were alerted by a group of people walking along the road towards them. It was soon obvious that they were fellow travellers, probably making for the coast. The only white man among them was none other than the Bishop of Bloemfontein, Dr Knight-Bruce. He was returning home after seeing two of his newly recruited English nurses settled at Umtali, where they were to supervise the building of a small hospital. They all stopped and brewed some tea while the parties exchanged news.

"I'm afraid you might be walking into a conflict," the bishop told the three men. "The Portuguese commandant at the garrison at Messi-Kessi has ordered Captain Heyman, the Member in Charge of the BSA Company's police at Umtali, to leave. He says the area is part of Manica, the name the Portuguese call that part of Mozambique. Heyman refused and is waiting for further orders from his commanding officer at Fort Salisbury."

Grievous frowned. "Heyman won't stand a chance. The Portuguese garrison is manned by four hundred men. How many policemen are there at Umtali?"

"Forty five, I think," replied the bishop. "Still, the majority of the garrison are not Portuguese, only the officers. The rest are local Manicas, not keen to fight someone else's war, I suspect."

"I think we'd better hurry up," said Pat. "The Umtali force is going to need every extra gun they can get."

Brian said, "I reckon now would be a good time to take a fishing holiday on the Pungwe. What do you think, Grievous?"

"Sorry. I'm here to report the situation on the ground, Brian. It wouldn't look good if I ducked out of this one."

Brian turned to the Bishop. "How long to reach Umtali from here?"

"If you move fast, you could be there by tomorrow evening."

Fort Umtali was first settled in 1890 when Rhodes sent the colonising column of two hundred hand-picked pioneers and four hundred heavily-armed British South Africa policemen north to raise the British flag at Fort Salisbury. A small patrol was despatched to the north east to contact Chief Mutasa, who lived near the Umtali

River. There they learned of the large Portuguese garrison at Messi-Kessi, only a day's ride away. They decided to base their camp on a hill overlooking the junction of the Umtali and Sarombi rivers.

From there they sent an emissary to the chief with gifts. He was tasked with trying to find out how strong the Portuguese influence was in the area. His report was startling. With the chief was a high powered delegation of high-ranking Portuguese officers, led by a Colonel Andrada who was anxious to sign a treaty confirming a verbal arrangement made some years earlier.

The situation was clearly serious and the patrol leader immediately sent for reinforcements from Fort Salisbury. Several days later a Major Forbes arrived with a contingent of men. He took one look at the fortified sacred mountain-top home of Chief Mutasa, called Binga Guru, and decided that storming tactics would be futile. Instead he walked around the base of the hill and discovered the end of a waste disposal channel that coursed down the mountain. He selected a small group of men and they climbed up through the channel. They emerged at the top filthy and smelling foul, but not far from the chief's hut. They burst into it and faced the chief, who still had the Portuguese delegation around him.

Forbes pointed his revolver at a shocked Colonel Andrada and said politely but firmly, "Colonel please keep your hands where I can see them, you are now my prisoner."

Andrada recovering his poise, replied equally politely, "You are mistaken, sir. This is the territory of the King of Portugal and I am his representative here. Go outside and see the flag of Portugal flying from the mast." He wrinkled his nose in distaste and added. "May I say that right now I would much prefer to be outside."

"Certainly," replied Forbes. "Let us go and examine this flag you speak of."

With the Major's revolver pressed against his back, Andrada was escorted out of the hut. There, fluttering from a pole, was the Union Jack.

An astonished colonel turned to Forbes and said, "It would seem that you have the advantage over me, sir – for now. But, remember that Portugal does not concede so easily. This matter is far from closed."

━━━┼┼━━━

The settlement of Umtali in 1891 consisted of several scattered huts built on individual mining claims with a concentration on top of a steep rocky hill where the Sabi Ophir Mining Company had built its offices and accommodation for its employees. In front of these buildings grew a huge fig tree. The area was known locally as the Hill of the Great Tree.

The fortified police camp was on an adjacent hill. Umtali, meaning gold in the local ChiShona dialect, was the name of the river that ran past the foot of the hill occupied by the mining company and was thus known as the River of Gold. Evidence of ancient mine workings was everywhere. The origins of these may well have dated back five thousand years to the time of King Solomon when the Queen of Sheba brought Gold of Ophir, meaning Gold of Africa, to him. She claimed it came from the Land of the Punt or *Punt wi*, which may have become Pungwe. So said many writers at the time.

The Portuguese were aware of the potential wealth of the area and understandably wanted the British out. It was little wonder that Captain Heyman had been told to leave. Those living there now wondered whether Colonel Andrada was busy plotting his revenge as he had promised.

━━━┼┼━━━

Pat and his two friends arrived early in May and were fortunate to find an empty hut for them to sleep in at the mining compound.

On the day after their arrival Grievous set up his camera under the fig tree while Pat and Brian went to visit Captain Heyman.

"Good day, sir," said Pat. "I'm Pat van Zyl and this is Brian Wood-Gush. We arrived from Beira yesterday. Two days ago we met Dr Knight-Bruce. He told us about your problems with the Portuguese so we're here to offer any help we can."

"Good day to you both." The captain shook hands. "Indeed we can do with any help we can get. Do you have any experience handling firearms? My orders are to march on Messi-Kessi to settle the dispute once and for all."

Brian said, "My friend here is very likely the best rifle shot you or I will ever see. He is also a gunsmith and a blacksmith and that is the nature of the business he owns in Ladysmith. I'm not much good with firearms; my only skills were with the hammer and shot putt on school sports days."

"There are three of us," said Pat. "Colin Grieve is a photojournalist with The Times. He could be useful as a reporter."

Heyman said, "We're seriously outnumbered by them but, apart from the officers, the rest are poorly trained locals. We need to unsettle them."

"What have you got as heavy armament?" asked Pat.

"Just one seven-pounder, a muzzle loader. I'm having a yoke made so that oxen can pull it."

"Has anyone spied out the garrison, captain?"

"I've actually been there. It's surrounded by a thick stone wall. There's a main gate and a smaller one at the rear leading to where they keep their livestock. They have five or six field-pieces and a couple of Gatling guns."

"Do they know what you have?"

"I reckon so. They have their spies too."

"I think we need to increase your fire power," said Pat. "How are you off for gunpowder?"

"Not much, I'm afraid. We've just enough for the twelve rounds we have left for the cannon."

"Are there any dassies in these hills?" Heyman looked puzzled so Pat explained. "That's what we South Africans call rock rabbits."

The captain looked oddly at Pat. "I've seen plenty around. Why do you ask?"

"Dassies live in communes and share their toilet facilities. Over time there is a build-up of droppings and crystalline urine on the rocks where they live. Scrape this off and mix it with charcoal and you have an explosive charge. Urine is a nitrate and has the same effect as saltpetre and that's the main ingredient of the black powder you use. Urine mixed with sulphur and charcoal was used as an explosive as early as the Middle Ages. Then it was refined from old sewage pits."

"I'm amazed. I read about old sewage pits when I was in officer training, but no one mentioned rock rabbits. I could send some workers off with my sergeant to do some harvesting."

"That would be a good start, sir. Collect as much as possible."

"Do you have any plan in mind, Mr van Zyl?"

"Not really. I'll leave the battle tactics to you though I think we should try to convince the enemy that our arsenal is bigger than they believe."

"I agree. As I said before, I'm going to need all the help I can get and that includes ideas."

I'm at your service, captain," said Pat. "Perhaps you could come with me to get some help from the mine manager. I'll need a few bits and pieces from him as well as the use of their forge. I'm sure you can convince him that it will be in his best interest to assist."

By that evening, with the help of the mine staff and Brian, Pat's armoury was starting to take the shape of six giant blunderbusses. The barrels were two and a half feet long, made from three-inch diameter steel piping and reinforced with a strong sleeve over the chamber/breech. This was mounted on a single yoke-shaped carriage made from channel iron with a coco-pan wheel at the apex, the whole shaped rather like a wheelbarrow. The barrel could be elevated by rotating it on its connection to the chassis. The complete unit could then be strapped to the back of an ox, barrel up.

Loading was simple. A measured amount of powder was wrapped in newspaper and pushed down the barrel. This was followed by a wad of wet newspaper and then the shot which was a mixture of horse shoe nails and any other available scrap metal. It was all tamped down before a final piece of wadding was added. It was fired by putting a match to the touch hole.

⇥‖‖⇤

The next morning the troop of Company police turned out for a demonstration and then training on the use of the weapon. They would work in pairs – a loader to prime the gun while his partner aimed and fired it.

Pat set up one of the cannons at the foot of the hill on the bank of the Umtali River, facing a steep bank about fifty yards away on the opposite side. He wanted to judge the impact and spread of the shot. Brian worked with him while Grievous set up his camera close by to capture the action. Pat put the match to the touch hole and they quickly covered their ears with their hands. The explosion was deafening. There was a flash followed by a cloud of smoke that enveloped the two gunners. The far bank erupted as gravel and dust filled the air for a radius of twenty yards around the impact point.

"That was bloody fantastic," exclaimed Grievous. "We've got to give this machine a name, Pat."

"You're the word man, you think of one."

"How about Pat's Peeshooter – dassie pee – get it?"

"Nice one, Grievous." They all laughed.

An excited Captain Heyman joined them. "I'm most impressed, Mr van Zyl. I'll tell Sergeant Johnson to start weapon training right away. Perhaps you gentlemen would like to join me and my number two for a strategy session at the camp?"

They all made themselves as comfortable as possible under a tree, sitting around a rough mud model they had made of the Portuguese garrison and the surrounding mountains. After some discussion a plan began to form.

As they were enjoying a break, each with a glass of whisky, there was a noise at the gate and a trooper arrived, holding a curious-looking battle axe made from hardwood which appeared to be inlaid with gold and silver.

"There's a woman at the gate, sir, the owner of this." He raised the battle axe. "She says she is Queen Marquaniqua, Chief Mutasa's aunt. Her interpreter verified this and said that she holds sway over most of the tribesmen around here, including the chief. She's asking to see you, sir."

"I think we'd better see what she wants. Bring her up."

Marquaniqua was a spectacular sight. She was very tall and built as if she could lift a wagon wheel one-handed with ease. Her face was ugly, almost brutal.

She squatted before the captain and eyed the bottle of whisky, Using the interpreter, she said she had travelled far and needed something to drink.

Heyman eyed her with suspicion. "What can we offer you, tea or coffee?"

She laughed loudly. Her voice was loud and harsh. "I want none of your white women's piss. I need more fire in my belly." She pointed to the whisky.

Heyman poured a generous tot into a metal mug and passed it to her. She gulped it down without flinching and held out the mug for a refill.

"Let's hear what you have to say first," sighed Heyman.

She shrugged her enormous shoulders and then told them that she knew about the Portuguese demands. "I and my people will fight with you against this enemy. The Portuguese have mistreated us for generations. Now is the time for revenge."

Heyman now refilled her mug and urged her to continue.

"I will offer you many of my best warriors. You will tell them what you want from them," she said.

"I hear you, my queen. First, do you have anyone who knows the area around the garrison well, people who know the paths?"

"I have walked these hills since I was a girl. I will be your guide and my men will follow me. Together we will drive these Portuguese back to the sea." Her voice had risen to a bellow. She leaned forward to retrieve her axe from the ground at Heyman's feet and waved it in the air.

The captain eyed her warily, but said, "Make your men ready, Queen Marquaniqua, and join us here the day after tomorrow before the sun rises. Do not tell them the reason. I want to keep our raid as a surprise." He was mindful of the possibility that one of her men might be a spy who would inform the enemy beforehand. After all, he had only just met this formidable woman. She rose, nodded her head, and left.

The next day at the camp was spent in preparation, including making harnesses for the oxen which would pull the seven-pounder as well as carry Pat's Peeshooters.

⟞╫╫⟝

The queen and her men joined them as promised on the day of departure and the whole column was ready to leave Umtali at 0700 hours. The early winter sunshine soon evaporated the mist that hung lightly around the mountains. An emerald spotted dove sent up its poop-ta-poop-ta-poop-poop-poop-poop from a thicket down near the river.

The route to Massi-Kessi entailed a wide detour to take them over two mountain ranges and then down into the Revue Valley south of the garrison. They followed only game trails to avoid meeting any one. Heyman imagined himself as Hannibal crossing the Alps, but with oxen rather than elephants. There were plenty of elephants around but they were unlikely to cooperate so lesser beasts had to do the work.

Two of Marquaniqua's husbands were at the front with Captain Heyman and half of his troops. A mile behind came the rest of the police troop and the queen's main contingent. Between these two groups the oxen pulling the artillery were being herded and encouraged to keep the pace set. Pat and Brian were scouting well ahead of all of them with the queen of the battle axe and one of her men. Their task was to scout the way forward without discovery so that the force retained the initiative. They were all on foot.

They made good progress on the first day, covering fourteen miles before they came to the first mountain range. Once they started to climb, however, there were difficulties with the seven-pounder. The trail was narrow. It wound between rocks and trees, necessitating a single file formation. The cannon had a six-foot wheel span and men were continually being sent back to help push it forward. The first night was spent only a third of the way up the mountain.

Pat and Brian based themselves in a saddle between two rocky peaks. On top of either of them they had a panoramic view of the land on both sides of the mountain range. What they saw ahead was a breath-taking vast basin at least half a dozen miles wide that gradually rose in the middle distance onto msasa-wooded hills. Beyond that were more towering mountains.

Pat said quietly, "You know, Brian, this place must have potential. I can see people wanting to settle in this valley. There must be water from the mountains which can be dammed. There's good grazing for cattle and one could plant trees like pine and gum on the hillsides. The problem will be getting the railway Rhodes wants to build over the mountains to Umtali, even if they move it to a new site, which has been suggested. It may be easier to bring it up into this valley through that saddle over there." He pointed to his right. "When we get back, I think I'll write to Rhodes and suggest that."

Brian nodded his agreement. "It certainly is a beautiful place. If we can settle this problem with the Portuguese, I could be tempted to tap my big brother for a loan. I wouldn't mind doing a bit of farming. He may fall for it, even if only to keep me at a distance."

"Any new community is going to need milk and cheese and they'll soon tire of eating venison. Done properly, I can't see how you can fail"

"What about you, Pat?"

"There'll be plenty of opportunities, I'm sure."

Night fell as the two men returned to their camp to rejoin the queen and her companion. They began to cook a meal over a small fire. Brian was about to toss some impala ribs into a hot pan when they heard a dry cough in the darkness, followed by another to the right of the first.

"What the hell was that?" whispered Brian.

"A leopard, I think, but not just one. There's a pair of them." Pat reached for his Winchester and threw another log on the fire.

"I thought they ate baboons, not humans."

"Maybe we smell like baboons. We're not at our cleanest after the day's toil. Anyway, I doubt that they'll worry us unless they're very hungry. If they are, they'll probably go for the fat lady first. Still, keep your shooter close to hand, just in case."

Marquaniqua looked unsettled as she pulled her cloak tight around her large body. She clutched her battle axe tightly in both hands, nervously scanning back and forth.

Perhaps the leopards had already eaten or feared the fire or were simply being inquisitive, but they moved on as nothing more was heard. They all ate and then covered themselves and drifted off to sleep.

CHAPTER THREE

As Marquaniqua guided them up the mountain, Pat and Brian, thinking of the cannon's width, left a trail of bright red knitting wool tied to bushes and tufts of grass for the rest to follow.

By midday the artillery group had reached the top of the mountain. Captain Heyman rested the men and the oxen through the hottest part of the day; when it was cooler, they would begin the descent into the valley. Before that happened, they would need to construct a braking system for the cannon. Again, Pat's blacksmith skills proved useful. He made a simple braking mechanism for each wheel. When a lever was pulled hard, wooden blocks tightened against each side of the wheels. It was slow hard work for men and beasts but it worked.

The path took them past Gomo re Mbira, named after the rock rabbits that had provided the source of the gunpowder. Chief Murahwa had a fortress nearby to protect his people from Gunganyana and his raiders.

That night the expedition rested in a quiet, well-wooded area next to a tiny crystal-clear stream at the foot of the mountain.

Heyman and his second-in-command sat with Pat and his friends opposite Marquaniqua and the interpreter, relaxing with a whisky each. In the queen's case, one tot was not enough as she downed the first and held out her mug for a second before the others had taken more than a sip.

"Talk about truffles for pigs," Grievous exclaimed. "I thought whisky was an acquired taste. It hasn't taken her long to adjust."

Pat grinned. "I don't think her taste buds have much to do with it, Grievous. If dassie piss charged her up, she'd as likely drink that too."

Captain Heyman intervened. "Gentlemen, to business. The old soak here says that the real challenge begins the day after tomorrow when we have crossed the valley. Then it's all uphill, figuratively and literally. She assures me it can be done and she will get us up and over the next range."

"You'd better ration her whisky, Captain," said Grievous, "or she won't know the difference between a footpath and a twelve -inch ruler."

They next faced the Bvumba mountains. Heyman would then join the reconnoitring party while his assistant found a suitable camp site on the far side of the valley and waited for him to return and guide them onwards.

The forward party was now reduced to Pat, Brian, Heyman and Marquaniqua. It took longer than they had thought, three days in fact, to find a suitable route through the mountains that would bring them down behind the Massi-Kessi garrison. They constantly came upon obstacles that would hinder the progress of the cannon. When they reached the top, they were faced with a wall of trees that covered the summit like a feathered headdress.

Heyman removed his hat and scratched his head. "How the hell do we drive our artillery through that lot?" he asked of no one in particular.

Marquaniqua seemed unperturbed as she strode purposefully ahead of them. Shielding his eyes from the sun Pat observed that she had now stopped and was sitting on a rock waiting for them. On reaching her he could hardly believe his eyes.

In front of him was a huge pile of elephant dung, surrounded by bluebottle flies. More surprising was that the heap lay in the middle of a path wide enough to drive a wagon along it. To his left, the path led back into the forest. To his right, it disappeared down the mountain in a southerly direction.

"What do you make of this? muttered Brian when he saw it.

"I think it's an elephant highway," Pat replied, "maybe a migration route. "My guess is that when the annual bush fires have destroyed the veld, they head south looking for greener pastures, so to speak."

Captain Heyman agreed. "It's the only possible explanation. The old queen is not just an ugly face, after all. Let's see where it takes us."

The forest was like a nature park, completely different from what they had experienced in the valley. Butterflies fluttered everywhere like rose petals while blue duiker sniffed the air with their moist noses. All around them were ferns and vines.

Now they made good progress and four hours later they emerged from the canopy of the forest and looked down onto the Revue Valley. Marquaniqua turned east and they followed her along the edge of the tree line for another hour before she stopped. Here the mountain dropped away steeply into the valley. Then she signalled to the men to drop to their knees and crawl to the edge of the ridge.

Two thousand feet below, clearly visible, was the Portuguese fort of Massi-Kessi, built with crenelated walls on a low rounded hill.

Captain Heyman agreed to accompany Marquaniqua back to the camp and bring up the main party while Pat and Brian were left to work out the best way down the mountain and to decide on gun emplacements. They estimated that it would take Heyman two days to reach his men and another four days to return with them and the artillery. Plenty of time, thought Pat, to organise with Brian their side of the operation.

The sharp drop in the evening temperature at the start of the winter months meant that they had to retreat into the tree-line to light a fire to keep warm.

They relaxed close to the fire, sipping coffee laced with whisky while they contemplated the task ahead of them.

"I must be mad," Brian thought to himself. "How did I get involved in throwing shrapnel at a bunch of Porks? This Man van Zyl is trying to make a gunner out of a number plumber, for God's sake."

Pat was lost in his own thoughts. He could visualise the valley below and was trying to think where best to place his artillery to best effect. Because of the enemy's larger numbers, he had to use deception and cunning to make the Portuguese think that they were up against a superior force. His biggest problem was how to manhandle the seven-pounder into the most effective position. He also had to consider the need to do everything at night to avoid discovery before they mounted an attack at first light. His thoughts faded as he drifted off to sleep.

⇒╬⇐

After breakfast the next morning, Pat and Brian went to the cliff edge. They lay prone as the sun rose higher before them. Brian reached for his field glasses but Pat's arm shot out and stopped him.

"We can't risk a reflection with the sun as it is."

Pat took out a pencil and note pad and began to sketch the scene below, placing an asterisk next to certain features which, he explained, were likely sites for the six Peeshooters, but they had to be inspected first for suitability and ease of access. The cannon was still their biggest problem. After an hour, he had an acceptable artist's impression of the valley. They moved back and sat in the sun to study the drawing.

"The other consideration is that these villages will have dogs around," said Pat. "This afternoon we'll follow the elephant trail down as far as we safely can. Then we'll branch off and look for the best sites for the Peeshooters. We need to set them up at the rear of the garrison and on at least one other side. I'm still not sure what we do about the dogs. You and I might make it on our own without detection, but a whole platoon of men won't."

"I'm starting to get an idea," said Brian. "It entails Marquaniqua's men." He explained further to Pat, who listened quietly, nodding his head in approval.

"Excellent!" Pat said. "Very workable and I like it. I'm sure Heyman will, too. Brian, you'll be signing up for officer training when this is all over."

"No, thank you. I still fancy myself as a gentleman farmer."

Around 3pm they picked up the elephant trail again and by dusk they were ready to descend further as soon as the moon rose to guide them. When it did, they walked for an hour before the trail suddenly turned north, away from where they wanted to go. It was obvious that the elephants had wanted to avoid the village ahead.

They could see the women preparing the evening meal around smoky fires while children darted about in the dust, chased play-fully by leaping barking dogs.

Amid so much noise it was easy to skirt the village undetected. They were still descending the hill, undisturbed by trees which had been cut for firewood over the years. Suddenly Pat stopped and Brian bumped into him. "What now?" he hissed.

"Get down on your belly, man. Someone is walking towards us. I can hear him. He's mumbling or singing or something." He looked frantically around for a bush or a boulder behind which to hide. "Over there," he whispered and pointed to a bush a few yards away. "Let's get behind that fast."

They scrabbled to cover mere seconds before a figure came weaving up the path.

"He's been to a beer-drink, he's pissed!" whispered Brian.

"Yeah, but he could still have blown our cover," replied Pat. "He still might," he added as the man veered off the path towards their bush. Pat tightened his grip on the Winchester.

The man, old and grey as they could now clearly see, stopped at the bush and then swaying from side to side, raised his front flap and proceeded to spray all over and through the bush, including the heads of the hiding men. Fortunately, they were wearing hats. As Brian pointed out, shaking his hat, when the man had gone on his way up the hill, the incident might raise a laugh at an old boys' reunion in the future, if they ever had one.

They skirted two more villages without mishap before they came to a point that Pat had marked on his map as a possible placing for the seven-pounder. They were directly behind the garrison on a knoll and well above it, which was about a thousand yards away by Pat's estimation. The ground around the walls had been cleared with just well-trimmed grass left.

From where they stood, there was a clump of bushes nearby which would hide the cannon. Within another five hundred yards they found two Peeshooter sites. The rear of the garrison would be covered. As they expected, there were no huts within rifle range of the fort. They then retraced their steps and worked their way round to the east side, looking for three more suitable sites.

When they had finished, they climbed back up the hill and by midnight they were drinking coffee around their camp fire, set well back from the ridge.

⊷╋⊶

During the days waiting for Captain Heyman and his troop to arrive, Pat and Brian searched for a convenient camping area for the whole contingent. They also spent many hours observing the garrison from the top of the cliff, learning the daily routine. They noted the positions of at least three of the dreaded Gatling guns which they would have to respect, even eliminate if possible.

After five days, Heyman returned with his men. It had been a hard trip and they were all exhausted. Grievous seemed less rotund and Brian remarked on this. "Lend me your camera," he said." I'll take a "now" picture for a "then and now" advert in your newspaper."

All Grievous could say was, "That was heavy going. The things one has to do to make a living."

Pat laughed. "Look on the bright side, Grievous. You're making history and recording it at the same time. One day you'll be known as a great journalist while the rest of us pass on unnoticed."

That night Captain Heyman called them together for a meeting. Marquaniqua was not included. "Gentlemen," he said, "My intention is to give the men twenty-four hours rest before we attack at first light on Wednesday. Pat, please give us the benefit of your observations over the past few days."

Pat produced his original sketch of the valley which now showed the positions for the seven-pounder and the Peeshooters. A second one, drawn from memory, showed the route down the mountain. At the same time he detailed the terrain and ground cover available. This was important to the patrol leader. Then, to please Grievous, he recounted the tale of the drunken old man and the unfortunate ending.

Grievous roared his delight. "He must have thought it was a lava-tree," he quipped, slapping Pat on the back.

Brian grinned at him. "If you'd been with us, it would have been a real hat-trick." Everyone enjoyed that retort.

Pat stopped laughing and said, "Seriously, my biggest concern is getting the troops into position without them being seen. The village dogs were the problem, but fortunately Brian came up with a solution and that developed into a sort of battle plan, which you may or may not agree to. I'll let Brian explain."

"Here's what I propose, Captain," said Brian. "We send Marquaniqua and her men in against the villagers just before dawn and clear them out of their homes. Hopefully, her people will be mistaken for Gunganyana's thugs. Limited pillaging can be allowed for authenticity, but nothing more violent than that. We have no quarrel with the locals. The Portuguese will be certain to send out patrols to investigate the disturbance. We will then follow closely behind our fat lady and take up position where we can observe the fort. As soon as the patrols have passed us, I will lead you, Captain, with three sections in to places at the rear of the fort and you will then open up with the seven-pounder and two of the Peeshooters. Pat will lead the other three sections into position. I'm assuming that when the enemy patrols realise their garrison is under attack they will do an about turn and head back fast and then run into Pat's ambush."

"You two seem to have thought of everything in our absence," said Heyman. "Well done. I like it. Tomorrow morning we'll brief the men fully. Until then I'm going to catch up on some sleep. I'm bushed." His troopers, too, were soon wrapped in their blankets that night after such a gruelling few days.

⟞⟊⟝

The next morning, all the men, having checked their kit, were fully briefed. They had already been divided earlier into six sections when training with the Peeshooters. Now they sat in their groups around the captain.

Pat, with Brian's help, had transcribed his drawings onto a tarpaulin with a piece of charcoal. He hung the large canvas between two trees for all to see.

In his briefing, Captain Heyman emphasised the need for stealth, No man was to carry anything that might rattle. They would also blacken their faces with charcoal. This did not go down well until Grievous' chubby face was used as an example to demonstrate the effectiveness of camouflage in the bush. Grievous had only agreed to be used in this way when Brian pointed out the credibility he would gain in his Times column which would carry a picture of him in his war paint.

The cannon axles were to be greased and the wheel rims muffled with grass. They assumed that any noise made by the oxen would be accepted as normal around villages.

⇥⊹⇤

The operation began to get underway when Pat was awakened by a guard at 2am. His first thought was to rekindle the fire and brew coffee, the smell of which soon woke up Brian and Grievous. Soon the sections were being inspected by their corporals for dangling noisy items and missed spots of face and hand blackening.

Marquaniqua's men listened intently to their queen's instructions as she strutted before them, waving her battle axe above her head, but for once lowering her voice. Her words seemed to inspire the warriors, judging by their body language and the galvanised looks on their faces.

Heyman had had difficulty convincing her about the need for restraint with the village raids; it took time and patience before he could persuade her that her performance as a decoy was vital to the success of the mission.

The queen led her men along the ridge towards the elephant trail. Fifteen minutes later Captain Heyman and Brian and their men began to shift the seven-pounder, while Pat guided the remaining three sections to their ambush positions. All of them, black and white, shivered as much from anticipation and excitement as from the early morning chill.

An hour later, Heyman and Brian branched off to the west with their artillery to set it up at the rear of the fort. As they did so, right on cue, they heard the noise of the first attack upon a village. It sounded very authentic. Pat suppressed a chuckle as he took his men down the hill to their positions. Dawn was breaking to reveal the activity below them at the fort.

The Portuguese reaction group poured out from the opened wooden gates. Pat estimated a force of two hundred men who formed up along the mown area in front of the wall ready to sweep forward. Their officers, easily identifiable by their bright elaborate uniforms, and with their swords reflecting in the sunlight stood behind the troops, who were ill-equipped with obsolete weaponry for the task ahead of them.

Brian and Heyman also saw the scene unfolding before them from a different angle. They were to wait fifteen minutes after the garrison troops moved forward before mounting their attack. When they heard the shots and shouts of the troops chasing off Marquaniqua's warriors, they fired their first shots. The cannon boomed, shortly followed by the slightly lesser explosive sound of the Peeshooters. The first cannon shot soared over the fort, but a quick adjustment of elevation saw the next one blast into the battlements, sending rocks scattering in all directions.

The reply was quick as the Gatling guns opened fire peppering the mountain.

Pat and his men were ready in their ambush when the troops chasing Marquaniqua's men realised that the fort was under attack, turned about to race back in disarray to defend it. As the first wave broke cover, Pat gave the signal to open fire. A deadly volley of nuts and nails spewed forth from his Peeshooter, quickly followed by shots from the other two home-made cannons. Confusion became panic as the soldiers skidded to a halt and cast about looking for a way out. Pat's marksmen began to pick them off with ease so that now some of them were throwing down their weapons and running back into the bush.

Meanwhile the seven-pounder was very accurately lobbing more shells into the walls of the fort. Now one of the Gatlings had identified Pat's position and he and his men had to get their heads down. As it happened the Gatling gunner was unwittingly helping Pat's cause because much of the firepower was high and overshooting his ambush position and cutting down his own men who were trying to return to the garrison. This prompted Pat to give the order for half of his men to take one of the Peeshooters across to the opposite side of the dry river bed and return fire.

The garrison commander was now under attack from two sides as well as from behind.

Marquaniqua by now was enthusiastically engaged in the battle as she wielded her great cudgel against the fleeing unarmed soldiers all the while bellowing encouragement to her warriors to follow suit.

Grievous had found the perfect spot to record much of the action with his camera. He cursed its limitations, but he consoled himself that his pen would complete the picture.

Captain Heyman had the upper hand at the moment with so many of the garrison's strength on the wrong side of the battlements and those within thinking they were being attacked by a large force. Nevertheless, he knew that the superior power of the

Gatling guns represented a stalemate in reality. They had to be silenced.

Pat suddenly had a thought, what had become of the Portuguese officers in charge of the sweep line that had left the fort to quell Marquaniqua's raiders. They would not have panicked like their troops, but they were nowhere to be seen. Then he reasoned that they would be circling round to the west in a wide detour to reach the fort undetected. There were only three of them, but if he could capture them, it could pressure the garrison commander to surrender. If he could act quickly, he could reach the opposite side of the garrison before them. Failing that, he would be no worse off. He sent a messenger to Captain Heyman to tell him that he intended to take half of his remaining force to enact his plan.

He and his group scrambled over the river bed and made their way to the thicker cover at the base of the mountain where they picked up a game trail. They then struck out for the other side of the fort. Suddenly there was a rustling in the bushes as if some bulky animal was moving down the mountainside towards them. Every man held his weapon at the ready. Then, from within the bushes, came a hoarse whisper. "Hey, Pat, it's me, Brian."

Pat was shocked. "Wood-Gush, you idiot, what the hell are you doing flailing around the bush like a wild pig with its nose stuck in a cooking pot?"

"If you think I'm going to sit up there with the drop-shorts while you have all the fun, you're badly mistaken. Now lead on with the peace of mind that comes from knowing that big Brian is covering your fat arse."

Pat grinned at his friend. "Ok, ok, just try not to trip over your big feet. I'd like to keep an element of surprise if I can. Now, let's get moving."

Ten minutes or so later, they were in a position on the west side of the garrison where they could look down on the cleared area. Only a few goats grazed there, oblivious to all the human activity going on, which had lessened. The heavy artillery was silent though they could hear sporadic rifle fire. Before them was the small gate they had recorded earlier as a possible livestock entry point.

"There should be a path from the bush to that gate, don't you think, Brian?"

"Yes, and you think our soldier boys will come strolling along and knock on the back door?"

"Exactly! So let's get down there and into the shrubbery alongside the path ready to welcome home the brass and hope we don't get pissed upon again."

"My bloody hat still smells a bit from the last time," grinned Brian.

"We must nab them without too much fuss. We don't want to kill them. Here's what we do." He quickly outlined his plan.

The path was well worn by cattle and goats, but the cover on either side was thick. Pat drove a stake into the middle of the path, split the top, and placed a sheet of paper from his notebook in it. He hoped that his theory about the curiosity of man was true. Then they retreated into the bush to wait. Pat and Brian hid just ahead of the cleft stick while the rest spread out on either side of the path behind it.

It was not long before they heard footsteps hurrying towards them. The three Portuguese were so intent on looking over their shoulders for signs of pursuit that they were almost upon the stick before they saw it. They stopped and stared at the stick and the flapping piece of paper as if it would strike them like a mamba. Then they began to argue and gesticulate without actually touching it. The troopers moved onto the path behind them and the corporal coughed lightly.

"Excuse me, gentlemen," he said mildly, "may I have your attention? You are now prisoners of the British South Africa Company police. Kindly drop your weapons and raise your hands above your heads."

The officers swung round and found themselves staring down the barrels of half a dozen rifles. Pat and Brian then moved on to the path to cut off any attempt to escape to the garrison.

"Just not your day, is it, sirs?" said Brian.

They tied their captives' hands and the whole party began to make its way back to Captain Heyman. Brian had a sudden thought.

"Hey, Pat, what did you write on that piece of paper?"

Pat laughed. "Sorry, no pork and beans for you tonight, Senhors, just bully beef stew and mealie meal porridge."

"Always the joker, hey?" roared Brian.

CHAPTER FOUR

They were back with Captain Heyman. Pat sat with the others, his back resting against the wheel of the seven-pounder. The heavy guns were all silent; there was only intermittent rifle firing in the area of Pat's earlier ambush.

"What do we do from here?" he asked. "As I see it, we now have the initiative. Half of their men are scattered to the four winds. The commander, Andrada, must believe they are under attack from a large force and we have three of their officers trussed up. How do we use this to our advantage to finish this business?"

Heyman's gaze had been shifting between Grievous and one of the Portuguese officers. Grievous was short and, despite being English, was swarthy and looked quite continental. "The resemblance is uncanny," he said suddenly.

"Who are you talking about?" asked Pat, sitting up straighter.

"Take a look at that little fellow, the one in the middle." Heyman pointed at the Portuguese officer.

"I see what you mean," exclaimed Brian. "With some hair under your nose, Grievous, you could be his brother."

"He's not nearly as good looking as me," retorted Grievous. "He's not as tall either."

"You flatter yourself."

"Still, what does it matter if he does look a bit like me?"

Pat said, "If the captain is thinking as I am, we might be looking at a solution – the last spoonful of beans to complete the stew the Portuguese find themselves in."

Grievous looked alarmed. "Oh, no, you can leave me out of this. I'm the journalist. I tell the story. I want no part in the action. Forget whatever you're thinking."

No one listened. A few minutes later, Grievous stood before them dressed in the officer's uniform with a thin moustache drawn with charcoal adorning his upper lip, ready for inspection. He looked a convincing double.

"From twenty feet, you'd fool the man's own mother," said Brian.

Grievous shook his head unhappily. "If I don't win over Andrada at a hundred yards, my mother is not going to see her favourite son again."

"All you have to do," said Heyman, "is create a good impersonation of one of the Portuguese officers returning with the ragged remains of his platoon so that they'll open the gate to you. I have total confidence in your natural acting ability, Grievous."

"Thanks for nothing, *sir.*"

Brian moaned that he could not fit into any of the uniforms and would miss all the fun. Heyman pointed out that he could not, in any case, double for any of the officers because of his size. A few troopers prepared themselves to look like the remnants of the platoon, blacking their hands and faces once more. Pat did the same. They were all taking a chance, they knew, but, barring Grievous, they all appeared confident of success when they set off.

Back at the place where they had arrested the three officers, Pat explained quietly, "Captain Heyman is going to fire a few rounds our way shortly. That's when we take off at a trot towards the gate. Grievous will be twenty yards ahead as he is the leading man in this scene. When we reach open ground, keep glancing over your shoulders to give the impression that you're being pursued. I'll return fire to complete the charade."

At that moment the first shots rang out from behind them and they trotted down the path towards the fort. The adrenalin was pumping through Pat's veins; he felt almost light-headed with excitement.

They broke cover and Grievous, well ahead of the others, began waving his arms urgently for someone to open the gate. Pat stopped, turned, knelt and fired into the air. They ran on, bellowing as loud as they could.

They must have made a convincing spectacle because the gate swung open and a white officer beckoned to them to hurry inside. Shots were fired from the battlements in the general direction of the imagined pursuers. Grievous and his men burst into the inner parade ground and came up against a group of waiting officers, one of whom Pat fervently hoped would be Colonel Andrada.

He was not disappointed. Grievous had acted superbly and drawn attention away from the others who would not have survived closer scrutiny. The colonel and his men belatedly reached for their side arms, but Pat shook his head and thrust the barrel of his Winchester into Andrada's chest.

"Colonel," said Pat quietly, "kindly order your men to lay down their weapons. The battle is over – no more shooting."

Captain Heyman and his patrol waited in the long grass at the edge of the clearing for a signal to enter the fort. He trembled in trepidation, imagining the many ways in which such a simple plan could go wrong, but knew he had to bide his time.

Inside, Colonel Andrada reluctantly gave the order for his men to place their weapons in the middle of the parade ground. He had no idea what force was outside. The mound grew as two hundred rifles were surrendered.

Grievous was finally enjoying himself, strutting about in his splendid uniform, waving his sword and using it to prod some of the laggards into faster capitulation.

"Instead of marching around with that pig-sticker in your hand, Grievous," shouted Pat, "will you please find a napkin or something white and raise it on the flagpole? Poor Heyman must be wetting himself out there by now."

"I know where I'd like to put a crappy nappy, too," Grievous called back, but he did as he was told.

"Mr van Zyl," said the colonel in English, "I must protest at your actions. It goes against the rules of conventional soldiering, does it not, sir?"

"I agree, but Mr Grieve is not a soldier even though he impersonated one so well. He is a photo-journalist with The Times of London and any minute his camera equipment will come through that gate with one of Captain Heyman's troopers and will ask me to take his picture beneath that white flag he has raised. That picture, colonel, together with his story, will make front page reading and make him famous around the world."

Just then, Captain Heyman entered with his men, their rifles at the ready.

Andrada looked puzzled. "Surely these are not the extent of your troops?" he asked.

"There are forty-eight of us plus about a hundred tribesmen under Queen Marquaniqua, and that's it." Pat watched the colonel's face redden as he accepted his predicament.

"This will be a disgrace that will end my career. We thought we were being attacked by a large force. What about all the artillery?"

"You may well ask. Apart from one genuine cannon, we pounded you with nuts and bolts from our own unpatented Peeshooters. I'll show you one later,"

Captain Heyman marched up and he and the colonel exchanged salutes. "I believe we have the advantage, Colonel," he said, "so if we can retire to somewhere more private, we can discuss the way forward. Would you gentlemen care to join us?" he looked at Pat, Brian and Grievous.

"I don't think so, captain. This is a military matter that we should stay out of," said Pat.

"As you wish."

The prisoners were sitting in platoon formation with their hands behind their heads under the watchful eyes of the sergeant and his men. The sun was heating up and it was obvious that they could not be left like that for long. Thirty minutes elapsed before Heyman and Andrada emerged. Heyman joined the three waiting friends.

"Well," he said, "first of all, my thanks to you. Without your help, I doubt we could have pulled this off on our own. I will report this in detail to my superiors in due course. I have informed Colonel Andrada that he and his men have permission to ration up and then he is to leave the garrison as soon as possible, unarmed, of course. We will claim everything else within these walls as spoils of war. The battle we have won today has established the boundary between the two countries permanently. I have given him a copy of the map Mr Rhodes drew up indicating this boundary with instructions that it be forwarded to the King of Portugal. Gentlemen, this is indeed a historic moment and deserves a celebration."

And so they celebrated, especially after they discovered the officers' well-stocked wine cellar. After the stresses and strains of the past few days, it came as a welcome release from tension and resulted in a few sore heads the following day.

Thus ended what was to become known as the Battle of Chua fought on May 11, 1891.

The next day, in spite of the hangovers, had its compensations as the spoils of war were itemised. It took three days. The three Gatling guns were especially prized as military acquisitions, but there were also crates of medical supplies and food. Then there was furniture and linen plus livestock consisting of cattle, sheep, goats, pigs mules and horses. There would, of course, have to be something from this hoard to give to Marquaniqua.

The return to Umtali would be more direct and therefore an easier journey, with no need for stealth. It was a road that had evolved over time as the best route through the mountains. Nevertheless, it would take more than a few wagon trips as Captain Heyman had decided to take much of the building material which would be used to construct better facilities at his headquarters.

⚔

Prior to departing with his men, Colonel Andrada asked Captain Heyman for permission to clear his desk. Heyman hesitated, and then Colonel Andrada quickly suggested that Pat accompany him. Pat shrugged. He had nothing else to do at the moment so he followed the colonel into his office.

The man seemed agitated as if his mind was elsewhere as he slowly sifted through his files. Suddenly he stopped and looked directly at Pat.

"Senhor van Zyl," he began, "I believe you are an honourable man and I know you are a resourceful one as you have shown over the past two days. I would like to make you a proposition. If you agree to it, we could both be wealthy men in time. Shall I continue?"

"By all means, Colonel. I came to these parts to seek my fortune and unless your proposition is unlawful, I'll listen."

"Thank you. Senhor, some six months ago one of my patrols met a Shangaan man who had been attacked by a lion and was in a bad way. They brought him here and our medic did what he could but the man was clearly dying. He asked to see me alone. He told me that he used to work on the mines at Kimberley, but had recently returned to his tribal home on the Nyanyadzi River, which he said was a two-day walk from here. Then he showed me a pouch that was tied around his waist under his loin cloth."

Colonel Andrada unlocked the bottom drawer of the desk, withdrew a game-skin pouch, and spilled the contents onto the desk. Sparkling in the morning sunlight coming through the window were twenty large uncut diamonds.

Pat let out a low whistle. "The bloody thief must have stolen them from a mine down south."

"No. He claims he dug the first one up near his home while visiting his family a year ago. Because of his working background, he recognised it for what it was and started digging. What you see here is the fruit of one week's labour, he told me."

"Go on," Pat encouraged the colonel.

"The man, Siyakonza, knew he was dying and he was concerned about his wife and young son at his home. He wanted to make a deal with me as I am now trying to do with you. If I agreed to adopt and care for his family, he would draw me a map showing where his diggings were and, more importantly to him, his wife and child. I immediately despatched a patrol and four days later we had them both under our protection. The poor man died two days later. Naturally I did not reveal to anyone here the details about the diamonds. The whole story could still be a fabrication and perhaps he did steal them from the Kimberley mine, as you said, but surely he would then have tried to sell them somewhere in the Cape rather than bring them back here to a country where he was unlikely to find a buyer."

"That makes sense," Pat said. "So what sort of deal are you suggesting?"

"The deal is, Senhor, that I give you the map and we become fifty-fifty partners. I would have to be a silent partner because I can hardly go prospecting in a foreign country, especially after what has happened here over the past few days. I have some savings and could contribute towards the start-up costs but you would be the man with his hands on the pick handle, if you understand me."

"I can see your position all right," said Pat. "This really is unexpected and my first reaction is that any deal would have to include my two friends because, without their recent help, you and I would not be having this conversation. What do you say to a four-way deal with twenty five per cent each?"

The colonel thought for a moment and then held out his hand firmly. "Agreed."

"I think, colonel, you should give me half the stones now because I'm going to have to convince my friends and perhaps some others that we are not embarking on a hopeless cause and that there is a probability that this place does exist. Do you trust me that far?"

Andrada did not hesitate. He counted out ten of the diamonds and handed them over. They shook hands again before he gave Pat the map and his contact details in Beira. Then he left the office and called to a junior officer to make final arrangements for their departure to the coast. The party would include Siyakonza's wife and son, whom he had promised to support.

That evening Pat told his friends of his talk with the colonel as they sat round a fire in a corner of the parade ground sipping whisky.

"It could be a load of old horse manure," said Pat, "or there could be lots more of these waiting to be dug up." He opened his hand and revealed the diamonds.

"I don't know anything about diamonds," exclaimed Brian, "but those look real enough to me."

"Where do we go from here?" asked Grievous?

"Nothing ventured, nothing gained is my view and I have no other pressing agenda." Pat said.

Brian chuckled. "The farm can wait a while."

"Count me in," said Grievous, "though I do have to get my story and film back to my editor and then tell him I'm extending my stay here. I'll say there's a chance of more good stories. That's not far from the truth – diamond discoveries always make big news. If we do strike it rich, I may be due for a career change anyway."

"So what's next?" asked Brian.

"Unless I do it myself and hold you two up for a few weeks, I need a reliable postman who can ship my package from Beira," Grievous said.

"Your best chance of that is from Umtali, and as we're in for some serious walking and carrying, perhaps we can persuade Captain Heyman to sell us a couple of his newly-acquired mules."

"Good idea!" said Pat. "We'll need tools and rations and he's got plenty of both at the moment. I'll go and talk to him right now." Pat stood up, but Grievous held up his hand.

"Should we tell him the whole story?"

"A half-truth will be enough," said Pat. "We're going off for a bit of prospecting. There's nothing unusual in that these days."

Half an hour later, Pat returned with a big grin on his face. "He's rewarded us for our efforts with three horses and two mules from the booty and as many rations as we can carry. We leave with the advance party for Umtali tomorrow."

They made an early start and were in Umtali by nightfall. Their first task was the delivery of Grievous' mail and they found a recommended trader who was leaving for the coast in a couple of days.

On the eve of their departure to Nyanyadzi River they discussed their knowledge of the diamond business which amounted to almost nothing. Pat had thought a lot about this since his meeting with Andrada. Now he shared those thoughts with his friends.

"I think our first job is to verify Siyakonza's story. If it is true and diamonds do exist there, I believe one of us must travel to Kimberley and consult with Mr Rhodes. He is the head of de Beers, but also his British South Africa Company is the only authority in Mashonaland or Zambezia or whatever they call it that can grant us a mining claim. We must play this thing straight or we could come unstuck."

"Fair enough," said Grievous. "If this turns out to be a rich deposit, we'll need a lot more money to exploit it so we'd require a wealthy partner or a hefty loan. De Beers can provide that and they would solve the marketing aspect as well. I agree with you, Pat."

Brian added, "Seems to me we've got nothing to lose by going that route."

The end of May was a good time for travel. It was the start of the cooler months when there was little or no rain though early mornings and evenings would be chilly and the days slightly shorter.

They hired three of Marquaniqua's tribesmen, one of whom knew the Marange area through which the Nyanyadzi River flowed.

However, Gungunyana also knew the area. Over many years he had stolen cattle from Chief Marange without any serious retaliation. Because of this, Pat took three of his Peeshooters, which he had modified by putting in a simple percussion mechanism that made them more like conventional muzzle-loaders. They could now be operated by one man and could be fired by a trigger or a trip wire. Any one sneaking up on the men at night would hear the bark and feel the bite of a hundred pieces of shrapnel.

When they left, the whole police troop came to see them on their way. Captain Heyman shook their hands and wished them well.

They had seventy miles to cover before they reached the river, hopefully in two days. The hard part would be after that as they looked for Siyakonza's village.

After they had passed beyond Brian's suggested site for the new Umtali, which they achieved on the first day, the mountains gradually gave way to flat open landscape with a few scattered rocky hills, called *kopjes*. It was what the Afrikaaners termed the *lowveld*. There were many great baobab trees, leafless now and looking as if a giant hand had uprooted them and replanted them upside down. Grass was sparse and the only other vegetation was the acacia karoo covered with branches with long thorns that groped and scratched if one passed too close.

The guide was Tendai. He led them along worn paths that linked the villages, which were far apart because they each relied upon the availability of water. This was country better suited to goats than humans. They saw a few oxen that were used for draught power.

Wildlife was more prolific. They saw herds of impala and several kudu groups. These were creatures that could survive many days without water as they could assuage their thirst through their food alone. Elephants had left their marks on the baobabs, having stripped the bark from them with their tusks during leaner years.

They reached the Nyanyadzi River on the second afternoon and they were extremely happy to see it was still flowing. They noticed several women from a nearby village drawing water so they decided to make camp further upriver. They found a good spot under a large Nyala tree where the grassy river banks provided grazing for the horses and mules.

Siyakonza's map had shown the route from Massi-Kessi, whereas Umtali was further north so they were not sure which way to proceed. Pat's instinct and coarse calculations suggested a downstream progress.

Pat said, "First we'd better pay our respects to the local chief and then we can ask if he or one of his people can point us in the right direction when I show him my sketch of the two hills."

It was still light when they reached the village after a thirty-minute walk. There were only about twenty huts and a kraal for the oxen, a few grain bins on stilts and plenty of hard well-brushed space in between where chickens ran and scratched without much luck. The chief emerged from the murky interior of the largest hut. He looked no different from any of the other male villagers other than that he carried a calabash, presumably containing some local alcoholic brew as he was unsteady on his feet.

"Why are so many of the local dignitaries we meet always pissed?" asked Grievous. "This one wouldn't know a hill from a hole in the ground."

"Just smile a lot, go through the clapping routine to greet him, and leave the talking to Tendai," whispered Pat. Greeting customs were always long, even more so when a chief was involved, so they waited patiently.

At last Tendai was able to put their request for help. He brought out the map which the chief snatched from him and examined it from every angle without showing that he understood it at all. He passed it to a group of elders who sat beside him. After much discussion over it, heads began to nod in agreement. However, the chief began babbling again, sniffing at his wrist like a wild dog on the scent. Pat got the message and produced a tin of snuff from his pocket and handed it to the chief, who shook out a generous heap onto the back of his hand before giving one repulsive snort.

Pat spoke from behind his raised hand. "If that doesn't blow his head off, nothing will. There's quite a few grains of our Peeshooter powder in it to add impetus." But they were amazed to see the man squint momentarily, shake his head, and break into a dazzling smile without the hint of a sneeze.

Pat was anxious to leave. He pulled Tendai aside and with both of them using a mixture of sign language and the few words of ChiShona he had picked up, he learned that his instinct had been correct. Their destination was less than a day's walk downstream. Now the chief wanted to know why they were going there.

"How did you answer, Tendai?"

"I told him you sought the teeth of the big elephant that lives in that place. And that's true."

"Good thinking,"

"He also said that until recently he had a woman relative living there with her small son and a husband who only visited sometimes."

Turning to his friends, Pat said, "Did you understand that? It sounds as if he was talking about Siyakonza."

As they walked back to their camp, Tendai said that the chief had also told him that they should be careful as Gungunyana and his gang of thugs were in the area. They had raided a village upstream and stolen cattle two nights ago. The chief thought that they might be tempted to include some white men on their visiting list.

Pat told Brian and Grievous about the chief's warning and suggested that they move further upstream where they would be better protected in the event of an attack that night. He did not think it likely at such short notice, but he still set up the Peeshooters so that they covered the whole area beyond the camp and could be triggered by one person, whoever was on guard at the time.

As it happened, the night passed peacefully with only a mix of Brian's snores and croaking frogs from the river breaking the silence. Grievous, on the final watch of the night, shook the others awake and told them to expect scrambled eggs for breakfast when the messenger he had sent to the village returned.

"An A for initiative," grinned Pat, "but then food is never far from your mind, is it?"

Worried about Gungunyana, Pat said, "It seems to me that we have two options. We can press on downriver and hope to stay ahead of him, but if he catches us, he'll have the advantage as our artillery will not be set up. Or, we move a short distance downstream, organise ourselves, and meet him on our terms. I favour the second choice."

"That makes sense to me," said Brian.

"I agree. Let's get the bastard sorted once and for all. If we do, the locals will love us and that can only be good for our mission." Grievous forked the last of his scrambled egg into his mouth.

They were packed and were ready to move out by 8 am. A messenger was despatched to the chief to tell him that should Gunganyana arrived at his village he was not to be afraid of telling him the direction the whites had taken. They then departed, following a path along the river line. An hour later Pat called a halt and they tethered the animals in the shade of a large fever tree.

"This will make and ideal campsite, only we are not going to camp here."

"I am confused Pat, what do you mean?" asked Grievous?

"We're going to use a little subterfuge. We make them think that we're camped here when in fact we'll be sitting up there." Pat pointed to the top of a slope about fifty yards away where a large anthill was lodged up against a fig tree. "We'll set up the Peeshooters and then wait for him. If he follows the usual pattern we've been told about, he'll come before first light."

"What about the animals?" asked Brian.

"All we can do is tether them down on that grassy patch at the water's edge below the bank and hope they'll be out of harm's way when the Peeshooters start spreading our good news."

By midday they completed their preparations at the camp, including a smouldering fire which gave off a tell-tale spiral of smoke. This had to last for the rest of the day and night.

The guide and the two porters each had rifles which Pat had taught them how to use before leaving Umtali. They could probably hit a baobab tree from fifty paces, but it added to their fire power. Now he briefed them on their role. They nodded their heads in understanding and moved into their positions.

As the sun set, a procession of wildlife made its way down to the river to drink. They were aware of humans around them as they sniffed the air and swished their tails, but they were not too perturbed, merely extra cautious.

When it was dark, Pat moved to the camp fire and rearranged the logs to last through the night. Again they all took turns to keep guard. The porters took the rear while the white men watched the front. They were connected by a length of string to tug which changed hands at the end of each three-hour shift. They settled down to wait.

CHAPTER FIVE

It was 4.30 am and Pat sat on a large rock scanning the area below him in the limited light of a fast sinking new moon. Already the francolin had started their ratchet-like call as they walked around pecking the ground for food. Suddenly there was a change of pitch as they became alarmed and began darting about, unable to see well enough yet to take flight. Pat was instantly alert. Silently, he crawled over and shook his companions while pulling on the string to warn the three porters. They all took up their pre-arranged positions. Pat laid the trigger wires close to hand. He had anticipated Gungunyana's men surrounding the camp before attacking and the Peeshooters were arranged to deal effectively with such tactics.

Nerves taut, six pairs of eyes strained for signs of movement below them. Pat was certain they were coming. Then he saw them, nebulous, almost surreal, as they crept, bent over, along the path through the early morning mist rising off the river. They spread out as they reached the clearing, encircling the camp. There were about thirty of them, armed with what looked like ancient flintlock rifles and knobkerries.

"Brace yourselves for the big bang," whispered Pat. Suddenly the marauders stood upright and, screaming hysterically, they fired at what they thought were the three sleeping white men and their porters.

Pat paused for a few moments and then activated the Peeshooters in unison. The noise was ear-shattering. Dust and shredded leaves blotted out the scene before them.

"Take that, you savages," yelled Grievous, hopping up and down.

"Get down, you idiot," shouted Brian, pulling at his jacket. "You'll get your bloody head blown off."

"Hold fire, everyone," bawled Pat. "Don't move. Wait for the dust to settle."

When it did, nothing moved at the camp site. All that they heard were the groans of wounded and dying men. There was nothing left to shoot at. No one spoke as they surveyed the devastation. They were awe-struck.

"I suppose it was us or them," Brian said softly. He was struggling with his conscience.

"Sit tight," murmured Pat. "Wait until light. If anything moves, shoot it."

When the full dawn came, Pat led them all down in an extended line, rifles at the ready. He told Tendai and his comrades to collect the weapons while he, Brian and Grievous assessed the damage. There were only seven left alive and of those some were unlikely to make it back to their kraals.

Pat examined the bodies, wondering which one was Gungunyana, until he came upon one, shattered and bloody, taller and broader than the rest. Around his neck was a necklace of blood-soaked monkey paws, shrivelled with age to the point where they looked to be carved from wood.

He called over Tendai and told him to confirm from one of the survivors if this was indeed their main man. It was confirmed willingly, almost with relief.

Brian said, "Judging by the reaction of his own men, I reckon there won't be too many tears shed when this news gets out."

"What do we do with the wounded?" asked Grievous.

"Patch them up as best we can and let them go," replied Pat. An hour later he said to Tendai, "Tell them they are free to return home but if they cross our path again, there'll be no second chance for them."

"Amen to that," sighed Grievous. "Now I suggest a brew-up with a touch of scotch to settle the nerves." They went back to their ambush position, lit a fire, and settled the kettle on it.

Draining his cup, Pat stood up and stretched, "Wait here while I go to the village to tell the chief that Gungunyana won't trouble him again. He may wish to pay his last respects or celebrate our success. Either way, it's good public relations."

"He should be grateful enough to supply a few gravediggers," said Brian.

"I'll suggest that." He put on his hat, picked up his rifle and the monkey-paw necklace, and strode off.

⇒‡‡⇐

Pat returned with the chief and his ululating tribesmen, who pounced upon the bodies with further mutilation in mind before they were restrained.

"He took some convincing," said Pat, "but the necklace did the trick and then he was delighted with our efforts. He sent messengers in all directions to spread the news."

The dead were finally buried according to custom before the chief told Pat they would celebrate the occasion the next day with a slaughtered ox and plenty of millet beer. This would be conducted at the battle ground and all were invited.

The day began early for the women as they collected firewood, cut up meat which they threw into large clay pots, pounded grain into flour with long wooden pestles.

By midday the party was underway. Pat's group, as the guests of honour, had to join in and this meant pretending to drink plenty of the foul-tasting, gruel-like concoction which passed as beer. Refusal would have insulted the hosts.

"The stuff people will swallow just to get drunk," said Grievous. "This swill must slosh around in the belly like shit in a bucket."

"Look on the bright side," Brian said, "Distillation follows fermentation. They'll learn that if they haven't already."

Then the complex rhythm of drumbeats began the dancing with much swaying and stamping of feet. Soon dust and the smell of sweat permeated the air.

"Now would be a good time to leave," suggested Grievous. "They won't miss us."

"What about our porters?" Brian asked. They were clearly enjoying themselves immensely.

"I'll let them know that we're moving further down the river and they must catch up with us tomorrow, whatever time that might be," said Pat.

They sneaked off unnoticed and walked downstream for an hour before setting up camp and preparing the evening meal. There was no urgency as they knew the porters would not arrive early the next day. They relaxed, discussing their latest adventure, secure in the knowledge that they were now safe from human attack and that night they slept well.

They resumed their journey when the porters arrived around midday looking a little the worse for wear.

The river took a bend and there before them, not more than a mile away, were the hill features they had been looking for. They soon found Siyakonza's empty homestead, another set of dilapidated pole, mud and grass huts set back from the river. The family grain plot was between the two, a collection of dead stalks entwined with creepers.

Leaving the porters to set up camp, they followed the map's instructions, anxious to find the diggings before nightfall.

"There it is!" cried Brian. He pointed at what resembled an alluvial terrace a few feet high and extending as far as the eye could see in both directions. The vegetation was sparse, the ground hard and full of rocks.

"This looks like it could have been the original river bank many, many years ago," said Pat.

Grievous agreed. "Look behind you. Across the river there's a similar ridge. It must have been one hell of a waterway in the distant past."

Pat stared at the two hills in the middle distance and began walking east along the bottom of the ridge, followed by his companions. He kept his gaze on the two hills. His map told him that when he reached a point where he could see through only a narrow gap between them, he would have arrived at Siyakonza's diggings.

He was so intent on looking ahead that he nearly fell into them. Suddenly he found himself standing on the edge of a ditch four feet deep, the same in width, and about twenty feet long. He let out a loud whoop and turned to his friends. "Gentlemen," he announced, "I think we have arrived."

Siyakonza had disguised his toil by spreading the piles of soil he had excavated and placing thorn scrub over the trench. They were lucky not to have fallen in.

"From the little I know about diamond mining from my reading about Kimberley," said Pat, "any diamonds Siyakonza found here would be alluvial, washed down river centuries ago. On the other hand, it could be that he hit upon a kimberlite pipe that became exposed by the water rushing down the river."

"I guess we'll find out soon enough," said Brian, jumping into the trench where he picked up a handful of gravel and let it slip through his fingers. "Anyway, for now let's get back to camp, get a good night's sleep, and make an early start in the morning."

After supper, around the fire, Pat told them a story he had heard about those legendary prospectors, Cecil Rhodes and Barney Barnato. "Just to whet your appetite, chaps!"

"Barney Barnato began as an East End barrow boy in London with very little education. However, he was street-wise and ambitious so he joined the early rush to the Kimberley fields where he prospered until his Kimberley Central Company became the largest producer of diamonds.

"Cecil Rhodes, as head of de Beers, was keen to join forces with Barnato so that they could regulate the sale of diamonds on the world market, thus ensuring the viability of the industry and the sooner the better as Barnato was planning to float his company on the London Stock Exchange. This was more for the prestige it would bring him than through good business sense. As usual, Rhodes eventually had his way. The end result came about because of Barnato's inferiority complex about his humble beginnings and his craving for social acceptance."

Pat paused for a swig from his mug before continuing. "Barnato once confided to one of his aides that Rhodes looked down on him because he had not been to college. If he had received Rhodes' education, he said, there would have been no Cecil Rhodes. But that's another story.

"Rhodes had asked Barnato to come to his office but Barnato, seeing the disadvantage of negotiating in his rival's arena, insisted that Rhodes came to see him. Rhodes agreed. He pointed out to Barnato that while he was loyal to his shareholders, they were selling their shares behind his back as the price rose. It seemed as if he was fighting himself. Barney Barnato knew about this but still he held out against selling the company he had founded.

"Rhodes was a stubborn man; he rarely took no for an answer. Shortly afterwards, he invited a number of dealers, including Barnato, to view a few parcels of diamonds for sale. He arranged them in piles on a long plank with raised sides in the de Beers' boardroom. Of course, the whole ploy was aimed at Barnato. 'Just a small selection from our reserve stock,' he informed them all casually. 'They were gathered like mushrooms in a field, only one day's workings, twelve thousand carats.'

Barnato was naturally impressed, but not overwhelmed. Rhodes then added to the piles a further two hundred thousand carats. Each pile of diamonds had been carefully graded according to size and value and placed on a square of tissue paper. Rhodes knew the total value to be half a million pounds but he had priced them at seven hundred thousand pounds to allow himself some bargaining space. He told the buyers that he was only interested in selling them all as one package. Then he left the room.

No one knows what was said in the room, but finally, when Rhodes returned, Barnato agreed to the asking price. Much as Rhodes was delighted by this turn of events, he urged his rival not to sell too soon as this would flood the market and drive down the price. Barnato said nothing though he planned an early sale with a quick profit before the market reacted. Then, without warning, Rhodes upended the plank and the diamonds cascaded into a bucket like some kaleidoscopic waterfall. "I've always wanted to see a bucketful of diamonds," he said. Too late, Barnato realised what Rhodes had done. It would take at least six weeks to re-grade the diamonds, thus delaying their resale and avoiding a market flood."

Grievous chuckled. "That must have been a sight to see – a bucketful of diamonds. £700 000! Hell, you could buy a kingdom with that much money. Even a farm, Brian!"

"I wonder what really lies up there," mused Brian, nodding in the direction of Siyakonza's diggings.

"We'll know soon enough, my friends," said Pat.

In the distance a lion roared and a hippo retorted with a snort of contempt from the river. The three men slept and heard nothing.

The porters, transformed into diggers, attacked the hard earth with their picks. They flung them back in a wide arc, and then crashed them down, embedding the steel fangs into the sun-baked crust. The loose soil and rock was then shovelled into sacks and dragged down to the river where the white men washed and sifted it. They were all soon sweating and it became obvious that they could only work before ten o'clock in the morning and after four.

The intention at this stage was merely to confirm the existence of the precious stones before they planned a new strategy. They had not long to wait. Grievous suddenly let out a mighty shout.

"Take a look here! If this isn't a sparkler, I don't know what is." He held up to the sun a pea-sized chip stuck into a piece of clinker-like rock.

"Are you sure it's a diamond?" asked Brian.

Pat said, "It looks very much like Siyakonza's stones so let's assume it is."

Brian was still dubious. "How the hell do we know if it's flawed or valuable?"

"We don't. All we can do is keep digging the damn things up until we have a sock full and then go and see an expert."

This seemed to be a breeding ground for the stones, whatever they were, for that afternoon shift revealed half a dozen more of varying sizes.

At dusk, Pat set off with a shotgun in search of guinea fowl, which would be making their way towards the river before perching for the night. He also wanted time to think about their next move in case they really were on to something big. His main concern was secrecy. If word got out about their find, there would be another uncontrolled diamond rush as had happened at Kimberley. They would have to tread carefully to avoid that.

His thoughts were interrupted when a flock of guinea fowl broke cover twenty yards ahead of him. He smoothly brought the shotgun to his shoulder and followed their flight for a brief moment before firing one barrel. Because these birds tend to fly in close formation behind the leader, it was not uncommon to bring down a brace with one cartridge. Pat, with his expertise, watched as three of them rolled and fell to earth in a polka-dot confusion of feathers. If only we had potatoes and onions to go with the meat, Pat mused. He retrieved the evening supper and sat down with his back against a tree to continue his thinking.

He recalled how Rhodes' business partner, Charles Rudd, had secured an agreement with King Lobengula, the son of Mzilikazi, the man who had brought the Ndebele people to their new land around Bulawayo in the west. Rhodes was granted sole concession for mineral exploration in the kingdom on the understanding that the limited number of Europeans allowed in were subject to Ndebele law and would defend the king from any other invaders. These were verbal pledges and Rhodes reneged on them all by forming the British South Africa Company. In October 1889 he received a charter from the British government which gave him sovereignty over not only Lobengula's land but also that which extended eastwards to include Mashonaland and Manicaland on the Mozambique border.

Dr Jameson was the local authority in the BSA Company and Pat realised that he would have to seek this man's advice about the way forward. He stood and returned to the camp.

"Can we trust these fellows?" Grievous asked, nodding towards the porters. "What's to stop them from blabbing about our find?"

"I spoke to Tendai," replied Pat. "When he asked what we were looking for, I told him it was pretty stones that white men give to their woman as a wedding present instead of cattle to the father, as he would do. He found this hilarious and then asked what use these stones were. I said, 'None at all'. He looked at me in amazement and said, 'You white men are lucky to get your women so cheap,' and he walked off, shaking his head. So, no, I don't think we have a problem at the moment. Still, when we get to Umtali, I reckon it would be wise to keep them on a retainer while we travel to Fort Salisbury so that we don't have to recruit a new bunch for the next stage."

⊱─━─⊰

On the first night back in Umtali, they dined with Captain Heyman, who already knew about their encounter with Gungunyana, as did the whole district.

"You lads have become a bit of a legend in these parts with your role in the Battle of Chua and now the routing of Gungunyana. This can only help the Company's cause and I've been sending my reports. In fact, I received a message from Dr Jameson himself two days ago. He wants to meet you in Salisbury as soon as possible."

Pat winked at his friends and smiled at the Captain. "That works out nicely for us. We were hoping to set up a meeting with him anyway."

After a brief stopover in Umtali, Pat and Brian bade farewell to Grievous, who was leaving for Beira. He had to sail to London to report to his editor. He planned to stay there, pending the outcome of the talks with Dr Jameson and Pat's future plans. He would then decide whether or not to rejoin them permanently.

"I don't know why, Grievous," said Brian, "but I think I might even miss having you around. Perhaps it's because of that vacuous aura which surrounds you and invites ridicule."

"And you, my friend, will look even more ridiculous if I bloody your nose as a parting gesture, you big ox."

They laughed and shook hands.

⊱─━─⊰

Dr Leander Starr Jameson, known affectionately as Dr Jim, was a highly competent surgeon. He had arrived in Kimberley from

71

England at the age of twenty-five, lured like so many others by the prospects of wealth on the diamond fields. Through his medical practice and his natural charm, he became a hugely popular character. Befriended by Cecil Rhodes, he had prospered to the extent that he was now a major shareholder in de Beers.

The doctor's Fort Salisbury office was hardly imposing for a man who was the sole authority over the white settlers in this new country. It looked like a large wooden crate with an iron roof. One of the roofing sheets was propped open like the flap of an envelope to give ventilation and more light. The Union Jack fluttered from a makeshift flagstaff outside – the only symbol of officialdom. Inside, the single room was partitioned by a linen curtain, suggesting that one side of it was used as his sleeping quarters. The floor was a mixture of cow dung and crushed anthill compacted until it was rock hard. A desk, a bookcase and three chairs was the only visible furniture. The office was otherwise bare except for a stand for a pen and inkwell and a photograph of Cecil Rhodes on horseback, both on the desk.

Dr Jameson rose and shook hands with the two men. He was of delicate stature, almost bird-like with a fringe of hair around a bald pate. Despite the gentle appearance which suggested a warm nature, his firm handshake demonstrated great strength of character.

"Please sit down," he said, offering the two chairs on the other side of his desk. "Thank you for coming to see me so promptly. I hope I haven't taken you out of your way."

"On the contrary, sir, we were planning to ask for an appointment with you," said Pat.

"Let me put my proposal to you first and then you can tell me what I can do for you. Your exploits since arriving in Mashonaland so recently are already known to the indigenous population, especially the ending of Gungunyana's reign of terror with the use of your, er, Peeshooters, as Captain Heyman called them in his report. Quite ingenious, Mr van Zyl, and obviously very effective." He smiled at them. "The Company would like to believe that it can call upon your skills as a gunsmith to assist against any insurrection, which is always on the cards. But first, let me ask you if you intend to stay in this new land."

Pat replied, "I have leased my business interests in Natal and I'm looking for new opportunities. A little adventure along the way to spice things up will be welcome."

"As for me," Brian said, "You could say I'm on an extended holiday, gratefully paid for by my family in England, with whom my outlook on life tends to differ. This country has great appeal. With the climate so suited to agriculture, I'd like to try my hand as a farmer."

"I like that, Mr Wood-Gush. Now, in the event of an uprising, would you both be prepared to offer your considerable skills?"

Pat paused while he considered what the doctor had said so far. "Before we answer your question, let me say that we wanted this appointment because it has some bearing on our decision."

"Fine! Go ahead."

Starting with the Battle of Chua and his encounter with Colonel Andrada, Pat related the events leading up to their diamond discovery on the Nyanyadzi River. "Our problem, Dr Jameson, is that we know nothing about diamonds, diamond mining, or how to obtain a mining claim."

"You have some samples with you?" asked the doctor.

Pat brought out the bag of diamonds and tipped them on to the desk. Jameson produced a jeweller's glass from his top desk drawer and examined the stones. Removing the glass from his eye, he leaned back and cleared his throat. "These are quality stones, gentlemen. You could be on to something important. The question is, where do you go from here? Pegging your claim can easily be arranged. Mining and marketing the stones takes expertise and you admit you have no knowledge there."

"That's why we're here," said Brian. "There are four partners so far in this venture." He mentioned Grievous' involvement. "Then, of course, we feel honour bound to include Colonel Andrada. The three of us are happy to roll up our sleeves and get stuck in, but we feel we're going nowhere without bringing on board your company for knowledge and further finance."

Jameson rose and paced up and down the office for a while. He stopped and said, "As it happens, Mr Rhodes is on his way here from Beira with some good news for the settlers. He'll be here in four or five days. I'm sure he'll be interested in your proposal, as I am. I'm also certain that if Barney Barnato hears of your find, he'll be here damned fast with a proposal of his own. Naturally, we don't want that to happen."

"I can understand that, sir," said Pat.

"I take it you can wait a few days for Mr Rhodes. Perhaps you wouldn't mind spending some time looking over our security arrangements here at Salisbury."

Pat, always looking for opportunities, said, "May I make a suggestion, Dr Jameson? I am also a trained blacksmith and I'd like to bring in a forge and install it here. I can see a definite need for one later in Umtali and perhaps elsewhere. I have a couple of competent and well-trained locals in Ladysmith who I'm sure would agree to re-locate if given the right incentive. I'd set them up here at the anvil. They'd require only minimum supervision, leaving me with plenty of time to spend on more lucrative work." He pointed at the diamonds.

"I had positive feelings about this meeting," said Jameson, "but this is more than I had anticipated. It's a very good idea. Choose your site and leave the rest to me."

Pat and Brian left the office to tour the settlement on horseback. The buildings were confined to the slopes of a small hill overlooking a vast plateau. Most of them were pole and mud huts with conical thatched roofs, but larger than those used by the local tribesmen. Here and there were wood and iron structures much like Dr Jim's.

A clean water supply came from a small fast-running stream on the western side. They followed it away from the hill for half a mile and camped under a msasa tree.

Brian said, "I suppose we will have time to inspect the security system while we're waiting for Mr Rhodes."

Pat grinned at him. "I wouldn't mind checking out the female talent as well, if there is any. I'm desperate to see something more shapely than you – and smells better too."

Without warning, Brian leapt to his feet, scooped up Pat in a bear hug, and ran with him to the water's edge and heaving them both into the river. Pat rose to the surface spluttering and coughing, trying to break loose from Brian's grip.

"Don't talk to me about body odour," roared Brian as he dunked Pat up and down. "No woman will let you within a mile of her, especially if she's downwind."

Soon they emerged laughing to strip off their clothes and return to the river, this time with soap and a razor. Lying naked in the sun while their washed clothes covered the surrounding grass, they agreed that the future looked promising. Content they drifted off to sleep.

⊶⊷

The unaccustomed sound of giggling women drifted through their slumbers. When they sensed it was real, they bolted upright, then promptly flattened themselves back on the grass. They were too late and caught only a brief glimpse of two young women retreating in a flurry of petticoats.

"Damn it, Pat, are we dreaming or did we just see two giggling females?" If we did, then they've seen every last bit of us. Naked as the day we were born and we don't even know what they look like. You know what that means? It means every time we pass a woman in the street, we won't know if she was one of them."

"You won't bump into them again, Brian. Having seen what you have to offer, they'll run a mile at the first sight of you."

"Listen to who's talking. You might be lethal with your rifle, but your personal weaponry is pretty shabby, to say the least." They both laughed.

"Seriously," said Pat, "if we do meet those two flappers again, we'll know who they are because they won't be able to keep a straight face."

That confrontation came sooner than they expected. They had finished eating and drinking at an eatery which served the bachelor community on the crest of the hill. As they made their way back to their campsite along a road that snaked through a maze of shacks, wagons and tents, they noticed a man struggling to remove one of the rear wheels from his wagon.

"Can we help you, sir?" asked Pat.

"I'd be more than grateful," answered the man. "Sometimes I think I would have been better served with sons instead of two daughters." He chuckled. "I'm Joe Graham and the scrubber over there is the love of my life, Madge."

"I heard that! Call me a scrubber, would you, Joseph Graham?" The lady swung the nightshirt she was washing once around her head and let fly. It caught Joe a good frothy swipe right across his face. "Take that!" she hollered, "Ye Scottish twit."

Joe, sporting his soapy scarf, cracked up laughing and made a lunge for Madge.

"Don't you dare lay a finger on me, Joseph, or you'll be on short rations for the next three weeks," she shrieked. Then she too was laughing.

So engrossed in this scene were Pat and Brian that they failed to see the two young women who had emerged from the other side of the wagon to investigate the uproar. Pat noticed them first and dug his finger into Brian's ribs. The girls were giggling and blushing and the two men realised that this hilarity was directed, not at their parents, but at them.

"What did I tell you, Brian?" said Pat, showing a rare blush while Brian's mouth simply opened and closed like that of a landed catfish.

Joe said, "I think I'm missing something here. Have you young people already met?" The girls laughed even more.

Once the mirth had subsided, Brian said, "I can honestly say that we have never laid eyes on your lovely daughters, more's the pity, but if they say the same about us, it will be a lie." The subtlety of this comment was not lost on the younger generation. present. "However, enough said by us. If the girls wish to elaborate later, that's their choice. Now let me introduce ourselves."

Joe looked puzzled, but said, I'm sure all will be revealed in time. (more sniggering from the sisters.) Allow me to introduce Sandra, our elder daughter. He indicated the taller, darker girl.

Her face did not have a classic beauty, but her light brown eyes, flecked with emerald, mesmerised Pat. Her crinkly smile left him weak at the knees. Of all the girls he had met, none had had this effect upon him, but he managed to say, "I thank God for bringing me to Mashonaland and I thank him for breaking Joseph's wheel spoke, and ..." Then he ran out of words.

Sandra, seeming equally attracted, responded with a mischievous smile, "God works in wondrous ways, Mr van Zyl."

"That he surely does, miss."

Joe sensed the mood and quickly said, "And this is Margery, the baby in the family."

Margery was fairer and shorter than her sister, more like her father, but very pretty.

"If she's a baby, sir, then I'll be back tomorrow when she's grown up," grinned Brian.

"Don't overdo it, Brian," whispered Pat.

"I'll try, but she's something else, hey?"

Pat tore his gaze away from Sandra and said, "Let's get this wheel sorted out now before it's too late."

The job done, they all sat around the fire sipping coffee as the sun's last rays bathed the veld in a deepening golden yellow.

"What brought you to these parts, Mr Graham?" asked Brian.

"I guess it was a desire to see new places and explore the possibility of a better life. Although both our parents were born in Scotland, Madge and I were brought up in the Cape and the girls were born there. We were both teachers, Madge with music and I taught geography and mathematics. Sandra has studied dressmaking and Margery is something of an artist. We think we're a fairly useful family unit in these pioneering circumstances and Dr Jim was happy to have us as settlers. The plan is to build a school here. I'll be the headmaster, Madge will look after the music, while Margery will help out with the little ones. As for Sandra, she's brought enough calico with her to keep her busy for quite a long time."

"How does your wife intend to make music when the only instrument around is a native drum?"

"The Africans do have more than just drums, Mr van Zyl. Still, let me show you something." Joe took Pat over to the wagon with a lantern and raised the flap. "You remarked on the size of the wagon when we were removing the wheel. There's the reason." To Pat's astonishment, wedged safely between some sea chests, was a piano.

"I can hardly believe it. Come and see, Brian."

"This is a bit of history in the making, the first piano in Mashonaland," said Brian. "When's the first dance to be held, Mrs Graham, so that I can claim in advance the first dance with your lovely daughter, Margery?"

"As soon as the school house is built, I would say. And if you've a way of hastening that matter along, the sooner you'll be dancing."

"I volunteer," said Brian quickly, "but first let me see if Margery agrees with this arrangement. I've a feeling my good friend Pat will also go along with this idea." They looked across at the girls, both of whom smiled and bowed their heads coyly. "Well, ma'am, it looks like you have a couple of volunteers."

"What about you two?" asked Joe. "Are you just passing through or are you thinking of staying around?"

"I'd say the chances of sticking around become more likely by the minute," replied Brian, glancing towards the girls. "But I have to say that we do have a proposition to put to Mr Rhodes when he comes. If we reach an agreement, it could prove mutually beneficial. Anyway, enough said for now. I think we should be getting back to our camp. Thanks very much for the coffee, Mrs Graham and it's been a pleasure meeting you all."

"We should thank you for helping us with the wheel."

"When you've replaced that spoke, call us in to help fit the wheel back on."

They were silent for a long time while walking to their camp until Brian said, "This is the stuff of story books, Pat. You'd walk all the streets of Cape Town without meeting two better-looking girls and we bang into them in the back of beyond. The chemistry seems to be right for both of us or am I missing something?"

"You're right, Brian. Sandra really does take my breath away, but slow down a bit. If there's one thing I've learned about women, it is not to appear too eager at first. You've got to use the right technique."

CHAPTER SIX

Rhodes' arrival was delayed for reasons unknown so Pat and Brian spent the next two weeks fulfilling their promise to Mrs Graham by helping to build a schoolhouse. It was no architectural wonder but it was functional and waterproof. The structure was forty feet long and twenty wide with walls of Msasa poles that were daubed with mushed anthill soil and were only three feet high. However, the high-pitched roof was designed so that the thatch overlapped the wall, leaving enough space for light and good air circulation while screening the pupils from outside distractions. Reed sleeping mats, used by the local Africans, hung from the side roof beams and could be rolled up for extra light and air and down to provide waterproof curtains. The floor was the usual local recipe of cow dung and anthill which, when dried hard, could be waxed and polished to a high sheen. The door was constructed from old paraffin boxes while rough-hewn planks of msasa wood were made into desks and benches.

"Job done!" announced Joe Graham as he placed a blackboard on its easel as the final touch. "I think this calls for a celebration. What do you say, Mrs Graham?"

"Of course! We promised these two young men a dance when the schoolhouse was finished and we can't break a promise, can we, Joseph? But I must ask Pat and Brian for one last favour." She looked at their puzzled faces. "Help us move the piano in." They nodded enthusiastically.

Word had just arrived by messenger that Rhodes was due to arrive the next day, a Friday. It was quickly decided to hold the dance on the Saturday, giving the women in the community two full days to prepare.

During the past fortnight, Pat and Brian and the two girls had got to know each other better and feelings had not changed though so far no physical contact had taken place. Pat hoped that dancing together would change that on Saturday night.

⊱⊰

The next morning, while Pat and Brian were enjoying a mid-morning cup of tea, a messenger delivered a letter from Dr Jameson, addressed to them both.

"It seems that the great man has arrived, Brian, and he wants to see us as soon as it is convenient."

"Let's not keep him waiting," Brian replied and, fifteen minutes later, they dismounted outside the building that served as Dr Jim's office and bedroom.

Mr Rhodes and Dr Jameson sat talking at a camp table under a large marula tree. They rose to greet the newcomers, Rhodes thrusting out his hand and saying, "The name is Rhodes, Cecil Rhodes. Dr Jim has been telling me of your discovery in Manicaland."

Here was a man who, at thirty-seven, was Chairman of De Beers, the biggest diamond mining company in the Cape and possibly in the world, and also Chairman of the Gold Fields Company, Managing Director of the British South Africa Company, and

Prime Minister of the Cape. Pat and Brian were more than a little awestruck to meet with such a man.

Cecil Rhodes was tall, broad-shouldered and loose-limbed. His auburn hair was combed back from a receding hairline while deep lines were already embedded above the curve of his moustache. Yet it was his eyes that dominated his face; they were bluish grey, kindly but strangely distant as if his mind was elsewhere. There was a determined set to his lips. Even all this belied the energy that lay within.

They all sat. Rhodes said, "While Dr Jim organises some coffee, please tell me all the details of your find. Take your time and don't leave anything out."

"Sir," said Brian, "most of the credit goes to my friend, Pat, so he's the best one to brief you."

"The floor is yours, Mr van Zyl," said Rhodes.

Pat began by briefly recounting the events at Chua. When he left out something through personal modesty, Brian filled in the gap. While the story unfolded, Rhodes examined the bag of diamonds Pat had shown him, turning them over almost reverently in his hands.

"So here we are," Pat concluded. "Our question to you, sir, is how do we proceed from here?"

Rhodes looked up from the diamonds. "First, we must know the extent of this discovery. Judging by the quality of these stones, it looks good. I'd like to send someone up from our Kimberley operation. He will be trustworthy because we want to avoid a stampede like the one that hit Kimberley when the first diamonds were discovered. If my man brings me good news, we'll have to sort out labour. Have you two given any thought to that?"

"Yes, we have," said Brian. "Old Chief Tafadzwa feels beholden to us since we got rid of Gungunyana. I'm sure he'd be delighted to supply labour. It would benefit both he and his villagers.

Pat added, "Plus nothing softens the old boy up more than a pinch of our special snuff." He then related the snuff episode which gave them all a laugh.

Rhodes stood up and began to pace up and down with his hands behind his back. Then he stopped and looked at them. "What we have to agree is an equitable share agreement which satisfies everyone involved – you two and your friend, Grievous, Colonel Andrada and, of course, the board of directors of de Beers."

"We've thought about that, Mr Rhodes, and we're happy to give you a twenty per cent holding in return for your company supplying the start-up capital and expertise."

"That more or less coincides with my thinking, Mr van Zyl. I'll have my lawyers in Kimberley study it all in detail once we have established the extent of your discovery. If things go well, it will go a long way to opening up this beautiful country. There is so much potential here. Having said that, one of the first priorities must be to educate the indigenous people, on whom a successful and prosperous future will so much depend. We must narrow the gap between our cultures through education, but this can only begin when the country generates some income."

Pat, though kindly disposed to the local people, had given little thought to educating them. In Natal, the whites from Britain tended to be paternalistic. The Boers saw things rather differently.

"Fundamentally," continued Rhodes, "the barrier to Union in South Africa is a disagreement between the British and the Boers over the native question. In the two Boer republics, no African has a vote. It's pretty much the same in Natal. The Cape is different. Since 1853 the franchise qualification for blacks and whites is an annual income of £25. It's not a race issue, which is as it should be."

It was common knowledge that Rhodes was well thought of by his native employees. He always remembered their names and never forgot a face. "However, before we can tackle education, I fear we will first face a conflict with the Ndebele. But enough of my prophesies, let's get back to the matter in hand."

Pat said, "I've been thinking about someone coming up here from Kimberley. Perhaps it might be better if Brian and I returned to Kimberley with you and do a hands-on course for us to grasp the fundamentals. At the same time, and as we'll be sailing from Beira, I can see Colonel Andrada there. I also need to go to Ladysmith to take care of some business matters, including persuading a couple of my workers to relocate here to open the blacksmith's business I spoke of with Dr Jameson before your arrival."

"That makes sense to me. I should be finished here by Wednesday so we can leave on Thursday and, if we make good time, we'll catch the steamer that leaves at the end of the month and that should see us in Durban in about four weeks' time. How long do you expect to spend in Ladysmith?"

"A week should be enough and then I'll go on to Kimberley, ready to start my apprenticeship."

Good," said Rhodes. "I'll be staying on board to Cape Town so I'm there for the opening of parliament, but I'll give you a letter of introduction to my business manager, Charles Rudd, who will arrange for your education, which should take about a month."

There was an air of excitement in the settlement before the dance on Saturday evening. This would be a first time event. A dance floor had been laid outside the school house, using the usual mixture of cow dung and anthill. Later it would serve as an assembly area and other outdoor activities for the children. Lanterns were hung from wooden poles that were spaced around the perimeter. There was a small stage at one end for Mrs Graham's piano, which stood as a symbol of culture strangely at odds with the general surroundings.

Pat and Brian bathed and shaved in the river and then gave each other a haircut before donning the suits that Mrs Graham had insisted on pressing with her charcoal iron. They nodded at each other with satisfaction.

Joe and Madge Graham went ahead to the school house while their daughters waited by the wagon for their escorts to arrive. They sat by a fire, looking beautiful in their dance dresses. When he saw them, Pat wished he had Grievous with them to take a picture of the scene, but contented himself with the knowledge that he would never forget it anyway.

The couples walked arm in arm to join the revelry, both men conscious of the envious glances cast in their direction. They knew there would be plenty of competition from other young men that night.

Dr Jameson stepped on to the stage and raised his hands. "Ladies and gentlemen, you'll all know that Mr Cecil John Rhodes is with us and he would like to say a few words before we start the evening's entertainment. Mr Rhodes."

Rhodes stepped up. "I will not distract you from your fun for long but, having enticed you to come to this land, I must first thank you for your pioneering spirit and confirm that the funds I promised before you came here have now been put in place and soft loans will become available to those of you who wish to start farming, mining and other essential business enterprises with immediate effect."

There was loud and long applause from the crowd. Rhodes continued, "Ladies and gentlemen, prosperity awaits you and it is your destiny to build a new nation but," he stabbed his finger skywards to emphasise his point, "be sure to take with you on this journey the indigenous people. Improve their lot as much could depend on that. I wish you all well. Now let us enjoy ourselves."

Mrs Graham sat down at her piano, looked around the revellers, caught Pat's eye with a wink, and began to play. Accepting the cue, Pat and Brian bowed to the Graham sisters and claimed the promised first dance, a waltz.

Most of the settlers, basically decent hardworking, adventurous types intent on improving their lives, were more inclined towards country-style dancing than the genteel sophistication of a ballroom waltz, but music of any sort had become a rarity to them and they were happy to dance to anything and with anyone, even if the partner wore breeches.

The men tended to drink even more than usual to celebrate the occasion, whisky being the favoured tipple, of which there were ample supplies available in Salisbury. It looked like being a raucous night.

Pat and Brian were conscious of the shortage of women in the community and selflessly relented to the stream of young men wanting to dance with Margie and Sandra. It was not easy for him and Brian, less so for the girls who were forever on their feet. After a couple of hours, Pat suggested a quiet stroll to Sandra. "At this rate, you won't be able to walk in the morning," he chuckled.

"I don't think I've danced so much in my life," she laughed, "but it's hard to say yes to one man and then turn another down."

Pat took her hand and led the way along the path to the top of the kopje. "It's been so long since I held a pretty girl in my arms so I know how they feel. Tell me something, Sandra. How do you feel about giving up the comforts of a normal home life in a city for this harsh primitive existence?"

She thought for a moment before replying, "You have probably gathered that Dr Jameson is a convincing character and when he offered my parents the chance to own their own plot of land and financial assistance to build a decent homestead in return for establishing a school, they thought that to be a very strong incentive. I enjoyed living in Cape Town, but we're a close-knit family and I couldn't bear the thought of being parted from them."

They stopped and turned to look down on the dancing below them, which was as lively as ever. Sandra said, "Margie feels as I do. We both have a touch of the tomboy in us and share our folks' love of nature. So, yes, there is much I miss that I have left behind but there is more to look forward to up ahead. Now let me ask you the same question."

Pat smiled at her. "Life was becoming mundane. My business was doing well enough but I was getting into a rut and I had an urge to get the wheels moving in a different direction. One doesn't get the excitement and advantage of opening up a new country every day or the opportunities that presents. It's the chance of a life-time."

Pat took Sandra's hand and led her to a flat-topped boulder where he brushed away some twigs and took off his jacket for them to sit on.

"Things are already looking good," he said, "and Brian and I and our friend Grievous could be on to something in Manicaland. I don't want to go into detail now but it does mean we'll be away down south for a while."

Sandra looked disappointed. "How long will you be gone?"

"Probably about three months." He looked at the expression on her face. "Does that concern you?"

"No," she stammered, "I was just curious."

"I was hoping it was more than curiosity." He edged closer to her and looked down into her lovely eyes. Then he raised her hand to his lips. "The sight of you, Sandra, breathes light into the very embers of my being and illuminates my soul. From the moment I first set eyes on you, I knew there was something between us. There, I've said it. It probably sounds foolish when spoken rather than read in some romantic novel, but I mean it, even though we've only known each other for a couple of weeks."

"You're not a fool, Pat. I feel the same way about you. I'm sure it's meant to be."

Pat drew her to him and kissed her eyes and then her mouth. It lingered sweetly and gently as a soft breeze on a candle.

Sandra spoke at last. "We'd best get back, Pat, before my father sends out a search party."

Pat laughed. "He's quite right! If you were my daughter in these circumstances, I wouldn't let you out of my sight at all. Anyway, it looks like dinner is being served so we'd best join the queue before those gannets eat the lot."

Brian and Margie were near the front of the queue when they arrived back and Pat received a knowing wink from his friend.

"Trust Wood-Gush to be near the front," he whispered into Sandra's ear. "The hyenas will have slim pickings tonight from what he leaves."

As his contribution to the feast, Pat had shot two impala and a young bush pig two nights ago, much to the delight of the catering ladies. The impala carcasses, skewered and threaded with strips of bacon to make them more succulent, had been rotating over the coals since the early afternoon. Below them in the embers were several three-legged cooking pots containing stewed guinea fowl and francolin steeped in rich red gravy seasoned with chilli. There were also pots of sweet potatoes, pumpkin and stiff maize porridge, cooked as the Africans liked it and the Europeans had become used to.

"It's amazing how the noise level drops when people hook the old nose bag over their ears," Brian remarked as the two couples sat opposite each other with their plates balanced on their knees.

"Now you know why he's got such big ears, Margie," said Pat. "It comes from his nose bag hanging over the front of his face more often than not."

"Keep that up and you might have something hanging from your face which you'll have some trouble blowing in the future."

"We've seen more than that hanging from you two," said Margie. The reference was all too clear to the men.

"We'll never live that down, Pat," said Brian.

"At least what was exposed doesn't seem to have been too off-putting, Brian."

"You could almost say there won't be any surprises left for the future."

"Stop it, both of you," said Sandra, trying to avoid blushing and giggling at the same time. "The conversation is deteriorating too quickly. Eat your food before it's cold."

"Yes, ma'am," the men responded in unison.

After the meal, Pat and Brian were relieved to note that the young men seemed to have accepted that they had little chance of competing for the attentions of the two girls and were instead pouring liquor down their throats.

Suddenly the music stopped and Dr Jameson once more stood on the stage. "I think it's time to give Mrs Graham a break from the piano and indulge in a bit of sport," he announced. "Mr Rhodes has suggested a game of bok-bok with two teams of ten. He has put up a prize of £100 for the winning team. In return he claims the right to nominate the captains. Will Mr van Zyl and Mr Wood-Gush kindly come to the front." There was a cheer from the crowd. "Now, can we have the able-bodied men step forward for selection, please?"

The game of bok-bok required one team to crouch down one behind the other similar to a scrum in the now popular game of rugby, but in single file. Meanwhile the other team lined up and, one at a time, with a running start and a warning cry of 'bok-bok' took off from the ground, leap-frogging as far forward as possible, the aim being to land as many of their team as they could on the backs of the opposition without toppling off. If the crouching team collapsed under the increasing weight, they lost, as did the leaping team if one of their men fell off. The first team to win two legs was declared the winner.

This was no game for the faint-hearted and a relaxed state of semi-inebriation among the players was almost a pre-requisite to boost courage and avoid serious injury. Being a bar-room sport, plenty of gamesmanship was used to gain advantage.

Pat thought how he had been hoping for a cultured evening of dancing and now found himself dragged into a session of bar-room antics and by no less a person than the Prime Minister of the Cape of Good Hope. He needed to use some guile if he was not to prolong matters.

Pat and Brian picked their teams alternately, trying to choose a mix of speed and brawn.

Brian called his team Big Brian's Bucking Bronchos and won the toss against Van Zyl's Farmers, choosing to crouch as the bucks first. The first man in the line was more than a little unsteady on his feet as he stood with his back propped against a pole to act as the cushion and anchor. Being drunk was no handicap as he could not fall over anyway. Like a giant caterpillar, the team crouched, nine backsides to taunt Pat's leapers.

Pat had his team tapered by weight, theorising that the lighter men would leap the furthest, leaving more room for the heavier tail-enders.

With a whoop and a 'bok-bok' the first man raced down the dance floor and agilely took to the air, landing on the back of Broncho 4 with his knees tucked up. Pat was pleased enough; that left five backs available. The next four Farmers did well and, despite the Broncho's efforts to unseat them, they all stayed in the saddle. Pat went next. He planned to land on the back of the heaviest of his men already in place and cause a collapse.

With a cry of 'Tally-ho, the jackal' and legs and arms pumping, he propelled himself up and over his already astride first three team mates, landing squarely on the next, who gave a yelp of surprise, then realising Pat's tactics he chuckled, as he heard the whoosh of air being expelled from the man beneath him as he took the double load on his back. He lasted less than four seconds before his legs buckled and he went down, bringing the whole edifice to the ground in an unruly heap.

"A lucky leap on your part," growled Brian. "Now it's our turn."

After an obligatory shot of whisky, the Van Zyl Farmers huddled for a team talk for Pat to explain his strategy. No one noticed two members of his team sneak off into the darkness and reappear a few minutes later with smug looks on their faces to re-join the circle. By now, bets were being placed by the excited spectators.

Down went the Farmers, waggling their backsides as they taunted the Bronchos. Brian strutted confidently back and forth, firing up his team and assuring them that it would take an extraordinarily stout pair of legs and a backbone of steel to withstand his 225lbs descending at speed. "As soon as the first three are in place," he mused, "I'll strike and they won't know what's hit them" Then, at the top of his voice, he yelled, "Prepare for doomsday, Van Zyl!"

The onlookers' excitement had reached fever pitch when Brian's first man took off fast, encouraged by the shouts of his team-mates and those who had backed the Bronchos to win. He landed well up the line, leaving plenty of space for the next two leapers.

"Now for the crunch," thought Brian. With a mighty roar, he took off down the hard track surprisingly fast for such a big man. He had chosen his victim, a man of average size who had perhaps had one or two drinks too many. Brian figured he wouldn't be able to manage the load and, with a triumphant smile, he leapt, leapfrogged and landed squarely on his intended target.

The rules of bok-bok dictate that the jumpers cannot let their feet touch the ground once they have taken off or the team forfeit that round, so Brian landed with his legs bent like those of a jockey saddled ready to start a race. He remained mounted for less than a second because within that time he found himself flat on his back on the dance floor with a look of utter disbelief on his face.

Pandemonium broke out as everyone burst into laughter. It took Dr Jameson ten minutes to restore order and then it was only by firing three shots into the air from a revolver.

"Ladies and gentlemen," he called out, "Let's have a little quiet while we get the winning team captain to step forward for the prize. Up you come, Mr van Zyl."

Brian appeared totally bemused as he brushed himself off while muttering under his breath. He could not understand how his unseating had been so emphatic. One moment he had been upright and then, like shit off a shovel, he was on his back.

Pat accepted the prize, sealed in an envelope, and then called for silence. "By unanimous vote," he said, "the Van Zyl Farmers have agreed to donate the winnings to Mr Graham's school." Amid wild applause, he handed the envelope to Joe. "Finally, I have a word to say to my good friend, Mr Wood-Gush. Remember, Brian, that the good hunter never lets the leopard out of his sight lest it sneaks up and bites him from behind."

All Brian could do in his confused state was mouth an obscenity at Pat.

"Don't take it too hard, my friend. I've had a bit more experience at the game than you have. We used to play it regularly in Durban."

Later, back on the dance floor, Sandra looked up at Pat and said, "There was something not quite right about that game of bok-bok. I've watched it a few times in the Cape but I've never seen someone unseated quite so – er – abruptly."

Pat looked fondly at her and told her what he had done.

"Shame on you, Patrick van Zyl, how could you? He's not going to be happy if he ever finds out."

"I love it when you pout like that," Pat said, squeezing her hand.

"Last dance, ladies and gentlemen," called Madge. "It's time to call it a night, I'm afraid."

Pat was surprised to realise it was two o'clock. "I have to admire your mother's stamina, Sandra," he said. "She's been playing that piano for something like six hours."

"She loves to see people dancing and enjoying themselves."

"What about you and Margie? Do you play?"

"A little. Mother only started teaching us recently, but when we're settled, I'm sure we'll continue our lessons. Now, would you and Brian and a few others help her by putting the piano back into the schoolroom?"

It was two days later when Brian found out how he had been tricked by his friend. Margie told him, having got the story from her sister.

"Your friend Pat is a cunning cur," she chortled.

"What do you mean?"

Still laughing, she explained to him, "The man you landed on was coated with axle grease from waist to neck under his shirt, as was the one behind him, in case you dropped short."

"The swine, the cunning dog, wait till I get my hands on him," Brian howled. "I'll have my revenge on him, you wait and see, even if I have to wait a year or more."

Thursday arrived and it was a tearful early morning parting as each man bade farewell to his new found love.

"We'll be back before you know it," said Pat, leaning down from his saddle to give Sandra a final kiss. "Look after yourself, my love. I'll bring you back something special from Natal."

"The entire settlement turned out to see Mr Rhodes and his party off to the coast. They wondered when they would see him again.

CHAPTER SEVEN

The trip to Beira was relatively uneventful and they stopped for only one night at Fort Umtali, where they were to leave their horses. They received a warm reception from Captain Heyman and his troop. The next morning they hitched a ride on the mine's re-supply wagon.

At Fontesville, Rhodes gave Captain Dickie a short sharp directive to lock up the liquor and to avoid the sandbanks, real or imaginary, as they wanted a speedy trip downriver to Beira.

During the voyage, Pat expressed his nagging concern to Rhodes over the possible hostile reception or even arrest by the Portuguese authorities when they learnt that they were in town. "Surely they'll still be smarting over the battle at Chua!"

"Don't worry," replied Rhodes. "Since then there have been a number of developments. In short, the Portuguese should be grateful we did not take Beira. If I'd had my way, we would have done. Instead, the boundaries between the two territories have been amicably agreed upon by Lord Salisbury on behalf of the British Government and the Portuguese Minister of Foreign Affairs. Part of the agreement gives us unhindered use of this corridor to the sea. It is my intention to build a railway line along the whole length of this route. Mr Pauling's company will start surveying the land shortly. Does that allay your fears?"

"It certainly does. Finding Colonel Andrada in a hostile situation would have made life difficult."

"I mentioned George Pauling," continued Rhodes, "so let me tell you a couple of amusing stories about the man. He really is a larger than life character with a hearty appetite for fun, food, drink and work. The story goes that he and two friends once breakfasted on a thousand oysters and eight bottles of champagne and then, on another occasion, with the same companions, they accounted for three hundred bottles of beer in two days. The stories may have been embellished in the retelling, but whatever the quantities consumed, they must have been impressive and excessive, otherwise it would not have been worth relating. His favourite party trick, which I actually witnessed once, was to lead his Basuto pony into the bar and then lift it on to his shoulders and carry it around the room. However, one night he attempted the impossible when he tried to climb some stairs burdened like this. Man and beast collapsed in a heap and the poor animal refused to cooperate again."

They were still laughing when Brian, looking behind him upstream, said, "He'll certainly have his work cut out constructing a railway line through some of that terrain. The best of luck to him."

At Beira they booked into the Grand Hotel, which was clearly mis-named, but was the best accommodation available. It was easy enough to find the garrison, where they reported their arrival to the duty officer, whose command of English was just sufficient for him to understand that they wished to see the Commandant. They waited half an hour before being shown into his office where another officer, a Captain da Sousa, explained that he would act as interpreter as his superior, introduced as Commandant Mendes, had limited English.

Mendes seemed to be the epitome of a colonial Portuguese officer with his neatly-trimmed beard, brown eyes, swarthy skin and upright bearing.

Pat explained that he was looking for Colonel Andrada. There was a discussion in rapid Portuguese before da Sousa said, "The Commandant is puzzled as to why two English gentlemen would be looking for the colonel."

"Please tell the commandant that it's a long story, but we met him in unusual circumstances at Massi-Kessi a couple of months ago," said Pat.

The Commandant frowned when he heard this translated and there followed another torrent of Portuguese. Da Sousa said, "The Commandant wants to know because he is a close friend of the colonel, who is currently under investigation and suspended from duty. This causes him much distress."

Pat was fairly sure he knew what the colonel's predicament was. He looked at Brian, who nodded to show he was of the same mind. "Have to tread carefully here," thought Pat.

"May I ask, sir," said Pat, "if the investigation has anything to do with the battle at the garrison at Massi-Kessi recently? If it is, I may be able to help you."

The Commandant had obviously understood some of what Pat said because he rose and began to pace to and fro in front of his desk. He stopped abruptly as if reaching a decision and spoke quietly and at length to da Sousa.

The captain then said, "On the orders of the King of Portugal, a court of inquiry is to be held into the circumstances surrounding the defeat of Colonel Andrada's garrison. The king wants to know how a fort manned by over four hundred officers and men could be overrun by what he understands was little more than a handful of British troopers. He has ordered an official investigation and until their findings are made, Colonel Andrada is under suspension and confined to barracks. Should they report that the Colonel has been remiss in his conduct, he could face a dishonourable discharge."

Pat's mind was racing. It would be easy to simply walk away and leave Andrada to his fate. That would rid the partners in the diamond deal of one shareholder which would be to the advantage of the others.

He asked for time for he and Brian to confer, which was granted. Outside, Pat looked at Brian and said, "You're thinking the same as me, aren't you? Do we walk away or do we do the honourable thing?"

"I believe we're on to something big at Nyanyadzi," Brian replied. "If we're correct, there will be more than enough wealth to share. And if the colonel hadn't followed up the Shangaan miner's story, we wouldn't be going to Kimberley to do a crash course in diamond mining. We have to honour our obligations, Pat, and also see how we can help this poor man."

"We agree, then. Let's see what we can do for him." Then a thought struck him. "Damn it, Brian, we're overlooking something here."

"What's that?"

"We're forgetting Grievous."

Brian was quick to realise what this meant. "The whole world has probably had a blow-by-blow account of the Battle of Chua through The Times."

Exactly! And if Grievous' story is disparaging of the colonel, then it bodes ill for him and there's little we can do to help. All we can do for now is proceed with caution and play things by ear."

Back in the office, Pat enquired, "Have there been any reports in the papers about what happened at Massi-Kessi?"

"Yes," said the Commandant, "it was in our papers but with little detail given."

"Was the colonel in any way personally ridiculed in those reports?"

"I don't think so. It's possible that the story was censored to avoid embarrassment to Portugal."

"Perhaps it's time for me to tell you that Mr Wood-Gush and I took part in that battle and had a hand in the strategy, as did another friend who is a reporter for The Times of London. Before we can help you with the details you have not heard about, we need to know how this friend wrote his story. It may well have been censored in the Portuguese press, but we must establish how The Times presented the version that the English public has read. If it is unfavourable and ridicules the Portuguese army, there is not much anyone can do. You see, Commandant, the fort at Massi-Kessi was taken by using guile and cunning, not brute force. The key to our success was largely due to the inclusion of Marquaniqua's people."

Mendes' face looked incredulous at these revelations. He took some time to answer. "And who, Senhor van Zyl, is Marquaniqua?" he said at last.

"She," continued Pat, "is the fat and exceedingly ugly queen who lives with her followers near Captain Heyman's post at Umtali. We wanted to give your garrison the impression that Gungunyana's men were plundering again in the villages under Colonel Andrada's control. It was Marquaniqua's men who in fact raided the villages but, I must add, without causing any deaths or serious injuries or even any looting. Colonel Andrada reacted quickly and honourably by sending a large contingent of his men out to help the villagers. And that move alone was half the battle won. When the attack on the actual fort began, he must have been totally surprised by the amount of heavy artillery we seemed to have and where we had placed it on a mountain ridge. Would it, do you think, influence your inquiry board if we, the enemy as it were, offered the view that the colonel acted no differently to how any other garrison commander might have done in similar circumstances?"

Da Sousa listened to his superior and then translated, "The Commandant says that it is rare for a member of an opposing force to submit evidence that commends his former foe's military conduct. It must surely work in his favour."

"So much depends on our friend, Mr Grieve." said Pat.

"I agree, but the Commandant is still puzzled about your interest in the colonel's welfare."

"Tell him that we merely came here to make a courtesy call and to pay our respects to a former adversary. We spent some time with him in Massi-Kessi, exchanging views after the event. We found him to be a gentleman in every respect and we parted amicably."

Brian interrupted. "I must remind you that we leave for Durban in two days and, unless the board sits tomorrow, we won't be here."

"We already have a problem then," said da Sousa. "The board is due to sit in two months' time on August 28."

"It's only a problem if our friend Grievous can't make it," Pat said. "He'll probably do a better job than us anyway with his gift for bullshit."

"Excuse me, senhor, I don't understand."

"Forgive me, captain, I was just thinking aloud. Please explain to Commandant Mendes that Mr Grieve might be persuaded to give evidence as he could be returning to Africa soon, but we'll need to send a letter to him before we catch the steamer."

"The Commandant says that it is indeed fortunate that you have come here today. Your request to see the colonel will not be difficult and I have been instructed to take you to his quarters here."

Pat and Brian shook hands with the Commandant, promising to keep him informed of any developments, and followed da Sousa out."

They found Andrada sitting in the shade of a casaurina tree in the gardens outside the officers' mess. On seeing them, he rose to his feet with a broad smile of welcome.

"This is an unexpected pleasure, senhors. What brings you to Beira? I hope it is good news."

"We certainly have much to talk about," Brian said. "Much has happened since we last saw you."

They sat and updated the colonel on everything, starting with Gungunyana's defeat, moving on to the diamond discovery and their deal with Rhodes and ending with their interview with Commandant Mendes.

"You've not been idle since we parted and I thank you for your integrity. My immediate problem is to clear my name and what you have told the Commandant may well make the difference. I am due to retire from the army shortly, but it is important to me that I do so with a clean record. I agree that much will depend upon Mr Grieve's version of events in the British press."

"We must first find the back issues of The Times," Pat said, "and I think there might be some at the Grand Hotel for English speakers who stay there. Then we'll write to Colin Grieve in London and ask for his help. We'll report back tomorrow morning. There is so little time."

"I am most grateful for what you are doing," said Colonel Andrada.

⇥✦⇤

They found Rhodes studying the menu in the hotel dining room. "What can you tell me?" he asked.

Pat reported everything about their morning and Rhodes looked up and smiled. "I've been reading the London papers. The story did indeed appear in The Times under your Mr Grieve's by-line. You'll be pleased to know that it was severely edited.

"How did that happen?" Brian asked.

"I told you in Salisbury that I was aware of the devious tactics the three of you masterminded to take the garrison. That knowledge and my connections with the editor of the Times gave me some leverage when it came to negotiating the terms for the Beira corridor with the Portuguese. The uncensored version of your efforts would have greatly embarrassed the Portuguese and this put them at a serious disadvantage. So the news was filtered, shall we say, and I got my corridor to the sea. Unwittingly, you have done me another favour."

"That must have upset Grievous, having his story more or less spiked," Brian commented. "He might be disinclined now to help Colonel Andrada."

"Don't worry. I'm told his editor explained the bigger picture and reeled off the old queen and country line and the important role he had played in it and that mollified him, as did the healthy bonus I'm sure he received."

"Does all this manipulation come naturally to you?" Pat asked with admiration in his voice.

"Perhaps. I also have plans for after the good colonel's retirement. My company will need a reliable Portuguese-speaking agent for a variety of reasons and he would seem, from what you tell me, to fit the bill."

It was a happier Colonel Andrada who received their report the next day and a contented couple of men who set sail for Durban with Rhodes on the next leg of their journey.

CHAPTER EIGHT

Pat and Brian stood at the top of the gangway about to disem-
bark at Durban. Rhodes, or CJR as he was often called, was
with them though he would continue on to Cape Town.

"Right, gentlemen," he said, "be aware that the people you will
be working with in Kimberley for a month are among the best in
the business. Learn as much as you can from them. That will be an
advantage to all of us."

"We will, sir, and thank you for everything," replied Pat. The
two men shook hands with him and went ashore.

They were quickly able to find seats on a coach travelling inland and two days later they were in Ladysmith.

While Brian explored the town and the surrounding area, Pat
was busy sorting out what items of equipment he would need for
the blacksmith's forge he would open in Fort Salisbury and what
needed to remain so that he could sell the Ladysmith business as a
going concern. He also had to purchase a wagon.

Maforga, his foreman, and one other were happy to re-locate
to Salisbury and run the forge once they realised that financially

it would benefit them more. They would take their families with them and meet up with Pat in Kimberley when his crash course was finished. Then they would all set off together to Salisbury with their equipment.

When Pat's work in Ladysmith was completed, he and Brian boarded a coach for the long ride west through the Drakensberg mountains and on to Kimberley.

Kimberley had been described as the ugliest place on earth in the early 1870's when Colesberg Kopje was being clawed apart in the search for diamonds. It was on a dusty treeless plain under an unremitting sun.

Without any civic order, there were piles of fly-blown garbage and discarded rotting animal carcasses everywhere. A place where humans relieved themselves in slit trenches with the accompanying stench assailing the nostrils of the weary traveller long before it came into view.

Now, twenty years later, it was still an ugly dusty place but more sanitary and orderly.

Charles Rudd, in charge of the Company management at Kimberley, was a business-like, reliable man who came from Northamptonshire in England. He had been educated at Harrow and Trinity College, Cambridge, where he had been an accomplished athlete. He left Cambridge without taking a degree to head for the warmer climate of South Africa where, for the next five years, he led a foot-loose adventurous life. Then he was drawn to the diamond fields and bought a claim adjoining that of Rhodes. The two became friends and soon decided to pool their resources, a partnership that led to their mutual prosperity.

Rudd appointed, as guide and mentor to Pat and Brian, Tony Johnson, a personable and friendly young man. He would educate them in the diamond industry over the next few weeks. He readily accepted the explanation that his students were management trainees who, along with a geologist, were to undertake exploratory work north of the Limpopo River.

Pat and Brian stood mesmerised, staring down into the massive man-made crater, where once had stood the kopje, and from which CJR had extracted the largest quantity of diamond-carrying dirt and with it the largest quantity of diamonds. Hundreds of pulley ropes extended into the depths, forming what looked like a giant cobweb.

"It's hard to believe that man has created that massive hole with just picks and shovels," said Brian.

"Yes, and all in search of pretty pieces of glass to decorate the female form," Tony added.

"It seems odd that the man who has more of them than anyone else doesn't have a woman in his own life to decorate. Right, shall we get started, Tony?"

Johnson grinned at them. "The first part of your education is to don your working clothes and dirty your hands to learn how to dig for diamonds. Two days of that down the hole and another two scrabbling around on the sorting table should be enough. Grading will take up most of your time. That will partly be with Mr Alfred Beit. No one knows more than he on the subject. He has agreed to give up a few hours of his time to give you an overview on grading, valuing and marketing. He will then pass you on to one of the Company's best people for more detailed training for about a week. The final few days will be spent on security, stores and equipment. Now, I think it's time for tea, over there." He indicated a wooden building with a long veranda that overlooked the diggings.

When they were settled with their tea, Brian said, "Tell us about Alfred Beit, Tony. How does he fit into the organisation?"

"He's not an impressive-looking character," Tony replied. "In fact, he looks a nervous, self-conscious little fellow. Don't be fooled by his appearance. No one in Kimberley knows more about diamonds than he does. He learned his trade in Hamburg. He is also probably a financial genius with an extraordinary mathematical brain. Apart from that, he is a kind and thoroughly decent gentleman. It's believed that he and Rhodes had the same ambition, which was to control the total diamond output. They decided to work together."

Tony sipped his tea and continued, "In the battle for control of the stocks and shares of the mines, Mr Rhodes was Commander-in-Chief while Alfred Beit was the Chief-of-Staff. So, listen carefully to whatever he tells you and remember it."

The next three weeks passed quickly with the trainees kept busy throughout each day. At night they had plenty of material to read, but they did manage some sort of a social life which mainly consisted of hard drinking. While Pat and Brian were out of practice from their time in the bush and on the road, others were not. So many men in such close proximity without much female influence around led to many disagreements which often ended in fights.

One evening they were having a drink with Tony in The Pick and Shovel when an argument ensued at the far end of the bar. At first they paid little attention to it, but then one of the brawlers tried to hit another with a bottle. It slipped from his hand and flew through the air, landing on Brian's head.

"Shit!" roared Brian as he turned and stared at the offending group of men. There was a silence. The music stopped and conversation ceased while everyone watched as this mountain of a man made his way slowly towards the group who had, a moment before, been pushing, shoving and cursing.

"Tell me," Brian said mildly, "which of you – er – gentlemen threw that bottle at me?" He looked at each man in turn. "I came in here for a quiet drink with my friends and one of you, without any provocation, decided to include me in your little argument. Now I have an unsolicited lump rising on my head. Now, I ask you, is that nice?"

"Feck off, you fool," said a big Irishman who was more than a little drunk. That comment was a mistake and so was his next move, which was to swing a fist at Brian.

Blocking the blow with his left arm, Brian shot out his right arm like a giant piston and grabbed the man's windpipe in a vice-like grip. His left fist then sank into the Irishman's midriff, knocking the wind out of him.

Brian's voice was still mild. "Now, from your aggressive response, I assume it was you who tried to render me unconscious and now you abuse me with profane language. You are a horrible man."

The Irishman's eyes bulged big, round and bloodshot in Brian's unrelenting grip around his throat. He couldn't admit his guilt even had he wanted to.

Brian turned to the barman and said, "Please bring me a piece of soap from your kitchen. This man has a dirty mouth that needs washing."

The atmosphere at that end of the bar had turned from vitriol to laughter while Pat and Tony stood and looked on.

The barman returned with a bar of blue laundry soap which he handed to Brian. "When you've finished with it, you might like to give it to the Irishman to wash his smelly body with." The onlookers roared with laughter. Brian released his grip on the man's throat and forced open his mouth with thumb and forefinger, before ramming the bar of soap into his mouth. Then he spun him round, caught him in a headlock and marched him across the room, through the batwing doors head first onto the walkway, and then into the street amid a chorus of cheers. He gave a slight bow to his audience and walked slowly back to join Pat and Tony.

"That was quite a performance," said Tony, "quiet, controlled."

"He probably won't remember a thing in the morning," Brian said. "Just as well or I'd be watching my back for the rest of my time here. Barman," he called, "another round, please." He tossed some coins on the counter.

"Keep your money, son." The barman pushed the cash back towards Brian. "This round is on Mr Barnato."

"Who?"

"Mr Barney Barnato," repeated the barman. It was then that Brian remembered Pat's story all those weeks ago around the fire at Siyakonzi's diggings. "Mr Barnato has asked me to invite you and your friends to join him." He pointed to a table in a corner where two men sat.

Brian looked and saw a small bespectacled man with blond hair and neatly-trimmed moustache beckoning to him.

Tony said, "This could be your opportunity to meet one of the real characters of the diamond fields. He's your typical cockney trader but his barrow is diamond-studded. This will be part of your education. Come, I'll take you both across, but be careful what you say. He doesn't miss a trick."

They were introduced by Tony and sat down with their drinks. The other man was Harry, Barney's brother and partner.

"I must say, Mr Wood-Gush, you sorted out that loud-mouthed Irishman well. It's about time someone did. A couple of years ago I put him down in the boxing ring, but that was when I was broke and I did it for the purse."

Pat said, "Wouldn't he be a slightly different weight division to you?"

"That may be so," said Harry, "but Barney has flattened bigger men than him before now." He went on to tell them how Barney had done some prize-fighting when he first came to Kimberley. "I ask you, does our Barney look like a man who can use his fists? Of course not, but this works in his favour. His opponents underestimate him and drop their guards. Add to that, our old man taught us every dirty trick in the book. That tends to help.

"Shortly after he arrived here, Barney took on the so-called Champion of Angola. He was huge, about your size." He nodded at Brian. "The prize for Barney was a gold medal and a refund of the shilling he paid to enter the ring to take this brute on - if he won. Barney, being the cunning dog he is, went around placing bets on himself and getting long odds as no one thought he stood a chance."

Harry took a long swig of his beer before continuing. "Come the day of the fight, there's plenty of excitement. The whole town turns up to see the little Jew take a thrashing. There are other bouts before his. When his turn comes, Barney walks up to the ring as bold as brass, wearing his bowler hat and his specs and, when he climbs into the ring, half the crowd is cheering him, the rest jeering. Barney bows to the crowd and his specs fall off the end of his nose into the dust and there he is, feeling around trying to find them. So what does this big ape of an opponent do? He walks over to Barney and bends down to pick them up. And that's when Barney gives him one from the floor into the solar plexus, followed by another punch to the jaw and the gorilla goes down like a sack of shit." Harry chuckled at the memory. "No one is interested in rules, apart from the punters who have lost a pile of money, and Barney gets the verdict by popular vote. It also gave him his stake."

"I'll remember not to throw any bottles in your direction," grinned Brian.

"So what brings you to Kimberley?" asked Barney casually. Tony shot Pat a warning look.

Pat said, "Brian and I have just returned from Mashonaland, where we have been looking at what the place has to offer. We met on the steam boat that travels up the Pungwe River from Beira and decided to throw in our lot together. While in Salisbury we met Mr Rhodes, for whose expansionist plans in that part of the world it seems we had done a big favour. But let's not pursue that part of the story. The eastern side of that part of the country lends itself to forestry and Mr Rhodes agreed to give us a concession on the Mozambique border and to help us finance the project. We are here to tie up the details with Mr Rudd and, while we're waiting, it made sense to learn a little about the diamond trade. Who knows what we might come across up there?"

"Good thinking, Mr van Zyl," said Barney.

They chatted for a while before Tony asked for them to be excused as they were to meet Mr Rudd at the Kimberley Club for dinner. They took their leave of the brothers.

"Mr van Zyl, Mr Wood-Gush," Barney called when they were halfway to the door. They stopped and turned. "Good luck with your venture. Perhaps one day our paths will cross again. I hope so."

As Pat and Brian left, Barney said to his brother, "Do you believe that bullshit story, Harry?"

"It sounds a bit rehearsed to me," replied Harry. "What do you reckon CJR is up to?"

"I think we should keep an eye on those two and see what's on their shopping list. That could tell us something."

The next morning Pat and Brian received a telegram from Grievous telling them that he was on his way back to Africa and had agreed to testify at Colonel Andrada's hearing. He had resigned from The Times full time, but would remain with them as a freelance correspondent. They would meet at Siyakonza's diggings.

"It'll be good to see him again, cocky little devil that he is. I miss his wit," said Brian.

"Yes, I agree, though I'm not sure that he's the mining type. Still, neither are we, really. Maybe he'll start the first newspaper in the country."

"Now that, Pat, could be a good idea. Talking of ideas, that story you spun to the Barnatos last night might not be such bullshit as you thought. In a new country, there's going to be a big demand for building materials."

By their third week in Kimberley, the two men felt confident in their ability to put a reasonably accurate value on a diamond and now they turned their attention to ordnance. Mr Rudd seconded one of his storemen to help them draw up the vast list of equipment they would need. Brian could deal with this better, so Pat concentrated on acquiring wagons and draught oxen. Without the de Beer connection, this would have been an impossible task; they needed six wagons and ninety oxen. The Company had the resources to replace them in due course from the Cape.

The distance from Kimberley to Salisbury via Fort Tuli on the Bechuanaland border was about nine hundred miles. If they could average fifteen miles a day, it would take them three months. Then it was around a hundred and eighty miles to Umtali, another twelve days. If they moved now and had a trouble-free journey, they hoped they could complete it before the annual rains fell.

Pat's two blacksmiths arrived on August 27 with their helpers so they now had six teenage boys to lead and tend the oxen. They took on three more locals for general duties.

A young Spaniard called Lou Corbi, who claimed to have had training as a chef on a steamship, offered to do the cooking if they let him join their party. Pat and Brian readily agreed; this arrangement would be a pleasant change from the diet that their limited culinary skills usually produced.

Weapons skills were important both for procuring meat and defending themselves if under attack from wild animals or belligerent tribesmen. Pat had trained his two workers from Ladysmith to a competent level and it remained for him to now do the same with Lou Corbi. The handsome young Spaniard turned out to be an eager pupil.

"We'll have to watch that lad in Salisbury," Brian said. "Given half a chance, he'll cut a swathe among the ladies, including ours"

"I wonder how they're doing?" mused Pat. "I haven't been able to get that girl out of my mind."

"I have to confess I feel the same way about the sister. I wonder what will ever come of it."

"We'll have to wait and see what reception we get when we return. Then we'll know." Neither man had anything to add to that thought.

On the last day of August, with their newly acquired skills, they took their leave of Mr Rudd and Tony and set off on the long trek to Salisbury. Their departure did not go unnoticed by the Barnato brothers.

"We'll give them a two week start and then our lads can follow," said Barney. "They thought they could bluff old Barney, did they? We shall see."

Harry slapped his brother on the back. "No chance of that. There were too many picks and shovels and sieves in their shopping bag. You were right, Barney, they're on to something. All we have to do is wait for our trackers to report back to us."

<hr />

The first stage of the journey along the Selous Road to Fort Tuli was a monotonous plod. The road was well-used and held few challenges apart from river crossings. There they had to negotiate a descent into the river bed and then haul themselves up the other side. North of Tuli would be a sterner test, difficult enough now, nigh on impossible during the rains. At least, in spite of the seasonal dryness, there was still plenty of game along the way so there was no shortage of fresh meat. Meat could also be bartered with the local people for vegetables.

Fort Tuli stood on a kopje above the Shashi River which, at this time of year, was a half mile wide stretch of sand interspersed with pools of shallow water. This was lowveld land, rocky with only stunted mopani trees and larger baobabs as cover. Game, including lions and big herds of elephants, was in abundance though it tended to keep its distance from the settlement. This left the water in the pools clean and drinkable. Domestic animals were taken further downstream.

The fort was the base for a troop of British South Africa Company police. It had a hotel of sorts and one trading store, run by a Portuguese man and his wife. This was surprisingly well-stocked, including a wide variety of whiskies.

Pat and Brian were anxious to move on and only allowed for a two-day stop at Tuli, during which they carried out repairs to the wagons and rested the oxen.

The rough road they set out on had been established only two years previously, in 1889, when Rhodes' charter from the British Government had given him almost total freedom to open up the land north of the Limpopo. It had been made by a Colonel Frank Johnson. With Frederick Selous leading the way, he had cut the road with his troopers and the first pioneer contingent as far as Salisbury.

They knew, from the briefing they had received from the commander at Tuli, Captain Dobson, the problems they would face. The track was punctuated by foot-high tree stumps and loose boulders which must be avoided. Either Pat or Brian would drive the lead wagon for the first few days. This meant actually leading and prodding the oxen around these obstacles. Hitting a stump would result in a vicious swerve which could easily result in a broken wagon pole – or worse. This would hold them up for at least a full day while they fashioned a replacement.

The first week passed without incident until they came to a particularly steep river bank. Surprisingly, the river was still flowing quite strongly and was about fifty yards wide. The normal drill in such a situation was for the driver to move to the rear of the wagon to operate the brake. Winding the handle clockwise tightened the brake blocks against the back wheels, slowing the wagon down. Failure to do this properly would send the wagon careering downhill out of control and smashing into the oxen, causing injury or even death. Only when one wagon was safely on the other side, would the next attempt the crossing.

Pat had noticed some large crocodiles lurking in the water so he positioned himself on an anthill with his Winchester at the ready, leaving Brian to operate the brake on the first wagon. It crossed without a problem, as did the next, driven by one of the blacksmiths. Already Pat had warned off a couple of interested crocodiles with his rifle.

The driver of the third wagon, one of the younger men, waited until the second had completed its crossing. Then he softly cracked his whip and the wagon edged forward. Halfway down, on the steepest part of the slope, there was a sharp crack, followed by another, moments later.

"Oh, shit!" yelled Pat. "The bloody brake blocks have popped."

The wagon, now unrestrained, lurched forward. The oxen, frightened by the unfamiliar sharp noise, did the same and there followed a chase between beasts and wagon, ending in a mighty pile-up as the lead pair hit the water and lost their footing. Those behind barrelled into them in a frothy frenzy of kicking and bellowing. The wagon teetered dangerously but, slowed by the water, came to a standstill, still miraculously upright.

Pat sprang to his feet to help with the turmoil when the bellowing from one of the front oxen became a scream and the water around it turned a bubbling red. He knew immediately that a crocodile had pounced. All he could see of the reptile was its upper body and threshing tail, but not its head. He judged where the head might be and fired. He was lucky. The tail stilled and the creature turned belly-up and slowly drifted downstream. The ox continued its pitiful bellowing and Pat knew he had no choice. His second shot took the poor beast through its ear and it became still.

The other wagon drivers on the south bank gathered at the water's edge. Pat ordered Maforga to free the remaining oxen from their traces while he watched for any more crocodiles that might show interest in the scene. Now that the screams of the stricken ox had ceased, the rest began to settle down.

Brian, who had been a horrified spectator across the river, first assuring himself that Pat was on the alert with his weapon, now waded through the river to supervise the freeing of the oxen.

Eventually the situation was under control and the animals were led across to the far bank. The dead one was dragged out of the water and up the bank to be butchered later. It was a pitiful sight. The right front leg had been ripped off near the shoulder, leaving jagged strips of bloody flesh hanging.

A fresh team of oxen had to be used to pull the foundered wagon across the river. It was nightfall when the last wagon was drawn up. Everyone was in a state of utter exhaustion.

"Bloody hard work, this pioneering business, eh, Brian?" said Pat as he poured generous tots of whisky. "I really thought that wagon was going to overturn."

Lou was stirring a pot on the fire. "I hear that crazy ox crying in my dreams for the rest of my life," he muttered. "Good that you keel that crocodeel, Patrick. He one big mean bastard, huh?"

Brian wearily said, "CJR should make this journey. He's going to have to do something to sort out the track. When this trip is finished, I'll have to concentrate just to walk in a straight line. I won't be long out of my bedroll tonight."

CHAPTER NINE

On his return to London, Grievous had wasted no time in having his film developed and the pictures printed. He was well satisfied with the results. He had brushed up his stories on the boat and they, together with the photographs should, he estimated, fill a four-page feature for The Times in their weekend edition. He was warmly greeted by his editor, James Robertson.

"Come in, Colin, sit down. This is really good stuff," he said, tapping Grievous' typed copy on his desk. You had some close calls, too, judging by this."

"Thank you, sir. It's been quite an adventure and I've met some amazing people and made some lasting friendships. The Battle of Chua was a tactical masterpiece, shades of Hannibal, I'd say."

"Er, yes, indeed. Actually it's that part of your feature we have to talk about. It's hard for me to say this, but I'm going to ask you to re-write the story, Colin."

"I'm sorry, I don't understand. Why? I've told the story just the way it happened without any embellishments."

"I'm afraid there are greater forces at play here and they go all the way up to the Prime Minister himself."

"Go on," Grievous prodded the editor.

"Your story in its present form would severely embarrass the Portuguese government," said Robertson. "It amounts to a handful of ostensibly British troopers overrunning a garrison manned by over four hundred Portuguese officers and men."

With all due respect, sir, so what! That's exactly what happened."

"And that is exactly what Lord Salisbury doesn't want. He is a great admirer of Cecil Rhodes and shares his dream of bringing central and southern Africa under British control. Mr Rhodes wants a safe corridor from Umtali to Beira with a railway linking the two. The PM goes along with this."

"You're saying that if we print the full story, the Portuguese will not agree to this?"

"Not quite. Rhodes and the PM are saying that if the Portuguese do not accept the corridor, your full story will be published. While this cuts across our ethical values, national interest takes priority."

"I must say, if nothing else, you have to admire the cunning of Mr Rhodes. Even so, surely we can't spike the whole story. After all, it did take place."

"I agree Colin. It's been suggested that we make it look less like a rout by increasing the artillery and numbers of the British forces and decreasing those of the garrison by having a large number of them out on patrol at the time of the attack. It's still our victory but it saves face for the Portuguese."

At that moment there was a knock on the door and the editor's secretary was invited to enter.

"An urgent telegram for Mr Grieve, sir," she said, handing it to him.

"It's from Africa," said Grievous.

"In that case you'd better open it." Robertson said.

Grievous tore open the envelope and read the contents, a smile broadening across his face. He handed it to Robertson.

"Perfect timing, I'd say," the editor said. "What do you want to do about this Colonel Andrada, testify or not?"

"Before I answer that, let me tell you that I have decided to resign my post here and return to Africa. I feel that is where my destiny lies. I'd like to play a part in opening up Mr Rhodes' new country. One day, perhaps I'll start my own newspaper there. Meanwhile, may I ask that you retain me as a freelance correspondent? I'll rewrite this story for you, leaving out many of the more triumphal details, and then I'll return to Beira to do my best for Colonel Andrada, who is, to my mind, an honourable man, deserving of all the help he can get."

"The paper will be sorry to lose you from the permanent staff, Colin, but I won't stand in your way. Do what you feel you have to do, and, yes, go as our central Africa correspondent."

A week later, Grievous had tied up his affairs in England and was once more on a boat bound for Beira. He had no idea where his friends were at the moment, but hoped there would be some word waiting in Beira for him.

The board of inquiry sat two days after Grievous' arrival at the port of Beira. The Governor of Mozambique chaired the meeting in the officers' mess on August 28. It consisted of four senior army officers. The Commandant assured Grievous that the result was already determined with Andrada being cleared of all charges of dereliction of duty. Grievous would give evidence based on his shortened version published in The Times, which the King of Portugal had seen and approved. The board, after a brief retirement, returned the expected verdict and issued a short press statement.

"What happens now, Colonel," asked Grievous as he and Andrada sat in the garden outside the officers' mess over a cup of coffee. "Where's your next posting likely to be?"

"Firstly, I must say how deeply indebted I am to you for speaking up in my defence. Without your evidence I would have lost my career and forfeited all my pension benefits. I have already been posted to Cabo Delgado province in the north of the country. It's not my choice of area, but I am grateful for it. Having said that, I'm not sure that I'll accept it."

Grievous reached into his inside pocket and produced two letters, one unopened. "One of these is to me from Patrick van Zyl. The other is addressed to you and is from Mr Cecil Rhodes. Before I give it to you, let me brief you on what he and Brian Wood-Gush have been up to since you last saw them."

He explained how all was going to plan and that Pat and Brian were en-route for Salisbury, suitably equipped for and educated in the mining of diamonds. He then passed across the letter.

"I think, Colonel, you may well find the contents of this letter well worth considering."

Colonel Andrada looked puzzled as he took the envelope and tore it open. A minute later he looked up and shook his head. "This is extraordinary. Mr Rhodes is offering me a position with his company as his Beira agent. I'll be responsible for the movement of goods and materials into Manicaland and Mashonaland and, if the new diamond find proves fruitful, he wants me to supervise their safe passage to de Beers in Kimberley or elsewhere as directed."

"Sounds like a good deal to me, Colonel. Are you going to accept it?" asked Grievous.

"It seems a better option than banishment to the bush, Senhor Grieve. It also better serves my interest in the diamond venture. I can be more useful here in Beira than wielding a pick and shovel out in the sticks. What do you think?"

"It looks to me like the perfect arrangement."

"Mr Rhodes has asked me to meet him in Cape Town so he can explain in more detail what he wants from me. What about your own plans, Mr Grieve?"

"It's back up the Pungwe for me and then on to Nyanyadzi to meet up with my two friends."

The Colonel bade farewell to Grievous the very next day from the jetty as Captain Dickie's paddle steamer left. He heard Grievous' comment, "Please confirm, captain, that this passage is straight through to Fontesvilla and we won't be returning to Beira later in the day."

He did not catch the skipper's muttered reply, "Hope you fall overboard again, you little bastard."

⏤┼┼⏤

Meanwhile Pat and Brian made reasonable progress with their entourage as they followed the route that detoured around Lobengula's headquarters. They did not want to antagonise him or more particularly, his lieutenants.

It was true that the British government had granted a charter that virtually gave the British South Africa Company a free hand to do pretty much what it liked, even beyond the northern border. However, Lobengula believed that he had agreed to prospecting rights only, not permanent settlement by the white men. He had received news of the charter from a patrol led by a corporal of the Blues in full dress uniform, whom he thought to be more important than he actually was and he had no idea of the significance of the charter or what it entailed. The fact that the king spent much of his day with his nose in his drinking vessel did not help him either. His *indunas*, those who commanded his warrior *impis*, did recognise the threat the white men posed and cautioned the king, who was hard-pressed to contain their savage thirst for blood against these intruders.

Pat and his party had no wish to draw attention to themselves and clash with such men. Brian commented, "One of these days the old bugger is going to see the light and realise that these whites who are swarming all over his country mean to stay. Then there'll be problems and the odds are not exactly stacked in our favour."

"I'm sure you're right. I think we have a few adventures ahead of us if we hang around these parts for long."

"So why are we here at all?"

"You know the answer to that, Brian, as well as I do. But you have to see the Ndebele point of view, don't you? Here they are leading a comfortable life without opposition. When a bit of sport beckons, they spread out and bash a few Mashona heads, rape their women, steal their cattle, and then return home and go back to feasting and drinking until they feel restless again. All of a sudden these white men come along with their magic sticks that they don't throw at a buck, but point at it. It then makes a bang and the animal falls down dead. I think they have a right to feel threatened and in time, yes, they will retaliate."

"What about the poor Mashona people? They were here before Mzilikazi brought his people up from Natal after his break with Shaka, the Zulu king. But, if we are to believe the historians, we can go back to the time of Christ when capoids and bushmen were here and driven out by migrating tribes from the north. Now, the poor sods are only found in the south west and in the worst regions where no one in their right mind would want to live. At least, they feel less threatened there."

Pat shrugged. "Now you see why I have no qualms about exploiting mineral wealth. Also, somebody has to bring these tribes into the nineteenth century. Rather the British than the Portuguese or the Afrikaaners, I say. As far as I'm concerned, Lobengula has no authority other than his own to cross the Limpopo. I have no doubt that he will have to be deposed if Rhodes is to achieve his dreams.

This is no man's land. It's for whoever wins it and we're here so it's now up to us to introduce the local people to civilised society."

Warming to his subject, Pat continued, "The white man will act as a wedge between the tribes. The savagery which exists now must be stamped out. I think, as we have reached a more advanced level of civilisation, we are destined to rule this new country until that gap is closed. It's nothing new to them. After all, the average man among them doesn't have a say in who rules him, does he?"

"So you think Lobengula is going to have to be defeated, Pat?"

"That's how I see it, Brian."

⟩⟨ ⟩⟨

The wagon train arrived in Salisbury ahead of the rains and they settled below the kopje by the river where Pat and Brian had first made camp on their arrival from Umtali.

Sandra and Margie had seen the wagons approaching when they were still an hour away and had ridden out to meet them. Sandra pulled up her horse in a cloud of dust in front of Pat who nimbly avoided being knocked onto his back.

He reached up and pulled her from the horse into his arms. "Well, my little dove, I was hoping that you'd missed me, but here you are trying to kill me."

"What's taken you so long, Pat? What have you been doing?" she gasped.

Brian, as he walked over to help down Margie from her horse, chuckled. "It took him some time to drag himself away from the fleshpots of Durban. Then he had the same problem in Kimberley. You have to admire his stamina."

"He's just jealous," was Pat's only comment.

Sandra hooked her foot around Pat's ankle and pushed him to the ground, falling on top of him and pinning his arms to the ground. "You no-good two-timing rat," she screeched. "If your friend is right, you're dead meat."

"I didn't know you cared so much," laughed Pat as he put his arms around her and rolled her onto her side, kissing her hungrily. Sandra returned his kiss with passion and that was the moment when Pat knew for certain that this was the woman who would one day be his wife.

Meanwhile Brian and Margie were similarly engaged, though a little more decorously, and by the time the four of them had finished their reunion, the wagons were almost at the settlement and the two men had to hurry after them to show the drivers where to outspan the oxen.

That evening, before joining the Graham family for dinner they bade farewell to Lou and thanked him for the benefit of his culinary skills over the past months and wished him well in his new endeavour. He had plans to open an eatery in opposition to the single facility that currently existed. He was to rather grandly call it The Granada.

"So, my friends," said Joe, when they all settled on the veranda after dinner, "I see you've returned with more than a little baggage. Care to tell me what your plans are now?"

Pat and Brian had already decided that they couldn't keep their discovery from Joe much longer so Pat told him their story from the finding of Siyakonzi's diggings onwards, without revealing too many details or the exact location of their find.

"That's quite a story," said Joe. "You could write a book about it."

"That's more in your line," said Pat, "but I believe that this tale is far from over."

"When do you intend leaving for Nyanyadzi, Pat?" asked Sandra. He could see that she was trying to control her emotions.

"In two or three days. First I have to talk with Jameson about where to site the blacksmith's forge so that I can send my two lads back here as soon as I can release them to set it up."

"But you've only just got here," exclaimed Sandra.

"That's right," wailed her sister. "It's not fair on us." Holding hands they ran off into the darkness.

"Dear me," said Madge to her husband, "I fear we have a double dose of love sickness on our hands. What are we to do?"

"My dear," said Joe, cocking an eyebrow at Pat and Brian, "I don't think you and I can do much about it. It seems to me that the only people who can influence things are these two young men. What you and I have to worry about, Madge, is whether they have the right intentions."

Brian cleared his throat self-consciously. "Speaking for myself, and I'm sure Pat thinks the same way, I have only the most honourable intentions towards your lovely daughter. One day, when I am established, and if she will have me, I will ask you for her hand because I know for certain she has stolen my heart. Before that happens, though, there is much work to be done at the diggings, expanding the mine operation and in building homes."

"What can I add?" Pat said. "I love Sandra and Brian is right. There is much work to be done first. The situation as it is at present is not suitable for a woman."

Joe smiled at them. "Instead of waffling on to Madge and I, you two should be spreading a little comfort so get on with it, lads. Don't keep the girls waiting."

Pat and Brian excused themselves and left. "I'm not looking forward to this, Brian. The first and obvious question will be, 'When do we see you again?' and I don't have an answer."

"I think we're going to have to plan to visit the girls at least every couple of months or we're going to lose out to someone who's here more permanently."

They heard the girls before they saw them. They were talking by the river bank. Brian spoke first. "Look, Sandra, Margie, this isn't any easier for us than it is for you. We've just been talking to your folks. They were rightly concerned about our intentions towards you and we've assured them that we are sincere in our intentions towards you."

"Come," said Pat and he led Sandra down the path so that each couple could have some privacy. When they stopped, Pat held both her hands. She looked up at him and said, "When will I see you again, Pat?"

"Brian and I have just been talking about that. We've decided that whatever happens we'll come back at least once every two months. I've had a lot of time to think on the road from Kimberley and I want you to know that I've never felt this way about a girl before. I love you and I want you to agree to be my wife. Will you marry me, Sandra?"

Sandra tore her hands away from his grip and flung them around his neck. "I love you, too, Pat, and yes, please, I will marry you." She pulled him down to her and kissed him fiercely on the lips.

Pat finally broke away and held her at arms-length. "You must understand, my love, that there are things that Brian and I must do first. We must see how this diamond find develops and then we can decide together where we'll live. Please be patient, Sandra."

"That you love me and want to marry me is enough for now, but you must promise to return every two months or sooner if you can."

"Nothing will stop me, sweetheart."

CHAPTER TEN

Nick Du Ploy and Eamon Colhoun were rough, hard men, pugilists who wore the battle scars of their trade on their faces, and whose features Barney Barnato had had a hand in rearranging in the ring when he was trying to make ends meet on arrival at the New Rush diggings.

Barnato had used the pair when he needed some muscle to recover debts or deal with anything else that required more than verbal persuasion. They were following Pat van Zyl's wagons north to find out why he needed so much mining equipment.

Eamon, the Irishman humiliated by Brian in the Kimberley bar, accepted the task with alacrity, partly for the money offered, but as much for the chance of gaining his revenge on Brian. Nick was willing enough to accept the job.

They approached Salisbury, eager to replenish their liquor supplies and perhaps add some food to their shopping list. Eamon couldn't wait to find a bar.

"Listen, you *bliksom*," said Nick, "you can't just go riding in to town. What if you run into Wood-Gush, hey? No, man, we find a place to camp and you keep your *skop* down while I go and get a re-supply of food and *dop*."

"I suppose you're right, but let's get a move on."

They camped in a thicket about two miles down-river from the kopje. Nick immediately set off to the settlement where he soon found his way to the canteen atop the hill and settled down with a bottle of brandy. Before he knew it, darkness was descending and he had yet to buy any supplies other than the brandy. He decided that food could wait a day. Instead, he bought another bottle of brandy and staggered off to retrieve his horse.

Being drunk on a moonless night in a strange town did not help Nick's orientation and he suddenly found himself in a wagon camp. Realising his error, he turned his horse and galloped away, but again in the wrong direction, as he found himself entangled in the camp's washing line. He cursed and thrashed around but that only made things worse.

Pat had heard the commotion down by the river and came rushing back with a lantern. When he saw what was happening, he yelled, "What the hell d'you think you're doing, you bloody fool?"

"Bliksom!" was the only response he got, as Nick finally took off, festooned with washing that clung to his body and trailed along the ground after him.

Brian arrived. "Who the hell was that?"

"I couldn't see who it was, but he was hopelessly drunk and obviously had no idea where he was."

"Never a dull moment," Brian sighed. "We'd better go and collect our underwear and put it back in the tub."

Nick eventually found his own camp, or perhaps the horse did, and he slid from the saddle, utterly confused, and barely able to stand upright.

Eamon was furious. "You useless fecking Dutchman," he roared, "I can't rely on you to do anything. You disappear for half the day and then return empty-handed, from what I can see. What are we meant to eat, you bloody useless hairyback?"

"Shaddup! If you hadn't started that bar fight, we could have ridden into town together. Be thankful I've brought you some dop," slurred Nick and he tossed the bottle of brandy to Eamon, who caught it and went off muttering and in search of a mug.

Nick left his horse untethered and still bearing its saddle as he staggered off to his blankets. Within minutes, he was snoring loudly.

With the oxen rested, it was time for Pat and his men to once more take their leave. Before they did, they felt they should pay their respects to Dr Jameson and fill him in on developments since their last meeting.

Dr Jim smiled as he said, "I've heard that you two gentlemen are planning to do some regular coming and going." He winked at them knowingly.

Pat looked serious. "We've got to protect our interests, haven't we, doctor?"

"Aye, that we do!" agreed Brian.

They left the office and, now that it was summer and the sun rose at five, they were ready to move an hour and a half later. The two men stood apart from the wagon train, involved in the complex departure process from their lady-loves..

"It's only for two months, Sandra. Remember, when you next see me, I could be well on the way to making a fortune," said Pat.

"That doesn't matter to me, you fool. It's you I love, not your money. Just make sure it's no more than two months or I'll be coming to look for you." Sandra was trying not to shed tears.

Pat finally broke their embrace, mounted his horse, and rode off after the departing wagons. Brian soon joined him.

"I must say I'm glad that's over," said Brian. "I can't handle these emotional farewells. Can you?"

"No more than you, my friend, but now we must concentrate on the business of mining."

Pat wanted to find a more direct route to Nyanyadzi. He felt they could leave the road to Umtali at the Odzi River. He suggested to Brian that he go ahead to Umtali, collect the horses along with Tendai and the labourers before backtracking to meet Brian at the Odzi River. Then they would cut across country, proceeding southeast to their destination.

"That makes sense to me," said Brian.

Because hostilities between the company and the Portuguese were now over, Pat found Captain Heyman moving his men and the whole community to a new site about four miles west from their original kopje. The new site, being on level ground, lent itself better to building and, equally important, was close to the Umtali River, which would give them a perennial source of water.

Captain Heyman mused, as they sat that evening over a drink, "My men won't miss having to forever carry water up this wretched hill. We'll be able start building something more permanent. Enough of that, though! What are your plans now, Pat?"

Pat was prepared to divulge a little more than he had the last time they had met but he still kept the exact location secret. He admitted the possibility of a diamond find and that Rhodes was backing the expedition.

"I'm just picking up our guide, Tendai, and his friends, whom we used last time," he explained. "By the way, has Colin Grieve passed through here?"

"No, but I have a letter for you that came to my office." Heyman fetched it and passed it over. "So, it looks like you'll be in these parts for a while."

"You can count on that," replied Pat, smiling with thoughts of Sandra on his mind.

He skimmed through the letter and said, "The good news is that Colonel Andrada has been exonerated and Grievous will be taking a leisurely cruise up the Pungwe and he'll join us at the diggings."

Before they set off the next day, Pat, with the help of sand diagrams and a few words of ChiShona he had picked up, asked Tendai about the possibility of a short cut through to Nyanyadzi. Tendai thought it entirely possible with the help of local chiefs in the area who would willingly direct them.

They left on horseback, Tendai riding nervously on Brian's horse, a new experience for him. The rest of the men trotted behind. They could do this all day, humming tunelessly as they went; this was their normal mode of travel. They were at the meeting place within half a day, but there was no sign of Brian. Pat was sure he would come the next day so he set up camp and then went fishing while Tendai dug for worms. An hour passed before he was grilling his fish lunch over hot coals.

As he did so, he reflected over the events of the past six months. There was plenty to think about. He had come north looking for adventure and found plenty of it, but aside from that he had found love and that made him feel good, as did the vision of making his fortune in diamonds. It was almost too good to be true, which was a little unsettling. Pat knew that there were still a few raging rivers to cross and that there was no room for complacency.

Brian and the wagons arrived as Pat had predicted, by which time Tendai had caught enough fish that he would smoked, and last him and his friends some time.

Dark clouds were beginning to roll in from the east and Tendai warned of the onset of the rains.

Pat said, pointing to flashes of lightning over the distant hills, "I think our problems are about to begin."

He was right. The deluge began as they rolled into their blankets for the night. It lasted seven days, only varying in intensity.

Damp crept into everything. Clothing was mouldy, as was saddlery and the oxen harnesses. When the sun finally reappeared, it took a whole day to dry everything out.

None of them were under any illusions about the difficulty of trekking through virgin bush. Tendai pointed out a feature each morning and then Pat and Brian would ride on ahead to reconnoitre. Where possible they followed game trails or footpaths between villages that led in the general direction they were heading in. The village chiefs, when they recovered from the shock of seeing white men and wagons drawn by oxen, were happily obliging. It was their advice that got them across many a river at suitable crossing points. Pat was prepared with a good supply of items such as fishing hooks and line, cloth, called *limbo,* and beads as payment for such help, without which they would never have made any significant progress.

Even so, it was slow and frustrating; the two men wanted to be at the site and digging for wealth. Neither were the nights easy. They were often disturbed by lions trying to break through their camp's defences to reach the horses and oxen. Too often they were shaken awake by a guard to deal with animal intruders.

On one occasion, Pat was shaken awake by an agitated guard shouting, "*Shumba, shumba,* come, come!"

Grabbing his Winchester, Pat ran across to the next wagon to alert Brian and they followed the guard to the far side of the enclosure where the blacks had been sleeping around the embers, but were now huddled together in fear while some of them built up the fire as the only deterrent available to them. Outside the perimeter, they could hear a man yelling. "At least he's not screaming," said Brian. "It means the lion hasn't got him yet. He was probably relieving himself."

Pat said, "Follow behind me, Brian, with your shotgun and a torch." Then he shouted, "Solomon! Get the torches lit, please." A torch was a stick with a ball of rags, sticky with fat from a bush pig, tied to one end. They had been prepared earlier for just such an eventuality. All Solomon had to do was thrust one into the fire.

Pat led the way, his rifle into his shoulder, safety catch off. They passed between two of the wagons, stepping over the *disselboom*, towards the noise. It was not far away; no one ventured too far from the fire at night for any reason.

The lioness had treed her victim and was halfway up the trunk of a marula tree. There it became a problem to go further as the trunk thinned and swayed, much to the alarm of the man hanging on to the upper branches.

Pat took careful aim. He had no desire to deal with a wounded lioness at close quarters. The bullet went through the beast's ear into its brain. It fell with a dull thud to the ground.

Pat was about to tell the man in the tree to come down when a deafening roar came from the long grass to their left. Brian nearly dropped his torch in fright.

The grass parted thirty feet away and a full-grown lion bounded straight towards them. What followed was a blur. Pat had to re-cock his rifle before he could fire again. He had not expected this attack. He worked the lever, took aim and fired in one fluid movement. Another second would have been too late. The lion caught the bullet in its brain in mid-leap and now lay dead at their feet, giving off a nauseous smell. There was a silence before Pat let out a long audible sigh of relief and lowered his rifle. "That was close," he muttered to himself, "too close."

The onlookers, realising that the drama and the danger were over, came out of their transfixed state and gave voice to their relief while one ashen-faced man slowly descended the tree.

Brian said, "I thought I'd seen it all when you won that competition back in Fontesville, my friend, but no one's going to believe this when I tell them."

"Better not tell anyone, then," replied Pat. "Right now I need a stiff drink."

After giving instructions to Tendai to organise the skinning of the two lions, Pat and Brian returned to the wagons, where an unsteady hand poured the first tots.

Two miles behind them Nick Du Ploy and Eamon Colhoun had been woken by the shots.

"What was that all about, Eamon?"

"Uninvited guests is my guess," replied Eamon, "of the four-legged kind." He threw a few more logs on the fire, rolled over and went back to sleep.

In the morning, Pat was approached by Solomon and a man whom Pat knew to be his relative. With them was the still visibly shaken young tree climber. Solomon crouched well away from Pat, a traditional sign of respect, and explained that the youngster wished to thank the boss for saving his life.

"What's his name?" asked Pat.

"Tembo, boss. He is the son of my uncle."

"Tell him we are both lucky to be alive. Also tell him and everyone else to attend to their ablutions before nightfall. Next time, we may not be so lucky."

As the wagons began to roll, Pat noticed that the two skins had been stretched out over frames made of young saplings and been tied either side of the kitchen wagon.

⇒‖⇐

Brian had taken on the job of mapping their route. He was producing a remarkable piece of artwork complete with illustrations of the diverse outstanding features such as hills, rivers and open savannah. The msasa trees of the highveld gradually gave way to the acacia and baobab of the *lowveld*. Every day brought some rain, but the intensity decreased as they moved further south. In the east they could still see heavy clouds hanging over the mountains.

Closer to their destination, Pat noticed certain landmarks that looked similar to those spotted on their first journey to the diggings. He pointed them out to Brian.

"It won't be long now, Brian. I'd say we're fairly close."

He was right and they found themselves once more sitting with the village chief, offering him their special snuff. Tendai explained why they were back and told him of the benefits that would accrue to the village in exchange for the supply of a work force.

The old chief showed great interest and asked about the form of payment for such a service. He was delighted when shown the array of cloth, knives, hoes, axes and especially the snuff. Pat presented him with an old muzzle loader as a sign of his good intentions. The chief leapt from his stool and began prancing about and stabbing the air with it as if it were a spear.

"Nice touch, Pat," said Brian. "It looks like you've made a friend for life. One thing's for sure though, I'm not going to be the one to teach him how to use it."

"Nor me. I'll ration the powder and give him no ammunition. That way the only damage the old bugger can inflict will be to blow the balls off a goat."

The next morning, they recruited twenty young men as labourers and started out on the final leg of their journey. Now that they had the wagons to deal with, they had to manoeuvre them along the top of the ridge overlooking the river instead of using the riverside path as they had done before. The Nyanyadzi had risen considerably with the recent rains and in places was a hundred yards wide.

Everything at the diggings was as they had left it; there were no signs of visitors. Pat divided the work force into two. Brian's team worked on building a kraal to pen the oxen and other livestock at night. This took the form of an inner pole fence surrounded by sickle thorn tree branches to keep out lions, leopards and other predators.

Pat's crew set to building huts for the workers. When this was done, they would start on a permanent homestead for themselves. Pat had spent several hours during the journey planning the house, using stone, of which there was plenty. However, this could come later as they wanted to get on with the mining as well and they were so used to sleeping in the wagons, that it was no longer any hardship.

⊶⊷

Meanwhile, Nick Du Ploy and Eamon Colhoun had made camp behind a kopje about three miles away. They ventured out each day to observe the daily activities at the diggings which, for the first week, was a boring exercise. Things changed when the sorting tables were set up and the workers began to attack the ground with picks.

Concealed behind a rocky outcrop above the site, Eamon whispered in Nick's ear, "Well, isn't it about fecking time something happened? I was beginning to think this was going to be a bloody nature study outing."

"It looks like old Barney might have been right," replied Nick as they watched the first coco pan run down the rails to the waiting sorting tables that had been placed in the shade of some big fever trees. "I reckon we give it another week to see how lucky they get."

"The sooner we get back to civilisation, the better as far as I'm concerned," Eamon moaned, "but I suppose you're right. We need to give it a bit more time."

⊶⊷

The diggings took the form of a trench running parallel to the river. Pat and Brian spent their days at the sorting tables below. It was absorbing work and they never tired of it as the rewards were generous and each stone they picked out created its own measure of excitement.

The workers were bemused, unable to understand the white men's pre-occupation with apparently useless stones and Pat and Brian saw no need to enlighten them. They knew that in time the value of these stones would be revealed one way or another and then the problem of security would become a serious issue, as it had in Kimberley. There, the work force contrived ingenious tactics to steal them, including inserting them into every orifice of their bodies.

Alongside the mining work, the house was beginning to take shape. It looked down on the river and took in the savannah beyond, taking in the two hills that had been their original guide to the site. Beyond that, in the far distance, were the blue mountains. To take in this magnificent view, a large veranda was planned. There would be three bedrooms and an open plan living room which included a dining area. The kitchen and ablutions would be separate structures away from the house. A wagon was sent to search for thatching grass and long timbers for the roof. They had brought with them doors and window frames. It had the makings of a weatherproof and comfortable home.

Nearer the river, Siyakonzi's vegetable garden had been revived and seeds sown. Within a few weeks of their arrival, the signs of success of their mining venture were becoming evident. The largest diamond they had unearthed weighed fourteen carats and six and seven carat stones were commonplace.

"You know, Brian," Pat said at the dinner table next to the kitchen wagon, "I think we are on the road to riches. It's a bit overwhelming, isn't it? I'm finding it hard to come to terms with the quantity and quality of the diamonds we've found in such a short time. What makes me uncomfortable is that it all seems a bit too easy."

"I know what you mean. I feel the same. It's like this whole thing is too big for us. I keep trying to envisage the repercussions once word gets out, which it will eventually."

Pat had another thought. "If we are to keep our promise to the girls, one of us should start thinking about returning to Salisbury. It's also important that we keep Dr Jim informed."

"You're right, Pat, but I've a feeling that Grievous is going to pitch up any day now, so let's give it another week and then we can decide."

Brian had barely finished speaking when a breathless and agitated night watchman ran into the lamplight. He jumped up and down, pointing along the track.

Grabbing their rifles, the two men, followed by the watchman, ducked into the shadows. They heard the sounds of someone approaching on horseback. The rider came to a halt before they caught sight of him and a familiar voice rang out from the darkness. "Hello! Any chance of a whisky for a weary traveller?"

"Grievous, you bloody word waster, it's about time," shouted Pat as he ran forward, followed by Brian, offering his own profanities.

"We were just talking about you," laughed Brian. He pulled Grievous from the saddle and held him in a bear hug. "Your bloody ears must have been burning."

"Put me down, you great ox," grunted Grievous.

"We were wondering how long it would take you to get here on those short stumps of yours," said Pat. He instructed the watchman to take care of Grievous' guide and the horse and then, with much backslapping, they made their way back to the table by the kitchen wagon.

"Seriously, Grievous, what took you so long?" asked Pat. "We expected to find you here when we returned."

"After the board inquiry, I thought I had a bit of time on my hands so I took a cruise down to Durban, did a bit of sight-seeing, then continued on to Cape Town."

"Good for you!" said Brian. "Now, this reunion calls for a round of drinks." He delved into a trunk under the wagon and produced a bottle of whisky and three glasses.

"Certainly," agreed Pat, "but first let me get the cook to organise some food for the man."

"Thanks, Pat," Grievous said. "I'm so hungry I could eat a decomposing baboon."

Seated round the table, Pat suggested that Grievous bring them up to date with his news and then Pat and Brian would follow suit with theirs.

"Before I do that," said Grievous, "I must tell you that I think someone is spying on you. About half an hour's ride away from here, my guide noticed a small camp fire, just a flicker, well concealed. You couldn't have seen it from here because of the hill in the way. I sent Tafadzwa forward to investigate. He crawled away far more quietly than I could have done. He told me there were two white men camped there with their horses. Now, tell me what you think two white men would be doing way out here in the middle of nowhere?"

"I can only think that you've already reached the only possible conclusion," replied Pat. "We're going to have to take a look first thing in the morning and have a serious chat with these two gentlemen."

"If they are spying on us," Brian observed, "they must have been on our trail from the start."

"All the way from Kimberley," added Pat. "The next question is who sent them?"

Grievous shook his head morosely. "My late arrival seems to have been fortuitous, doesn't it?"

"I suppose," said Pat, "that they legally have as much right to be here as we do. Following us is hardly a crime. We'll think on that one. Now, tell us your story, Grievous."

Grievous related all that had happened to him from his resignation from The Times to Colonel Andrada's clearance of all charges against him and his own resignation and subsequent appointment as Mr Rhodes' agent in Beira. "So," he concluded, "everything seems to have worked out well for him. Now, it's your turn. What's been happening here?"

It was midnight by the time Pat and Brian had brought him up to date and, with the whisky bottle empty, they were glad to roll into their houndsfields with Brian's final comment: "I wonder what will happen next!"

It happened four hours later when Pat shook them awake. "Sorry, chaps, but we've got an interview on our hands and we don't want to be late for it."

He then woke up Tendai and Grievous' guide and by four o'clock they were ready to go. They walked briskly behind Tafadzwa. Half an hour later they were motioned to stop and crouch. Tafadzwa held Pat's shoulder and pointed to a large tree. Pat nodded his head and gathered the others around him.

"The plan is simple," he whispered. "We creep in and encircle the camp. I'll announce our presence and we'll take it from there. No force, but if one of them goes for a gun, leave it to me. We crawl in to avoid any trip wires they may have placed. Grievous, tell the two lads to stay here until we call them up."

The three of them made their way forward. The only sound was a gentle wind blowing through the trees. They were close to the tree the guide had indicated. There was no sign of life, no dying embers, no sleeping forms, no nervous horses.

Pat stood up. "It looks like we're too late, chaps. As soon as it's light, we'll look around and see what signs there are to help us."

They were able to ascertain that two men and three horses had been there and, judging by the amount of ash left from fires, for some time.

"Now we'll never know who they were," Grievous said.

"That's what's worrying me," said Pat. "Come. I'll bet we find a path through the grass leading to that kopje. That's where they could have easily watched us."

They soon found the path of trodden grass that went where Pat had predicted. "There's the evidence," he said. "Who sent these snooping bastards? I don't think we can put off this trip to Salisbury any longer. If neither of you object, I'm heading back to camp to prepare to leave immediately. I must get word to Mr Rhodes on the extent of the find and also this latest development. It will be up to him to get his own sniffer network into action. Agreed?"

Brian sighed enviously, "Pat, as much as I'd like a change of company, you're the best man for this job so get going – you lucky dog."

"What do you mean by a change of company?" snapped Grievous. "I haven't been here twelve hours yet. What d'you think I am?"

"You're not the change of company I had in mind. You're not good looking and you don't wear skirts."

"The chubby little fellow has breasts though," chuckled Pat.

"You've been peeping!"

Brian turned to Grievous. "It's good to have you with us again, Grievous." He gave him a slap on the back. "I mean that."

On the way back to camp, they took turns telling Grievous about the Graham sisters. Grievous sighed, "A pity there's only two of them."

At the diggings, Pat yelled first for some porridge for breakfast and then for Maforga, whom he wanted with him on the journey as he could both ride and shoot.

The last thing he packed, in the bottom of his bedroll, was the game skin pouch that held the diamonds, about a thousand carats of them. He estimated five days for the trip.

"I don't know how long I'll be gone," he said as he swung into the saddle. "As long as it takes to get some guidance from Mr Rhodes, I guess. The other thing I must do is set up some form of communication between here and Salisbury."

"Go well, Pat," said Brian, "and don't forget to give my love to Margie."

"Of course. Now be sure to keep Grievous busy; we don't want him getting fat and flabby."

"You look after your body and I'll look after mine, you cheeky sod," came the retort.

CHAPTER ELEVEN

On the evening of the fifth day, weary and saddle sore, Pat and Maforga rode into Salisbury and made immediately to where the Grahams had parked their wagon. They were faced with an empty space. There was a moment of panic before it occurred to Pat that in the weeks he had been away, they had likely moved to somewhere more permanent. Wheeling his horse around, he headed for the schoolhouse and was relieved to see that an extension had been built on to it. The melodious tones of Madge's piano coming from the school part of the building confirmed his thoughts. He tethered his horse and pushed open the classroom door. It was Sandra sitting at the piano. She was absorbed as she practised a new piece of music.

Watching her sitting with a slight frown of concentration, Pat thought he had never seen anyone more beautiful or more desirable. He was certain that this woman had stolen his heart and that he loved her more than he had thought possible.

Sandra sensed a presence in the room, stopped playing and looked up. An expression of such happiness spread over her face that Pat could bear things no longer. A moment later they were in each other's arms.

"Oh, Pat, Pat," she cried. "How I've missed you!"

"Me, too, my little dove." Pat looked down into her lovely eyes.

A voice behind them said, "I wondered why it had suddenly gone quiet in here so I came to investigate." It was Joe Graham.

Breaking the embrace, Pat self-consciously shook Joe's hand. "Good to see you again, sir. How are you?"

"Fine! It's good to see you, too, but clearly not as good as it is for this young lady," laughed Joe. "I'll leave you two to catch up and go and tell Madge to lay another place at the table – or is it two?"

"Only me this time, I'm afraid," said Pat.

As they ate, Joe told Pat about developments at the settlement, dwelling a lot on his own new premises. Over coffee, Margie could contain herself no longer. "Please, Pat, what news of Brian, for goodness' sake?" she burst out.

"Oh, he's fine, Margie, he's fine,"

"And … was there no message for me?"

"Actually, no. I did leave in a hurry." Pat paused, looking at Margie's crestfallen face. "But he did ask me to give you this." He held up an envelope.

"You sadistic beast! You've let me sit here and stew throughout dinner. I hate you sometimes, Patrick van Zyl. Let me have it."

"I might consider it if you ask nicely." He held the envelope tantalisingly away from her.

"You ba …"

"Watch your language, young lady," interrupted Joe, who was enjoying the moment. Margie jumped to her feet and snatched the envelope from Pat's hand. "Er, yes, you're excused from the table," he added as his daughter disappeared, clutching the letter.

Pat spent the next hour relating the good news about the claim being a rich one and then the bad news about them probably being followed all the way from Kimberley and the secret being out and the ominous times that could lie ahead as a result.

"We've got to find out who is on to us," said Pat. "We're fairly sure the answer lies in Kimberley and that someone influential there hired those two fellows to follow us. I must contact Mr Rhodes and warn him so that he can try to find out the identity of this individual. In two days, I'll ride to Tuli and send a message on the telegraph."

"But you've only just got here, Pat, and you're off again," wailed Sandra.

"I know, but what else can I do? There's too much at stake."

Pat hoped that his timing was right as he took out an impala skin pouch and shook out an eight carat diamond onto the table.

"Whew!" enthused Joe. "That's a beauty."

"A beauty for a beauty, Mr Graham. With your and Mrs Graham's permission I would wish to present it to your daughter, but only after I have had it cut and mounted on to a gold band."

"Patrick van Zyl," said Sandra with a quizzical look, "are you in some roundabout way proposing marriage to me?"

Grinning hugely, Pat knelt before her and took her hand. "I most certainly am, Sandra, because I love you. Will you consent to be my wife?" Turning to Joe and Madge, he said, "Mr and Mrs Graham, please agree to giving me your daughter's hand in marriage."

Sandra, throwing her arms around his neck, half laughing, half weeping, stammered, "Yes, yes, yes, please." Looking over her shoulder, Pat saw Joe nodding and Madge smiling and he knew it would be all right with them.

⇥⊹⇤

Early the following morning Pat was once again sitting opposite Dr Jameson beneath a tree outside his office, telling him about the latest news from the diggings.

"Communications really is a problem," sighed Dr Jim. "I've started a courier service to Tuli twice a month which helps, but the sooner we have a telegraph line erected, the better. This issue before us now highlights that need, doesn't it?" Stroking his moustache, he continued, "Assuming that these two fellows are still unaware that you have discovered their presence at Nyanyadzi, they'll be in no great hurry to get back to Kimberley. With luck, you'll be able to contact Mr Rhodes before they report back to their principals. That will give us an edge."

He stood up and began to pace back and forth with his hands behind his back. When he stopped, he pointed to the bag of diamonds and said, "I'm sure that Mr Rhodes will want to deploy some sort of a guard force to protect our interests down there now that it seems fairly certain that you've made a substantial discovery of diamonds, Pat."

"I'd be more than happy to go along with that. Still on communications, though, we're going to have to improve them from the diggings to you here in Salisbury. We need to think about that."

"We've also started a weekly mail service to and from Umtali. It's just a question of extending that. How long would it take a horse and rider to reach Nyanyadzi from Umtali?"

"Two days is possible, depending on the weather," Pat replied.

"Good. That means I can get word to you there in seven or eight days."

"With a reply in just over a fortnight."

"I'll get on to it right away. Now, tell me, does the Nyanyadzi River flow all year round?"

"According to the chief, it's never dried up in his lifetime, and he must be over sixty."

"That's good news. Apart from being essential for the mine, it's a real bonus if the area can sustain crops like maize and vegetables. Feeding the staff becomes a problem when everything has to be carted in. "The land on the opposite bank of the river to mine would seem, to my inexperienced eye, suitable for cropping and, given adequate protection from wild animals, cattle might also be an option. My side is very rocky. All it could sustain is goats and they'd need to be rugged creatures to survive."

"I wish I could escape from my wretched desk and get down there myself. It's exciting, isn't it? There's so much potential in this beautiful land. The hard part will be managing it. We must put the right structures in place so that all the people benefit from its resources. It's that educational gap that needs to be narrowed. The white man can provide the technology, but it needs the black man's physical effort as there aren't enough of us. If we are to live in harmony with the blacks, they must be protected from exploitation. Sorry, I'm on my hobby horse again. Let's work out your message to Mr Rhodes. We don't want to arouse any unwanted curiosity. We'll go through to the office and make an inventory of the diamonds and then work something out."

"I've already given the wording some thought," said Pat and he handed over a draft which read, 'Siyakonza producing an excellent carrot crop but cultivation being observed by others, possibly from Kimberley. Please advise. Communications to be improved in near future so that a message from Salisbury could reach me at the farm in two weeks. Regards. P.V.'

"That will do nicely, Pat. It sounds ambiguous enough," said Dr Jim. "Now, you'll be anxious to get back to your young lady, but before you go, I'd like to show you something, if you'll give me a minute to saddle my horse. I'll do the diamonds later."

Shortly, they were looking out over a twenty acre or more field of healthy maize standing about two feet high.

"It's an experiment, Pat, to see what we can grow and how well we can grow it. Further over, inside a fenced enclosure, we've sown a variety of vegetables. On Mr Rhodes' orders, we're trying to grow some tobacco on a five-acre plot. Cotton growing is also on the cards. So far, the results are encouraging. The plan is to appoint a suitably qualified person to supervise and run short courses in agriculture for those settlers opting to take up farming. I hope we can extend into livestock management as well. What do you think of the idea, Pat?"

"It's an excellent idea, doctor. I also think that we should find the right person to teach the *ChiShon*a language and customs to the settlers." Jameson nodded in agreement.

Pat set off with Maforga the next morning on the long monotonous journey to Tuli.

CHAPTER TWELVE

Nick Du Ploy and Eamon Colhoun arrived in Kimberley a week before Pat reached Fort Tuli. They immediately made for the Pick and Shovel and that's where Barney and Harry found them much later, worse the wear for alcohol.

From the doorway, Barney said, "Shit! We'll get no bleeding sense out of them tonight. It'll have to wait 'till morning."

"Too true, Barney. I just hope that if they've discovered something important, they keep their vile mouths shut. I think you should remind them of the 'squeal and no deal' clause. Talk to Eamon. He's probably a fraction brighter than Nick, but that's not saying much."

Nick and Eamon saw the brothers and weaved their way over to them. "Hey, man, have we got news for you," blurted out Nick.

Cursing under his breath, Barney took Nick by the arm, indicating that Harry should do the same to Eamon, and they steered them to a corner table of the bar room.

Barney leaned forward and addressed the two drunks. "Listen, you dickheads, whatever you have to tell us can wait until the morning when we're more likely to get a little less fiction. For now, finish your drinks and take yourselves off to bed. Be at my office at ten tomorrow morning. Understood?"

It took them another half hour to empty the bottle and glasses and guide them safely to bed in a nearby doss house where Barney slipped the owner a few coins to make sure they both bathed before they left for the office. Both Barney and Harry were glad to return to their own cottage in a better part of the town.

"I can't remember anybody smelling as bad as those two," said Barney. "I'll bet they haven't bathed since they left here."

"Not unless they got drunk and fell in a river," Harry replied.

When they arrived at the office, the men were blurry-eyed but cleaner and looking more human. Barney sat them down and called in his brother, who closed the door behind him.

"Right, who wants to start?" said Barney.

"You do the talking, Eamon. Your English is better." Nick sniffed and wiped his nose on his sleeve.

Eamon began by talking about the road conditions to Salisbury. Nick interrupted to describe the extent of the Salisbury settlement before Eamon took over again with details of the scene at the diggings. "To be sure," he concluded, "it's as you suspected. There's diamonds like fecking sugar lumps at a duchess's tea party."

"Do you think they were on to you?" asked Harry.

"No, man, they was none the wiser," said Nick.

"There's no reason for them to suspect they were followed," Eamon said. "One strange thing happened the night before we left. After dark, we took one last look at the camp and there was a third man there, a little chubby fellow. I don't know how he fits into the picture. Anyway, we decided not to hang around any longer and broke camp straight away rather than wait till dawn."

"Interesting," said Barney. "I never saw anyone of that description in their company while they were in Kimberley. I wonder who he is? You've done well, both of you." He crossed to a steel safe, took out a wad of notes and proceeded to count them out into two piles. "Remember, not a word to anyone about this if you want any more work from me. Now, me and Harry have got some thinking to do so we'll be in contact later."

Harry said, "Before you go, confirm you've drawn up a map showing how to get to this place."

"Here it is." Eamon produced a grubby rolled up sheet of paper. "I'm no artist but if you follow this, you'll get there."

Closing the office door, Barney turned to Harry. "Right, let's look at what we know. We can be fairly sure that Van Zyl and company have what sounds like a rich strike. The fact that they spent some time with Rudd tells us that they are working with Cecil Rhodes so we're not up against a bunch of novices. I've thought a lot about something like this happening and I have a plan – I think."

"Let's hear it."

"We know that when Rudd signed the original mining concession with Lobengula, the sweetener was to supply the king with a thousand guns and plenty of powder and shot. Understandably, Rhodes has been nervous about that part of the deal and so far he's been making excuses to delay supplying the goods. I think it would be to our advantage to make a presentation to the king now. The problem is how we lay our hands on that many guns."

"We'll have to put out feelers, Barney. There's always somebody selling something."

"One final thing, Harry. We'd better arrange for that man Nick to fall down a hole or he's sure to start blabbing at some stage. I don't trust him. Eamon is more reliable and will keep his mouth shut as long as we keep him on the payroll."

———◄┼┼►———

Pat was weary when he arrived at Tuli after such a long ride. Still, he made straight for the telegraph office to send his message to

Mr Rhodes. That done, he led his tired horse to the Shashi River, finding a suitable pool downstream from the settlement to clean himself up and sooth his aching muscles in the sun-warmed water. The horse drank further downstream before turning to nibble the lush grass on the bank.

That night, even the Tuli lions did not disturb Pat's sleep at the little hotel he booked into and he awoke refreshed. Breakfast on the veranda consisted of two freshly baked scones and plenty of strong coffee. He looked out at the river that ran from east to west as far as the eye could see and felt ready for the challenges ahead. He spent some time with the proprietor catching up on news from the south and then enjoyed the luxury of reading old copies of The Times that were clamped together at the spine by two strips of wood sewn with thin copper wire.

He found the issue that contained Grievous' shortened account of the Battle of Chua. The evidence of political expediency was apparent to him and he felt that such censorship was worth the deception. The result was an honourable discharge for Colonel Andrada, a railway line between Beira and Umtali, and the British and Portuguese back on speaking terms. A satisfactory outcome.

It was almost noon and Pat went to see if the telegraph office had received a reply to his message. The smiling telegraphist handed him a message form.

Pat read, *'Delighted to hear Siyakonza doing well. Have my suspicions about who the watchers are. Please remain at Tuli while I make some inquiries. Will be in touch again within two days.'*

Colonel Andrada was settling in to his new job as Cecil Rhodes' Beira agent which so far had entailed procuring materials needed by George Pauling for the Beira-Umtali railway line. Through his work, he had befriended many of the shipping agents and others who ran the docks. As a result, he was well-informed on the movement of cargo.

The morning after the exchange of telegrams between Rhodes and Pat van Zyl, one of the colonel's friends mentioned that he was puzzled by a consignment of muzzle loaders that was, according to the manifest, destined for Kimberley via the port of Durban. The consignor was the Portuguese army while the consignee was one Barnett Isaacs.

"Who in his right mind would want to buy so many obsolete guns?" said the official. "The Portuguese army must be laughing up its sleeves to get rid of that lot."

Colonel Andrada thought, "I have no idea who this Barnett Isaacs is, but I know of someone who will be very interested to know more about this matter."

He lost no time in sending the news to Cecil Rhodes, who was still in Cape Town for the sitting of the Cape Parliament.

⟞⟝

That same night, sitting in his office at Groote Schuur, a glass of port in his hand and his trusted personal assistant, Neville Pickering, opposite him, Rhodes indicated the telegram on the table beside him. "What do you make of that, Neville? You know, of course, that Barnett Isaacs is Barney Barnato's original name. He became Barnato as it sounded more flamboyant for his career as a pugilist when he first arrived at the diggings."

"I know about that," replied Pickering. "Whatever it is he is up to, you can bet it's not good. When is that ship due to dock in Durban, sir?"

"In ten days. Add on a week and the consignment should be in Kimberley around the beginning of next month."

"One thing is sure, sir, if Barnato was going to raise an army and start a war, he wouldn't be buying a load of obsolete weapons."

"I agree, which means they must be going to someone who doesn't know any better. Let's ask ourselves why Barnato would want to give these guns to the natives. There are two possibilities, I think: one is that he wants to start an insurrection or two, he wants to curry favour."

"I would go along with that, but I don't see him doing either in Kimberley."

"Right again, so if he is the busybody we suspect he is, add this latest information about the arms shipment and we must conclude that it is going further north and he is going to try currying favour with Lobengula."

"You suspect he is going to try to influence him?"

"We have to accept that the king doesn't like the charter so by bearing gifts, Barnato hopes to persuade him to disregard the agreement or negotiate his own agreement over mining rights, enabling him to muscle in on our claim. The fact that I haven't supplied Lobengula with the promised guns is in Barnato's favour. He's a cunning devil, which is why I can't abide him. Armed with this information, we must now seize the initiative."

Rhodes stood and stared at the floral carpet for several minutes. Then he looked at Pickering. "What we must do, Neville, is capture those wagons and stop the guns reaching the king. It's as simple as that. I think Van Zyl should head the operation as he has a vested interest and he's currently on the spot. The best place for an ambush is, I think, just after they have crossed the Shashi River at Macloutsie. As the Company is the authority in Mashonaland and Matabeleland, it has the right to protect its interests there. The importation of weapons constitutes a threat to security so the law enforcers have a right to confiscate them." He paused for effect. "And we, or rather Captain Dobson, is the law, is he not? We must get a coded message off to Dobson, explaining what is required from him and Van Zyl."

At around the same time, the Barnato brothers were in their Kimberley office discussing the imminent arrival of the arms shipment from Mozambique.

"How many cases are there, Barney?"

"About thirty, each containing thirty guns. Although the manifesto describes the cargo as obsolete weaponry, the cases are marked otherwise to avoid undue attention."

"We'll need three wagons, then, two for the cases and one for supplies for the journey."

Barney nodded, happy to leave those sort of arrangements to Harry. "Sounds fine to me."

"I'm having reservations and sleepless nights over this plan of yours, Barney. You must tread carefully. We don't want to start a war up there."

"Don't worry. Lobengula can hardly start a war with nine hundred muzzle loaders, especially as I intend to – er – tamper with the shot a little. What I have to do is convince him that he shouldn't put all his eggs in one basket. I'm not going to bad-mouth Cecil Rhodes or anything like that, just convince the old bugger that there's room for a second operator and the Charter Company shouldn't hold a total monopoly. If I can get a signed concession out of him, we can go there and peg a claim next door to Van Zyl's and there's nothing Mr high and mighty Rhodes can do about it."

"We shouldn't have to be so manipulative, Harry," he continued, "but what else can we do? The Charter Company is hardly likely to grant us a claim, is it? I just wish the trip wasn't going to be so time-consuming. I'll tell you this much, I'm not returning with the wagons; they can make their own way back. As it is, I'll have to take Colhoun along with me as a guide, more's the pity. I don't expect much scintillating conversation with him."

"Why are we doing this?" asked Harry. "We're already wealthy beyond our dreams."

"It's not the money that drives me, it's the challenge. Life's getting a bit mundane. We need a bit of adventure in our lives. And we can't pass up the opportunity of getting up old Cecil's nose, can we?"

"I'm sure that's nearer the truth," sighed Harry.

Barney looked at his watch and reached for his hat. "Look at the time already. Let's continue this conversation over at the Pick and Shovel."

As they walked out the door, Barney poked Harry in the ribs and said, "Did you see that short piece in the Advertiser? It seems our old friend Nick Du Ploy got pissed and fell down a mine shaft. Pity about that, hey?"

Captain John Dobson found Pat reading more back copies of The Times on the hotel veranda.

"What's up, John?" asked Pat, looking up from his paper. "Something's on your mind?"

"Perhaps we should take a walk, Pat. I've had a coded message from Mr Rhodes."

Away from the hotel, they stopped and Dobson read out the message. Pat whistled softly. "That Mr Barnato is one slippery character. You'd think he'd be content with his lot in Kimberley. He's already a very rich man."

"You'd think so, Pat," replied the captain. "You know what it is with these rich and powerful people. It's never enough. Mr Rhodes is an exception. His money is for different purposes. It's more for queen and country and the expansion of the empire."

"Confiscating the weapons shouldn't be too much of a problem for you. I'm puzzled about why he wants me involved, though."

"You can be sure he has his reasons. He always has."

"We need to know when and where. Presumably Mr Rhodes will have the railways watched and, when the consignment arrives in

Kimberley, he'll wait for the Barnatos to make a move so that he can give us a date of departure. As far as the where is concerned, surely Barnato will use the road to Macloutsie, cross the Shashi, and make his way through the Matobo hills to the king's kraal at GuBulawayo."

"That's my conclusion, too," said Dobson, "and, yes, Mr Rhodes will send word when the wagons depart."

Pat said, "There's no point in me hanging around here just waiting, especially as there's a lady in Salisbury who will be worried about my extended absence. No offence meant, John, but I'll find her company better than yours so I'd rather wait it out with her. Rest assured I'll be back in time for the action."

"Lucky dog," grinned John. "How on earth did you find a girl in these parts?"

"Pure luck, John, pure luck. She also has a pretty sister but, before you get too excited, let me tell you that my good mate, Brian Wood-Gush, has already laid claim to her."

"You don't think she could be distracted by a dashing young army officer?"

"Under normal circumstances, it's very likely, but it would be an uphill battle as things are – and you'd lose. So, if we've finished massaging your ego, let's get back to business and devise a plan to relieve Mr Barnato of his cargo."

⥤⥢

In recent times Barney Barnato's lifestyle had changed and he was running to fat. No longer did he have to keep himself in trim for a fight that might suddenly present itself to earn him a few shillings to survive. He was now very wealthy, so sitting up on a wagon behind a toiling team of oxen in the heat and dust, week in and week out, was not his idea of fun. After a few days, he was regretting his decision to do his own dirty work. A more agreeable companion than Eamon Colhoun would have helped.

Others who took the road north would saddle a horse in the evenings and search for guinea fowl or francolin. It provided a welcome change of diet while at the same time breaking the monotony of the long tedious trek.

This did not work for Barney. He was no horseman. His first attempt to ride was shortly after his arrival in Kimberley. It brought forth a string of ribald comments, the worst being, "Hey, Barney, old son, better stick to pushing a barrow. It's not so far to fall." He never tried again.

His answer was to bring a modified two-wheeled buggy with him. The wheel rims had been strengthened and extra springs added to cope with the rugged conditions. It could be drawn by a single horse or a pair. When not in use, it was towed behind his wagon. This extra vehicle was mainly for the return trip when Barney intended to take his leave of Eamon and the ox-wagons and hurry home.

Progress was slow but eventually they reached Macloustie and crossed the Shashi to make camp. The intention was to linger a couple of days on the river bank to rest and water the animals before embarking on the final leg to the King's kraal.

<hr />

Captain Dobson knew of their departure and sent for Pat to join him. They took four troopers and two helpers on an unhurried trip, following the Shashi River westwards. The huge trees on the river bank gave them shade for their midday breaks and the deeper pools allowed them to wallow in comfort at the end of the day. There was game of every description with great herds of impala, wildebeest and zebra and many groups of kudu. Elephants were on the move, trunk to tail; several prides of lion lay basking in the sun. More than once they had to detour around a snorting rhino. In the evenings, as they sat around a fire, the silence was broken by the giggling of hyenas and the roar of lions on the hunt.

"It makes you feel like an intruder, doesn't it, Pat," said Dobson, "sitting here in the midst of all this nature."

Pat agreed. "We really are privileged. What makes it more special is that we haven't seen another human in two days."

They crossed the Shashi the following afternoon and rode on for a while before starting to look for a suitable site to intercept the oncoming wagons.

———

When they left their Shashi camp, Barney and his wagon train had been on the move no more than a couple of hours before they met resistance. Just as they were about to make the steep ascent from a dry river bed, four horsemen appeared at the top of the rise. The man leading the oxen stopped abruptly and looked back enquiringly at an astonished Barney and Eamon, who sat side by side driving the leading wagon. Barney looked behind and was relieved to see that the next wagon, in line with the established river crossing procedure, had not moved from the top of the southern bank.

Leaving the others training their rifles on the stranded wagon, Captain Dobson approached. Barney was convinced this was a hold-up but Eamon thought otherwise. "It's the fecking troopers, man. If they search the wagons, we're in big trouble, that's for sure."

"Well, if it isn't Mr Isaacs, alias Barnato," said Dobson. "A little far from your usual patch, aren't you, Barney? There must be something out of the ordinary in those wagons for a city lad like you to venture into the sticks and get his finger nails dirty. Care to enlighten me, sir?"

Barney tried to bluff his way out of his predicament. "If you must know, I felt like a break from city life and I thought an outing in the countryside, far away from my desk, would be good for the soul. I have nothing to hide inside the wagons. They contain farming implements. I thought I might as well make my holiday pay for itself – er – captain, is it?"

"Captain Dobson, at your service. I heard a different story, Barney, something about you carrying arms of war with the likely destination being King Lobengula's kraal at GuBulawayo. As I represent the law in these parts, I'm going to insist in taking a look inside those wagons."

Pat, watching from behind a thicket overlooking the river bed, shook his head and smiled at the spectacle of the little cockney sitting on the wagon seat in obvious discomfort.

Eamon kept muttering oaths and blasphemy. "Fecking soldier boy with bird shit on his shoulders! What right has 'e got to be ordering us about?"

John Dobson laughed. "I can't say I approve of your choice of travelling companion, Barney. In fact I find his foul mouth offensive and you had best tell him to shut it."

"Shut your stupid face, Eamon," snapped Barney. Then he said to the captain in a more placatory tone, "What can I say? You have the initiative." With an exaggerated sigh of impatience, he climbed down from the wagon and led the way up the bank behind him. Dobson's troopers joined him and they followed the little man.

Barney's mind was working overtime. He soon concluded that somehow Rhodes had learned of his plot. What puzzled him was how he had done so. It was a question that was to occupy his thoughts for a long time.

"Let's see what we have here, Mr Barnato, or is it Isaacs?" said Dobson, dismounting and climbing into the back of the first wagon. "Wooden crates, I see, all with padlocks. As you said, they are all marked 'Farming Implements'.

"What did I tell you, captain? Everything's ligit," chirped Barney.

"I'd better make sure, though, hadn't I? After all, me and the lads have spent three days getting here. If you'll give me a key, I'll take a peek inside."

Barney shrugged his shoulders theatrically and nodded to the driver who produced a bunch of keys. Barney took them and joined Dobson at the rear of the wagon. He opened the nearest crate and threw back the lid, revealing the muzzle loaders, tightly packed in cotton waste.

"I don't know a lot about agriculture and I probably couldn't tell one farming implement from another, but I am a military man and I know the difference between one shooter and another. I can declare with certainty that these are muzzle loaders, not a lot of use in farming. Barney, my lad, it looks like you're in a pickle. You and I had better sit down and have a little chat."

"Why am I getting the feeling that this will not be a happy sunny day in Africa?" muttered Barney to himself as the two men walked away from the wagon and sat on a log under a mopani tree.

Dobson heard the remark and said, "I'm afraid there are some dark clouds closing in, Barney. You know what's going to happen, don't you?"

"I guess I'm going to lose my investment here."

"To be sure, Barney, but I'm also going to have to take you in. Illegally importing weapons of war is a very serious matter."

"You mean you are going to lock me up?"

"Yes. I'll take you to Tuli, where you'll get a fair trial. Never mind, it's not all bad news. The circuit magistrate is due next week so you won't have to wait long."

"That's bloody convenient, isn't it?" said Barney. "Friends in high places, hey?"

"I don't know what you're talking about, of course," said Dobson, "but I do know that things will be easier for you if you come clean and tell the full story. I might be able to get you off with a fine. On the other hand, if you don't cooperate, you could find yourself part of a road gang for a spell. That prospect might prompt you to hire a lawyer, but that would delay things for three months until the magistrate gets round to visiting us again. You can think it over as we make our way back to Tuli."

"Bloody hell, you've really got me stitched up tight, haven't you, you ..." Wisely, he did not continue. He did not want an additional charge of abusing an officer of the law.

Barney's imprisonment awaiting his trial was very relaxed. He was permitted to book a room in the hotel and was free to move around, guarded by a trooper. His only discomfort was at night when he was handcuffed to his bed. Nevertheless he was not a happy man and, when he came face to face with Pat, he vented his indignation. "What a coincidence! You're here, too, Van Zyl. What's your part in this conspiracy?"

"Good day to you, too, Mr Barnato," said Pat. "What brings you this far north?"

"You know bloody well what I'm doing here. Don't give me that Mr Innocent bullshit."

"Why don't you concede gracefully, Barney? You were caught with your snout in the trough so stop bellyaching and cooperate."

"I haven't much option this time, Van Zyl, but remember that this is round one. There will be others and you'd better believe that Barney Barnato shouldn't be counted out yet."

The following day Barney went in search of John Dobson. "Ok, captain, you win. I'll make a full statement."

"That's a wise move, Barney," replied Dobson. "Let me call in Pat van Zyl as a witness."

"You mean call him in to gloat, don't you?"

Barney spent the next ten minutes dictating almost verbatim what Rhodes had deduced. The gift was to curry favour from

Lobengula in the hope of influencing him to grant the Barnatos a mining concession. He was emphatic that the guns could not be turned on the settlers as they would prove to be ineffective and were more likely to advantage the settlers in any conflict.

"How so?" enquired Pat.

"If you will tell Colhoun to fetch any one of the guns and a box of ammunition, we will demonstrate."

On the rifle range used by the troopers for practice, Barney picked out one of the rounded shots and explained, "As you know, these muzzle loaders are in fact musket rifles that use conical ammunition for greater accuracy and distance. With this shot, it would be difficult to hit a backyard latrine from ten paces. What's more, the powder has been pacified."

He handed a gun to Eamon and told him to prime it and fire it from thirty paces at his hat, which hung from a knife stuck into the centre of a large baobab tree. The shot rang out, but Pat knew that the sound was clearly muted. The hat did not move and the bullet marked the tree well below it.

Barney said, "I may have been a pugilist in my time, but my tactics don't extend to mass murder. That you've got to believe."

"So how were you going to convince Lobengula?" asked Pat. "I suppose you have a small supply of good shot and powder."

"Exactly!"

"You'd better give me a weapon and a sample of the ammunition, Barney," said Dobson. "They'll be exhibits at the trial and will play an important part in your defence."

The trial was held on the hotel veranda with no public allowed in. Troopers surrounded the area to ensure this and they also guarded the wagons from curious eyes. Apart from the magistrate, Pat, Captain Dobson and the accused, no one else was there or even knew what was happening. Eamon was told to keep his mouth shut or be charged as an accessory to the crime and end up doing a spell with a road gang.

The case lasted less than fifteen minutes. The charge was read out, along with Barney's statement, the magistrate then asked Barney if he had anything to add.

"No, sir." Barney said.

"How do you plead, Mr Barnato?"

"Guilty."

"Very well," the magistrate announced, "sentence will be delivered after lunch. Until then the court is adjourned." He rose and made his way to the dining room. The others followed suit and a leisurely lunch proceeded with conversation about a variety of topics, none of them to do with the case in hand.

When they returned to the veranda, replete and content, the Magistrate looked over the top of his glasses and said, "Will the accused please stand while sentence is passed?" Barney complied. "Barnett Isaacs, you have been found guilty of importing weapons of war into Matabeleland, the purpose for which I can only speculate on. The evidence leads me to believe that the conclusion could, in the worst case scenario, be extremely serious. However, in view of your cooperation and your clean past record, I believe that your intention was not violence so I will exercise my prerogative of leniency. I sentence you to a fine of 100 or four weeks hard labour. Furthermore, this court orders the forfeiture of your wagons and their contents to the British South Africa Company as the administrating authority in Matabeleland." He gathered up his papers and promptly headed to the bar.

Barney, rather than being relieved, was seething. The fine was nothing, the loss of the cargo was bearable, but the confiscation of his wagons really hurt because he could foresee their eventual destination. It meant that Rhodes had scored heavily against him. That was the worst of it.

Dobson came across to him and said, "If you accompany me to my office, I'll give you a receipt for the money and the wagons with contents. You can then be on your way as soon as you like."

"You're loving every moment of this, aren't you, Captain Dobson?" Barney growled.

"I must admit it's one of the highlights of my career, but look on the bright side. You've still got your horses and smart buggy to take you back to Kimberley."

"Thanks for nothing."

Both the captain and Pat were up early the next morning to see Barney depart. They watched as a hung-over Eamon Colhoun, with the help of two of the wagon drivers, harnessed the horses to the buggy under Barney's jaundiced eye.

John Dobson said, "We thought we'd just stop by and wish you *bon voyage*, Barney, and suggest that you stay on your own patch in future."

"You're all heart, captain. Round one may be to you and your master, but I was known as the come-back kid in my boxing days. Remember, Mr van Zyl, that I know where your diamond mine is. We'll meet again." He pulled himself up into the buggy, shook the reins and was off down the track without a backward glance.

Pat said, "He's right. I don't think we've seen the last of Mr Barnato."

As the dust from the buggy's wheels settled, Dobson said, "Do you remember, Pat, asking me why Mr Rhodes wanted you here for the interception of Mr Barnato?"

"Of course, but I still don't know why."

"The answer came through on the telegraph last night. It's addressed to you." He handed it over.

It read: *'My congratulations to you and Captain Dobson on completion of a successful mission. I must now prevail upon you further. I'm sure you will agree that my request is in the best interests of our joint venture. I am asking you to proceed with the wagons and their cargo to the Royal Kraal at GuBulawayo and make a formal presentation of the "farming implements" to King Lobengula as a gift from me to him. However, before doing so, and en route, I would also ask you to apply your special skills to the effectiveness of these tools, bar one for demonstration purposes. I suggest that you take the opportunity to ingratiate yourself with the king during your visit, for obvious reasons. Concerning the wagons, if you will deliver these to Dr Jameson, I will be most grateful.*

Yours truly, CJR.'

Anxious to be on his way, Pat called for Maforga and told him to recruit some new wagon drivers and be ready for an early departure the next morning. The wagons were already well-victualed, even after Barnato had taken sufficient for his needs for his return to Kimberley in his buggy.

CHAPTER THIRTEEN

GuBulawayo stood on a treeless dome-shaped hill overlooking the Umguza River. A large circular assembly area in the centre was surrounded by row upon row of tightly-packed beehive-shaped huts. The innermost dwellings within a stockade consisted of two brick buildings, built for the king by two former sailors, and these housed Lobengula's favourite wives. Close by stood the royal wagon, his own preferred sleeping accommodation. Also within this precinct was the king's cattle kraal.

This was a fearsome place where the king performed his traditional religious rites and where he also consulted with his witchdoctors to reveal those who were perceived to have evil intent before they were subsequently put to death in the most brutal manner.

Surrounding these buildings were the huts of his indunas, witchdoctors and other attendants. The entire area was enclosed behind a strong stockade of mopani poles.

Pat made camp before he sent word to the king to request an audience with him.

The king's curiosity must have been aroused. Sometimes it took several weeks of waiting before a visitor was granted permission to speak to the king but Pat was seated before him within three days. The fact that he was an emissary from Mr Rhodes and had a mysterious wagon convoy in tow may have influenced him.

Pat had no need of an interpreter because the Ndebele people were an offshoot of the Zulu nation in Natal and, having been raised in that area, Pat was fluent in their language. This could only be to his advantage in any negotiations.

He had heard differing descriptions of Lobengula. His skin colour was described as intensely black by one while another called it fine bronze. He was reported to have a benign smile that illuminated his face but also as being gross, fat and unsmiling with cruel restless eyes. The only common thread was tales of his cruelty and the gruesome way he punished any miscreants.

Pat did not know what to expect as he sat on a low stool in the courtyard between the king's wagon and the brick buildings, the area which was reserved for meetings. The morning sun was pleasantly warm on his back and, totally lost in his own thoughts, he did not hear Lobengula approach. Suddenly he was confronted by a big black belly bulging over a short curtain of cowhide. He sprang to his feet and apologised before going through the greeting ritual. His manner was polite but less servile than that of one of the king's subjects as this would be seen as a sign of weakness. An attitude of polite aloofness to the local population usually made a better impression on them, whether they be kings, chiefs or ordinary tribesmen.

The two men were of the same height, about six feet, but the king's girth was far greater. His bearing was proud and his eyes glowed with intelligence and cunning.

King Lobengula," said Pat, "I bring you greetings from that great friend of the queen across the sea and indeed your friend too, Mr Cecil Rhodes. He sends you tokens of his gratitude for allowing him and his people to dig for the bright metal in your empire."

The king's smile looked so benign that Pat found it hard to believe that this was the face of man capable of such beastly deeds.

"What is it that Mr Lodie has sent me?" he asked. Pat was used to the mispronunciation, knowing that the 'r' sound did not exist in the Ndebele language and all syllables ended in a vowel sound.

He said, "I will show you soon, but first I must give you the message that comes with these gifts from Mr Rhodes." The message was a half-truth as he warned the king against the dangers presented by Mr Barnato, a former partner of Mr Rhodes who had cheated him in Kimberley and was now planning to enter Lobengula's kingdom to ask permission to prospect in the area that Pat's group was currently mining, close to the Mozambique border. "This man, Barnato, and his associates are not the sort of people you want running loose in your kingdom. They are trouble-makers," he concluded.

Lobengula sat quietly listening to this story, nodding occasionally. Then he said, "That is an interesting story, Mr van Zyl, but I know Mr Lodie. I think he may be protecting his fishing spot on the river bank. It does not matter. If this Mr Barnato comes wanting to see me, my warriors will turn him back. Now show me what is in your wagons."

Pat was hard pressed to smother a grin at the king's astuteness as they made their way through the rows of huts to the point by the river where he had outspanned the wagons. "Wily old blighter," he thought, "you won't catch him dozing in the early morning sunshine with both eyes closed like an ageing lizard bumping up its body temperature."

When they reached the wagons, Pat shouted for Maforga, who came running, recognised the visitor, and promptly prostrated himself on the ground with a look of fear on his face.

"Get up!" the king ordered. "You can't show me what you have in your wagons while you're lying down as if between the thighs of a village slut."

Maforga called for two helpers and between them they lifted out one of the crates and laid it at the king's feet.

The king bent down and threw open the lid. His eyes lit up. "What have we here? Yes, this is just what I want. With my warriors armed with these, the Ndebele will be invincible."

Pat expected to have to train a few chosen warriors, he thought about ten, who could hit a biscuit tin at twenty five paces. This would require correct ammunition and full-strength powder. Lobengula beamed and ordered some men to carry the boxes to the royal enclosure. He and Pat followed and resumed their seats, Pat on the stool while the king relaxed his bulk in an intricately carved chair which left him with a height advantage, no doubt intentional. He clapped his hands and a woman, bare to the waist, brought a calabash of traditional millet beer.

Pat winced at the thought of this unpalatable brew being passed back and forth. It looked like regurgitated thin porridge and smelled and tasted much the same.

The woman dropped on her knees some way off and shuffled forward until she was close enough to offer it to the king. Lobengula took a healthy swig, smacked his lips, belched loudly and, as Pat had feared, passed the calabash across to him. Pat smiled feebly and raised it to cover his mouth and swallowed saliva so that he gave the impression he was drinking. Even with this pretence, he found it revolting but he could not afford to offend the king. He put on a convincing display, smacking his lips after each swallow as if he was drinking nectar.

"Mr van Zyl," said Lobengula, "I am grateful to Mr Lodie for his generous gift, but I now have a favour to ask of you. These guns are useless unless my warriors are trained to use them. Would you train me first and then some of my ndunas?"

"Pick out nine men and I'll begin tomorrow," replied Pat. "If you wish, I'll start with you now."

The king clapped his hands like an excited child. "Good, good!" he cried. "Let us begin."

Pat thought, "I hope he can hold his liquor or this is going to be hard going."

The crates had been put in one of the brick buildings, but Pat had ensured that the one containing the cone-shaped correct shot was easily accessible and surreptitiously marked. He had a tin of full strength powder with him.

Pat sat with one of the guns across his knees and explained the workings and the loading of the weapon. Lobengula sat watching and slurping from the calabash while his indunas looked on.

"Nothing will work if the powder is wet, so always keep it in a dry place." He then placed a biscuit tin he had brought from the wagon on a post that formed part of the cattle kraal and strode fifty paces before marking a line along the ground with the heel of his boot. He brought the gun to his shoulder, took a deep breath, aimed and fired. There was a metallic twang and the tin spun into the air and landed on some dung in the middle of the cattle kraal. Pat breathed out, thankful that his demonstration had been successful.

The king clapped with delight while two young boys rushed into the kraal and brought back the tin for inspection. He was impressed and wanted his turn. It was perhaps unfortunate that he had drunk a lot of beer by now and was unsteady on his feet.

Pat groaned at the thought of what might happen next but he primed and loaded the gun and once more showed the king how to pull it into his shoulder, lean forward, and aim. He estimated that an arc of fire of forty-five degrees was more than enough for safety and the people had been warned to keep away from the area. However, he had not taken into account that just outside this arc the last half dozen of the king's fine herd of heifers were waiting to be milked. A woman squatted, squirting milk into a clay pot.

Lobengula squared his shoulders and leaned forward as Pat had shown him and then brought the gun up and into position.

For half a minute the barrel waved from side to side as he struggled to bring the weapon onto the target. Then he lowered the gun, lifted one leg off the ground and let rip a thunderous fart, the force of which blew his heavy skirt back. Pat jumped involuntarily and turned away, biting his knuckle to control his mirth, the tears rolling down his cheeks.

Feeling more comfortable, the king repeated the firing routine but still the barrel continued its aimless search for the target. Suddenly he tensed as if he had found the target and pulled the trigger. He looked up at the biscuit tin which was still steady on its post. As he did so, there was an ear-shattering bellow from the cow pen.

Pat stared horrified at the scene that had unfolded. The milkmaid lay flat on her back with the upturned pot on her chest while the cow was running amok around the pen, bellowing in agony. Unbelievably, the bullet had blown away the poor beast's udder.

The king dropped the gun and looked at Pat. "What is wrong with this thing that I, King Lobengula, with the eye of an eagle, shoot at a tin while the gun shoots one of my finest cows? How can that be, Mr van Zyl?"

The indunas were trying to smother their laughter with their hands while Pat still had his fist in his mouth and had a sudden urge to relieve his bladder. How could he explain to a king that with the amount of beer he had consumed, anyone would be hard-pressed to stand up straight, let alone shoot straight? He searched frantically for a solution to this conundrum as he picked up the rifle and began dusting it with his handkerchief. Then it came to him. He discretely unscrewed the bead from the end of the barrel and concealed it in the handkerchief.

He turned to the bewildered king and said, "See, o slayer of elephants, the bead is missing it must have worked loose on the long trip from Kimberley and fallen off when I fired just now. That is why your shot went wide. I will take the gun and repair it. Tomorrow, we will continue." He added the thought, "But it will be earlier in the day before the bugger gets into his cups otherwise things could go badly for me and the project."

Meanwhile, the stricken cow had been caught and mercifully killed. The meat would not go to waste.

The next morning, Pat arrived early at the king's kraal and sat waiting for him. He noted that the cow pen was empty. When the time came, he took the first shot and hit the tin.

Lobengula took his stance, his left foot on the line. Pat stood close to him, correcting his grip slightly and checking that he was on the target, hoping all the time that his pupil would not decide to pass wind again. He then made him lower the gun and rest for a minute, while he prayed silently before telling the king to prepare to shoot. His prayer was answered. The shot was true and the tin somersaulted into the air.

The king raised the rifle into the air triumphantly and strutted around the enclosure, accepting the congratulations and adulation of his indunas, wives and children.

Pat spent the rest of the day with the ndunas and by the evening they were as proficient as they would ever be. They would never be great marksmen; the best they could hope for was a reasonable possibility of hitting a man at forty paces. An enemy further away than that was safe. There were only a few rounds left of the correct shot and the full-strength powder was finished, effectively rendering each gun in the consignment as harmful as a catapult.

It was with a feeling of relief that Pat departed for Salisbury the following day with promises from the king to keep a watchful eye open for Barnato or any of his cohorts and to close the road to anyone who did not have an authorising letter bearing the seal of the Charter Company, a sample of which had been left with him.

It was a weary man who drove his wagons into Salisbury where, before he had stopped, he heard a squeal of delight. "Pat van Zyl, you beast, what's taken you so long?" Then she was in his arms, her satin soft cheek against his rough stubble and he could feel her tears trickling down his neck. He thought his heart would melt and he held her tight. "Yes, my darling, and I've missed you, too." And then he his lips met hers.

After a splendid meal with the family, Pat and Sandra walked down to the river where Pat told her about his escapades in Tuli with Barney Barnato and then of his time with Lobengula at GuBulawayo. His description of the king's first attempt at firing a muzzle loader had them both laughing.

"The poor animal," said Sandra. "We shouldn't be laughing. It'll be a story to tell our children though, when they're old enough. You do want children, don't you, Pat?"

"Of course. As many as you like. I'll enjoy making them, too."

Sandra fetched him a blow on his chest which nearly knocked him onto his back. "What are you saying, Patrick van Zyl? Are you telling me that you've had plenty of practice in the past?"

"Ouch! Where did you learn to pack a punch like that?" Pat said, laughing and rubbing his chest. "I am as pure as a lamb in such matters."

"I don't believe you, but better we leave the matter there but God help you if you are so inclined in the future.

"That's hardly likely to happen out here, is it? The bush is hardly teeming with beautiful eligible young women. Even if it were, I would have eyes for none but you."He drew her down onto the grass and pulled her closer, slipping his hand inside her bodice. Sandra caught her breath and felt her breasts respond and the nipples harden and then his mouth was on them and she felt a sensation in her loins that she had never experienced before. She pulled away from him breathlessly and sat up.

"No, Pat, my love. I don't want you to stop, but it must, until we are wed."

"That's easier said than done. I don't know how I'll be able to keep my hands to myself. It seems I'll have to work hard to bring that great day closer."

━━━━

Pat rose early the next morning, shaved and made himself a bowl of maize porridge. As he did so, he thought how being wed would bring an added advantage of having skilled hands preparing his meals.

Dr Jameson welcomed him warmly and Pat brought him up to date on recent happenings over a cup of coffee. "I don't think, doctor, that we've seen or heard the last of Barney Barnato. It's a sort of game to him, I reckon. He'll be looking for revenge. We may have closed the front door on him by using the charter and appeasing Lobengula, but I can see Barney trying to sneak in through the back door."

"You may be right, Pat. We must remain vigilant, speaking of which, there's another problem to consider. You know of John Moffat, who also has the ear of the king. I've heard from him that the Boer general, Viljoen, has been making subtle suggestions to Lobengula on the instigation of President Kruger. We know that Kruger wants to expand his Boer Republic. He's crossed the River Vaal successfully. Why not cross the Limpopo? The old man considers that Rhodes' total control of the mining concessions here to be unfair. I've passed on this information to Rhodes. He'll know best how to handle it. Meanwhile, instead of worrying about the future, let's get back to the present. Barnato's wagons are going to come in handy for us. Having to forfeit them must have got right up his nose."

"I think the fact that he was beaten at his own game annoys him more. I can see him now sitting in the Pick and Shovel with

Harry, crying into his beer." replied Pat. "By the way, there was something else in one of Barney's wagons, a cage full of pigeons."

"Why on earth would he carry pigeons?" asked Dr Jim. Then it dawned on him. "He must have wanted them as couriers."

"I would think so, which is why I brought them with me. Maybe we could use them for communication between Nyanyadzi and Salisbury. They'd have birds of prey to deal with, but it's worth a try."

"I agree, though they'd have to be retrained for a new route, if that's possible. I know someone here who would know."

"What news have you had from Nyanyadzi, sir?" asked Pat.

"Your friend, Mr Wood-Gush was here two weeks ago with a satisfactory quantity of good quality diamonds. If the mining continues at this rate, you gentlemen are going to be extremely wealthy."

"That's good to hear, but how are things otherwise?"

"There have been no problems that he and Mr Grieve haven't been able to solve. While he was here, Mr Wood-Gush spent most of his time with the sister of your sweetheart. They make a nice couple, I'd say. When are you returning to the mine, Pat?"

"I intend to stay here for a week. Any less than that and I'll be in trouble with Sandra. I also have to get the forge up and running. My blacksmith, Maforga, will stay here to run it and train a couple of local lads to help him. Sandra will do the bookkeeping for me."

"There'll be no shortage of work at the forge, I can assure you. Please call in again before you leave."

"Of course. I have to come round to sort out a loft for the pigeons."

The Barnato brothers were indeed in discussion, as Pat had forecast, but not at the Pick and Shovel. They were in Barney's office where he was explaining to Harry the details of his trip, his arrest and the loss of the wagons and the contents.

"Somehow, Rhodes got wind of what we were up to. How he did it is a mystery to me. Anyway, that door is closed to us for now as you can be sure he has had Van Zyl queer our pitch with the fat king. We're going to have to make another plan."

"Hell, Barney, why don't you leave it alone? We're doing all right here in Kimberley. We've already made more money than we can ever spend."

"That's not what it's all about. Don't you see, it's between me and Mr Bloody Rhodes. Why should he, one man, decide who will or who will not dig for gold or diamonds or anything else up there on the other side of the Limpopo? This is a battle of wits and right now the scoreboard shows that I'm one down. Somehow I've got to get even. Start thinking about that, Harry. Van Zyl and company are picking up diamonds like they were pebbles on a beach, if Eamon is to be believed. We need to get a piece of that action."

⇥⇤

Cecil Rhodes was dining with his partner and trusted advisor, Charles Rudd, at Groot Schuur in Cape Town. Mining discussions were rarely out of their conversations.

"You know, Charles," said Rhodes, "Van Zyl and his companions are extracting an inordinately large amount of stones at Nyanyadzi. We're going to have to proceed cautiously to avoid flooding the market. Naturally Van Zyl's group have expectations of fast profits, but that leaves us sitting on the diamonds which will put a strain on our cash flow, surely, Charles?"

"That's true, Cecil, but we can always go to the banks if we run short. We'll have the collateral."

"What!" Rhodes retorted, "And pay those thieving bastards interest? Not bloody likely!"

"Steady on, Cecil. Think about it. Yes, we'll be paying the banks, but all we have to do is sit on the stones until such time as the selling price offsets the interest."

"I suppose you're right. That's why you and I make a good team, isn't it? I see the obstacles and you find the solutions. Nevertheless, we will be talking big numbers." Rhodes visibly relaxed. "By the way, I had word from Kimberley yesterday that Barney is walking around like he's got a carrot stuck up his backside. It must be from all the bouncing up and down on his buckboard. I'd pay a lot to see that."

After a week in Salisbury, Pat again bade farewell to Sandra and headed for Nyanyadzi, his mind full of thoughts of a political nature. The news from John Moffat was of grave concern; it was one thing having to contend with Barney Barnato's avaricious scheming, quite another taking on the President of the Transvaal Republic. If Kruger chose to pursue the issue, the implications could be dire.

Brian and Grievous had not been idle during the three months he had been away. The house was completed and, though it lacked a woman's homely touch, the interior had a certain rugged but artistic ambience. The furniture was hewn from indigenous trees, animal skins adorned the floors and walls, while various native clay pots were scattered around, some containing plants transplanted from the riverside.

"Who's the mother here?" Pat enquired.

"Who do you think? Who here is halfway there, complete with breasts? Need I say more?" said Brian.

"If I was halfway there, you big ape," retorted Grievous, "I would have had your money long ago. However, even if I do say so myself,

I do have a discerning eye due to my cultured upbringing, which is more than can be said for you, Wood-Gush, you ignoramus. I also have an appreciation for the comforts of life and I'd rather sit in a comfortable chair than cross-legged on the floor."

"I agree, Grievous, and I fully approve. You'll make some woman a good wife one day," said Pat.

"And I need to be more careful about how I choose my friends in future," replied Grievous.

"Tell me, Brian," said Pat, "what have you been up to while Grievous has been working his fingers to the bone."

"Come, and I'll show you." Brian led the way outside. "Look up there, Pat."

A few hundred yards upstream a large weir held back a stretch of water some one hundred yards long by fifty at its widest point.

"Hell, Brian, I'm impressed. That should supply us with water throughout the dry months."

"I also want to start an agricultural project on the far bank, vegetables but also citrus. Oranges should do well in this climate."

"The vegetables make sense, Brian, but what will you do with the oranges?"

"Transport them to Beira where I believe there'll be a ready market, especially with the shipping lines. When George Pauling completes his railway line getting them to market will be easy."

"It sounds good in theory. Either way, the weir was a useful idea, Brian."

The next few hours were spent discussing production issues and the number of stones recovered from the diggings. There were now three parallel trenches and extraction was in the region of 175 to 200 carats a week, an exciting prospect.

"Something that we must now take into account is that this mine is no longer a secret," sighed Pat. He told them of his experiences over the past three months and the arrest and sentence of Barney Barnato.

"So word is out that we are sitting on a lot of wealth here," summed up Grievous, "and old Barney isn't going to sit back and accept defeat. He wants a slice of the cake and he'll find a way around Lobengula, however fat he is. And now we may have General Viljoen to contend with as well. So, what are we going to do about it, Pat?"

"We must upgrade security first by erecting a fence around the claim and hiring some guards."

Brian interrupted. "That's easier said than done. I mean, it's not everyone's idea of the perfect lifestyle to be stuck out here in the middle of nowhere."

"We'll erect the fence and Mr Rhodes will recruit a dozen guards. We can afford to pay well with bonuses. We'll have to build a bunkhouse and a mess to accommodate them. Your vegetable garden is already paying dividends, Brian, and you should start thinking now about adding livestock."

Grievous was the self-appointed diamond sorter and he was good at the job. First the earth was put through a fine wire sieve which eliminated the lime dust. The remains were loaded onto a wheelbarrow and dumped at the side of the sorting table which Grievous had installed under a shady tree. A worker then deposited a shovelful of diggings where Grievous was ready with a scraper to spread it out and examine it and deftly remove any diamonds. What was left went back into the wheelbarrow to be carted away to be used as foundations for one of the buildings.

Grievous loved the work. Occasionally, to rest his eyes, he handed over to one of the trusted workers. Every now and again he let out a whoop of joy when he found a significant stone and everyone nearby would run to his table to fondle the latest discovery. On average, this happened every second day and it broke the monotony of the work for everyone.

When he had a spare moment, Grievous turned his self-proclaimed aesthetic talents to the landscape around them by planting grass and shrubs and building rockeries and even a fish pond, which he stocked from the river. He was meticulous in everything he did and harangued anyone who was less so, including Pat and Brian. He screened off the working area from the homestead which made it look more like a farm dwelling. Pat and Brian were impressed with his efforts.

Brian, away from the agricultural plot, supervised the labour. With his size and strength, he had little difficulty doing that. He led by example when it came to lifting or carrying and any worker wanting to shirk from his duty only tried it once. He had, in fact, a good rapport with his work force and they worked well for him in a good-natured way.

Pat busied himself erecting the perimeter fence, using sturdy mopani logs. He built bunkers at the four corners to take his Peeshooters which, in case of attack and until the arrival of the security guards, would be manned by Tendai and his team.

Sitting out on the veranda one evening enjoying their sundowners, the stock of whisky now replenished by Pat while in Tuli. They still rationed themselves to two a night and three on Saturdays. Brian suggested that Grievous should take a turn at civilisation and go to Salisbury.

"What for?" said Grievous. "Unlike you two, I don't have a damsel waiting for me, more's the pity. No, you take yourself off for a few days, Brian. When you return, I'd like to go to Beira and contact The Times to let them know I'm still alive and ask if they want anything written. I can also see how Colonel Andrada is getting on. He might know a few Portuguese ladies who, once they see me may lust after this magnificent body of mine."

Brian snorted. "The only ladies who might do that will be those who frequent the dingy waterfront taverns and then only if they're half-sloshed with alcohol and hard up for more."

Pat broke into the argument. "That's actually a good idea. We need to make personal contact with the colonel and brief him on developments here and the money that may be coming his way. Also, as Rhodes' Beira agent, he will deal with the diamonds we send via Beira to Kimberley. We now have enough to justify such an arrangement. I've also got a long shopping list of things we need here. So, yes, when Brian gets back from his love break, you should take off for the seaside, Grievous."

"It'll be good to catch up with world events. As a news man, that's the one thing I miss stuck out here in the bush."

"That's settled then," said Pat. "When do you want to leave, Brian?"

"If it suits you both, the day after tomorrow," Brian replied.

"Oh, I nearly forgot," grinned Pat. "I have some news of my own."

"Out with it, then," prompted Grievous. "It might make a story."

"Not for you, Grievous. While I was in Salisbury, I – er – proposed to the lovely Sandra and I'm delighted to say that she accepted."

"You sly dog!" cried Grievous. "Why didn't you tell us sooner? Wait until the young women of Ladysmith hear this, there won't be a dry handkerchief to be found. You think I haven't heard of your reputation as a womaniser, Patrick? I've a mind to notify the editor of the local paper there when I get to Beira. It'll make headlines on the sports page. In fact I'll do just that."

"You're exaggerating again, Grievous, but as you're going to Beira anyway, I would like an announcement in the paper, but only as a formal engagement notice, please."

Grievous stood and walked across to Pat, his hand extended. "Of course I'll do that, my friend, and let me be the first to congratulate you."

Brian jumped to his feet and rushed at Pat, lifting him with ease onto his shoulder, and marched off the veranda with Pat flailing his arms and pounding Brian on the back.

"You beat me to it, Van Zyl," Brian shouted. "I meant to pop the same question to Margie on my next trip. For getting in first, the punishment is a good dunking."

"Put me down, you bloody great ox, before I do something I may regret later. You've no chance that such a sweet girl will ever marry you." Pat was spluttering and trying to take in air. "She's got better taste. She's stringing you along until someone better shows up."

Brian charged to the fish pond with a roar. He stopped at the edge and heaved Pat into the middle of a clump of water lilies. He stood there panting, but Grievous had crept up behind him and jabbed his fists hard against the back of Brian's knees. The giant teetered, windmilling his arms, finally lost his balance and, with a mighty belly flop, he hit the water, creating an awesome tidal wave.

Grievous quickly went back to the veranda, picked up the bottle of whisky and three glasses and returned to the fish pond. Brian and Pat by now were frolicking about like a couple of three year olds in a tin laundry bath.

He carefully placed his cargo on the edge of the pond and, after a moment of dignified contemplation, he launched himself into the water, surfacing between his two friends.

After squirting out a stream of water through the gap between his two front teeth, Grievous said, "Enough of this horseplay! Let's have some order. I think this latest news from Pat calls for a drink or maybe two, so let's be charging our glasses, gentlemen."

One thing led to another as one bottle led to another and it was three bleary-eyed miners who greeted the new day and then cancelled it and took themselves off to bed.

Brian soon headed off to Salisbury and, on arrival, with trepidation and plenty of rehearsal beforehand, he asked Margie to marry him. She accepted without hesitation to his great relief and deep joy and, after a blissful week, he returned to Nyanyadzi, a happy man.

Grievous took off for the coast and Brian and Pat were once more sitting at the dinner table without the little man's banter and verbal abuse.

"With both of us engaged," Brian said, "you and I are going to have to give some thought to our future accommodation."

"I know. What thoughts have you had, Brian?"

"I suggest we build further along the ridge. There's more breeze up here and the view is great."

"My thinking too," said Pat. "There is another matter. Have you thought of a wedding date? It may be a good idea, and more convenient for a lot of reasons, if we make it a double occasion."

"I like it, Pat. Now all we need is an exact date."

"Not too exact. The girls must have a say. Everything depends upon how long we take to build the houses and furnish them. I'd say we're looking at twelve months."

Brian nodded. "That sounds about right."

"I'll put it to the family when I'm next up there in a few weeks."

CHAPTER FOURTEEN

The track between Umtali and Fontesville had become more defined with the increased traffic and Grievous made good time with two wagons, arriving without incident. Having made arrangements for the safe keeping of the wagons and the animals, he went to search for Captain Dickie, hoping he'd be around or at least on his way up the river. He was lucky. The captain was in the hotel bar. Grievous informed him that he'd have a passenger the next day.

"Sit down, Mr Grieve, and join me in a wee drink as there's nothing else to do in this wretched backwater. Tell me what you and your two friends have been up to."

Grievous made a mental promise to have no more than two, three at the most. He did not fancy a boat ride with a hangover.

"As you say, Captain, there's nothing else to do here and you can bring me up to date with happenings in the outside world." Grievous got it all while waiting for the dinner drum to beat.

"And ye'll be wanting to know too, Mr Grieve, that the Natal newspapers are carrying stories about President Paul Kruger of the Transvaal Republic making overtures to Lobengula, wanting to get his foot in the door to his lands."

Grievous became alert. "What exactly are the papers saying, Captain?"

"They're reporting that Kruger thinks it is unfair that one company has the sole right to look for minerals there, that being the Charter Company. There's no love lost between Kruger and Rhodes. Now Mr Rhodes is warning Kruger publicly to stay away from his area of influence."

"I wonder how that story got out!" Grievous said softly. He concluded that a third party could be involved, one who knew how Rhodes would react to the news and the effect his response would have on Kruger.

"I've no idea, Mr Grieve. Newspapers have their sources, as you well know."

The dinner drum beat and Grievous excused himself. "Goodnight, Captain Dickie, and thank you for the update. My grumbling stomach leads me on."

The captain had no interest in food. "We sail at seven, Mr Grieve. I'll see you then." He called for a refill of his glass.

As it turned out there were no other passengers on board. The cargo consisted of vegetables and fruit for the Beira market. The river was docile and the boat was mostly carried along by the current with the odd spurt from the engine to assist steering.

Grievous rode to the Grand Hotel on a rickshaw, had a hot bath in a real bath, and headed for the reading room to peruse the newspapers. A waiter appeared with a tray.

"Is it six o'clock already? Yes, please, I'll have the coldest beer you can find." He loved his beer but it was bulky and difficult to transport, which was one reason why whisky was so common inland.

He found the story about Kruger's disgruntlement with the Charter Company in the Natal Mercury. He knew of the well-documented animosity between Kruger and Rhodes. The president had already been thwarted by his rival in his attempt to annexe Bechuanaland in the west and now the same had happened in the north. There was also a problem over Delagoa Bay, which Rhodes wanted to buy from the Portuguese and Kruger coveted as a port for his own landlocked country. It was clear to Grievous that if Kruger pursued a new initiative, the situation could become ugly.

Suddenly, Grievous, wrapped up in his thoughts, was aware that he was overdue for a meeting with Colonel Andrada. Returning the newspaper he was reading, he hurried through to the bar.

"My apologies for keeping you waiting," he said. "I was engrossed in the newspapers. It's three months since I saw one."

"I understand," Andrada said. "It's good to see you again."

"Likewise, my friend. We've plenty to talk about. First, let me get you a drink."

They sat at a corner table. Grievous began, "Did Mr Rhodes brief you on that shipment of arms you reported to him?"

"All he's told me is that the outcome could have been disastrous for his plans if he hadn't been forewarned. I would like to hear the details."

Grievous enlightened him. "So, Colonel," he concluded, "knowing something of the reputation of Barney Barnato, we're going to have to be extra vigilant because you can bet he'll want to even the score. The other matter concerning me is the recent reports about President Kruger's expansion plans."

"I agree, but it's political and there's not much you and your friends or I can do about it. We have to leave that to Mr Rhodes."

"True, though political manoeuvring can be disguised. It may be an idea to keep an eye on the passengers travelling inland up-river. Would that be difficult?"

"No, Senhor Grieve, I could manage that."

"On a happier note, let me tell you how things are progressing at Nyanyadzi."

"Please do," Andrada replied.

"We've already handed over three thousand carats of quality diamonds to Dr Jameson for onward transmission to De Beers and I have a thousand with me now, which I'll leave with you. That's the result of four months mining. Not bad, hey? All our transactions are through De Beers and money from the sale of diamonds is deposited into a joint account – that's you, Rhodes, Pat, Brian and myself. Withdrawals require three of us as signatories. We should soon be wealthy men, though I foresee a few problems along the way."

"What are they, apart from what we have already discussed?"

"We don't know the full extent of the field so cannot peg an accurate claim yet. It stretches along the terrace above the river for some distance and we've picked up stones half a mile away from our present working site. The area needs to be fully and properly surveyed. Until then, all we can do is occupy the land and defend it if need be. Legally, there is nothing to stop anyone setting up next door to us so you'll understand the need to keep on the right side of King Lobengula. As soon as you have some leave due, I think you should visit the diggings and see for yourself."

"I would like to do that. In fact, I am due some leave so as soon as I've delivered this parcel, I'll look forward to making such a trip."

"That's great!" said Grievous.

"On another matter, you will remember Siyakonza's widow and child. They have been living here comfortably as I promised they would, but she now wishes to return to her people. It would be convenient if they accompanied me inland."

"Quite so," agreed Grievous. "How old is the child?"

"He's about ten and he seems to be a bright boy."

"We owe it to his father to give the lad a decent start in life. He needs an education, but I don't know how we'll do that for him. Perhaps, as the mine develops and we employ more people, a school will become viable."

They went into dinner and Grievous was happy to order *garoupa*, the Portuguese name for rock cod, as a welcome change from the endless game meat and vegetables he was used to. It was cooked with plenty of garlic, onion and tomato. Ironically, Andrada had guinea fowl casserole.

"Has Mr Rhodes been keeping you busy, Colonel?" asked Grievous.

"There's been plenty to do. It's hoped that this railway line project to Umtali will start some-time next year so there is much preliminary work to be done."

"That will be a huge undertaking with flood plains and rivers to be crossed and then the border mountains."

"It will actually start from Fontesvilla to cut out most of the flood plain. Use of a narrow gauge will reduce the cost, though over two hundred miles of track must be laid. The mountains will present the biggest problem. Umtali may need to move to the railway rather than the other way round."

"How long will it take to build?"

"Mr Rhodes wants it done in two years, but George Pauling, the contractor, estimates five. My job will be to procure the materials. I'll take you round the yard tomorrow and show you, if you like."

"I'd love that, but tell me, when do you realistically hope to start?"

"When we have enough materials and enough workmen. Despite top wages being offered, recruitment has been slow. When you consider the extent of the task and the working conditions, that's understandable."

Grievous was busy making mental notes, thinking of a future feature article. "What do you know about Pauling?" he asked.

"He's definitely a character of note. It seems he comes from a long line of construction engineers. He served a tough apprenticeship as a navvy on railway and other construction projects in Britain before he came to Southern Africa and worked on the railway extension to Grahamstown. After he'd gained experience of local conditions, he began contracting work on his own account. He made rapid progress. By the time he was twenty-four, he was quite rich, but he then lost most of it by dabbling in other enterprises. I understand he has since recouped his losses and has built many miles of railway down south. He has a reputation as a party animal with a good appetite for liquor, food and fun, but he's not afraid of hard work and he gets the job done."

"We do live in interesting times," Grievous commented. "By the way, the food here is much better than it used to be. The rooms are a vast improvement too, since my last visit."

"It's the old story, Senhor Grieve. There is another hotel being built which is going to be bigger and more impressive than this one. If the owners here want to compete, they must improve the standards."

"They're certainly trying." Grievous said. "To business, Colonel. I'll hand over these diamonds to you now. I'm sure you have a safer place for them than under my pillow."

"I do. Where are they right now?"

'Around my waist, but this is the last time I'll do that. In future they'll come under armed escort. I took a chance this time, but word will get out and we'll be a target for highwaymen. Rhodes and Jameson will recruit suitable security personnel for both the mine and the transportation of the diamonds to you. Now, I'm ready for bed."

"Me, too. I'll settle the bill and call a rickshaw. We'll go together to my lodgings, make the exchange, and then the rickshaw will bring you back here."

"Thank you for an excellent meal, Colonel. I'll meet you in the foyer."

As they trundled along in the rickshaw, dodging the many potholes, Grievous asked, "What about security on board ship?"

"The diamonds will be locked in a steel box with a wax seal, for which the captain will sign. I retain one key, Mr Rhodes has the other. The box is then placed in the ship's vault in the captain's cabin. In Durban I retrieve the box and hand it over to Mr Rhodes' representative who is then responsible for its safe arrival in Kimberley. That's about as safe as we can manage at the moment."

Grievous was fascinated as he was shown around the Charter Company's Beira premises. All the materials were laid out meticulously like in a quartermaster's store. The colonel was highly organised and Grievous told him so.

"I have one request to make," he said. "Can you loan me a wagon to do my shopping and then some covered space to store it all for a few days until I leave?"

"Of course. I'll organise it straight away."

Grievous, with the help of Colonel Andrada, was able to procure everything that the mine needed, thanks to some working capital provided by Dr Jameson. There was even enough left over to include a few luxuries like a case or two of whisky.

At the post office, he collected the mail for himself and Pat and Brian. He drove his wagon under an old casaurina tree and opened the letter from James Robertson. Most of the contents was an inquiry about Grievous' activities and the chances of receiving any good stories as a result. He ended with, 'How's your new master, CJR, reacting to the latest utterances from President Kruger?'

Grievous had already written a report about Barney Barnato's attempt to influence Lobengula, referring to Barney as a cockney barrow boy rather than by name. It was ready to post to Robertson.

Two days later, Colonel Andrada set sail for Durban while Grievous boarded The Kimberley once more for his return journey. The colonel would follow in three weeks, on his return to Beira, with Siyakonzi's widow and son. When they reached Umtali, an employee of the mine would be there to guide them safely to Nyanyadzi.

On the river boat, Grievous went over Brian's plans for a water reticulation system to the homestead which included some water features along its way. The galvanised piping for the project took up most of the deck space.

There was a handful of other passengers so Captain Dickie was looking for sandbanks to delay the journey and boost his whisky sales, but Grievous kept to himself until sundown. It was Saturday which meant there would be a dance at the hotel and he wanted to arrive reasonably sober.

When they docked, he found the wagons and oxen in fine shape and there was enough light left to unload his cargo and set up camp. He was happy to spend the night in a wagon rather than in a room at the raucous hotel. Water was heating on the fire as he made his way to the river to enjoy the sunset and watch the hippos having a final frolic before they moved onto the bank to begin their nocturnal grazing.

His reverie was interrupted by one of his workers rushing towards him, gesturing wildly to the wagons. Grievous got up, wondering what the problem was, and returned to the campsite.

Wary and not sure what to expect, he stood outside the circle of firelight and saw someone sitting at the table. Judging from the bonnet and shawl he could make out, it was a woman. He cleared his throat and strode forward.

"Good evening, madam. My name is Colin Grieve. How may I help you?"

She was short, slightly plump but by no means fat, and attractive in an impish sort of way with a pert nose and a lovely smile. Her handshake was firm and her gaze direct as she introduced herself. "I'm Margaret O'Reilly, Mr Grieve, and I'm very pleased to meet you. I've been referred to you by the parish priest who says you may be able to help me. I'm a nursing sister looking for safe transport to Umtali. I'm taking up a post at the new hospital there."

"My friends and I met Bishop Knight Bruce on the road early last year when he was returning to Bloemfontein after conveying two nurses to Umtali."

"I should have been with them, but I was delayed by a death in the family."

"How long have you been waiting in Fontesvilla?" Grievous enquired.

"Ten days. There have been a couple of departures during that time, but the local priest advised me that they would not be suitable companions. When he saw you arrive, he contacted me and suggested that I approach you. He remembers how you and your friends came to the rescue of a poor widow who was having some trouble with bees at her husband's funeral."

Grievous chuckled. "Forgive me, sister, but the circumstances were somewhat unusual."

"I found it funny myself when the priest told me."

"Sister, you may certainly join me. I'll be glad of your company."

"You are very kind, Mr Grieve. I'm quite prepared to work my passage. I can cook."

"That sounds like a fair deal to me. My culinary skills are very limited."

"I expect you'll want to make an early start in the morning."

"First light, I'm afraid. The further we can travel during the cool part of the day, the better."

It was then that Grievous remembered the dance at the hotel that night. "Aren't you going to the dance tonight, sister?"

"I think not, Mr Grieve. An early night will be a better idea if we're to get off at sunrise."

Grievous decided at that moment to cancel his plans for the dance. After all, his main reason for going was to meet with some female company. "May I suggest that the hotel might be a difficult place to rest in tonight. Why don't we fetch your things now and you can sleep in the wagon?"

"That sounds like a good idea, but only if I'm not putting you out."

"Not at all, madam, not at all." Grievous had realised that he was going to have to give up his own sleeping space in the wagon for one next to the fire as the second wagon was full. He decided that he could not have it both ways – the promise of decent meals and a roof over his head. Anyway, it was not the rainy season and he had a spare mattress and his houndsfield.

In less than an hour she was comfortably settled. "Goodnight, Mr Grieve, and thank you," she said. "I am so happy to have made your acquaintance."

"I, too, sister. I look forward to your company over the next two weeks."

As the francolin wakened all within earshot with its impatient squawking, the first rays of the morning sun reflected off the Pungwe River. The camp roused itself from its slumber and preparations began for the long trek inland.

Sister Margaret was already flipping pancakes on the griddle over the fire; the enticing smell alone was enough to waken Grievous.

He realised that he would need to change some of his vulgar early morning routine like passing wind, scratching his nether regions while wandering around in his underwear. It had been some time since he had had any relationship with a woman and he would have to tread carefully. Still covered as he lay by the fire, he wriggled into his trousers and pulled on his socks and boots. Hot water was ready and he completed his ablutions.

After a delicious breakfast, they were ready to depart. Grievous helped Sister Margaret onto the wagon seat and, joining her, he took up the whip and cracked it over the oxen. They were on the move.

Sister Margaret, Grievous was relieved to note, was dressed sensibly in a light cotton dress and a large straw hat with a blue ribbon. She seemed relaxed and he thought he would enjoy her cheerful company on the arduous journey ahead and he was determined to make her life as comfortable as possible.

This was his third trip and he knew the road, if one could call it that. Various night stops were still in place and used regularly. Running water was usually nearby and rubbish and latrine pits had been dug by previous travellers.

He spent much of the first day explaining to his companion the noises and situations they might encounter on the way – lions, hyenas, snakes and insects, both crawling and flying. He told her about Pat's hyena trap on their first journey, but her look of horror at the cruelty involved made him regret it. Feeling embarrassed, he ended with a note of warning. "Shake out your clothes and shoes before you put them on and don't go wandering into the bush alone. If you're unsure about anything, ask."

With little else to do while travelling, Grievous and Sister Margaret talked a lot, revealing to each other more than they might otherwise have done. "If you'd have asked me a year ago what I would be doing now, I would have said that I'd be sitting behind a desk, typing out a story on the latest coal miners' strike in South Wales or something. I would never have dreamed that I'd be sitting on a wagon beside a pretty Irish nurse, headed to some remote part of Africa, full of colonialist ideals and thoughts of nation building. But that's enough about me. What about you, sister? What brings you to this part of the world?"

"It's not an exciting story, Colin. My father was a doctor and my mother a librarian. I had a comfortable middle-class upbringing. I was an only child so I never lacked parental attention. I admired my father and his work greatly and he encouraged me to train as a nurse in Belfast. Then I had the urge to see something of the world and saw Bishop Knight Bruce's advert in our parish newsletter for nurses to work in Manicaland. I applied and here I am, with you on the way to Umtali to take up a two-year contract."

Grievous, plucking up courage said shyly, "Dare I ask if you left any broken hearts behind in Belfast?"

"There was a man a year or so ago, but that's all over now, thank goodness."

"Why do you say, 'thank goodness'?"

"He was too demanding and I enjoy my independence too much. It would never have worked. What about you, Colin? Is there a woman in your life?"

"There have been one or two over the years, but no one I would want to settle down with permanently."

Grievous discovered that he and this Irish girl had much in common aesthetically. They were acutely conscious of the natural beauty that surrounded them, the colourful butterflies, the array of birdlife, and all manner of flora and fauna. He expressed his love of the arts, which led to his career in journalism and photography. Margaret had not thought of photography as an art until he explained the creative input needed to compose a good picture. He told her how he believed that the invention of colour photography was only a step away.

He then told her about his adventures with Pat and Brian, including the Battle of Chua, and, begging her confidence, he explained how they had made their diamond discovery at Nyanyadzi and their subsequent association with Cecil Rhodes.

"Our claim is on a beautiful stretch of river," he enthused. "Perhaps you would like to visit us there one day, Margaret."

"I think I would like that very much." She squeezed his arm.

"I would, too," he replied.

⇥⇤

One morning a few days later, Margaret told Grievous she was going to the river to bathe. On her way along a well-used path, she heard a rustling sound in the short grass close by. She stopped to listen, expecting a small creature to cross in front of her. What emerged was a large black snake. On seeing her, it rose upright until its head was a yard off the ground. Margaret froze, more from fright than standard safety instructions, and then let out a piercing scream. The snake observed her, swaying slightly from side to side, and the area around its head spread into a hood. She found herself perspiring all over and wondered whether the snake was angry or bemused. She hoped she was not trembling; there was no way she could protect herself if it struck. All she could do was pray.

A deafening noise exploded close behind her making her jump involuntarily. The snake disintegrated into a psychedelic eruption and the serpent's blood splattered over her. She turned to see Grievous lowering his shotgun and rushed into his arms and clung to him, shuddering and whimpering, while drawing comfort from his closeness.

"It's all right, my dear," said Grievous. "It's dead. It can't hurt you now. You were very brave. You did exactly as I told you and stood still. That's what saved you."

"I don't feel brave, Colin," Margaret stammered. "I hate to think what might have happened without you there."

"The chances are that it would have got bored just staring at you and slithered off, but that wasn't a risk I was prepared to take."

"I'm grateful for that." Margaret blushed slightly as she broke the embrace and took out a handkerchief and dabbed her eyes.

"If you're all right now, I'll get back to camp. And Margaret ..."

"Yes, Colin?"

"You don't have to wait for an emergency if you're ever in need of a hug at any time in the future." He smiled to himself as he strode off.

———

Not long after this incident, Grievous was walking alongside the lead wagon. He looked up at Margaret on the high seat and realised that shortly they would be parting. He did not want that to happen. It was a new feeling for him with a woman and he wondered if this was what love was all about. If it was, he wanted more of it. He wanted to see more of this Irish lass, but was not sure what her feelings were. He would have to talk to her and time was running out.

The opportunity arose on their final night on the road as they sat drinking coffee in front of the fire. It was a chance remark that started it.

"How long will you stop over in Umtali, Colin?" she asked.

"Only two nights, unfortunately. The wagon contents are urgently wanted in Nyanyadzi."

"Oh!" She sounded disappointed and that was all the encouragement Grievous needed.

"Margaret," he began and he took her hand. "I'm not sure how to put this because I've never said it to a woman before, but the truth is I'm not looking forward to saying goodbye to you. I want to go on seeing you and I know that will be difficult under our circumstances. If you feel the same way, I'll do my best to visit you as often as possible."

"I would like that, Colin." She squeezed his hand. "I'll count the days until we meet again." They drew closer and she looked into his eyes. "At this moment, I would like it very much if you were to kiss me." He responded obediently with enthusiasm. "I think I'm falling in love with you, Colin."

They broke the embrace. "That's exactly the way I feel," replied Grievous, breathing heavily.

=≺∤ ∤≻=

The next day was spent making the difficult crossing of the mountain range and they reached Umtali by nightfall. Grievous suggested they spend the night in the wagon and seek out the other two sisters the following morning. He knew where the hospital was and wondered how Margaret would react to it. It was a far cry from anything she had been used to working in.

It occurred to Grievous that there was a story here for The Times. This was the first hospital to be built in the country so he took his camera along with him to record the meeting of the three nurses. Over breakfast he asked Margaret if she objected to this.

"It's a wonderful idea, Colin."

"Then let's be off and brace yourself, my dear, for a hospital which is really different."

A short walk took them to the hospital which was built into the side of the hill overlooking the beautiful valley.

"There's your hospital, Sister Margaret," Grievous pointed out.

Margaret put her hand to her mouth. "Oh my. It is different, rather … rustic."

It was a long rectangular building of msasa poles and mud under a thatched roof. Grievous set up his camera while Margaret went inside to find her two new colleagues. A chorus of shouts and squeals told him that the nurses had met. When they emerged arm in arm, he recorded the moment. It made a fine picture.

Grievous was then introduced to Sister Rose Blennerhasset and Sister Lucy Sleeman. "Very pleased to meet you, sisters," he said.

"Thank you, Mr Grieve, for delivering Sister Margaret to us," said Sister Rose. "She has not come a moment too soon."

"It has been my pleasure, I assure you," and he glanced at Margaret with a smile. "I'll leave you to get acquainted while I organise the unloading of her baggage and some medical supplies I've brought."

Grievous left the next day for Nyanyadzi, after promising Margaret he'd be back within a month.

━≼♦ ♦≽━

Pat and Brian were pleased to see him as they had run out of flour and sugar among other basics and, critically, whisky, which they had been without for a week.

That evening Grievous told them about his time away from them. "The colonel has matters well under control. It's like a military operation. He should be in Durban by now, waiting for a ship back to Beira. The consignment I handed over should be on its way to Mr Rhodes." He refilled his glass and continued, "More serious is that the papers in Cape Town and Durban have recently reported that Paul Kruger has been making overtures to Lobengula and trying to get concessions from him. The man tasked with the job is General Viljoen. There's nothing much we can do about it except wait and see what happens, if anything. It's worrying, though. So I asked Colonel Andrada to keep an eye on the traffic on the river in case someone tries to do some spying through the back door."

"Not a bad idea, Grievous," said Pat. "There's something else you haven't yet told us, isn't there, old friend? In spite of all this solemn news, you've been looking as if you've backed the winner of the Grand National."

"Well, in a sense I have hit the jackpot. I've found a pretty little Irish filly."

"You crafty dog!" cried Brian. "How on earth did you do that?"

With a wide grin, Grievous told his friends about how he had met Sister Margaret O'Reilly and the progress he had made with her.

"And now she's with her colleagues in Umtali," Brian said. "You can see what's going to happen, Pat, old Romeo here is going to scuttle off to Umtali at every opportunity."

"We might have to build a third house on the ridge soon," laughed Pat. "Grievous, we're truly happy for you."

"I'm happy for me, too," declared Grievous.

⟫⟪

Umgandan, a strikingly handsome and well-built fearless young man, had been one of Lobengula's trusted indunas until he fell out with the king. He hated white men, whom he thought wanted to drive the Ndebele from their lands. He remembered the stories from his father about King Mzilikazi's impis being driven out of the Transvaal by the Boers. He resented Dr Jameson's censure of Lobengula for raiding the Shona people. He expressed his views strongly to his king on many occasions and thus fell from favour.

Still he made his opinions widely known and several other indunas expressed the same misgivings. They all agreed that the white man should be driven back across the Limpopo.

Word of this resentment reached General Viljoen in Pretoria and he dutifully passed it on to President Kruger.

"This is a situation which can be exploited," mused Kruger when he heard the news, "handled the right way."

Viljoen then said, "You'll also be interested to learn that there has been a rich diamond strike near the border with Mozambique and Cecil Rhodes is directly involved in it."

At the mention of diamonds, Kruger's normally bland expression changed dramatically. Although the economy of the Transvaal was vastly improved with the recent discovery of gold on the Witwatersrand, Kruger knew that money fuelled the furnaces of power and anything that fed the fiscus and his own ambitions was welcome. This was the reason he had tried to annexe Bechuanaland but Rhodes had outwitted him. Mashonaland presented another such opportunity.

"That is very interesting. How did you learn about this, General?"

"You may have heard of Barney Barnato, *meneer*. He has made a fortune in diamonds but has lost out to Cecil Rhodes a few times and is seeking revenge by staking a few claims of his own up there. Yesterday I had a visit from Harry, his brother and the junior partner in their business. It seems the two of them arranged to have Rhodes' men followed from Kimberley to the mining site and they reported back that these new prospectors were picking up diamonds like hailstones in a storm."

Paul Kruger leaned back in his chair and, locking his fingers behind his head, he stared at the ceiling for a long time. Then he said, "So the Barnato brothers came to us because they knew we had an interest in Mashonaland, hey? And this dissension among the indunas, General? Tell me more about that."

"You're right about the Barnatos. They knew of our interest. As for the indunas' dissension, that came from the mines here. Many of their workers come from the north and they hear things from their wives and families when they return home. Harry Barnato also told me that he and his brother had tried to influence Lobengula with a gift of muzzle loaders, but something went wrong. He wouldn't go into details."

Kruger stuffed tobacco into his pipe. "We must find a way to exploit a situation that is against Lobengula's policy of treating the white men with kid gloves. What's your opinion, General?"

Viljoen looked nervously at his master. "If we do that, are we not scattering turds on our own veranda, if you'll excuse the vulgarity?"

"Perhaps not, general, perhaps not. Tell me, do you think you could recruit a band of, say, ten high calibre men with combat experience who, given the right incentive, would be prepared to go north on a special operation?"

Viljoen was surprised at the question, but he said, "I don't think that would be a problem. What exactly have you in mind?"

"If my plan works, we could even the score with Mr Rhodes and at the same time get our hands on a mining concession, perhaps even take over these diamond fields in the east that you speak of. Broadly speaking, I want your men to infiltrate the country and make their way to about a day's ride from Fort Victoria. As I understand it's a sparsely inhabited area and the group can establish its headquarters there without much chance of detection. Your men will then start harassing this Umgandan by rustling the king's cattle, a few at a time. Your men must be seen doing it so the thieves are seen to be white men and not Shonas. We want to get the man so angry that he starts drumming on his shield and then down on his knees begging Lobengula for revenge against the settlers. Faced with such provocation, Lobengula is bound to agree."

"If the Ndebele go on the warpath, Jameson must retaliate"

"He'll have no choice. He'll have to contain what could become a full scale rebellion. I will then make official representations to the British Government to complain that Mr Rhodes' settlers are abusing the charter by deliberately causing a confrontation to completely subdue the Ndebele. Remember, there were many influential Westminster parliamentarians who were against the charter because, in their view, it was undemocratic for a company, more specifically one man, to rule a country. The objective is to get Lobengula to repudiate the charter and create outrage in Britain at the behaviour of Rhodes' settlers. If it works, Lobengula becomes again the sole authority over who settles on the land and who gets the mining rights.

"While this is happening, I want you to go to Matabeleland and offer your commiserations and express our sympathy for the Ndebele cause. Inform the king that we are taking the issue up with the British government. If the king questions our integrity, tell him the truth. We think that he alone has the right to decide who should get mining rights and not Rhodes. You can also suggest that he should be demanding payment of royalties from any mining venture in his kingdom. Tell him that if we can mine there, we will be more than happy to pay for the privilege in any way he likes. He'll probably want cattle but that's no problem."

"It's easy to see why you rose to such a high office *meneer*," said Viljoen, "but tell me what we are to do about the Barnato brothers. Harry is still in Johannesburg in case you want to see him."

"I'll think about that. As they seem to be the only people who know where this mine is, we don't want to lose contact with them. Thank him for his information and tell him we'll be in touch later if anything develops. The fewer people who know of our plans, the better."

"Oom Paul, the Barnatos have sent you a gift as a token of their esteem."

"Oh! What's that, general?"

"Come outside and I'll show you."

On a flat-bed wagon drawn by mules and waiting at the gate were a pair of life-sized marble lions.

"They would look good guarding your entrance here, wouldn't they?"

On the way back to his office, a name popped into General Viljoen's head. He now knew the right person to lead this operation and he would waste no time contacting him.

CHAPTER FIFTEEN

The work on the water reticulation project from Brian's weir was complete. Water was now available at the house which, apart from the domestic benefit, would also speed up the building of the bunk room block for the security personnel. The sooner they were on site, the better. Pat supervised the work while Brian now concentrated on agriculture across the river where his gang were digging a furrow to carry water to the field to irrigate the crops. Grievous resumed his sorting duties and every day reaped a more than satisfactory harvest.

Colonel Andrada had given Grievous an approximate date for his arrival in Umtali and, as the day approached, Grievous brought the matter up at the dinner table. "He'll be here soon. We should think of sending out a guide to bring him to us."

Pat agreed. "Tendai would be the best bet. He speaks better English than the others and can ride a horse. I'll tell him to leave tomorrow."

It was just as well he did because it was not too many days before the gate guard rushed up to Pat to say there was a party of people approaching. Pat went to the gate and saw Tendai and the colonel, followed by a native woman mounted on a mule and leading another on which sat a young black boy.

The colonel dismounted and shook Pat's hand warmly.

"Welcome, Colonel," said Pat. "It's good to see you again. It's about time you came to see us and check on your investment."

"I never doubted for a moment that matters here were in good hands. My only regret is that I'm not here with you all to share the workload," Andrada replied as he gazed about him at the buildings and the activity everywhere.

"You're far too valuable to the operation by being in Beira. If it hadn't been for you, we'd never have learnt of Barney's plot and we might have had him as a neighbour by now. Your timing is perfect; lunch is ready."

Pat asked Tendai to take care of the woman and the boy. It seemed obvious that he was more than willing to comply.

As Pat and Andrada walked towards the homestead, Brian and Grievous came out to greet him and shook hands with their visitor.

"How was your trip, Colonel?" asked Brian. "How long can you stay?"

"Without incident, thank you, but I can only spend a week with you before I have to get back."

They enjoyed a lunch of freshly caught fried catfish with new potatoes and spinach.

"What of the woman and the boy, Colonel," enquired Pat. "What are their plans for the future? From what I gather, they're from the local village where she has relatives."

"We know all about the village," Brian said.

"That's where we get our work force from," Grievous added.

The colonel smiled. "The plan was for her to return here and I would arrange to build some accommodation for them and provide tools and seeds to set them up. When the boy is a little older, he would return to Beira where I'd make sure he received the best possible education. However, I suspect that things may turn out differently in the future."

"Why do you say that?" asked Pat

"I sensed a touch of romance developing on our way from Umtali. Your man, Tendai, showed a lot of interest in her and she seemed to respond favourably. Something permanent could develop there."

"I'll take you to the village in a couple of days," Pat offered. "It's time I spoke to the old chief, but I must first make up some of his special snuff as an offering or we could lose his favour."

"That will suit me fine," said the colonel, "but what is this special snuff?"

"It started as a bit of a prank, but the addition of a little crystallised rock rabbit urine to ordinary snuff turned out to be a winner with the old chief. It almost blew our heads off but he loves it. Now we daren't visit him without a supply."

Andrada laughed. "You must give me some to take back with me. I know a few snuff-takers who might see it as a challenge."

They then talked about the mine production and related problems. Pat brought up the subject of security. "Colonel, Grievous tells me that you have the Pungwe River dockside under observation and I wondered whether any suspicious individuals have been spotted."

"There's nothing to report as yet, but we remain vigilant."

"I feel it won't be long before something happens. We're sitting on a fortune here and man's greed will result in blood being spilt. I also believe it will be the indigenous people who will suffer most."

They moved out on to the veranda. Pat continued, "Our present tenure here relies upon our good relationship with Lobengula. If something happens to convince the king that it is in his interests not to put all his eggs in one basket, it will spoil Mr Rhodes' and the Company's plans."

"He wants to run the country like a company, doesn't he?" said Grievous.

"Exactly!" replied Pat.

Brian interrupted, "Whether it is the British South Africa Company or the Transvaal government, at some point in the not too distant future I fear the Ndebele people are going to say, 'Enough, we are being overrun by these *mukiwas*, these whites, and it's time to put a stop to it'. It will happen and then we'll have a rebellion on our hands."

"I believe you are right, Senhor Wood-Gush," said Colonel Andrada. "It's only natural that they should rebel."

"Unfortunately," Pat said, "we cannot influence the situation. Still, the bunk room is ready and our security contingent should be arriving soon from Salisbury. All we can do is await developments. At least we are not entirely cut off and have some communications with the rest of the world."

"How?" The colonel looked puzzled.

"Come, and I'll show you." Pat led the way to a small building at the back of the kitchen house and pointed to a loft on stilts under the overhang. "There's our communications, colonel, and very efficient carriers they are too."

The colonel peered in through the wire netting to admire the four pigeons perched within. "Yet another revelation, Senhor van Zyl!" he said.

"Providing the pigeon doesn't get taken out by a raptor, we can exchange information with Salisbury within a couple of days thanks to an unintentional donation from Barney Barnato. These are not the original birds, but they come from good breeding stock which he provided and they have been well trained on the route we require them to fly."

⪥⟨⟩⪤

On the way to the chief's village, Pat stopped at the tree beside the river where they had ambushed Gunganyana and recounted the story. "This helped our cause a lot," explained Pat. "The gang had been terrorising not only travellers to and from Beira, but the locals as well. Because we eliminated the problem, the chief has been friendly towards us and has kept us supplied with a good work force. This has also brought prosperity to his village.

On arrival at the village they dismounted and made their way towards the chief's hut. They found him sitting on a stool in the shade of a tree and on seeing them he smiled and rose to greet them. Suddenly his expression changed to one of astonishment and he ran to where Siakonza's wife stood off to one side with the boy. Much hand clapping and excited conversation ensued.

It was a while before Pat was able to learn from Tendai that the woman was related to the chief and that he had given her and the boy up for dead.

Colonel Andrada had brought with him a quantity of foodstuffs, household items, seed and implements. These were contained in canvass lockable holdalls for safekeeping. She would be fine for the foreseeable future, in more ways than one if the Colonel was correct in his observations.

Before they left the village, Pat told Tendai to ask the chief to spread the word for people to be on the lookout for any white people who might infiltrate the area and to notify them at the mine immediately.

As Pat and Andrada rode away the chief was already issuing instructions for a new sleeping and kitchen hut to be built.

With the colonel's departure imminent Pat thought it might be a good idea to investigate a short cut some of the locals had told him about which would avoid going through Umtali and meet up with the Beira road in Mozambique. This could shorten the journey by up to a week. To verify this, he decided to accompany Andrada along this part of the route.

"Beira is going to be our main source of supplies so any time saved in travelling is an advantage," Pat said when he suggested the idea.

"Where do you expect to intercept the road?"

"Close to the Revue River crossing." Pat turned to Brian. "I'll have to forfeit my trip to Salisbury if I go with the Colonel. That won't please Sandra so you go in my place and explain to the girls and suggest, through Madge and Joe, of course, that they return here for a few weeks. One of us can give up his room and sleep on the veranda."

"And what about me?" Grievous piped up.

Brian grinned at him. "You'll have to eat your little heart out."

"Never mind, old son, your turn will come," Pat consoled him.

"You two had better watch out. The ladies could find my natural charm and good looks hard to resist."

"I was forgetting that the little man has become a lady killer, Pat," remarked Brian. "We'd better find something for him to do that takes him away for a few weeks, hadn't we?"

The banter ceased when Pat said, "The pigeon post arrived earlier from Dr Jim telling us that the security team is ready and waiting. They can come back with you, Brian."

"How will you use these people?" the Colonel enquired

"Apart from camp security, they will do escort duties when we send the gems to you. This will be fairly frequent as I'd rather avoid large shipments in case of highway robbery. These men will be employees of the Nyanyadzi Mining Company, which has now been incorporated, and they have signed a one-year contract with the option to renew. They've all had military training at some time and have been handpicked. They'll be well paid so hopefully we'll have a loyal bunch."

Barney and Harry routinely took their first cup of coffee for the day in Barney's office, when they discussed current topics. Today they talked about Harry's recent trip to see General Viljoen.

Harry said, "When I told General Viljoen about the diamond find, he was all ears, I can tell you. I gather he was in the president's office in a flash, reporting to him. He kept me waiting for two days before summoning me to say that the president was grateful for the information and that if they were to act on it, they'd be in touch. He naturally asked about our intentions and I said that we would like to extend our operations if possible and hinted that this was what we expected in return."

"How did he take that?"

"He said that one good turn deserves another."

"My guess, Harry, is that Kruger, being the shrewd old bugger he is, will see this as an opportunity to be exploited. I wonder, though, whether his conscience will extend to seeing us right."

"Colhoun and ourselves are the only ones who know the location of these diamonds," Harry reminded his brother.

"For now, yes, but it won't take for ever for someone else to sniff it out, will it? I'm banking on Kruger acting like a typical politician and being a devious bastard. I think we'll see some interesting developments. We just have to keep cool heads, keep our ears to the ground, and be patient."

"Incidentally, your two marble lions went down well, Barney. That was a clever move."

Four men saddled up and set off eastwards very early in the day. Pat and Colonel Andrada were accompanied by Tendai and the colonel's personal manservant. There was a chill in the air as the sun glistened off the dew-soaked savannah. A group of impala made its way from their morning drink at the river to the grazing pastures.

Pat wondered where else in the world could one experience such peace and unspoilt beauty. This had to be a good place to start married life and bring up children.

His thoughts were unsettled by the colonel asking, "How do you think your future wife will take to this life of isolation, Senhor Pat?"

"You must be a mind reader, Colonel. I was just thinking what a perfect place this is to be married and rear children. Can one be any closer to nature than this? Sandra is that rare being who sees interest in everything around her, not just in people. It's one of the things I love about her. She is never lonely in solitude."

"That's a rare quality, my friend. You are a lucky man to have found a woman like that."

"Have you never married, Colonel?"

"No. I was nearly married once, but it was a long time ago."

"What happened? A bold question, I know."

"It's a sad story, but I will tell it to you."

"Not if it pains you too much."

"Shortly after completing my officer training in Lisbon, I met a lovely young woman who came from a wealthy family. We fell in love. We'd been seeing each other for two years when I received news of my first overseas posting."

There was a pause as his mind drifted back fifteen years.

"I asked Maria to marry me and she happily agreed and had no qualms about coming out to Mozambique. Her parents were not so happy. They refused to let her accompany me under threat of disowning her. She was an only child and they had heard so much of diseases that killed those who lived here. I could see their point and we agreed to wait until my four year posting was completed. Are you sure this is not boring you, Senhor?"

"Not at all. Please continue."

"After twelve months I was granted leave and returned to Lisbon. Nothing had changed; we still felt the same about each other. But another man was after her. Maria told him to stop bothering her, but he persisted.

"I arranged a meeting with this man and asked him to leave Maria alone because she and I were engaged to be married. He then told me at length that I was not in her class and unworthy of her affections. His father and Maria's were business associates and it was in both their interests that he and Maria should wed.

"It was hard for me to remain calm under this verbal onslaught, but I managed and took pains to explain to him that parental connections made no difference. The real issue was what Maria wanted and not what he wanted. I could see that I was wasting my breath. In fact, I was beginning to think that the man was unhinged."

"You must have been worried about leaving Maria in such a situation while you had to return to Mozambique," said Pat.

"Indeed, I was. I went to Maria's father to explain what was happening and suggest that Maria and I be married before I left."

"Did he agree to that?"

"He did, but on the condition that she remain in Portugal after the marriage. Maria had discussed this possibility and agreed that we would comply if necessary. A date for the wedding was set. There was little time for preparations as my leave was running out."

The colonel paused and pointed to a small herd of eland grazing nearby. They reined in their horses and watched in silence for a few minutes before moving on.

The colonel's voice was now charged with pain. "The wedding day arrived, the weather was perfect, and Maria arrived at the cathedral steps in an open carriage drawn by four horses. She looked radiant, beautiful, as always. She had just stepped down when this man emerged from behind a pillar. He ran to her and, from what I was told later, he appeared to be pleading with her. Maria was shaking her head and then, before anyone could react, this mad man pulled out a knife and stabbed her, three times. She cried out but once before she collapsed on the flagstones."

"My God," Pat muttered. "Where were you when this happened?"

"I was waiting for her at the altar." Tears welled up in his eyes. "I was aware that something was amiss because of the screams from outside. My best man, the groomsman and I rushed down the aisle. I will never forget that moment when I stared at Maria lying there, her blood seeping out and soiling her beautiful white gown. The picture will haunt me to my dying day."

They were quiet for a few moments before Pat asked gently, "What happened to the mad man?"

"He stood there for a time, rooted to the spot, looking down at what he had done, perhaps in shock or disbelief at his own behaviour. Close by were two policemen who, ironically, had been asked to attend by Maria's father in case this man tried to disrupt the ceremony or cause trouble. They pounced on him, too late, and arrested him. But the drama wasn't yet over. The three of us – Miguel, the groomsman and myself – were in full dress uniform. Miguel drew his sword to run the wretch through. It took all the strength the groomsman and I had to restrain him. In the end, he went to the gallows anyway, despite his father trying to use his considerable influence to have him acquitted on mental grounds."

"It's a tragic story, Colonel, and I'm so sorry. I should not have pried and put you through all that hurt."

"It was a long time ago and the pain has subsided, though not gone. I've never wanted to look for romance again. Instead, I dedicated my energies to soldiering."

They made camp at the foot of the range of hills. Tomorrow they would search for a way over them.

They soon found a well-worn trail leading over a saddle, probably one used by elephants making their way between rivers. Judging by the amount of droppings seen, it was still in use. They all dismounted and Tendai took the lead.

"This looks fairly easy, Colonel. All we have to worry about is whether the elephants decide to commute today."

"I never thought of that, Pat. What happens if we meet a herd head on?"

"We give way, do an about turn, and retreat fast."

The words were hardly out of his mouth when they heard a sound like heavy wooden barrels being rolled down a hill. Then came the unmistakable screech that resembled a bugler trying to blow rain water out of his instrument. The wind was blowing their scent up the hill towards the herd.

"Time to move," Pat. "Let's quietly turn round and get back down the hill."

They all beat a hasty retreat back to the level ground and re-grouped behind an anthill far to the left where their scent would not carry but they could observe the elephants' progress.

Three cow elephants appeared, each with a protesting and squealing baby underfoot impeding them. They stopped at the foot of the hill and the cows tested the air with their trunks. Satisfied, they resumed their journey to the river.

"I reckon it's safe to continue now," said Pat. "Perhaps we should put up a sign here saying 'Beware – elephants ahead – give way.'" He took a compass bearing and wrote down their position in his notebook.

They reached the saddle and tethered the horses in the shade while they climbed to the top of the taller of the two mountains above them. The view ahead was spectacular. They could not see the Revue River but Pat recognised three low hills in the distance which he knew were close to the Beira road and took bearings again and made another note before they returned to the horses. The two Africans roasted maize cobs over a fire until they were golden brown while Pat carved onto a tree trunk the compass bearing and a large arrow to point the direction.

On the third day they met the Beira road and could see the tree line that bordered the Revue River not far away.

The colonel said, "You were right. This will cut at least five days off the journey. Well done."

"All I have to do now is draw a map for future reference."

Colonel Andrada pointed to the young man who had accompanied him from Beira and said, "If there are any developments, I will send Antonio with a message as he now knows the way." They shook hands and the colonel and Antonio continued to Beira while Pat and Tendai returned to Nyanyadzi.

Brian had departed for Salisbury where he had met Sergeant Major John Erasmus, who was in charge of the security team. Erasmus asked Brian for directions to Nyanyadzi and decided to make his own way there with his men rather than wait for Brian. When Pat arrived, they were already settled into the bunkhouse and Erasmus had put in place his plans for securing the whole area. Grievous was full of praise for the man.

Pat had plenty to do while he looked forward to the arrival of the two girls. He had so much to discuss with Sandra, plans to make.

He learned that John Erasmus had worked for De Beers as a security officer on the mines. Prior to that, he had served in the British army, which was apparent from his military bearing, immaculate turnout and fastidious attention to detail. He expected the same attitude from the six men he had brought with him. He had a sense of humour which appealed to Pat and they seemed to have much in common, not least an interest in musketry.

John was fascinated with Pat's Peeshooters and thought them hugely innovative. He was impressed when Pat told him of the roles they had already played. "Give me a run-down on their workings and I'll start drilling my men on them," he said.

Pat said, "Let's do it now," and he led the way to the nearest emplacement. "So far we've used nature's gunpowder of crystallised rock rabbit piss but now we've got the real stuff, so we don't have to go sniffing around kopjies anymore."

The lesson over, they sat on the veranda sipping tea and pouring over Pat's map of the shorter route to Beira, which John and his men would have to take when delivering diamond consignments to Colonel Andrada.

"When's the next shipment ready to go?" the Sergeant Major asked.

"With the current rate of production, it should be in about four weeks," Pat replied.

John Erasmus had plenty of experience in mine security and it was a relief to Pat to hand over this responsibility to him because there would come a time when his labour force would realise that what they were digging up had great commercial value.

※━━※

Pat was sitting next to Grievous at the sorting table when they received news from the guard that riders were approaching.

"It must be Brian with your sweetheart, Pat," said Grievous.

They rushed to the gate. Standing on the high observation platform, Pat watched four riders approach and his hopes soared. When they were nearer, his heart sank as he realised that all four horsemen were dressed in breeches and wide-brimmed bush hats. He climbed down to the ground and leaned against the gate.

It was Brian; no one could mistake his size. "Why look so glum?" said Brian. "I thought you'd be happy to see us."

"I am, but I was expecting …." He never finished the sentence as an unmistakable high-pitched giggle came from beneath the hat of one of the riders behind Brian. Then Sandra laughed out loud, threw off her hat, and jumped down from her horse into

Pat's arms. Pat buried his face in her hair and then she was kissing him again and again. Pat was overcome by a feeling of great happiness.

Brian and Margie stayed in their saddles laughing at the scene while the workers fell in behind Grievous, all wanting to meet the newcomers who brought such joy with them.

Grievous was first in the queue and Pat had to tell him to stop gawking and close his mouth. Grievous spluttered, "I don't know how you both do it. Two of the ugliest sods in Southern Africa and you find two of the loveliest women."

"That's hardly true, Mr Grieve," teased Sandra. "My man mistook my sister and I for men a few minutes ago, which doesn't say much for our supposed good looks, does it?"

"What do you expect?" protested Pat. "You arrive wearing pants instead of petticoats and floppy hats instead of bonnets."

A groom led the horses away while the party made its way to the homestead, arm in arm, the men carrying the baggage.

Grievous had made a special effort to ready the house for the arrival of the sisters. The place was spotless and he had even placed bowls of wild flowers in their bedroom and in the living room.

Sandra came back from exploring the house with Margie. "I'm impressed," she announced. "Not bad at all for a bunch of bachelors."

"We have to thank Grievous for that," said Brian, slapping the little man on the back. "He's the one with the housewife's touch, aren't you, Gretchen?"

"If I was a woman, I wouldn't touch either of you. I would be more particular about who I kept house for. You deadbeats wouldn't feature on my possible employment list even if you paid me double the rate for the job." Grievous' retort caused the girls to break into peals of laughter.

"He's only joking, ladies," said Pat. "Actually, Grievous has found himself a lovely Irish lass. Tell them about Sister Margaret."

"Please do, Colin," urged Margie. Grievous smiled as he related the story of his journey from Beira with Margaret.

"Have you popped the question yet, Colin?" asked Sandra.

"Steady on. I've only known her for a few weeks and not seen her for most of them. I'll say this though, the idea is very appealing."

"We might have a triple wedding yet," quipped Brian.

"Then you'll have to hurry up and ask her," said Margie.

The girls were enchanted with their surroundings and they took an interest in everything that was happening around them. They all discussed the homes that had to be built and the school for the workers' children. Sandra and Margie inspected Brian's gardens and offered suggestions. They went on picnics and marvelled at the wildlife around them.

They also talked about the problems and difficulties that the men faced and the sisters were clearly aware of the possibility of a confrontation with the Ndebele.

The month passed quickly and it was time for Sandra and Margie to return to Salisbury. Pat would take them as he had financial matters to discuss with Dr Jim. He needed to make funds available for the girls so that on their next trip they could go on to Beira and from there to Cape Town to buy whatever household goods were wanted to set up homes. Pat also wanted to check how Maforga was managing with the blacksmith's business. Sandra had been in charge of accounts and she reported that things were going well. The forge was providing a useful service and prospering. If the mining venture somehow went sour on them, he would still have a source of income.

CHAPTER SIXTEEN

O nce more Pat sat across from Dr Jameson discussing production and developments at the mine. "We've just had Colonel
Andrada with us for a week. He brought with him the widow of
Siyakonza and the young boy, returning them to her home area,
which is what she wanted. The colonel seemed more than happy
with his investment and his partnership with us. Incidentally, we've
found a short cut from the mine to the Beira road and I've drawn a
map of it. John Erasmus will use this route when he takes the gems
through to Andrada."

"Excellent news!" commented Dr Jim. "How are John and his
men settling in?"

"No problem there. I'm so glad not to have to worry about security any more. He's a good man and we get on well together."

"I thought you would. As the last consignment went out through
Beira, I need to know your total carat production sent to Kimberley
to date so that I can compare it with Mr Rhodes' receipts."

Pat took out his notebook, found the relevant page, and gave
the doctor the number he had recorded.

"That's the figure I have - 4150 carats," said Dr Jim. "That equates to £12 450. Expenses to date amount to £2 150, leaving a surplus of £10 290. Split five ways, that's roughly £2 000 each. Not bad, eh?"

"Music to my ears, Dr Jim. Could I have a copy of that statement to show Brian and Grievous?"

"I'll have one typed for you before you return."

"When I was last here, Dr Jim, you told me of Rev. Moffat's news about General Viljoen's approach to Lobengula. Has anything further been heard about that?"

"No, but Mr Rhodes has hired a private detective agency to keep an eye on the Barnatos. Harry recently visited Pretoria and had two meetings with the general. We don't know what was said but it does not bode well, Pat."

"Could the Barnatos be trading information for favours? Don't forget they are the only other people who know of our discovery."

"I know," agreed Jameson. "Rhodes' thinking is that Harry may well have spilt the beans about the mine, in which case we have to assume that Kruger is not going to sit on his big backside and do nothing. He's far too cunning for that. What he has in mind, we have no idea."

"While Colin Grieve was in Beira recently, he read of Kruger's complaints in the papers and he's asked Colonel Andrada to watch the departures of steamers up the Pungwe in case spies are sent in by that route."

"Good thinking on Grieve's part. I am presuming that Kruger is planning an initiative to influence Lobengula so we have to keep an ear to the ground and hope we can take pre-emptive action."

"It would help if John Dobson did the same at Tuli," said Pat.

"Mr Rhodes has already done that. There is little else we can do now except wait until Kruger makes a move, which I'm sure he will, sooner rather than later."

The population of Fort Salisbury had grown considerably in recent months and buildings were now being erected at the foot of the hill and had better access to water from the river. They were being laid out in a more orderly fashion and the place was beginning to look like a small town instead of a makeshift community.

Maforga and his helpers seemed to have settled into their new environment well enough and Pat saw that more substantial premises needed to be built. There was sufficient income from the business for him to engage a contractor for the job. Maforga had trained his assistants well; they could already competently do shoeing and other simple work. This was as he intended as Maforga's skills would in time be wanted at the mine to help Pat to make the crushing machinery he had designed to increase production.

A new and bigger schoolhouse was being built to cope with the growing population as well as a better house for the Grahams, money for which had been provided by Mr Rhodes. He had reasoned that to attract more settlers, good facilities for education and health had to be available.

Madge and Joe were completely caught up in this pioneering spirit and were enjoying life immensely. They were pleased to see their daughters happy and soon to be wed. Pat and Brian always enjoyed a warm welcome at their table.

Joe enquired of Pat how things were going at the mine?

"Exceptionally well, Joe. If we're left in peace, there's a fortune lying there on the banks of the Nyanyadzi. I'm afraid it won't stay that way, though. There's big money at stake and that creates avarice. That's when the nastiness begins." He told the Grahams what was troubling all the partners.

"I understand your concerns, Pat, but what can you do about them?"

"Nothing that we haven't already done. We must just wait and see. Dr Jameson is alert to the possibilities. In the meantime, life must go on."

"There have been a few incidents in outlying areas involving the Ndebele, but I don't know any details. Dr Jameson will tell you. I'm sure you'll see him again before you leave."

"I'm seeing him tomorrow morning, as it happens, so I'll ask him then."

They talked some more about the mine and then Pat brought out the drawings for the house he and Sandra had planned. It would be built of stone, of which there was a plentiful supply. The design was open-plan and airy but it would also provide security.

"It's unusual to have a dining and living room combined," said Madge. "I haven't seen that before, but I admit it sounds sensible."

Sandra said, "The fewer internal walls, the greater the atmosphere, I think."

"What are all these little circles on the floor area?" asked Madge.

"That was Pat's idea. There is an abundance of lovely shiny pebbles in and around the river. If Margie can come up with a design, it would make for an unusual and robust floor, don't you think?"

"It will certainly be unusual, my dear."

"The other idea we've had," enthused Sandra, "is to do without a bath, which would be difficult to obtain anyway. Instead, we'll have a shower arrangement where the water is released downwards from a pipe through a rose while we stand underneath it to wash. We'll also have a boiler for hot water."

"Another advantage," said Pat, "in the intensely hot summer months down there, it's a quick way to cool off."

"Now that's ingenious," Joe said. "You youngsters seem to have thought of everything."

When the others retired to bed, Pat and Sandra sat late into the night compiling a list of basic items they would need for their new home. Brian and Margie had already done this on his last trip.

"Is that everything, Sandra?" Pat put down his pencil.

"I can't think of anything else, but there are bound to be items that crop up between now and when we leave in four weeks."

"I'll leave some leeway for extras for us and Brian and Margie and ask Dr Jim to make funds available to you both."

Sandra sighed. "Oh, Pat, I wish we didn't have to wait and could get married now." She came round the table and sat on his lap to hug him tightly. "I love you so much."

Pat undid one of the buttons on her bodice and slipped his hand inside. "It won't be long now, my love," he whispered, "and then we will be together always."

Their kisses were long and passionate and she could feel his manhood awakening beneath her. Suddenly she broke the embrace and stood up, panting hard. She whispered, "I think we had better retire to our separate beds while I still have enough willpower to resist. God forbid that I succumb to your charms and we both end up in mine."

"I wish!" Pat was equally breathless. As he got up, he put his hands into his pockets to hide the result of his wishful thinking from her. "It's times like this when I wish we could marry tomorrow. It's perhaps as well that we live so far apart. If I were around you all the time, keeping myself under control would be impossible."

Reluctantly, he kissed Sandra goodnight and made his way to the Graham's wagon, where he was billeted for the night. Sleep came slowly as a dozen thoughts mulled around together in his head, but when it did come, it was sound and deep.

At Pat's next meeting with Dr Jim, he arranged for the money to be made available to the girls without difficulty. Hearing the cooing of pigeons coming from the loft behind the office, reminded him to take back with him four more trained birds. They had proved their worth and they had only lost two so far to birds of prey. Better still, they were multiplying well.

He asked about the doctor's market garden project and was told it was having some success but there were difficulties because the

Mashona people were reluctant to work on it. "We've been trying to encourage them to learn and expand their own gardens from just producing millet and pumpkins. They will only grow for their immediate needs never mind if next year there may be a drought, for which they will be totally unprepared. They seem to have a strange attitude to regular employment, Pat. They only want to work when they are hungry and abandon their jobs as soon as their stomachs are full. Are your tribesmen at the mine the same?"

"So far we've had no problem and they're a cheerful lot. All our labour was recruited from the chief of the nearest village. We did him the favour of ridding him of Gungunyana and he is beholden to us for that. He and his people have seen an improvement in their living standards. They use their wages to buy little luxuries which were unimaginable to them before. Brian Wood-Gush has just started a programme where he encourages and teaches them to grow a variety of crops. We sell them the seeds at cost."

"Long may that continue, Pat. Here, there is a change of attitude towards the white man. Originally they held us in awe, but that's wearing off. They now see us as people like themselves and apply what seems to be a principle of their culture, which is to take what they covet. We're going to have to teach them a lesson soon."

Pat then asked about the Ndebele situation. "Joe Graham mentioned the possibility of problems but thought it might be better if you told me."

"Joe's right. There have been a few disturbing incidents, particularly to the south of us. Despite Lobengula's instructions to leave the white men alone, that does not apply to the workers and quite a few have been speared. On top of that, because the Ndebele consider that all the cattle in Lobengula's kingdom belong to the king, they have been helping themselves to cattle belonging to our farmers."

"What do you intend to do about that, doctor?"

Dr Jameson frowned as he thought about this for a few moments. "Up to now, all I've done is write letters of complaint to Lobengula, which I hope someone is able to read to him. Clearly I'm going to have to resort to stronger measures if the problem persists."

"I don't envy you your job. There must be times when you wish you could go back to full-time doctoring."

"You're right. At least then I only had people's medical conditions to deal with. Now I have to solve all their problems. One thing that Mr Rhodes, and probably all of us here, have been slow to realise is that a black king in GuBulawayo and a white settlement here could not remain peaceful for long. The European and Ndebele ways of life are poles apart. How can we expect Lobengula to understand British laws of property and how can the white settlers comprehend the workings of the minds of the Ndebele people? Lobengula accepted the Charter with misgivings and the presence of the pioneers with suspicion and he still believes that the country is his. He is told not to interfere with white men who come to look for gold for the Company and turn away all other white men. How fair is that? And what about the Mashonas? Lobengula sees them as his vassals and he believes he can deal with them as he likes, as he has always done. The white men have their own laws, but he is the law for those he considers as his property, his 'dogs' as he has been known to call them. So, where are we headed, Pat?"

"I'm afraid we're heading for conflict. We were talking about it the other evening at the mine. When and where was the last incident of harassment of white farmers, Doctor?"

"Three days ago and not far from here. You could ride to Norman Sparks' place in about four hours. Why do you ask?"

"Can I ask first if you think the marauders are still likely to be in the area?"

"They will have moved on, but with six stolen cattle, their progress will be slow."

"With your permission, I would like to follow them and try to recover the cattle and also give these thieves a bit of a fright, humiliate them to discourage further acts of banditry, but without resorting to violence. With no blood shed, we might gain a psychological advantage, if Mr Freud is to be believed."

"I'll agree to that, Pat. How many of my troopers do you want to go with you?"

"Actually, I'd prefer to go alone. The plan I'm hatching will require stealth and surprise."

"As you wish, but I don't think your young lady will like the idea."

"Neither of us will tell her, doctor. I'll say I'm going to see a farmer with a problem that I think I can solve."

"It's up to you, young man. Just don't incriminate me. I've enough problems with the settlers as it is."

"I won't add to them. I'll slip out at first light tomorrow if you'll give me directions. Oh, one last thing! Can you let me have a couple of pounds of dynamite from your armoury – as a noise factor, that's all."

"I'll take your word for that, Pat."

Pat left the office and collected the dynamite and a few feet of fuse from the armoury with his requisition order. Then he searched for a monkey orange tree, of which there were plenty laden with fruit, and picked a dozen of them. They were the size of a small orange, hence the name, and the ripe insides, when liquefied, were eaten by monkeys and men alike. Outwardly the difference between them and the citrus variety was in the skin. These fruits had a hard green pod-like shell which made handy receptacles for snuff, local medicines, beads and could be used as drinking vessels.

Pat took them to the forge to cut off the tops and he then scooped out the flesh before drying the shells near the fire. In each he placed a small quantity of dynamite and filled up the rest of the cavity with grass. Then he inserted a length of fuse, packed with wet newspaper to prevent spillage and he had twelve reasonably harmless bombs that would make a loud noise but cause little damage. He placed them in a small sack and put the other items he would need in his saddle bags.

Sandra was not happy when she saw Pat packing. "Patrick van Zyl, for goodness sake, you're not going off again, are you? You can't sit still for a minute."

"Sorry, my love, but there's a farmer called Norman Sparks who needs my help with a security problem he has. I'll only be away a couple of days."

"I know Norman Sparks. What worries me is the nature of a security problem that needs your involvement. Don't even answer that; I don't want to know. Just hurry back in one piece."

Pat rode away before first light and, as Dr Jameson had predicted, he was at the Sparks' Farm in time for the morning tea break. Norman was a tall, lanky and affable man who came from farming stock in England. With four brothers, he realised early in his life that his father's farm was too small to sustain all the sons should they want to be farmers. He decided to come to Africa where he worked for five years on a mixed farming estate in Natal. His preference was in rearing cattle and, hearing of the opportunities offered by the Charter Company in Mashonaland, he applied and was accepted and helped to buy his herd.

He married Joyce, the daughter of one of the estate managers prior to the move. They had arrived a few months earlier so their homestead was still fairly primitive but clean and orderly. There was a cluster of round thatched huts, two of which served as bedrooms. The living area was large and rectangular with the usual clay and cow dung floor and thatched roof, while the sides were rolled down reed blinds, similar to the schoolroom he and Brian had helped to build. A cast iron wood stove stood at one end. The chairs and table were made from a combination of wooden paraffin boxes and sawn mopani timber. There was also a storeroom, which doubled as a workshop, and a cattle kraal.

Pat explained why he had come. Sparks was surprised that a stranger should want to assist him, but was grateful nonetheless. He offered tea and food which Pat was more than ready for.

"I'm here to help you recover your cattle, of course," Pat explained, "but also I want to warn these Ndebele rustlers that they cannot roam the land helping themselves to other people's cattle whenever they feel like it."

"I'll be glad to join you," said Norman Sparks.

"Thank you, but that won't be necessary. I intend to use some harmless home-made explosive devices which, if my plan works, should have the desired effect. As a gunsmith, I'm trained in this sort of thing. I do need your help in finding the thieves and I thought one of your herdsmen might know something."

"I can tell you exactly where they are, Mr van Zyl. The culprits are so confident in their invulnerability that they wander around the district from their base, harassing locals and farmers alike with impunity."

"Could I walk there?" Pat asked.

"In no more than two hours."

"Good. I'll plan to be there an hour before last light. What I want you to do is to take a couple of herdsmen with you and be prepared to move at dawn tomorrow, about fifteen minutes after you hear a series of explosions, to round up the cattle, which would have scattered in all directions with the noise."

"You can count on me being there," replied Sparks.

Pat left in the afternoon with his sack of thunder flashes, a bottle of water, a few sticks of biltong, a telescope and his Winchester rifle. It was an easy journey and he blended in well with the tawny winter grass in his khaki clothing and soft ox-hide boots, so favoured by the Boers because of their comfort, lightness, and the stealth they afforded.

Sparks had told him that the Ndebele raiders were camped at the foot of a low hill, identified by a row of three large anthills before it. The cattle thieves were on the other side of the hill.

When he saw the hill, Pat took out his telescope and surveyed the area to check there were no sentries on lookout duty before proceeding, crouched low, until he reached the anthills. He stopped again, this time both looking and listening. Nothing! He climbed the hill and looked down. Ten men squatted around a fire grilling strips of impala meat taken from a carcass which hung from a nearby tree. Norman Sparks' cattle were grazing peacefully close by. He plotted a way down the hill before rolling himself into his blanket and going to sleep for a few hours.

Pat was up and ready for action shortly after four o'clock. He drank some water, picked up his sack and rifle, and moved silently down the hill. Every few minutes he stopped and listened, but heard no sound. At the bottom he settled behind the broad trunk of a marula tree. Nothing moved so he emptied his sack onto the ground.

He had worked out the burning time for each inch of fuse and cut them to create a set time delay between each explosion. The monkey oranges were numbered and he selected the first six and put them in his hat before placing the rest back in the sack. Then, with his rifle over his shoulder, he edged forward closer to the snoring men. Monkey orange number one had the longest fuse and this he placed behind a small rock directly in front of his own cover tree. He lit the fuse, covering the instant flame with his hat. Speed was now essential and he scrambled from there to his next selected spot, lit the fuse, and moved on.

He had just lit number four when one of the men threw off his *kaross* and stumbled to the edge of the clearing to urinate into the undergrowth. Pat froze. The man stood where Pat planned to place his next bomb. He seemed to be half asleep so Pat decided to toss the next two bombs into position. He lit both and threw the first towards where the man was shaking off the last drops. It bounced off his shoulder and fell to the ground at his feet, causing the man to cry out in alarm.

"Damn!" muttered Pat as he sent the last monkey orange further to complete the circle. He jumped to his feet and ran to the marula tree where he retrieved his sack and raced up the hill. Behind him there was much shouting and running about before the first explosion came with a mighty bang. It sounded like half a dozen shotguns going off simultaneously. Then came the next ear-shattering noise, followed by the next until all six had detonated. For good measure, Pat lit two more and tossed them down the hill.

There was pandemonium below as the men ran about in complete confusion colliding with one another. Eventually they came together and headed off fast away from the hill.

With the tension relieved, Pat had to laugh at the spectacle and was still chuckling when three figures strode around the side of the hill. It was Norman Sparks and his herdsmen coming to round up the cattle.

Pat went to meet them. The two herdsmen ran off to retrieve the cattle. Norman was delighted. "Man, you pulled it off. It's unbelievable. I don't know how to thank you."

"There's no need. Call it a community service. It's a long time since I had so much fun."

"You have to tell me how you created so much noise?" Pat showed him one of the remaining monkey oranges. "Ingenious! The shrapnel is the orange skin which isn't going to cause serious injury."

"That's right. If you want to pep it up, all you do is add a few nails or other bits of metal. Then it becomes lethal. Here, take these for farm protection." He handed over the sack.

After a good lunch, Pat took his leave of the Sparks and rode back to Salisbury, leaving behind one grateful farmer who had not expected to see his cattle again. Pat doubted that this would be the end of cattle rustling by the Ndebele, but he had given a few of them a fright and issued a warning.

Dr Jameson chuckled when he heard the story and expressed his thanks. "The local farmers will feel a little better now so you've done me a big favour," he said.

The next morning Pat said farewell to a tearful Sandra and, collecting his pigeons, he once more took to the road.

CHAPTER SEVENTEEN

General Viljoen knew exactly whom he would recruit. The man was a thirty-year-old career Captain in the army named Schalk van Driel. He had broad shoulders and stood six feet tall. His serious demeanour was that of a man much older. He hated the English for what he saw as the injustices meted out to his family and burghers in general. Currently he led a small clandestine commando of special forces which specialised in reconnaissance and sabotage, using bush craft to achieve their aims. Like his fifty men, he came from Boer stock and was brought up in the bush. These men were trained to live off the land and to blend in with it. They could operate on foot or as a mounted unit. They were the types to have behind you in a battle rather than marching towards you.

Captain van Driel appeared in the General's office in full dress uniform and saluted smartly.

"How are you, Schalk, and your ma and pa? It's been a long time since I saw them," said the general.

"All is well on the farm, sir."

"Sit down. I have a task for you and some of your men which requires your special skills. The order comes from the highest authority and it's extremely confidential."

An hour later Captain van Driel emerged from the office with the suggestion of a smile on his face, quite different from the morose expression he wore when he had entered it.

He had decided to infiltrate through Tuli for logistical reasons and decided on six men for his team instead of the ten suggested by the general. The patrol would cross the Shashi River below Tuli at night. They would then travel during the day in pairs an hour apart, parallel to the road but preferably out of sight of it, and meet up at night.

He had asked for a guide who could also act as a translator in the local language as well as have a moderate knowledge of either Afrikaans, English or Fanagalo, the lingua franca used by all mine workers, whatever their origin. There were many such men from the north employed by the mines. Such a man could move freely amongst the local people and discover the whereabouts of Umgandan and his impi. That was when the operation would really begin.

The patrol left Johannesburg quietly one morning. Their guide, Farai, had been taught to ride and they had three mules to carry food and extra ammunition. A spare horse was included in the entourage.

It took twelve days to reach the Shashi which they crossed below Tuli before backtracking to the road that led north east to Victoria.

Five days later, Farai proclaimed in Fanagalo that Victoria was 'duze', close, about a day's walk ahead. Few people lived here and Farai, who knew the area well, detoured around several villages.

The captain was keen to make a base close to water and instructed Farai to find a suitable site. They found a thorn thicket on the bank of a fairly large river which would make a good hideout.

Farai was sent on a 360° foot patrol to check their isolation while the others watered their horses and bathed. The immediate area was declared uninhabited and they set about hollowing out the thicket enough to accommodate both men and horses. This would provide cover and protection from wild animals.

Next, Farai was sent out to try to establish where Umgandan's present kraal was. Three days later he had not returned and Captain van Driel began to worry about defection in spite of the large bonus promised. He said to his second-in-command, Sergeant de Kock, "We'll give him two more days and then assume we've lost him for good. One of our own scouts will then have to capture a local to point us in the right direction."

The following day around noon, Farai appeared. He was hot, thirsty and hungry, but smiling. Van Driel told him to report after he'd eaten and cleaned himself up.

He had covered a lot of ground while he'd been away but eventually he had found a kraal that had been raided by Umgandan's warriors, who had taken some cattle only two days previously. Farai posed as a miner returning home and was fed and made welcome, as was the custom. The kraal head told him that the raiders had arrived early, before the cattle had been released for grazing. They set fire to some of the huts, forcing the villagers to flee for their lives. The warriors had then moved east almost in the direction of van Driel and his men.

It was not difficult to follow the spoor of rustlers herding twenty steers. He followed them all day until he came to another village, less permanent than others he had seen. This was what he had been looking for. The huts were of grass construction and the kraal was full. The cattle were surrounded by thorn tree branches and Farai guessed that other villages had been similarly invaded. Farai's next task was to find out how many there were in the raiding party. He could not count effectively so he had been instructed to use his fingers and thumbs, one digit for each man, and then place a pebble in a leather pouch he had been given. He did this before he retired and climbed a tree to spend the night.

Van Driel estimated that the Ndebele village was a six or seven-hour walk, far quicker on horseback. He emptied the pouch and found five stones. He knew now what he was up against.

The intention was to attack the Ndebele and drive them from their village before taking the cattle and bringing them back to their own camp where there was plenty of water and grazing for them. His men would then backtrack to set up an ambush in case of a follow-up. He was not interested in what eventually happened to the cattle as long as the Ndebele no longer had them. The main objective was to infuriate Umgandan. When the current exercise was completed, they would repeat it with other Ndebele raiding parties.

Farai could not confirm whether Umgandan had been with the men he had seen, but the captain felt sure he would catch up with him in time.

He briefed his men on their mission and the numbers they were up against. "We'll move out tomorrow at noon and camp an hour's ride from the target and attack at first light the next day. I don't anticipate too much resistance as we have firearms against their spears. I suspect they'll run away."

Dr Jameson received a letter from the Rev. Moffat at GuBulawayo. He frowned at the envelope, wondering what bad news he was about to read. The reverend's letters more often than not related to problems. He began to read.

Dear Doctor Jameson

I have been requested by King Lobengula to write to you over a matter that is causing him great concern and which, if not corrected, could lead to circumstances of a most serious nature as they affect the relations between your Company and the Ndebele people.

The king has learned from one of his indunas in the Victoria area that a band of white men are murdering his people and stealing the king's cattle. To date there have been five incidents of this nature.

This band of mounted men are operating in the Victoria area and each incident is a duplication of the previous one, whereby the attack is mounted at first light, most times with casualties, and the cattle herded away.

I urge you, Doctor, to take steps to discover the identity of these criminals and put a stop to their nefarious activities before the king succumbs to the pressure of his more militant indunas, particularly one by the name of Umgandan, who is keen to retaliate against the whites in general.

Meanwhile I await your urgent response.

I remain, yours sincerely,

John S. Moffat (Reverend)

Dr Jameson sat stunned as the implications sank in. The likelihood that the cattle had been stolen from the Shona in the first place was immaterial. Lobengula considered all the cattle in his kingdom to be his and the penalty for cattle rustling was death.

Who were these individuals? He could not believe that any of the settlers would be so stupid as to provoke a situation which could only be to their detriment. Could this be an act of retaliation by the farmers in the Victoria area who had recently had cattle stolen by the Ndebele? It was feasible that the thieves could be from south of the border and they intended to drive them across the Limpopo and sell them.

The first move was to pacify the king. He must be reassured that the Company would do all it could to establish who these people were and bring them to justice.

It was in emergency cases like this that Dr Jim wished he had a telegraph system to use. A written message to Moffat would take a week to reach him. He also had to contact Rhodes, which meant sending a rider to Tuli for onward telegraphic transmission to Kimberley or wherever Rhodes happened to be at the moment.

A despatch rider was due to leave for Tuli the next day and now another would have to go to GuBulawayo.

He composed both messages before calling in Captain Pierce, who led the British South Africa Police contingent at Salisbury. He showed him Moffat's letter.

"I want you to investigate, captain. Are we up against aggrieved settlers or a bunch of bandits? Ten troopers should be enough. Go to Victoria first and see if there's any more to learn. If you need more men, you can second them there. Your primary task is to stop whoever is responsible. If they are bandits, you know what to do, but try and establish a motive for what is happening."

Captain Pierce's patrol and the messengers left the next day. All Dr Jameson could do now was wait.

Lieutenant Blake was the senior officer at Victoria. He told Pierce what he knew.

"There have been reports of cattle raids by the Ndebele on the Shona. A few women have also been abducted. I received a garbled report about white bandits but it was third or fourth hand, very vague, I'm afraid. I'm sure none of the farmers around here would take the law into their own hands. If they did, I would hear about it."

"I think I must first visit Umgandan's village to establish what's going on. Can you spare someone to guide me there, Lieutenant?"

"I know the place. He moves around so his villages are temporary affairs. It'll take half a day to get there. Yes, I can give you one of my men to guide you."

"I'll also need an interpreter."

"That's no problem, sir. When will you leave?"

"Tomorrow," replied the captain.

When they reached the village, Pierce and his men dismounted and were greeted with open hostility. He managed to establish that Umgandan was in GuBulawayo and asked to speak to his deputy. A well-built warrior, carrying his shield and stabbing spear, stepped forward, announcing himself truculently as Nyati.

Pierce explained, through his interpreter, his mission, telling Nyati that Dr Jameson saw cattle rustling as a grave offence, even more so if committed by white men.

The reply was long and accompanied by a lot of emphatic gesticulating. Pierce knew from experience that his patience would be tested. His men stood nervously beside their horses, their hands never far from their rifles.

He and Nyati sat facing each other on stools. Nyati's speech took a long time, partly because of the structure of the Ndebele language and this was compounded by the need for translation. Captain Pierce's patience was tested to the limit.

The subject of cattle stealing was an emotive one in any case. Nyati's anger was increased by the fact that white men had invaded several of his temporary villages, killing and wounding several of his warriors and, worse than this, they had stolen the king's cattle. Pierce listened without visible reaction, but could not help thinking that double standards were being displayed. It was acceptable for Nyati to steal cattle from the Shona and kill and plunder the people, but it became a serious crime when the same herds were stolen from him with far fewer casualties.

"What can you tell us about these white men?" asked Pierce.

"They came in the early morning on their horses, riding through the village like the wind, firing at anyone they saw. Then they drove off the cattle."

"How many of these thieves were there?"

"They were many." Pierce could get no further than that simple answer.

"Do you know where these white men are with your cattle?"

"One of my men knows where to find them. He says it is not far from here."

"How does he know?"

"He followed them after the last attack."

"Why have you not tried to recover the cattle?"

"King Lobengula has ordered that the white men are not to be attacked. That is why Umgandan is with the king now. He is begging him to allow us to attack and kill these white thieves. He has only to give the word and we will rise up and destroy the enemy and take back that which is the king's."

Pierce said to the interpreter, "Ask Nyati if he will provide us with someone to guide us to this place. Tell him that, as policemen, it is our job to follow up this crime and arrest the criminals."

A long discussion ensued between Nyati and three of his senior advisers before they reached a consensus.

"We have agreed that Dube will guide you to where the white men sleep and cook their food, but he will not incur the anger of the king by helping you further."

Pierce ended the meeting with a promise to return the next day to collect the guide.

Dube was trotting ahead of the troop when he stopped, paused as if to get his bearings, and then headed towards a small kopje to their left. He stopped again and motioned to the horsemen to dismount.

He took Captain Pierce to the top of a large boulder and pointed out the meandering river, distinguishable by the large trees which followed the banks. Then he indicated a solitary dead tree.

Using hand signals he revealed the thicket which hid the men and horses they were seeking. It was just over a mile away.

Dube made it known to the captain that his work was now done. Shaking his spear in the air, he turned and trotted back the way they had come. But he had no intention of returning to the village; he was to meet up with Nyati half an hour's run back along the route.

Captain Pierce needed to establish the lay of the land and the size of the opposing force. He took one of his best bush trackers with him and made for the dead tree through the long grass, stopping and listening every now and again. All was quiet. They approached the thicket downwind from the horses. The grass was shorter under the canopy of trees and they began to crawl, hoping that the noise of the flowing river ahead would cover their progress. At one point they reached the river bank and saw the stolen cattle grazing on the far side.

They watched a man collecting water in a bucket before withdrawing silently and moving in the direction where they expected to find the camp site.

Suddenly they heard the restless stamping of horses' feet and knew they were close. Pierce moved nearer to his companion and whispered, "Stay here and keep your eyes peeled. All the men should be in camp by now and I want to get closer and count them."

He crawled, adrenalin pumping, on his belly like a leopard towards the sound made by the horses. Then he saw the thicket, as Dube had described it, about one hundred yards ahead.

He knew there would be a sentry somewhere and he asked himself where he would position one. The obvious answer was up a tree and there were plenty of those about. He scanned the upper branches in front of him and sure enough there he was, perched high in a fork where he would have a clear view of anybody who approached without caution.

Then he heard men's voices inside the thicket and, crawling closer, he saw flames flickering from a cooking fire. Short of walking brazenly into the camp to make his count, there was little more he could do at this point. Better to be in position when the men led the horses out to drink and feed in the early morning. Slowly, Pierce made his way back to his companion and explained his decision to him.

With darkness closing in, they felt it was safe to turn and walk away. That was a mistake. They opted for a short cut to save time – another mistake. Neither of them saw the trip wire attached to one side of a roughly constructed cage with a number of live francolin inside. The door swung up and the francolin flew out, making a raucous din.

Both men froze, undecided about what to do next. The camp quickly came alive and an extended line of men ran towards them. Pierce realised that this was no rabble; these were disciplined men acting in an orderly fashion. All of them were armed. One carried a lantern. A voice barked and the men, six in all, knelt and took aim. The same voice called out, "Stand still. Who are you?"

Pierce's position was hopeless. Both men dropped their rifles and raised their hands.

Captain van Driel came forward and again demanded, "Who are you?" Pierce recognised the guttural Afrikaans accent.

"I could ask the same of you. I am Captain Pierce of the British South Africa Company Police. I've been instructed to arrest you and your men for cattle rustling and other acts likely to endanger relations between the settlers and the Ndebele."

"That may be so, Captain, but right now I have the advantage and neither I nor my men have any wish to be locked up. Where is the rest of your patrol as I doubt whether you planned to arrest us on your own?"

Captain Pierce had already reasoned that he was dealing with military personnel whose first language was Afrikaans which meant that they were part of the Transvaal army. The implications of this did not bear thinking about. There was no point in trying to bluff his way out so he chose to play along with his captors and see what opportunities developed.

The two men were forced at gunpoint to lead Van Driel's patrol to the camp site. From 25 yards out, Captain Pierce hailed his men and, receiving the correct response, he moved forward. Fifteen paces away, Van Driel ordered a halt. "Throw down your arms," he called into the darkness. "We have your captain and his man in our custody and will not hesitate to shoot if you do not comply."

The troop sergeant answered, "Captain Pierce, sir, what do I do?"

"We have no choice, Sergeant. Lay down your weapons and tell me when you have done so."

When the sergeant confirmed the order obeyed, Van Driel re-lit his carbide lamp and led the way into the camp, where Pierce's men stood looking stunned. Their weapons were collected.

"Captain Pierce," announced van Driel, "tell your men to break camp. You are now our prisoners and you will come with us."

Van Driel now had a serious problem to solve. His orders from General Viljoen were discretionary. He was to continue the campaign until he was satisfied that the Ndebele were incensed to the point of revolt. He did not know the political ramifications, but he could guess at them. Now he wondered what he was supposed to do with his prisoners and this kept him awake long into the night.

There was only one possible solution. He wished he had a superior officer to make the decision and relieve his own conscience. He was a hard man and ruthless to a degree, but he was not a cold-blooded murderer and his decision was not made lightly. His orders had come from the highest level of authority. He considered the consequences if his mission was compromised and his country hugely embarrassed as a result.

Having reached a conclusion to his dilemma, he next thought was how to carry it out, but then he chose to leave that until the morning. His last thought before he finally fell asleep was that he must now accelerate his programme.

Captain Pierce found it no easier to sleep. He wondered about the motive behind stealing the king's cattle. Unless politics was involved, it made no sense. Then he thought of van Driel's predicament concerning the fate of he and his men if politics was indeed behind it all. He was not comfortable with these thoughts.

Nyati and Dube had witnessed the capture of Captain Pierce's patrol and they too were bemused. To the Ndebele, the white man was the common enemy. They assumed that they all worked towards the same goal which was to take the Ndebele land for themselves. They were confused when they saw conflict between these two groups of white men. Nyati decided to continue to observe and see what happened.

Van Driel's camp woke early. The atmosphere was sombre as they sat drinking coffee and eating rusks.

Suddenly Van Driel stood and cleared his throat. "I think that you all know what must take place next. As a professional soldier, this distresses me, but there are bigger issues at stake so let us waste no more time." He then ordered Pierce and his men to be ushered outside the thicket.

Captain Pierce spoke. "Captain van Driel, what madness is this, sir? I cannot believe your intentions. Do you intend to execute us like traitors or deserters? We are policemen doing our duty. Have you no honour, man?"

"I have a mission which is important to my country. I must do what is necessary to accomplish that mission. My personal feelings are of no consequence. I am very sorry, sir."

"You surely cannot hope to get away with this cowardly act."

"Please do not make this any more difficult than it already is. I have my orders."

"May I at least have a word with my men before you carry out this slaughter, because that is what it is?"

"Certainly you can, Captain Pierce."

Pierce gathered his men in a circle around him. He looked at their faces and saw a mixture of fear, consternation and hopelessness while detecting more than one quivering lip.

"Gentlemen," he said, "this man would have us die without honour, standing before a firing squad. If we are to die with some semblance of dignity, we have only one alternative and that is to run and force them to shoot us in the back. You all know that our chances of escape are zero, but better to die trying to escape than standing and waiting for death. What do you say?"

Each man in turn nodded his assent. Captain Pierce saluted them one by one and shook hands. "The river might be the best option so, on my word, make a dash for it and may God bless you."

"Now!" came the command – the last order the officer would ever give as they all, including the interpreter, ran for the river screaming their defiance.

Half of them never made it that far as Van Driel's men cut them down. Those who did were picked off one by one from the bank as they swam with the current.

The bodies of those that perished on land were carried down to the river and thrown into the water without ceremony. None of the executioners showed any emotion; they had all killed before and these were the hated Englishmen. The crocodiles would devour the evidence of the massacre within a very short time.

Knowing that a search party would be sent out to find the missing patrol, Captain van Driel decided to continue with his raids for a while longer. Two or three more should be enough to complete his mission before he returned to Johannesburg to report to his master.

When Umgandan returned from GuBulawayo, he was puzzled to hear from Nyati of the demise of Captain Pierce's patrol but, if the white men wanted to kill each other, he was happy. It was that many fewer to contend with.

The raids on the king's cattle continued and each one chipped away at Lobengula's tolerance. This, combined with the pressure from his indunas, finally broke his resolve not to attack the settlers and he gave the order to do so. He told Umgandan to commence raids on outlying white farms in the Victoria area. His reasoning was to restrict these retaliatory measures to one area to serve as a warning to other settlers and it would stop his cattle being stolen.

The raids took place at first light and the white farmers were slaughtered along with their workers. No one and nothing was spared, including children and family pets. All died by the spear or knobkerrie and all were butchered horrifically. The last act was to torch the homestead and drive off the cattle. It was not long before the remaining farmers took refuge in Victoria where they prepared for an attack on the settlement itself.

Lieutenant Blake was kept busy seeing to the welfare of the influx of farmers while worrying about the fate of Captain Pierce's patrol, whose return was long overdue. Pierce had said that he would be away for a week at a time, returning for a short rest before continuing his investigations. This plan would go on until he had the evidence he was sent to look for. He had now been away for two weeks without a word.

Blake had informed Dr Jameson of his concern and had despatched two search parties. A few villages reported a recent visit from Captain Pierce asking for information of Umgandan's whereabouts. He learned also of the patrol's finding of a deserted temporary village that had been occupied by the Ndebele. The captain's spoor had been picked up and followed until it petered out on hard ground.

President Kruger was reading a newspaper in his office when General Viljoen was ushered in.

He pointed to the newspaper on his desk. The headline read 'Settlers Stealing the King's Cattle in Mashonaland'. He asked, "Have you read this, General?"

"I have. It is what you wanted and the news is reaching the outside world. I must tell you that I did tip off the press shortly after Van Driel and his men departed."

"Good thinking. It says here a reporter has been sent to interview Lobengula. Things are going according to plan. Did they work out right for Van Driel?"

"Not quite, sir. I heard that there was one hitch. It seems that their camp was compromised. Van Driel does not know how, but he was visited by a Captain Pierce with some BSA Company police that Dr Jameson had sent to investigate the stock thefts. Van Driel captured the whole patrol and – er – eliminated them."

"Are you saying he wiped out the whole patrol?"

"That is correct, *Meneer* President."

"How many men did he kill, for God's sake?"

"Eleven troopers and one black interpreter."

Kruger thought about this for some time. Then he said, "I have to assume that Captain van Driel had no other option or he would never have resorted to such extreme measures."

"The captain expressed his deep regret that, as a professional soldier, he had to make such a decision and for the manner in which it was carried out."

"I'm sure he did, General. It distresses me no less. Tell him from me that I understand that he had no alternative if he was to complete his mission. I hope there were no witnesses to this incident."

No, sir, none. They were camped in an isolated area away from any villages on the banks of a large river teeming with crocodiles. They would have taken care of the evidence."

"I hope you are right because the consequences of this ever becoming public knowledge would be devastating." Kruger paused and then added, "It's now time for us to play our parts."

CHAPTER EIGHTEEN

Cecil Rhodes was in a foul mood. He strode up and down in front of his desk, waving his arms to make his points. He was with Charles Rudd at De Beers and had just finished reading a story in the Diamond Fields Advertiser reporting the unrest in Mashonaland. It attributed the cause to the abuse of the Ndebele by the settlers who were stealing their cattle and callously murdering the people. What really irritated him was to read that Kruger had complained to the British Prime Minister about settlers who, under the Charter, should be defending the rights of those they were supposedly abusing.

"Who the hell does this bloody man, Kruger, think he is?" raged Rhodes. "What a hypocrite, suddenly championing the cause of the Ndebele! Nobody has been more callous in their treatment of the black people than the Boers. Kruger himself, when he was fourteen, was part of a force that inflicted a devastating defeat on the Ndebele regiments which drove them over the Limpopo fifty years ago."

"Calm down, Cecil. It's not good for your blood pressure," said Rudd.

"You're not the one being vilified here, Charles. What I cannot come to terms with is this accusation that the settlers are killing people and stealing cattle. That's plain bloody stupid. It could lead to a full-scale rebellion. You do realise that, don't you, Charles?"

Charles Rudd did not respond immediately. When he did, he said, "I do, Cecil, and I too find it puzzling. They can only be a band of opportunists."

"I'm beginning to wonder whether this whole thing hasn't been orchestrated. It's too simple, the way it's got into the press and all. I wouldn't be surprised if that bastard, Barnato, hasn't got his hand in this somewhere. I wouldn't put it past him. He's still smarting from our last encounter. Perhaps I should pay him a visit and confront him with it to see his reaction."

"Why not? I'd like to come with you when you do."

"Good, so let's do it – straight away."

Barney was studying some documents when Rhodes and Rudd entered his office. He looked up, surprised to see them, but recovered quickly.

"To what do I owe the honour of this visit, gentlemen?" Noticing the newspaper under Rhodes' arm, he continued, with a smile, "I see you are in the news again, Cecil, and for all the wrong reasons."

"That's not funny, Barnato," Rhodes retorted, "but as you've brought the subject up, I must say that Rudd and I are beginning to think this is a conspiracy. The whole story is out of character with the reality of the situation as we know it. The thing stinks and where there's a bad smell, we normally find the Barnato brothers."

Barney's face was beginning to redden and he was finding it difficult to control his temper. Then he shouted, "Harry, come in here. We've got visitors and I may need a witness for a defamatory case."

Harry came in, looking concerned, but he relaxed and smiled when he recognised the visitors. Rhodes and Rudd remained standing.

"Harry," said Barney, "this gentleman is suggesting that we might have something to do with the troubles over the northern border."

"How ridiculous!" replied Harry looking the picture of innocence. "Why would you and I stoop to stealing cattle?"

"Credit us with a little more intelligence than that, Harry," said Rhodes. "I've never known you to get your hands dirty. You two always get someone else to do the dirty work for you. You really are a couple of smug buggers, aren't you? I don't care what you say, you've both had a hand in this somewhere and I intend to find out what it is."

"Happy hunting, Rhodes, but I think this time someone has beaten you at your own game and that makes me happy," Barney said grinning.

"We shall see, Barnato, we shall see. It's early days yet."

Walking back to de Beers, Rhodes said to Rudd, "What do you think, Charles?"

"I don't know, but the news is certainly music to the ears of those little shits."

"We must find who is doing the dirty work soon. Unless we can stop it, everything could blow up in our faces."

"Have you any ideas?" asked Rudd.

"About who should look into the matter? Yes, as a matter of fact, I do."

Reactions to the press reports came quickly and Rhodes received a telegram from Lord Salisbury, the British Prime Minister, demanding an explanation and warning that unless there was an immediate end to the hostilities, the Charter was in danger of being revoked.

At the same time news arrived from Dr Jameson about the disappearance of Captain Pierce and his troop. This did nothing to improve Rhodes disposition and prompted him to telegraph Jameson, asking him to personally contact Pat van Zyl at Nyanyadzi to enlist his help in tracking down the bandits. As he told Charles Rudd later, "If anyone can discover what is happening up there, it will be Pat van Zyl."

Rhodes then wrote to Lord Salisbury, explaining that he was undertaking an instant inquiry, but expressing his disbelief over the circumstances as they were presented in the press and suggesting that, in his opinion, there was treachery at play.

General Viljoen arrived at GuBulawayo with a platoon of soldiers and requested an urgent audience with King Lobengula. He brought many gifts with him, including an intricately carved chair which he explained to the king was a throne like those used by royalty in Europe. This would add greatly to his prestige.

The king accepted all these gifts with delight, but remained astutely aware that there must be an ulterior motive. He had not forgotten that the man who stood before him was a burgher, one of the people who had beaten his father in battle and driven him out of the Marico Valley to live in exile at GuBulawayo.

Viljoen showed Lobengula the newspaper stories and had them read out for him. "Where was the English Queen Victoria?" he asked the king. "Why has she not come to the aid of your people? Did she not promise to protect you?"

He then showed him the letter President Kruger had written to the British Prime Minister complaining of the treatment of the Ndebele. The President's seal seemed to impress the king.

The translation was a lengthy process but the selected interpreter was up to the task. There were words in English that were untranslatable in Sindebele, phrases that required complex interpretation. Finally, Lobengula said, "What is it you want from me, white man? Why are you here?" He gestured to one of his wives to refill his beer vessel.

"Only that you allow us the same privileges that you have granted Mr Rhodes."

Lobengula said to his interpreter, "Ask the soldier if he is aware that, as we speak, my impi in the east is attacking the settlers in retaliation for the theft of my cattle and the murder of my people."

"I did not know that," said the general, concealing his delight at the news and congratulating himself on the apparent success of his plan. "I can understand your reaction and agree that you have no alternative but to do this under such provocation."

It was now time to play his trump card. He reached into his top pocket and pulled out a tobacco pouch from which he removed two small diamonds. He showed them to the king.

"Do you see these shiny stones? They have made Mr Rhodes a very rich man in Kimberley. Each of these is worth many cattle."

The king displayed considerable interest. "How many cattle?" he asked. Viljoen held up both hands and spread his fingers. "Let me tell you that Mr Rhodes is digging up enough of these to fill a calabash every day in the east of your country near Mozambique. They are enriching themselves from your land. What do they pay you for this privilege?"

Lobengula thought about this before answering, "One of Rhodes' people, a Mr van Zyl, brought me many guns as a present." He gestured to two of his wives and sent them to his wagon. They emerged from it, carrying what was obviously an extremely heavy chest and laid it before him before backing away on their hands and knees.

The king opened the chest and revealed what must have been many thousands of gold coins. Even Viljoen was impressed.

Knowing that the king had no idea of the value of this hoard, the general said, "This is nothing, mighty one. Rhodes is cheating you. You are owed far more than this. Change your decision to allow Rhodes all the mining rights and let my men dig there instead and we will pay you with many cattle, not shiny stones that are worthless."

Then he had a thought. He could not imagine Rhodes arming these people with accurate modern weapons which might be turned on his own people. Perhaps he could further his cause. He asked, "Will you allow me to see these guns that Van Zyl gave you, O Slayer of Elephants?"

The king shouted another command, this time to one of the guards who stood with their short stabbing spears, shields and knobkerries in a circle around the two conferring men and their assistants. The man ran off and returned with a muzzle loader which he respectfully placed in the king's hands. Lobengula passed it over to the general with an air of pride.

Viljoen recognised it for what it was, an obsolete Portuguese musket. He wondered how Rhodes had procured them and, more importantly, how he might have tampered with them. The obvious answer was to subdue the powder to reduce the range of the weapon. He had to admire Rhodes' astuteness, but how could he tell the king without causing him to lose face? Lobengula was no fool and the general was sure that Van Zyl would have demonstrated the effectiveness of them with a workable version.

Laying the gun down, he asked, "Can you bring me the ball and powder?"

"Why?" The king was becoming impatient.

"I would like to check, that is all. I am a soldier and know about these things."

Lobengula agreed and a box of powder and one of shot was brought forward. Viljoen opened them and smiled at the cleverness of what had been done. It was the shot used for an even older musket, one without rifling.

"So what do you say?" asked the king.

"I say that this is the wrong ammunition for this gun and it will not shoot true and straight. I also suspect that the powder is not strong and will not throw the bullet far. Did Van Zyl give you a demonstration and did it go well?"

Another barked order to a wife brought forth the biscuit tin with its holes, which he displayed with pride. He then stood, took the gun and beckoned the general to follow him. He placed the tin on the same post that Pat van Zyl had used and paced out the same distance from it. He announced, "It was from here that I blew away that small thing. I, the king of the Ndebele, with the eye of the brown snake eagle, hit the piece of *simbi* – one time." This meant his first shot; he conveniently forgot the results of his real first effort.

Walking over to the king, Viljoen loaded the weapon and held it out to him. "If you please, show me how you did it," he said.

Remembering everything that Van Zyl had taught him, Lobengula brought the gun up to his shoulder, leaned forward and took aim. The shot went way wide of its mark. He looked on in disbelief as Viljoen took the gun and reloaded it, before taking his own stance and firing. The result was the same.

"You see, sir, that even I, a soldier who uses guns all the time, cannot hit that target. I will never be able to do so with this gun, loaded with that round ball so do not blame yourself for bad marksmanship. Now I will shoot the tin into the sky."

Viljoen, when first examining the tin of shot, had found a couple of conical bullets remaining and slipped them into his pocket. He reloaded with one of them and hoped that the powder was strong enough to reach the tin. He fired and was relieved to see the tin fly off the post.

Lobengula shook his head at the deception he had been subjected to and Viljoen hastened to assure him that his own military training was the only reason that enabled him to spot what had been done.

Mustering as much dignity as he could, the king offered his conclusions. "It would seem that you are right. I have been deceived by Mr Lodie and his men in front of my own people. That is not to be forgiven. I shall give thought to your proposition. Return to me in two days and I will give you my answer."

The general returned to his camp site and pondered the outcome of the day's events. He knew the man and his people were unpredictable. Just when you thought you were beginning to understand them, they did something totally at odds with realistic reasoning. All he could do was wait and hope.

His mind went back further to Harry Barnato's visit some months previously where he had been told of a scheme his brother had hatched to ingratiate himself with Lobengula, only to be outwitted by Rhodes, while landing himself in court at Fort Tuli., where he had been fined and had his wagons and goods confiscated. The contents had been nearly a thousand muzzle loaders. He reasoned that it was possible that the Barnatos had rendered them docile. He thought it ironic that the spoils of Rhodes cunning were back-firing.

Another problem was what to do about the Barnato brothers. If Lobengula ruled in favour of the Transvaal Republic's proposition, they would seek some reward.

When he presented himself back at the royal enclosure, he asked if the king had reached his decision.

"I have," he replied. "I will banish Rhodes' men from my country. My indunas want to drive all the white men back across the Limpopo. They are tired of having cattle stolen and their warriors slain by white men who tell them to stop their raids on the Mashonas. First, we will rid ourselves of those amongst us now and then you may return and we will talk again."

General Viljoen left the kraal thinking it was two steps forward and one back

━┥┝━

Rhodes' letter did little to mollify Lord Salisbury and his cabinet as criticism from the opposition increased. He summoned Rhodes to London to put his case in person. Anything short of that could jeopardise the whole Mashonaland venture.

Rhodes saw no alternative to making the voyage and making his case as best he could. As he explained to Pickering, "My real problem, Neville, is that I don't know what is going on up there and all I can ask for is time to investigate."

Pickering agreed. Just then a messenger arrived and delivered a telegraph for Rhodes. He took it and handed it to Rhodes.

As he read it, Pickering saw his face getting redder then he threw it across the desk to him before rising and beginning his fretful pacing back and forth.

When at last he spoke, he had regained some of his composure. "This is a bloody conspiracy, Neville. It must be. First we have Kruger complaining to Lord Salisbury about our treatment of Lobengula and then we hear that his right hand man, General Viljoen, is having talks with the king in GuBulawayo. Why this sudden interest in Mashonaland? It wouldn't surprise me if this Viljoen has something to do with the recent banditry. Think of it, Neville. If he can turn the Ndebele against our settlers, which is already happening, it opens the door for the bloody Dutchmen to move in, doesn't it?"

"But how can we prove it?"

"I've already sent a message to Jameson to ask for help from the only man I think may find out the answer. That's Pat van Zyl. I know it's irregular to ask a civilian to deal with a police matter, but no one can tell me what happened to Captain Pierce and his patrol. They simply disappeared. This is work that calls for special skills."

He sipped from a glass of water before continuing, "Do you know who masterminded the Battle of Chua? It was Van Zyl, not Captain Heyman. The captain himself told me that. Van Zyl also disposed of a savage called Gungunyana who was attacking villagers and traders alike, in fact anyone on the route between Umtali and Beira. As far as I'm concerned, this man has the right credentials."

"Will he help you, sir?"

"I think so. After all, if our suspicions are correct, he has as much to lose as any of us. Meanwhile, book me on the first available ship to Southampton and get me a train ticket to Cape Town as near to the sailing date as possible. I have a lot to do before I leave."

The day before his departure a telegram arrived from Dr Jameson. Pat van Zyl had just been in Salisbury seeing his fiancée and, despite her resistance to the idea, he had agreed to follow up on Captain Pierce's disappearance and try to track down the bandits. He had chosen three troopers from the Salisbury contingent and would supplement them if necessary from his own security team. The message ended, saying that by the time this telegram was delivered, Van Zyl should be on his way to Victoria.

Sandra had expressed her resistance to Pat's decision in no uncertain terms. "Why you, Pat?" she argued. "This is police work. Why doesn't Mr Rhodes tell Dr Jameson to use his own men?"

"I suppose it's because he knows I have a vested interest with much to lose. Don't forget that Brian, Grievous and I have a good record of successes since we have been here and we operate less conventionally than the police can and maybe that's what's needed in these circumstances."

"I still don't think it's fair."

Pat foresaw another tearful farewell. "Sandra, you'll remember me telling you that there would be hurdles to overcome before we can settle down and get on with our lives. This is one of them, so please try to understand. This is something I have to do."

Sandra softened a little. "What are your immediate plans, love? Who will you take with you?"

"I'm not one for working with large groups if it can be avoided. I find I'm more effective with just a few, using surprise and stealth tactics, so I'll take only three troopers from here. Then I'll return to the mine, tell the others, and ask one of them, probably Brian, to join me and leave the other to run the mine. I will also respect Brian's point of view if he declines."

"What then?"

"We head for Victoria and see if we can pick up some leads on Pierce's patrol. They can't have disappeared into thin air. There must be clues, some explanation. The Victoria police have their hands full with the local unrest. The settlement is flooded with fleeing farmers and unless we can put a stop to the people causing the problem of cattle theft and the murder of tribesmen, the whole situation will escalate until it is out of control. I must try to stop that happening."

Pat took both her hands and continued, "I understand how you feel, Sandra. All you can do is sit here and wait and that will be hard for you, I know. One day this will all be over and we can live normally. I also know that I can't sit and do nothing about it."

"I can see that nothing I say will change your mind so I'll say no more, except this: Patrick van Zyl, as soon as this is all over, I'll never let you out of my sight again. Is that clear?"

Pat burst out laughing. "My love, if that isn't an incentive to get back quickly and in one piece, I don't know what is." He pulled her close and held her tightly.

Sandra looked up. "One more thing, Pat. I'm going to have to tell my sister about this and I'm not looking forward to that."

"Must you? We don't even know if Brian will agree to come. If he does, well … what she doesn't know won't hurt her. He's due to visit in a month and if this mission isn't over, Grievous will have to pigeon-post an excuse."

"You are a devious blighter, Van Zyl. You've always got an answer for everything."

⊷⊱⊰⊶

Pat called on Dr Jameson before he left to inquire about any further instructions before he went to Nyanyadzi.

"I can't think of anything. How did your lovely young lady take the news?"

"Not well, but she's intelligent enough to see the bigger picture."

"She's a bright girl, Pat. I bet she asked you why I'm not sending policemen on this job and she's right, I should be."

"I told her that the task required unconventional tactics and that I had some experience with that."

"I'm sorry to have to impose on you like this."

Don't let it worry you, doctor. One thing I would like is your opinion on whether this is a conspiracy of sorts."

"It could be a band of opportunists out to steal as many cattle as possible and take them back across the Limpopo, but I don't think so. There's a larger force at play here."

"Do you think our friend Barnato has a hand in it? He has a score to settle with us, doesn't he?"

257

"It could well be so, Pat. The more I think about it, the more I believe there is a bigger, more resourceful hand conducting the orchestra which is why we must quickly establish who it is."

Pat went to see Sandra one last time and pay his respects to Joe Graham. He told him how he had been working with Maforga at the forge on three small cannons which, if he ever decided to patent the design, he would call The Vital Organ because it looked like a set of organ pipes. Each consisted of five pieces of two-foot pipe of two inch diameter. The breech end was plugged, a small igniter hole was drilled and the pipes were then welded together on a bracket. Finally, the cannon was mounted on a tripod which would have to be weighted to hold it down. The tripod could be dismantled for ease of transport.

Like the Peeshooter, it was to be muzzle-loaded, the shot would be small pieces of shrapnel. As he had explained to Joe when demonstrating it, "What we lack in manpower, we can make up in fire power."

"I hope you don't have reason to use the damn things, but if you do, there isn't going to be much left of anything standing in front of them."

"Yes, Joe, so do I, but I fear we could be dealing with a ruthless and clever bunch of bastards."

"Just bring yourselves back in one piece. If anything should happen, there'll be no living with those two daughters of mine."

"We'll be back, Joe. We've got too much at stake. I'm not just talking about us, our immediate circle, but everyone who has invested in this country. We won't fail. Sandra knows the score, but I don't think you should mention it to Margie that Brian may be accompanying us because that isn't certain yet."

They shook hands and Pat went to say goodbye to Sandra before setting off to Nyanyadzi

On his arrival, Pat called a meeting with Brian, Grievous, John Erasmus and the three troopers he had brought with him. He first introduced the newcomers, Troopers Norman Stiles, George Brown and Tom Bentley. Then he cleared his throat and said, "Gentlemen, while I was in Salisbury, Dr Jameson received a message from Mr Rhodes. Before I reveal the contents, let me tell you that theft of King Lobengula's cattle has been rife. The rustlers, who apparently are white, have had no compunction about killing those who impeded them. So far it has been confined to the Victoria area but it has been going on for some time. It has infuriated induna Umgandan, a nasty piece of work, I'm told. The suspicion is that he now has the king's authority to exact revenge and he is causing mayhem on the white-owned farms. The result is that the farmers have all moved to Victoria and are preparing for an attack."

There was silence around the table. All eyes were focused on Pat.

"There's no need to tell you what will happen if this goes on unchecked. Or maybe I should spell it out. There could be a full-scale revolt leading to all-out war." He paused for effect. No one moved or spoke. "Mr Rhodes' message to Dr Jameson asked me to investigate and discover who is behind these raids, what the motive is, and if possible, put a stop to it."

"That's a tall order," exclaimed Grievous. "Why you?"

"With no disrespect to present company, it seems we have the right credentials due to our - past record."

"What's this 'we' bit, Pat?"

"I was going to ask if you'd like to come along for the ride, Brian."

"And what about me?" Grievous sounded more aggrieved than usual.

"Someone has to stay behind to keep the mine going. As much as I would like you with us, we have to be practical. In any case, aren't you expecting a visit from your lady nurse very soon?"

"That's true, but you'll need more brains than Wood-Gush can provide if you get into trouble."

"Cheeky little man," retorted Brian. "If we had a brain cell count on you, the fingers on one hand would be enough."

"Very funny! Seriously, Pat, what's going through Dr Jim's head about the motive?"

"Mr Rhodes and Dr Jim agree that there could well be something more sinister behind this and they suspect that bloody man, Barnato, could be an influence, stirring it up behind the scenes out of vindictiveness. Stories have appeared in the press down south as well as overseas that have labelled us all as thieves and murderers."

"Which hack has been churning out this rubbish?" wondered Grievous.

"There's more to come, I'm afraid. President Kruger is playing the champion of the downtrodden and making representations to Whitehall."

"Listen, Pat," said Grievous, "there's no way you can leave me behind. If you do track these bandits down and politics is behind it, Mr Rhodes will need evidence and me, my pen and my camera can provide it."

"I hadn't thought of that," said Pat, "but you're right. You should be with us, but who is going to mind the shop?"

"If I spend the next two days showing John the ropes on the sorting table, he can look after things while we're away."

"If John has no objection to that but, bear in mind, John, strictly speaking your brief covers security only."

John said, "I was rather hoping you would take me with you, but you're the boss, Pat, and I don't mind looking after things while you're all away. Will you be taking any of my men with you?"

"I don't think so, John. There's enough of us. Any more and it gets a bit cumbersome."

Grievous said, "Any sortie with Wood-Gush has got to be cumbersome."

"Keep it up, Grievous," said Brian, "and you'll find yourself back in the pond."

The banter and laughter continued for a while until Pat brought the meeting back to order.

"Right, my friends, let's start working on our tactics, shall we?"

Barney Barnato and Harry were at their usual table in the Pick and Shovel bar and were just starting on their second whisky when Barney spoke. "Yes, old Cecil is right to label what's happening in the north as a conspiracy if Kruger has written to the British Prime Minister."

"It looks like he's starting to play the political card. Hypocritical bastard, isn't he?"

"Aren't all politicians a bunch of hypocrites, Harry? But he's a wily old jackal too. It's pure speculation, but I believe it's possible that Kruger could be behind these cattle raids. He could be planning to get Lobengula so annoyed that the whole Ndebele nation rises up and boots Rhodes and his prospectors back across the Limpopo and at the same time embarrasses the British to the point where they're unlikely to defend the Right Honourable Mr Cecil Bloody Rhodes. "

"You could be right, Barney, and that worries me because we could be labelled as accessories, if that's the right word. If the whole thing blows up in Kruger's face, we could find ourselves caught up and then where are we?"

"I haven't thought that far ahead yet, but it's a possibility. We've actually committed no crime and all that would suffer would be our reputation in the diamond business. On the other hand, if Kruger is up to what we think he is, we should be reminding him that we are the only people who know the way to this mine and it's time to start negotiations for our share of the spoils."

"So what's our next move?" asked Harry.

"It may be right to pay the general another visit, but this time we go together. Two heads are better than one."

Barney took another swig of his whisky and said, "We must proceed carefully and keep cool heads."

"What is our share of the spoils, Barney?"

"I'm hoping that Kruger will be grateful enough to give us a claim or two close to Van Zyl's mine. Getting one over Rhodes will be a greater prize though."

Harry said, "I'll get a letter off to the general to make an appointment."

Paul Kruger and General Viljoen sat opposite each other enjoying a brandy in the president's reception room. It was an informal meeting for the general to brief the president on his visit to Lobengula.

"Van Driel has been doing a first class job, Oom Paul. He has caused chaos in the Victoria district and, as you predicted, Lobengula is retaliating by giving his indunas in that area orders to exact revenge on the whites. This has been so successful that many whites have moved into Victoria. Maybe now is the time to move the area of operation."

"Let me think about that while you carry on with your report."

Viljoen told Kruger about Barnato's muzzle loaders and how they had ended up with Lobengula and how a man named Van Zyl had tricked the king by rendering them inaccurate. This had earned Rhodes another black mark in the king's book and hopefully enhanced Kruger's cause by exposing the ruse.

"What was Lobengula's reaction to the proposal to pay royalties with cattle in return for mining concessions?"

"The mention of cattle worked, *meneer*, but he was not prepared to make a commitment until he has sorted out his current problems. I emphasised that if he granted us a concession, we would limit the number of whites entering his kingdom and confine them to the east of the country where they would only do mining. I think he will come round to our offer. The cattle will do it."

"I hope you're right, General, but I must keep up the political pressure. We must work to make the British revoke the Charter. I would prefer a political victory to a blood bath up there."

"What news has come from the British government after your letter of complaint to them."

"I received a polite reply from Lord Salisbury expressing his concern and saying that Cecil Rhodes was being summoned to explain. He would keep me informed. We must wait and see what happens next. Just now, you asked about Van Driel's next move. I think he should sit tight for now. How will you communicate that to him?"

Viljoen said, "Communications were always going to be a problem, but I have set up a link. Originally I ordered Van Driel to operate for a month and then lie low and maintain a watching brief until I made contact with further orders."

"That means he is presently observing," said Kruger."

"Correct!"

"So something must happen within the next month one way or another."

"Harry Barnato has sent me a letter requesting another meeting. This time he wishes to bring his brother, Barney. Shall I see them?"

"I think you have to, General. They are the only people who know where this mine is. They must know from the newspapers about my letter to the British government, but they don't know about our involvement with the unrest. They can speculate, of course, but they have no proof. They must never find out or we will be at their mercy."

"Do you want me to string them along further, *meneer*?"

"Let's think about that more. If things progress as we would like, it will be something we'll have to deal with."

"Harry Barnato hinted to me at our first meeting that they would like to extend their mining activities into Manicaland and be rewarded with mining claims adjacent to the one that Rhodes has an interest in."

Paul Kruger picked up his pipe and stuffed it with tobacco. Putting a match to the bowl, he puffed it into life to the point where the room was thick with acrid smoke. "I think you can go along with that request," he said. "Apart from the fact that they know where the mine is, the Barnatos also have expertise in the diamond business, something which we lack."

Viljoen's eyes were beginning to water with the smoke swirling around his head in the enclosed room, but he nodded his agreement.

They discussed military matters for a while before the general took his leave, pausing in the corridor at an open window to gulp some fresh air into his tortured lungs.

He wrote his reply to Harry Barnato by hand, agreeing to meet both brothers two weeks later in a local hotel. He then sealed it in an envelope which he addressed; he wanted no one, including his secretary, to know about this meeting.

Gazing out of his window into the garden, he thought deeply about the president's plot. It was ingenious but there was danger attached to it. He hoped the rewards were worth the risk. But what was the risk? He thought that the only possible concern about his part in the plan was that if Van Driel or one of his men were to be captured and it was discovered that they were regular soldiers in the Transvaal Republic army. How likely was that? Van Driel was a high-calibre professional and his men had been hand-picked. It was right for them to keep a low profile for the time being. Let the dust settle and then take stock of the situation. The overall strategy seemed to be working so they would have to wait and see what transpired politically. Despite his assurances to the president, he wished that he had better communications with his men on the ground. It would make decision making so much easier.

⊷⊶

Barney and Harry arrived for their meeting at the appointed hotel before General Viljoen. They chose a secluded table in the lounge, ordered a whisky apiece, and settled down to await his arrival.

"Ah, Mr Barnato, we meet again." The general smiled and extended his hand to Harry.

"My pleasure sir. Let me introduce you to my brother, Barney." Then motioning to a passing waiter, "What will it be General?"

"Thank you. I'd like a brandy, please."

They took their seats and made small talk until the general's drink arrived.

Viljoen said, "You asked to meet with me. What exactly can I do for you?"

Barney took the initiative. "Harry and me was wondering, General, if there had been any developments in the north about getting concessions from old Lobengula?"

"This is confidential, of course, but I have personally visited the king and he is much troubled over the problems he is facing in his kingdom."

"Are you referring to the theft of his cattle and the murder of some of his people?"

"I am. He has become highly agitated and, as we speak, his *impis* are reacting against the settlers in the Victoria area."

"So did you have a hostile reception, General?"

"It was a bit strained, to be sure. Having said that, I think you'll enjoy hearing about it. I discovered how you, Mr Barnato, had, let us say, interfered with that consignment of Portuguese muskets. Quite a clever move, I must say. I demonstrated how he had been duped and that really hit a sore spot. These Zulu or Ndebele indu-nas don't like to lose face."

"That gives me great satisfaction," said Barney. "I would give a thousand pounds to ensure that news reaches Rhodes' ears and another thousand to see the expression on his face when it does."

"Stranger things have happened, Mr Barnato."

"We live in hope. Your little demonstration to Lobengula wouldn't have endeared him to Rhodes so that's a big plus for the cause."

"Yes, but there's a big minus as it could affect Lobengula's per-ception of white men in general. That's why I didn't press him on mining concessions. We must give him some space."

"We read about your president's letter to the British Prime Minister. We assume this is part of his strategy, but you need not answer that."

The general smiled. "I will tell you that President Kruger hopes to win a political victory and I'll leave the rest to your imagination."

"We understand what you're saying, General, but can I tell you what most concerns my brother and me? If everything goes accord-ing to plan and you receive the king's permission to prospect and to mine for minerals, we would like to know what compensation we could expect in return for our assistance."

"We anticipated that question. In fact, we discussed it only this week. The president has agreed that you will be granted mining rights adjacent to the diamond claim at present being worked by Cecil Rhodes and his accomplices. Is that reasonable?"

"Very, thank you. What do you say, Harry?"

"It sounds most satisfactory to me, Barney." He turned to the general. "Please convey our respects and thanks to President Kruger."

The general continued, "There is one other matter we should touch upon. It concerns the Transvaal's Republic's involvement in future mining operations in Lobengula's territory. There is one condition to President Kruger's offer."

Barney looked suspicious. "What would that be, sir?"

"Nothing sinister, I assure you. The president would like you and your brother to act as consultants. He recognises that you have much experience in the diamond industry through your business in Kimberley, whereas we have no one with such qualifications. Would you be prepared to help us?"

Barney breathed out in relief and smiled. "Of course, General. That would be no problem, would it, Harry?"

"No problem at all, Barney."

"The whole matter would be formalised from the start of any association between us so you can rest easy on that score."

"We don't doubt your word for a moment. Now that's settled, let me propose a toast. Here's to a mutually beneficial partnership."

Viljoen drank and placed his empty glass on the table before rising. "If there are no further questions, I must be going."

The brothers stood and shook hands with their guest. The general assured them he would be in touch as soon as he had something positive to report and took his leave.

"We've just heard what we wanted, wouldn't you say, Harry?" said Barney.

"So far, so good. Now we simply have to sit back and wait," replied Harry.

CHAPTER NINETEEN

Cecil Rhodes sat in the office of Lord Knutsford, the British Colonial Secretary, sipping a glass of sherry while waiting patiently for the man's tirade to end.

"The Prime Minister is mightily annoyed with you, Cecil. Your people in Mashonaland have embarrassed him a lot and when Kruger's cable was revealed in the press, he was apoplectic. You know how much he dislikes that Dutchman. Now, of course, he's on my back, spurs and all."

"I take it you've set up a meeting with him, Knuttie. When will it be?"

"We're due in his office in one hour."

"There's no time like the present, so let's not keep him waiting."

"I hope, for all our sakes, Cecil, that you've got the right answers for him," Knutsford said as he collected his overcoat.

"I'll do my best. I must as there's so much at stake here."

They were ushered into the Prime Minister's office after a short wait and were barely seated before he vented his wrath. "At this moment, Mr Rhodes, I am hugely embarrassed that you chose to name your first settlement in Mashonaland, Salisbury. It can hardly be called an honour."

"That's a bit harsh, Prime Minister, isn't it?" Rhodes retorted. "One day it will be a big city, very likely the capital of Matabeleland, Mashonaland and Manicaland."

Lord Salisbury said, "Bah! That doesn't impress me. Why couldn't you just content yourself with making money in Kimberley and legislating in Cape Town? Why must you complicate matters with dreams of colonising new lands? Now, having got your Charter to virtually govern the country, you go about abusing it by ill-treating the very people we have promised to protect, these Ndebele."

"If I don't do it, Lord Salisbury, someone else will and that person might not be an Englishman. We can't have that, can we? Before we deal with what you have said, can we be a little more civilised about this? If you visited my Prime Minister's office in Cape Town, the first thing I would do would be to offer you a glass of sherry. So, Prime Minister, can we try to discuss our topic more amicably?"

Lord Salisbury first looked astounded at Rhodes' effrontery and then flustered as he realised that he was being less than courteous to his high-ranking visitor. "Forgive my bad manners, Mr Rhodes, you are right. I've been under a lot of pressure lately about this saga. It's come from the opposition, the general public and even some of my own party. Her majesty is also agitated as the document carries her signature. To be fair, I have asked you here to hear your side of the story. I hope you have something to tell me that will keep the wolves at bay or I may have to seriously think of revoking the Charter."

Rhodes had half-expected to hear this, but it unsettled him nevertheless. He thought of Salisbury as a hypocritical man, a politician to his finger-tips. He wanted to bring as much of Central Africa as he could under British influence, yet he distrusted empire-building by private enterprise. As long as things were progressing well, he was sympathetic and encouraging, but this benign approach disappeared when there were complications, like now.

"I wish I could say that I have all the right answers for you, but I can't," Rhodes said. "All I can tell you at the moment is what I suspect has been happening in Mashonaland."

He cleared his throat before continuing, "When Dr Jameson, the Company's administrator, first learned of the raids by these unknown white marauders, and I emphasise the word unknown, he sent a troop of Company policemen under an experienced officer to the Victoria area to investigate. That patrol has disappeared without trace.

"Before I proceed, I must tell you that associates of mine have discovered a rich alluvial diamond deposit in the east of the country, close to the border with Mozambique. You will understand that this puts a different perspective on things."

"I assume," said Lord Salisbury, "that you have an interest in this find, Mr Rhodes."

"I do, Prime Minister, and it is my fervent hope that my interest will help to further the development of the whole country. Unfortunately, word has got out about this new mine. You may have heard of a cockney gentleman called Bernard Isaacs who is more commonly known as Barney Barnato."

"Isn't he another of your Kimberley 'cousins' who has struck it rich?"

"That's right, sir. He's a former barrow boy and pugilist and he's as sharp as a razor. Like me, he has done well in the diamond business. By somewhat devious means, he has discovered the location of this mine and used this knowledge to try to influence Lobengula to grant him concessions by bribing him with some muskets, a plot which we heard about and foiled. Had we not done so, he would now likely be digging right next to our claim."

"I won't ask for details, but knowing your reputation, I would wager that you somehow turned that situation into an advantage."

Rhodes ignored that comment and said, "Barney Barnato and I are old foes. Sometimes he wins, but on the whole I think the overall score is in my favour. I do know that he won't take my latest victory lying down. Not only does he want revenge, but he also wants some of those diamonds.

"So far I've given you facts. What comes next is speculation. I hope to convince you that it is not of the wild sort. I think that he and his brother, Harry, but mainly Barney as he is the brighter one, have realised that they need some help. Knowing that Paul Kruger has always had ambitions to expand his country beyond the Limpopo, my guess is that he has contacted him and tried to make a deal."

Lord Salisbury looked across at Lord Knutsford, who had been most attentive to Rhodes' narrative, and said, "The plot of a best-selling novel, eh, Knuttie?"

"I can't wait for the next chapter, sir. Pray continue, Cecil."

"We know that Kruger is no slouch and he would have fired up his smelly pipe and put on his thinking cap. He then probably conferred with his favourite general, Viljoen, and hatched a plan to satisfy his ambitions. But the Charter is blocking his way."

Knutsford burst out, "You're not suggesting that Kruger has anything to do with cattle rustling, are you, Cecil?" He reached for his glass, contemplating what he had heard. "My God, I do believe you are."

"It's preposterous, Mr Rhodes," said an agitated Prime Minister. "This is all a figment of your over-active imagination."

"I told you I was speculating, but if you think about it for a minute, it's not outside the realms of possibility. Were you to succumb to outside pressures sufficiently to cancel the Charter, it would play right into Kruger's hands, wouldn't it?"

"Look here, Rhodes, even if you are right, you have no proof."

"Not at this moment, I don't, only strong suspicions, but I already have someone trying to discover who is stealing Lobengula's cattle and harassing his people. I have every confidence in this man being successful."

"Who is this person?" asked the Prime Minister.

"You may not have heard of his name but you will be aware of what he did because of the politics that came into play soon afterwards,"

There was a flicker of interest on Lord Salisbury's face. "This gets more intriguing by the moment. Please carry on."

"You will recall the Battle of Chua and the re-scripted version of events that was printed in the papers to save face for the Portuguese?"

"Yes, though officially I know nothing about the details. Unofficially it was the best approach in the interests of international diplomacy and, if I'm not mistaken, in your interests as well."

"I admit that, because I'll have my railway through Portuguese territory. Getting back to the battle, a Captain Heyman was in charge but he was not the tactician who devised the battle plan. That was a Patrick van Zyl, who is a gunsmith and a first class shot. He had with him two friends, a journalist from The Times, and another Englishman called Brian Wood-Gush. In the short time this trio has been in the country they have accounted for other undesirables as well. They are also my partners in this diamond venture. I have appealed to Mr van Zyl for help and he has agreed. If anyone can get to the bottom of this problem, I believe he can."

Lord Salisbury moved to the window, looked out, and turned to Rhodes. "How can you be so sure that these raids on the Ndebele are not the work of a rogue element among your own people, Mr Rhodes? They could be common criminals looking to drive the cattle across the Limpopo to sell them."

"That is a possibility, sir, but I don't think so."

"That remains to be seen. Tell me, has Lobengula reacted at all yet?"

"I'm sorry to say that his *impi* in the Victoria area has gone on the rampage and murdered several families. This has resulted in the whites in the outlying areas moving into the settlement for protection."

"And if they fight back from there, you'll be looking at an all-out war. You can't let that happen."

"Believe me, I am not underestimating the gravity of the situation. I have ordered Dr Jameson not to retaliate until I give the word. That is why it is imperative that I discover exactly who the perpetrators are."

The Prime Minister was becoming irritable again. "Mr Rhodes, the very last thing I want your people to do is retaliate. I would rather evacuate them than have a war on my hands. The British public would not stand for it."

Lord Knutsford thought it was time for him to intervene. "Prime Minister, may I interrupt and ask Mr Rhodes how things stand there at the moment?"

"Only yesterday I received a cable telling me that, as of two weeks ago, there was a lull in activities in the Victoria district, including the cattle rustling, but that is not to say that it won't start up again at any minute."

Knutsford said, "I believe, Prime Minister that we should buy Cecil some time by issuing a press statement that gives the public something to think about, though I'm not sure what."

"I have a plan which will give me that time, gentlemen," said Rhodes.

"Then let's hear it," urged Lord Salisbury.

"What I would like you to do, Prime Minister, is issue a statement to the press saying that you have asked me to call a Special General Meeting of the British South Africa Company shareholders to discuss the way forward. You would be seen to be taking the initiative and it would shift the focus off of you and onto me. At the meeting I would explain that things were being thoroughly investigated. Then I would propose a resolution that the Company suspends its operations, including its immigration initiative, for a period of three months. This will mollify the stake holders and give me the time I need to complete my investigations. If my suspicions about Kruger are correct, such a resolution would help to convince him that his little plan is still moving in the right direction."

Knutsford said, "That will take some of the heat off you, Prime Minister. There's nothing complicated about it."

"I think you're right, Knuttie. Mr Rhodes' suggestion should stop the jackals snapping at my heels. I'll tell my press secretary to issue a statement straight away. That matter concluded, Mr Rhodes, tell me about this diamond business you alluded to earlier."

Rhodes proceeded to give the Prime Minister a shortened version of Siyakonza's death and Pat van Zyl's deal with Colonel Andrada and subsequent events leading to the discovery of the diggings at Nyanyadzi.

"The plan is," explained Rhodes, "for my share of the profits to firstly fund the railway line from Beira to Umtali. I'm also thinking of another line from Mafeking through Bechuanaland to GuBulawayo. This would be the next step in my proposed line from the Cape through to Cairo."

"Ambitious, indeed, Mr Rhodes, but there will be a few obstacles in your path to overcome first, starting with this Lobengula debacle."

"Granted, Prime Minister, which is why I urge you to consider the politics should it be proved that Kruger is implicated."

"I will do that, Mr Rhodes, but I ask you for one thing in the best interests of international diplomacy. If Kruger is part of this conspiracy that you talk about, I would like you to inform me first and let me handle it, otherwise it could be explosive. Will you give me your word on that, sir?"

"I will, Lord Salisbury."

The Prime Minister's statement appeared in the press the following day and two weeks later Cecil Rhodes sailed for Cape Town, having convinced a jittery bunch of shareholders that his resolution at the Special General Meeting was the best course of action.

When Paul Kruger read the statement published in the press by the British South Africa Company, he allowed himself a moment of self-congratulation. It was time for Van Driel to continue his work. He would give the order to Viljoen but he was aware it would take a while for the message to get through.

CHAPTER TWENTY

E ver since the demise of Captain Pierce's patrol, which still weighed heavily on his conscience, Captain van Driel had felt the need to distance himself from the killing ground. On top of this, the number of cattle accumulated from their raids was becoming overwhelming and eventually a passing tribesman was bound to notice them. On one of their raids, they had come across what must once have been a settlement belonging to some ancient civilisation. It was totally different from anything built by the present inhabitants of the land. Although there was no evidence of complete buildings, they must have been constructed within protective walls of granite blocks. The walls were about twelve feet high and six feet thick. There were no people around, nor had there been for a long time. He decided to move his men there. It was a good tactical move because it occupied high ground and a sentry sitting on a wall would have a good all round view and anyone approaching could be spotted at a distance. There was a source of water nearby. It would be difficult to find a better place to wait out the time until the second phase of the operation, which was basically to be the same as the first, but dependent upon the prevailing situation.

Van Driel sent out a scout who spoke English without a trace of an Afrikaaner's accent. He was disguised as a prospector. He was to meet their contact man, the link to Pretoria, in Victoria and find out if any messages had arrived and assess the situation. He was also to ascertain what form of retaliation, if any, the administration was taking.

On the scout's return, Van Driel learned that the surrounding settlers had moved into Victoria and that all able-bodied men had been recruited to assist the police, who were engaged in follow-up skirmishes against the Ndebele. There was a degree of frustration over the lack of reinforcements from Salisbury and Dr Jameson was being blamed for this.

Dr Jameson's inaction puzzled Van Driel because by reputation Jameson was a man of action and it seemed out of character for him not to be sending extra men, especially as his first troop had disappeared. Van Driel concluded that the man was hatching something but had no clue as to what it was. As there was no word from Pretoria, he followed his instructions, which were to stay put and check every ten days with his contact man.

Pat and his party began their trek to Victoria. They took two pack horses to carry extra provisions and the Vital Organs. It was an uncharted route, but one of Dr Jameson's officers in Salisbury had given him rough compass bearings and there were locals along the way to ask. He was looking at a five to six-day journey. Once there, he would see Lieutenant Blake before deciding his next move. His first priority was to find out what had happened to Captain Pierce's patrol, though he suspected that this was somehow linked to the cattle rustling.

As they travelled south west with dew still glistening on the grass in the early morning sun, Pat reflected ruefully that life since his arrival in this new land had been anything but uneventful and he wondered what lay ahead next. He hoped that whatever it was, it would be without bloodshed and that a major confrontation with the Ndebele could be avoided.

They arrived at Victoria as planned after six days and made camp in a copse three miles from the outskirts of the settlement.

Over his guinea fowl stew, Brian sighed and said, "What I wouldn't give for my mother's mutton stew with potatoes, onions and carrots. One can tire of wild fowl and bush meat day in and day out. When we're back in Nyanyadzi, my priority will be to import some breeding stock. A good idea?"

"Listen to old Farmer Giles, will you?" said Grievous. "Thoughts of food and breeding occupy ninety per cent of his waking hours and even in his sleep, he snuffles like a pig at the trough and groans like a rutting boar."

"Keep that up, Grievous, and I'll have your rump sizzling in a pan."

"Shut up," said Pat, "or you'll both be on a vegetarian diet. If I left the hunting to you, we'd be living on roots and berries."

Pat raised his hand for quiet, "Tomorrow I'm leaving you lot to entertain yourselves while I go into Victoria to speak to Lieutenant Blake. He commands the fort and should be expecting me. No one else knows we're coming. Our little operation is strictly confidential, which is why I'll go alone. Tongues will wag if people see all of us together.

He brought out a small bottle of whisky and laced each man's coffee. They clinked mugs and toasted the success of their mission.

Secrecy was so vital that Pat slipped away before first light to avoid the possibility of being seen and revealing the whereabouts of the camp.

When he arrived, he saw wagons drawn up in a large orderly square which encompassed the entire fort. Women were cooking, washing and cleaning. Children played on the veld, chased by barking dogs. Chickens ran around aimlessly, pausing to scratch and peck at the ground. No one paid him any attention as he weaved his way through all this activity towards the fort. He asked a trooper for directions to Lieutenant Blake's office.

Blake looked relieved to see him. "I won't ask why Dr Jim sees fit to call on a civilian to do what is plainly police work but I'm sure he knows what he's doing. If you can find Captain Pierce's patrol or even discover what happened to them, it will be more than I've managed to do," he said.

"Looking around, Lieutenant Blake, I'd say you've already had to cope with more than any one man should be called upon to do. You haven't been told the full extent of why we're here. We've also been tasked with finding out who is behind the cattle raids that have stirred up things between the Ndebele and our people."

"I've seen reports which suggest a band of renegade settlers trying to make quick money selling cattle over the border is responsible. I've also heard that President Kruger has entered the fray."

"So you are in the picture. Let me tell you, in the strictest confidence, that there are those who believe that there is more behind these raids than meets the eye. There could well be a political motive behind them. If that's correct, you can see that the implications are enormous. That's why I cannot afford to fail. What I need from you is a starting point. Have you any sort of map of the area?"

The lieutenant pointed to a hand-drawn map on the wall. "There you are."

They walked over to the wall. Pat studied the map for a few minutes, "This is better than I had hoped for. I see that the allotted farms are mostly north east or west of here. I suppose the land is flatter there. I also note that all the cattle thefts are in these areas. Hardly surprising, I suppose."

"That's right, Mr van Zyl. South east and south is mainly rocky hills, kopje country. That's where the mining claims are. Umgandan, the local induna, has his *impi* scattered throughout the villages in the farming area."

"If you were leading the rustlers, once you had raided a village or a farm, where would you drive the cattle?"

"Into the kopjes, of course, and that's what Captain Pierce and I deduced."

"Dr Jameson told me that the cattle thefts have lessened recently. Is that still the case?"

"Yes. The last reported theft was about a month ago. The Ndebele are still angry though, so for the time being those who have taken refuge here will remain."

"What you've told me narrows things down. My starting point must be in the direction of the kopjes."

"I wish you luck, Mr van Zyl. Is there anything else I can do for you?"

"Yes, there is," said Pat. "You can let me make a copy of that map. Perhaps, by the time we've finished here, I can add a few details to it."

Pat copied the map carefully, expressed his thanks to the lieutenant, and left, promising to report back in about three weeks. And then as an afterthought he added, "If we're not back by then, report to Dr Jameson that the mission has failed and we must be presumed dead, but not to worry, we'll meet again."

He took a circuitous route back to camp where he arrived just before dark. As he slid from the saddle, Brian arrived with a cup of coffee while a trooper took his horse.

"Thanks, Brian. I needed that. I'm first going to wash some of the dust off and then I'll fill you in on what I've learned today."

He set off with mug in one hand and bucket, soap and towel in the other. At a small pool he filled his bucket and stood on a flat rock. He poured half the water over his head, letting it run down over his body, lathered himself with the soap, and rinsed off with the rest of the water. He felt greatly revived.

That evening Pat told the others what he had gleaned from his visit and then told them how he intended to begin the search.

"First, let me remind you that we have a two-fold task to accomplish. We are looking for Captain Pierce and his men and these so-called bandits. I have here a copy of the map Lieutenant Blake has on his wall. It is going to be very useful and already has been by showing the geography of the district. It narrows down the search area. We'll need one more copy. We'll work in a pattern that will cover the land which is interspersed with kopjes. That's where I think the gang will be lying up. Any questions so far?"

No one spoke. Pat laid out his map on the grass and pointed to their present position. Then he ran his finger over the search area.

"These four black dots represent the four points of the compass. If we draw a line between these points we have four wedges. Divide those in half and we have eight." Pat proceeded to draw the lines. "We will work in two patrols of three. Each patrol will walk out from the central point in extended line, but within sight of each other, on a compass bearing for seven hours. They then turn to their right and walk for one hour and make camp for the night. The following morning, we return to the starting point, having completed one wedge each. On this basis it will take eight days to search the area. I realise we won't cover every inch of ground but the chances of picking up some sign are pretty good, especially when you remember that these bandits have been herding cattle. Any questions now?"

Brian raised a hand. "You did say walk, didn't you, not ride?"

"That's right, Brian. Horses are too noisy and more conspicuous."

Grievous couldn't resist it, "What an idle sod, no consideration for his poor bloody horse that has had to haul his considerable bulk all this way and deserves a rest."

Brian shot back, "You might end up regretting you're not on horseback when you lose your way in the long grass, little man."

"Let's be serious," Pat admonished them. "If there's nothing else, let's split as follows. Troopers Bentley, Brown and Brian will patrol together. Grievous will be with Trooper Styles and myself."

Pat handed a sheet of paper and compass to Trooper Brown and told him to start copying the map.

"Let's be clear on one thing. If any of us encounter these bandits, don't try to engage them. You'll be outnumbered. If they are on the move, make a note on the map where you think you are and take a compass reading of the direction they are travelling in and then get back to the starting point. If you come across any rivers, check the bank as well as the river in either direction for signs. Before you cross any open land, check the way ahead from a height. The grass is long and dry at the moment and where a horse or human has passed through will become obvious if you get into the right position in relation to the sun. I'll show you tomorrow as we make our way to our location."

The men had listened carefully with occasional nods of agreement. "Another point," said Pat, "is to blacken up before we move out. I don't want to see any white skin. We'll carry charcoal from the fire in our kit. When you're on patrol, leave nothing in your pockets which will jangle as you walk. One last thing! We'll move into position after dark. You'll have to trust my night compass reading. I think that's all I've got to say." He yawned. "I'm going to turn in now. We start out at first light."

⊨⊢⊩

Pat's map indicated villages and these they avoided as they rode on a compass bearing towards a distant feature which would be the central and reference point from which each patrol would take its own bearings. About an hour's ride away from the feature he called a halt and they tethered the horses with sufficient length of rope to permit grazing. When darkness fell they moved forward to their starting point.

Pat, Grievous and Trooper Styles would cover the first half on the first wedge Troopers Bentley, Brown and Brian the second half of the first wedge, thus covering 45 degrees.

The universal and persistent alarm clock of the bushveld, the francolin, had them up at daybreak. Each pair took its compass bearing and they set off on the outward walk which would take them until noon.

Pat walked at his usual steady pace which left the shorter Grievous struggling to keep up, but which to his credit he managed stoically, with no more than a few mutters. At noon, the hottest part of the day, they rested for two hours and ate. They then continued further until it was time to turn right. After half an hour Pat noticed a line of larger greener trees to his left, a mile beyond their intended limit. They decided to investigate and found they were on the bank of a river, which was still running strongly in spite of the time of year. They split, Grievous and Styles going downstream while Pat walked in the opposite direction. They agreed to walk for thirty minutes and then return.

Some shallow rapids proved too inviting for Pat and he stopped, shed his clothes, quickly and permitted himself a luxurious few minutes' wallow. Crocodiles were not known to frequent shallow waters and he would quicken his pace to make up for the lost time. Wading back to the bank, something caught his eye. The sun was reflecting off something caught in a dead tree that had fallen into the water. He stumbled towards it. Whatever it was, it was out of character with the natural surroundings. At first he thought it was a belt with the sun shining off the buckle. He pulled it free and realised that what he had in his hand was a Sam Brown, the belt and shoulder strap worn by officers to support a sword and scabbard.

Clutching it tightly, he waded to the bank and sat down to examine this strange find. The belt looked chewed, probably by a wild animal, even a crocodile. He turned it over and noticed lettering stamped into the leather. A closer look revealed a name and number, N.W. Pierce, 37438. He felt sick as the awful reality struck him. He was handling the property of a dead man. There was no other explanation. Officers did not throw their Sam Browns into a river. No, this was more likely all that remained of a man thrown into the river and eaten by a crocodile. What of the others? Had they suffered the same fate? Pat finally surmised that Captain Pierce had caught up with the bandits, lost the initiative, and he and his men had perished.

He could hardly believe what he was thinking. He dressed and walked back to meet up with Grievous and Stiles who was waiting for him.

"What have you got there, Pat?"

Pat handed over the Sam Brown without speaking. Grievous turned it over and over in his hand. "I don't believe this," he said. "What do you suppose happened to the poor sod?"

"Think about it for a moment and you'll both reach the same conclusion that I have.

"You're thinking murder, aren't you? You think he was bumped off and his body tossed into the river," said Stiles.

"Correct, my friend, and I'll bet the same thing happened to his men. It explains why no one has found a trace of any of them. The bastards killed the entire patrol."

"I can't take this all in, Pat. Surely at least one of them would have escaped an ambush and been able to report back! They were professional soldiers."

"That's something we're going to have to try and find out. We'll head back tomorrow, collect the others, return to this spot, and patrol upstream. That's where it must have happened, close to the river."

They took a direct route to the starting point and arrived long before the others.

Brian came in and said, "I see you didn't manage to lose the little man in the long grass."

"This is not a time for flippancy, Wood-Gush," said Grievous. "Shut up and let Pat fill you in on what he's found."

Pat handed the Sam Brown from his pack to Brian, who turned it over to seek identification. His face paled and he handed it to Bentley for examination.

"Where did you find it, Pat? It looks like some wild animal has chewed it," exclaimed Brian.

"You're right. My guess is a crocodile because we found the belt in a river."

He related the details to them and gave his conclusions.

"So what's the next move?"

"We'll all go back tomorrow to where I found it, break into our two teams and patrol both banks upstream until we find something that might tell us what happened. At the same time keeping a sharp lookout for any other items of kit that might have been snagged on rocks or fallen trees."

The six-man patrol, now on horseback, arrived at where Captain Pierce's belt had been found by mid-morning. Before they continued, they took advantage of a quick dip in the shallow part of the river to cool off and wash.

"Listen to me," said Pat. "You're all too clean so blacken yourselves up again. I don't want to see any pale faces."

Grievous could not let this comment pass. "No matter how much make-up Wood-Gush applies to his mug, it doesn't make him look any prettier to look at, does it?"

"And I know who's looking for a facelift that won't improve his looks if he makes any more wisecracks," muttered Brian.

The men collected their horses and Brian, Styles and Bentley led theirs across the river. Fortunately, the noise of the rushing water did not impede a shouted conversation across it.

They had not gone far when Brian's voice halted them all. Brian was already wading into the water where he pulled out the shredded remains of a pair of trooper's breeches. Before long they had retrieved several items of military apparel. They also disturbed a large basking crocodile which splashed from the banks back into the river, and had the men hastily heading for the bank.

Then, in the afternoon, Brian waved his hat. "What have you found, Brian?" shouted Pat.

"Cattle," Brian shouted back. "I'm seeing hoof prints and dung, and plenty of it."

"Take the other two and search the area in a circle to see if you can find anything else," yelled Pat. "We'll do the same on this side. When you've finished, find a safe crossing point and join us here."

Pat's party turned away from the river but had gone less than fifty yards when Trooper Brown gave a shout and pointed to what appeared to be a dense copse of thorn bushes. Urging his horse closer, Pat found himself looking at what he could best describe as a natural *boma*. There was an entrance which led into a fairly large hollowed-out space big enough to conceal at least a dozen horses and their droppings. There were plenty of signs of human habitation: the remains of a fire and footprints. Pat even found a covered rubbish hole but the contents revealed no clues about whose debris it might have been.

Walking back to the river, Pat stumbled over a small rock but caught himself before he fell. He would have missed it if he had not tripped because there, partially covered by sand, was a brass cartridge case. He called the others and showed them his find and they scoured the area on hands and knees. They had to scoop deep into the sand as an obvious attempt had been made to bury the evidence, but they unearthed between them another fifteen shells.

Pat called a halt to the search and decided it was safe to build a small fire in the enclosure. He asked Grievous to prepare a meal; they had not eaten cooked food for a few days and even a plate of stiff maize porridge with gravy concocted from onions, a few sticks of biltong and some dried vegetables that Grievous had brought, would be a welcome change from their usual fare. Some strong coffee afterwards, laced with a tot of whisky, would also go down well.

Pat opened the discussion. "It's time to put our heads together and examine the facts. I think all of us have considered the evidence that we've discovered and reached a conclusion on what we believe has transpired. Let's start with you, George Brown. What are your thoughts?"

"Frankly, Pat, I think there's only one conclusion and I agree with you. Captain Pierce and his patrol were massacred here and, from the empty cartridge cases we've found, it happened on the bank of the river and the bodies were thrown into the water in the hope that they would be devoured by crocodiles. The cattle on the far bank indicate that this was the holding area for the stolen cattle and it would seem they have now been abandoned."

Pat looked at the others. "Does anyone have any different ideas?"

It looked as if they were all in accord. "Well," Pat continued, "the first part of our mission must be considered completed. The items found, together with Grievous' photographs of the area will provide exhibits in any future inquiry. Our next objective is to find these murdering bastards. We'll start tomorrow but I'm not optimistic about finding anything which tells us which direction they took. All we can do is move on to the west to our next reference point and adopt the same patrol pattern that led us here. That is unless anyone has a better idea."

The next reference point on the map was fifteen miles away and now there was an air of expectation amongst the men and they were anxious to get on with the task of finding the culprits. Their sense of eagerness saw them up early, throwing off of their blankets and wasting no time in saddling up.

The geography in this new area was different inasmuch that there was a greater profusion of granite kopjes. Massive boulders were piled haphazardly as if sifted through the fingers of a giant hand to create a spectacle of nature's architecture.

It was Brian and Tom Stiles' patrol that arrived late in the evening of the first day's exploration in a state of excitement. They drank thirstily from Pat's water bottle before joining the rest, who sat waiting for their report.

"It's hard to believe, but we found some ancient buildings from a bygone age, maybe a thousand years or more ago."

"Very nice, Wood-Gush," said Grievous, "but we're not on an archaeological expedition."

"Shut up, Grievous, before you become an archaeological specimen yourself," barked Brian.

"Yes, stop yapping, Grievous," said Pat. "Get on with it, please, Brian."

"We were on some high ground when we saw these ancient structures which, on first sight, seemed to be uninhabited. Then we thought we heard a horse neighing, but we couldn't be sure. Because of that, we decided to hang around for a while." Brian stopped for another long swig from the water bottle. "Sorry, but I'm parched. Anyway, after an hour, a man carrying a bucket emerged from an opening in the wall. He returned shortly with it full of water."

"Did you see any other signs of life?" asked Pat.

"No. We hung about for another hour and then it was time to make our way back here."

"What do you make of it?" Pat was becoming impatient.

"Pat, the man was white. He can only be part of the gang we are after. Why else would a white man be living in an ancient dwelling in the middle of the bush?"

"I'm sure you're right, Brian. Right, tomorrow we move towards this place. When Brian thinks we're about an hour away, he and I will go ahead on foot and the rest of you will follow two hours later. If we run into anything on our own, we'll backtrack and wait for you. The last thing we want now is to compromise ourselves. All being well, we'll find a suitable base and leave the horses. From then on, we'll work in pairs and take shifts to observe until we can ascertain their numbers and spot anything else which will help us to make a plan."

That night Pat slept fitfully as he wrestled with the events of the last few days. He felt that the next two would be decisive and he worried about the consequences should he fail. Unless these bandits were stopped, the whole territory could erupt into a war between Lobengula's *impis* and the white settlers. This would jeopardise all Rhodes' plans for the whole country. Failure for this mission was out of the question.

They moved to their new base without incident. Pat and Brian went forward to the observation point and made themselves as comfortable as possible by burrowing into a conveniently placed bush.

Below them, a half mile away, stood this ancient stone structure standing in an open space about the size of a cricket field. Close on one side was a wooded area. Pat used his binoculars to search for a sentry. It was some time before he spotted him, perched on the highest point of the perimeter wall in a section shaded by a single tree with an overhanging branch. Any approach on horseback would have been easily seen.

Occasionally a man would come into view within the walls, sometimes two, but never more together. By the end of their watch they had counted six individuals, including the sentry. Add to that a man on water duty, who was seen several times during the day.

The next day Bentley and Brown counted the same number. If Grievous and Styles came up with the same number or less, Pat figured it was safe to assume that seven was the number in the gang. Again the water detail emerged more than once.

Grievous reported seeing four men, including the sentry. He had also identified one black man, whom Pat concluded must be an interpreter or a guide. That left six whites. The descriptions Grievous gave of the white men he had seen tallied with his own observations.

"It looks like a one-on-one situation, Pat"

"You're right, Grievous. I think we can safely assume we're up against six men. Now let me ask George something. George, did you notice anything special about the men down there?"

"Yes, I did."

"What was it?"

"They're not your average run-of-the-mill cowboys. They have a definite military bearing about them."

"Thank you, George. That's exactly what I thought, but I wanted a military man to confirm it."

Grievous said, "Hell, it sounds like Mr Rhodes' suspicions could be right. If these men are part of General Viljoen's army, this is dynamite. What a scoop!"

"Correct, Grievous, so be ready with your camera. We now know a lot more of what we're up against."

Brian rubbed his stubbly jaw and said, "Now all we have to do is find a way of winkling them out."

"We did it at Chua so there's no reason why we can't do it here. Remember, we were greatly outnumbered there," said Pat, "but if these are Viljoen's men, they'll be some of the best. So, let's consider the facts. If we're right and these are the villains we're after, they are guilty of cattle stealing and murder, including Captain Pierce's patrol. What else do we know?"

We know," said Brian, "that there's been a lull in their operations, probably under orders, and that they are holed up here, likely awaiting further instructions. How would they receive those instructions, stuck out here?"

"They must have a contact in Victoria who is at the end of a communication chain that stretches back to Pretoria," Pat suggested. "Their masters have the resources for that."

"So what do we do?"

"I think we'll have to use Trojan Horse tactics again. We must capture the man with the bucket when he goes on his first trip of the day, but he won't return with the water. I will. And it won't be water in the bucket because it will be full of surprises."

"You sound confident," said Grievous. "When do we move in on them?"

"The day after tomorrow. We need another day to study their movements and I need time to fill that bucket with the surprises I have in mind and to make some plans. Grievous, start taking some pictures while the rest of you alternate on the observation point."

An addition to his arsenal, apart from the Vital Organs he had fabricated in his forge at Salisbury, was what Pat called his Saucer Bomb. This looked like an oversized saucer and was primed with a charge of sawn up horse shoes. The explosive was packed up against it and held in place by a flour sack cut to size and tied up like a suet pudding. When ready for use, the bomb stood on edge and was triggered by a pull-string percussion cap. The blast would blow forward, that being the area of least resistance. Pat had enough materials to make two of them. His original thought was to use them in an ambush. Now they would have a different role.

There was an interested audience as he assembled them. That done they had a training session with the Vital Organs and made sure their own weaponry was in good working order.

That evening, he was told that the water detail, though irregular with his trips, had also carried a bundle of firewood back.

"That's perfect," said Pat with enthusiasm.

"Why?" asked Grievous.

"Let's sit down and I'll give you my plan of attack. As I said yesterday, it's the old Trojan Horse trick again. It's the best I can come up with, but any alternative ideas will be welcomed. A conventional frontal approach is too risky and that includes sneaking up on them at night. The water detail is the key. Tom and I are going to ambush him. Brian, you will be my back-up, carrying a Vital Organ, and Tom will then join you.

"Once the bucket man has been overpowered, we strip him, gag him and tie him to a tree. If all goes to plan, he could be the only survivor and we'll definitely need one prisoner to take back with us. I will make a small hole in the side of the bucket and thread through some thin cord which is attached to the detonator and then inserted into this hole in the saucer. The bucket is a quarter filled with pebbles and the saucer bomb is placed in it with the pebbles placed around and under the bomb. This will ensure that the bucket stands upright when placed on the ground."

Using their own canvas bucket, Pat demonstrated the procedure. "George, this is where you come in as you're the best marksman, according to John Erasmus. You will be the sniper. It'll be your responsibility to take out the sentry on the wall. When Tom and I move out tomorrow, you'll come with us. I'll place you where you'll have a good all-round view as well as a clear line of fire to the sentry. You will initiate the attack. When you see me enter through the side door with the bucket and a bundle of firewood on my shoulder, which will help to disguise me, you take out the sentry. This will create a diversion as I enter. While attention is drawn towards the sentry, I'll have a few seconds to assess my surroundings and place the bucket where it can do the most damage. I'll then beat a hasty retreat. The long detonator cord will lessen the likelihood of injury from the back blast. Brian, you and Tom will have followed me, but wait for the detonation before making an entrance. Drop the tripod and let rip into the melee with the

Organ."   Turning now to trooper Stiles, Pat said, Norman "Your job is to cover the front entrance. Set up your Organ and shoot anyone trying to break out that way. Grievous, you'll be behind Norman with your camera. George, you come down from your sniper's post and pitch in with Norman. Think about it and let me know your thoughts."

Brian asked, "What happens if your ruse fails and they see through your disguise early or if the black man is the water carrier?"

"You've identified the trickiest part of the operation, Brian. If they see through the disguise, then all I can do is chuck the bucket in their direction and hope I don't end up kicking it, if you'll excuse the pun. If I'm out of action, Brian, you take over and abort, because the element of surprise will be over. The signal to abort will be two short blasts on a whistle I'll give you. Wait a few seconds and repeat it. You will not have failed as you'll still have your captive. Take him to Victoria and message Dr Jim. If the water detail is the black man, Tom, Brian and I will remain hidden and return here. The rest of you will have seen the black man exiting so you too will return here. We will try again the next day."

"I can see why you were chosen ahead of a military man, Pat," said George. "I think you have a very workable plan."

"Not bad for a blacksmith!" Grievous added. This comment relieved some of the tension. The men mulled over the plan, looking for flaws.

"If there's nothing else, we'll break until daylight," said Pat.

Pat checked that the men were well blacked up before they left, tense but eager to get on with the job. They started out in single file.

Grievous and Norman diverted to their allotted cover position which faced the front entrance to the enclosure. George was perched in a tree before first light. Pat, Brian and Tom were in position by then. They had taken a wide detour through the woods and were in cover behind some bushes a few yards off the path that the water carrier would take.

Pat's plan for overpowering the man was simple. He would let him pass, break cover behind him, before hitting him behind the ear with a cosh. The man would be stripped and gagged, with his canvas bucket tied over his head before he was handcuffed to a stout tree. Brian had collected firewood earlier in case of need and they carried their own bucket, already primed.

It was mid-morning before Pat heard the sound of booted feet approaching along the path. No native wore boots in the bush so the waiting was over. The adrenalin coursed through his cramped muscles and he was ready for action.

The moment the man passed, Pat rose silently from the undergrowth and his cosh found its mark dully but effectively on the man's skull. He fell without a sound. Within a few minutes he was stripped and his hands were handcuffed behind him around a thick tree trunk. Next came the gag and finally the bucket.

Pat, now dressed in their prisoner's clothes and hat, picked up the firewood and Brian passed him the bucket with a mark on it to indicate the business side. "How do I look, Brian?" he asked.

"You're about the right size so you should have no problem."

"Wish me luck." He began his walk up the path towards the entrance. Before he broke cover from the woodland, he felt perspiration running down his back and his mouth was so dry, his lips seemed stuck to his teeth.

He was about to enter the opening in the wall when, right on cue, the shot rang out and Pat, in spite of anticipating it, was startled by the noise. Then he was inside. Before the dead sentry's body hit the ground, Pat had taken in the scene. On his right, men were scrambling for their weapons. He checked that the bucket was facing correctly in their direction before he dropped his firewood, placed the bucket down, turned and ran towards the opening with the cord unravelling from his index finger. Five, six, seven paces, but where was the big bang? Then the heart-stopping reality hit him. The detonator must have failed.

Brian and Tom were at the entrance as Pat placed the bucket; Brian had the Vital Organ while Tom had the butt of his rifle into his shoulder. Pat was bolting towards them, pulling at the detonator cord but nothing was happening. Pat screamed, "Shoot the bloody bucket, Tom!" Without hesitation, Tom aimed and fired. There was a mighty thunderclap that shook the ground and a great cloud of dust enveloped everything. Pat reached the other two and Brian, who had his Organ trained on the area where he had last seen the enemy, began to let rip. He fired one barrel and then altered the angle slightly before letting loose the next. He emptied three barrels before he stopped. There was one left, as planned. Pat's rifle was off his back and he and Tom strafed the area furiously, the heat from the ejected shell cases searing their cheeks.

A gust of wind suddenly dispersed the dust and the horror was revealed like the curtain-up, final scene of a macabre play.

Pat saw the other half of his team standing across the way looking for a target that was no longer there. They converged on the shrapnel shredded bodies of what had once been men and horses. Pat felt sick in his stomach at the devastation he had wreaked. It would take a long time for this awful picture to recede from his mind, if it ever did. Grievous was in action with his camera, shuffling about to satisfy its hungry lens.

Pat gripped Tom's shoulder. "You saved the day, Tom, and probably our lives with it. Thank you."

Tom nodded and they moved forward to look for any possible survivors. One man weakly raised an arm and Pat and Brian went over to him. Pat propped the man's head on a saddle and began to examine his wounds. He was beyond help. Pat bent down and asked him if he would like some water. The man nodded feebly and Pat held up his head and poured a little into his mouth, but he coughed most of it up.

"Who are you?" Pat asked gently. "Where are you from?" The man turned his head and Pat put his ear next to his mouth. "I'm sorry, men …" but he never completed his final word. His head suddenly lolled back. He was dead.

Pat looked at Brian. "You know what that final word was, don't you?"

"Aye, Pat."

Looking down at the man, Pat whispered, "And I'm sorry too, *meneer*, but we were both following orders."

The others gathered round but no one spoke for what seemed a long time. Pat stood up. "Our work isn't yet finished, gentlemen. Before we bury these people, let's search them and their belongings for further evidence of who they are."

They each took a body to search. Pat chose the one who had just died. The pockets revealed nothing. He picked up the wide-brimmed hat, looking for a name on the inside leather sweat band and was about to discard it when he noticed the edge of a piece of paper protruding from it.

He took it out and unfolded it and there was the evidence they were looking for. Why the man had kept it was a mystery and open to speculation? It read in freehand Afrikaans, *'Op 15 November kan julle aangan met julle werk'.* Pat translated it for the others. "On November 15 you are to resume operations." It was signed V. There was no heading to the paper, nor any watermark, but Pat was in no doubt who the author was. A handwriting expert would prove it conclusively, he was sure.

The men worked long into the night burying the soldiers for to leave the work unfinished would be to attract the hyenas.

⊶⊷

Nearby, Nyati and his companion, who had concealed themselves in the bushes, slipped quietly away into the darkness, stunned by what they had witnessed. Picking up the game path and with their spears at the trailing position, they trotted off in the direction of their kraal.

><+ +>

The moon was full and high as Pat and his men made their way back to their camp. Too tired to eat, they secured their prisoner and then, to a man, they fell upon their blankets and were instantly asleep.

One of Van Driel's mounts had miraculously escaped the carnage and they found it grazing outside the walled enclosure the following morning. George Brown was delegated to find a halter and catch it. It would be put to good use carrying the weapons and anything else worth taking back to Victoria with them. Lieutenant Blake's men could collect the saddlery later.

CHAPTER TWENTY-ONE

P at sat opposite Lieutenant Blake a week after their last meeting. He had ridden on ahead of his returning party of men.

"I bring good news and bad news, lieutenant," he said. "The bad news is that Captain Pierce and his patrol perished, shot down in cold blood. The good news is that we have accounted for the men who did the deed. I won't elaborate now, but I'm sure you'll hear the full story in time. I have indicated on your very useful map where the stolen cattle are located. They won't have strayed far from the river. I suggest you round them up and return them to Gungunyana and tell him that the thieves have been found and justice meted out. Emphasise that these were not our people, but opportunists from across the Limpopo. Hopefully this will help to convince him to leave our local farmers and miners alone and allow them to return to their homesteads."

Blake was shaking his head in disbelief, "I am greatly saddened to hear of the loss of Captain Pierce's patrol, Mr van Zyl, but I had begun to fear the worst. I am grateful to you and your men for tracking down the perpetrators and I am optimistic that returning the king's cattle will allow life to settle down here. I'm sure I speak for everyone by thanking you most sincerely."

"We're all in this together and I have as much at stake in this new land as anyone, perhaps more than some. I've updated your map as best I can. This dot is where we made contact with the people from across the border. It is an interesting archaeological site with ancient stone structures. We've left there a lot of equipment which you may like to recover after you've rounded up the cattle."

The weary saddle-sore men arrived in Salisbury four days later and there would be at least two overjoyed young ladies in the community that day.

Before they entered the town, Pat led them to the spot where he and Brian had first been spotted naked in the river by those same young ladies and they were all soon stripped naked, splashing in the water, and passing soap back and forth as they removed several days of grime from their bodies. They all sported plenty of facial growth so water was heated over a fire and razors were applied.

The three troopers and Grievous saw their prisoner safely behind bars before making for the beer hall at the top of the hill for some food and drink. Brian headed for the Graham's house.

"Brian, please tell Sandra I'll be along as soon as I've finished reporting to Dr Jim."

Dr Jim sat in his favourite place under the big tree, enjoying a sundowner with one of his aides. On seeing Pat, his look of surprise changed to a broad smile and he rose and shook hands warmly.

"I'm so pleased to see you, Pat," he said, "and not a little relieved. Sit down and have a drink. I'm sure we have lots to talk about." He introduced his friend, who after an exchange of pleasantries excused himself and left the two men, sensing that they were about to discuss important and probably confidential issues.

Pat described the events of the past couple of weeks and Dr Jameson took it all in without interrupting once. Only his eyes registered the level of his emotions.

"So Mr Rhodes' hunch, yours too, was correct," Pat concluded.

"Just confirm you have the prisoner in the cells. What's his name, by the way?"

"Pieter van der Berg and, yes, he is safely locked up at the police camp."

"The name alone is evidence enough. My sincere congratulations must go to you and your men. You did a great job. The evidence of Viljoen's note, the captured soldier, combined with Mr Grieve's pictures will give us a watertight case. You've completed your mission and from now on it's a political matter. It's up to Mr Rhodes how he proceeds with the information. I'd like to interview *Meneer* van der Berg. Has he confessed to anything yet?"

"No," replied Pat. "We haven't actually questioned him. I thought it best to leave that to you. Your powers of persuasion are probably better than mine and a lot more subtle."

"Let's hope so, Pat. I'll report all this to Mr Rhodes immediately. The task of taking this evidence to Lobengula will likely fall to me. If so, I'll take Moffat along to help me convince the king that there has been a conspiracy. This should avert any more bloodshed and we can get on with our lives."

"If that's all, doctor, I'll leave you now and go to see Sandra before she comes looking for me."

"I rather think you'd better do that. We'll talk some more in the morning."

Pat did not see Sandra sitting on a log in Dr Jim's garden, waiting for him. She came out of the dark and threw herself at him. Had it not been for her perfume, he might have struck out in defence. His nerves hadn't yet settled after his latest adventures. He landed on his back with Sandra on top of him.

"Patrick van Zyl, you wretched stay-away, why have you been so long?" she cried.

He exclaimed breathlessly, "I see you've been building up your strength while I've been away. Believe me, I took not a day longer than was necessary and I've missed you beyond words. Every night for these past few weeks, I have fallen asleep with thoughts only of you. The vision of you was what kept me going. Now it's all over and there should be no more parting. Well, perhaps only briefly." He drew her close and kissed her lips, again and again. He could not have enough of her, nor she of him.

At last he said, "If you'll let me up, I think it's time I paid my respects to your family, young lady. Don't you think so?"

Reluctantly, she agreed and they got up and brushed themselves down.

Joe and Madge Graham and Brian and Margie were sitting out on the veranda. Pat embraced Madge and shook hands warmly with Joe.

"Welcome back, Pat," said Joe. "It's good to see you lads back in one piece."

Pat smiled. "Thanks, Joe. I just hope that the politicians can sort out their side of things. There's not much else we can do."

"I won't ask you now what you've been doing. It's not the right time. I'm sure you'll tell me when you're ready."

"We'll do that, Joe. Thanks for your understanding. It's not a pretty tale."

"How long before you're off somewhere else?" sighed Margie.

Brian looked at Pat. "You're the best one to answer that," he said.

"We could be here a while. I have to see Dr Jim again in the morning and he has to communicate with Mr Rhodes and await his reply. That will determine our next move."

***

Pat, Brian and Grievous sat in the cramped space in front of Dr Jameson's desk.

"Our first task this morning," said the doctor, "is to interview the prisoner, so let's get started on that."

Throughout the journey from Victoria to Salisbury Van der Berg had spoken only when necessary and none of them had made any attempt at conversation with him. He was neither sullen nor cheerful, merely resigned. It would be interesting to see how he responded to questioning.

The police station was primitive but more substantial than any neighbouring buildings. It was made of brick under iron roofing. There were two cells and their prisoner was the only occupant. They crowded into his cell. Dr Jameson sat opposite the man while the other three stood against a wall. The interview began.

"Good morning. My name is Dr Jameson and I am told you are *Meneer* van der Berg. I understand you are a regular soldier in the Transvaal Republic army. Is that correct?"

"I am not a soldier. I am a hunter. My friends and I were on a hunting trip when, without provocation or reason, we were attacked and my friends were killed by those men." He pointed at Pat, Brian and Grievous.

"That is your version, *meneer*. Their version is that had they not acted as they did, your group would have killed them as you killed Captain Pierce and his patrol, who were trying to find out who was behind the theft of Lobengula's cattle."

"I don't know what you are talking about."

"And I'm sure you do, *meneer.*"

Jameson reached into an inside pocket of his jacket and brought out a sheet of paper. He passed it across to Van der Berg. "Look at that. It's in Afrikaans, but I'm sure you can read it."

Van der Berg's face turned ashen. "Where did you get this?"

"Mr van Zyl found it in the sweat band of your commander's hat." Without waiting for a reply, he said, "You see, my friend, when these cattle raids commenced, we figured that there was some sort of a conspiracy. If it hadn't been for Mr van Zyl and his men, your masters may have got away with it. I'll also tell you that this matter goes higher up the ladder than your General Viljoen. There were a couple of other things that gave away your identity, your horses' shoes, for example. Mr van Zyl is a blacksmith who has lived in South Africa and he recognised the distinguishing characteristics of the shoes that belong to your army. We have one of your horses, remember? The ballistics will also prove that it was your weapons that killed Captain Pierce and his men." Dr Jameson opened his hand to reveal six empty cartridge cases.

"Now, what are we going to do with you?" he continued. "The evidence we have is certainly enough to get a conviction for murder and for that you will hang. On the other hand, a confession together with a signed statement confirming that you were acting under orders from General Viljoen would make our case watertight and this would be to your advantage. I'm sure, given time, we could arrange a change of identity for you."

Van der Berg had been listening quietly and Pat could almost read his thoughts. At the mention of hanging, the man's face had registered horror, but had visibly relaxed when Dr Jim spoke of a change of identity. "He'll go for this," thought Pat. Then he had another thought.

"Excuse me, Dr Jim. I'm sorry to interrupt, but there is one other thing."

"What have I forgotten, Pat?"

"*Meneer* van der Berg must also agree to help us resolve things with Lobengula by admitting to him in person that he and his comrades were responsible for the theft of the king's cattle. Grievous' photographs will provide evidence that retribution has been meted out."

"A good point! Thank, you, Pat. What is your answer, *meneer?*"

"*Ja*, Doctor Jameson. I will do as you say for a change of identity and your protection until I am released."

"So be it." He turned to Grievous. "Mr Grieve, I have one last request of you. Please take this man's photograph, both with his beard and after he has shaved. I will need that to send with the statement."

Back at the office, the doctor again addressed Grievous. "I was wondering, Mr Grieve, if you have typed up your story yet."

"I haven't, but it shouldn't take me long. I wrote the outline in pencil on the way to Salisbury."

"How long would it take you?"

"If I can borrow a typewriter, no more than a couple of hours."

"Good. You can borrow mine and start straight away. Use the table outside. The sooner we get everything off to Mr Rhodes, the better. Last night I wrote a report based on what you've told me, Pat. All I need to add are the details of our talk with van der Berg. As soon as that is completed and Mr Grieve has written his story, the despatch rider and his escort will leave for Tuli."

"Where exactly is Mr Rhodes now?" Pat enquired.

"He's still in Cape Town."

"Would it not be quicker to send the despatch to Beira for on-ward transmission to Cape Town by mail ship? You see, we have discovered a short cut from the diggings to the Beira Road and we're now using it to transport the diamonds. It cuts out Umtali. I can probably be in Beira in two weeks. Allow another week at sea and Mr Rhodes should receive the envelope in about three weeks' time. Because of the importance of these documents, I would pre-fer to see them on board ship myself. What do you think?"

"It's a logical solution, but what is Miss Sandra Graham going to say about that?"

"I'll take her with me if she'll come."

"I think she'll probably insist on going with you, Pat," chuckled Brian. "Why don't Margie and I join you and make a party of it? We could all benefit from a bit of sea air."

"Sounds good, Brian, but what about old Grievous here?"

"Seeing that you two are womanising, I think I'll deviate on the way back to the mine and see Sister Margaret and check on the value of my shares there. That is, if you two have no objection."

Pat said, "A good idea, Grievous. It's about time you had a bit of sympathetic nursing."

"Huh!" said Brian. "Is that what you call it?"

Grievous broke in, "Please excuse the vulgar innuendo, doctor. He is a depraved soul and it never ceases to amaze me how he managed to hoodwink the lovely Margie into believing he was a man of flawless character."

The banter and laughter continued a while longer.

CHAPTER TWENTY-TWO

Rhodes was at his home at Groote Schuur when Pickering delivered the envelope from Dr Jameson and placed it on his desk. Seeing who it was from, he stared at it for several anxious moments as if trying to guess its contents.

"Do you want me to open it for you, sir?" asked Pickering, beginning to feel impatient.

"Never mind, Neville. I was just wondering about the surprises that lie within." He picked it up, slit it open and placed the contents on his desk. There was a small parcel marked 'Photographic film; open only in a photographic darkroom', along with two envelopes, one addressed to Hon. C J Rhodes Esq., the other marked 'News story by Times correspondent, Colin Grieve'.

Rhodes read the one addressed to himself first. "Bloody hell, Neville!" he exclaimed loudly. "It's as I suspected. The whole thing was a conspiracy. That bloody dung-smoking Dutchman is behind it, as I thought. The evidence is right here." He held up the piece of paper Pat had found in Van Driel's sweatband in one hand and in the other he had the confession by van der Berg.

"What do you intend to do with the evidence, Mr Rhodes?" Pickering took a seat opposite Rhodes.

"With this evidence, I have Kruger right where I want him. I'm going to screw that Dutchman right into the ground."

"I would expect nothing less from you."

"Read it all for yourself, Neville." Rhodes handed the documents across to his assistant, who examined them closely.

"This is red hot stuff, sir," Pickering said and handed them back.

"You can say that again and do you know what else, Neville? I bet that bastard Barnato has his finger in this somewhere as well. I don't know the precise details about how Van Zyl pulled it off, but I knew that if anyone could, it would be him. I owe him and his friends a great deal."

He continued, "We still have to square things with Lobengula and get him back on our side and I think I might do that myself. It won't be easy. If my information is correct, Viljoen has already been up there to reveal how we hoodwinked the king with Barney Barnato's guns. Still, in our favour is that the king has had his cattle returned to him and there's Van der Berg's confession and Grieve's photographs, which I'm sure will be revealing when we see them. I just have to convince him that he's better off dealing with Queen and country through me. He's been the victim of so much subterfuge that he's bound to be wary of any proposition put to him by a white man, whoever he is. I'll have to find a good argument from somewhere, Neville."

"You'll think of something, I'm sure," Neville said quietly.

"Get that film to a photographer, one who knows how to keep his mouth shut. I want three prints of each and make sure you get the negatives back. I'll also need three copies of Viljoen's note and Van der Berg's statement."

The photographs were sensational when he saw them. Colin Grieve certainly knew his craft. The pictures told a story, starting with a shot of the men involved in the mission, one of Pat holding up Captain Pierce's Sam Brown, followed by the other items recovered from the river. There was even a picture of a huge crocodile basking on the river bank. There were shots of Van Driel's camp with its natural thorn camouflage and of the empty cartridges lying in the sand. There were even photographs of the stolen cattle grazing across the river.

The next batch was of the ancient stone dwellings taken from the high ground of their observation post. Then came an elevated view of the battle ground with the gory remains of Van Driel's men lying scattered and torn apart. There were pictures of all six men and the prisoner, Van der Berg, and finally a close-up of a horse's hoof with the shoe showing the tell-tale markings of a mount from the stables of the army of the Transvaal Republic.

Colin Grieve's story was concise; he had made no attempt to embellish it. The events were sensational enough.

Rhodes sat late into the night mulling over the matter. He would use the power of the press to humiliate Kruger, of course. He tried to imagine the outcry when this story appeared in The Times. There would be plenty of denials from Viljoen, but the weight of evidence from his own note and Van der Berg's confession would be overwhelming. Rhodes and his settlers would be exonerated and his detractors in Britain, especially those in the Houses of Parliament, would be silenced and shamed for doubting his integrity. Surely, the Company's share value would then soar.

He knew that Kruger had designs on the trans-Limpopo territory but why the sudden interest? Could this be where the Barnato factor crept in? Had Barney gone running to Kruger with news of the new diamond field? Was that the motivation? If true, it would be sweet revenge for Barney, but he had also probably negotiated a claim for himself as his reward. He couldn't prove this, but he was fairly sure he was right. Either way, any dreams Barney had of further riches from the new territory were now shattered. Rhodes smiled in satisfaction. The next time he saw Barney, he would rub some salt into the wound.

His last waking thoughts were about how to deal with Lobengula.

━╬╫╤━

Cecil Rhodes was enjoying his favourite breakfast of Scottish kippers, his Saturday morning treat. He picked up his copy of The Argus. The three column headline at the foot of the front page caught his eye: 'Total Eclipse of the Sun on July 18'. The story explained that when the sun and the moon perfectly crossed paths in the sky, the moon, being closer to the earth, blots out the sun's rays and casts its shadow over a small part of the earth's surface. It went on to say that the likelihood increases when the earth approaches its furthest distance from the sun, which is usually in July. In this instance, the eclipse track would fall not too far north of Tuli. That would put it around GuBulawayo, King Lobengula's royal kraal.

His mind raced as he pondered the significance of this and how he could best use it to his advantage. He knew that witchcraft played a big part in the daily lives of the black people and all sorts of spiritual interpretations were read into scientific phenomena such as this. They were omens.

Here was the advantage he was looking for, a fortuitous windfall. Today was June 28 and it was imperative that he be in the presence of Lobengula on July 18 at all costs when the eclipse occurred, which would be around 1100 hours. He had to move fast.

He first mailed Grievous' story with one set of pictures to James Robertson at The Times. Another copy of both the story and the pictures went to the editor of The Argus in Cape Town, but later as he did not want to pre-empt The Times publication.

The Cape parliament was in recess which conveniently allowed Rhodes the time he needed to travel north. He telegraphed Captain Dobson to send a message to Dr Jameson, telling him to meet him at GuBulawayo on July 17 at the latest, without fail, and to prevail upon John Moffat to be present too. He then asked Pickering to book him on the train to Johannesburg the next day. From there he would proceed on horseback to GuBulawayo, carrying his equipment and provisions on mules. This was the quickest way to reach his destination. He must get there on time if his plan was to succeed.

Accompanying Rhodes was his manservant, Tony de la Cruz, a Mozambican of mixed race, and Pickering. They travelled without mishap and made good time. A night stop at Tuli with a comfortable bed in the hotel was their only indulgence during the hard ride. Captain Dobson and one of his troopers joined the party for the final leg.

Both Moffat and Jameson had already arrived at the royal kraal and were settled under the trees on the banks of the Umgasa River. Rhodes took a hot bath and dressed in clean clothes before he joined them.

He opened the conversation by addressing Rev. Moffat. "Reverend John, let me first apologise for dragging you away from your work. Thank you for being here. Your influence with Lobengula could be vital. Perhaps Dr Jameson has already told you of the recent shocking events and Kruger's undoubted involvement through his agent, General Viljoen."

"I must confess to being dumbfounded when I heard the news," replied Moffat.

"Let me tell you all how I intend to proceed. Confirm that we have a meeting with the king tomorrow."

John Moffat nodded his head. "Everything's arranged, Cecil. Tell, me, why is it so important to meet with the king tomorrow?"

Rhodes outlined his plan. There was silence for a while. Then Moffat said, "As a man of the cloth, I suppose I should condemn your claim to supernatural powers, however hypothetical they are. Still, if it brings a halt to the current wave of unrest and bloodshed, it serves a useful purpose and so I must go along with it."

Rhodes noticed a man sitting in leg irons not far away. "Is that Van der Berg, Jim?"

"It is, Cecil. We brought him along to corroborate our story."

"Good thinking, Jim."

It was half past ten the next morning when Rhodes, Jameson and Moffat sat in the royal enclosure awaiting the arrival of the king. Tony de la Cruz stood behind them. Rhodes had met Lobengula twice previously and made a good impression because of his reputation, which may well have been embellished, but was awesome enough without that. The king did not keep them waiting.

As Lobengula approached, the three men, wearing suits and hats, rose together, doffed their hats, and made a bow that was little more than a nod of the head. Tony, who spoke fluent Zulu, of which Ndebele was an offshoot tongue, would interpret.

The formalities completed, Rhodes checked his fob watch. It was 10.45 am.

"O Slayer of elephants," he began, "I have come to speak to you about the theft of your cattle and the harassment of your people. I want to prove to you that those responsible are not my people."

"Who is responsible, then?" Lobengula growled.

"It is the people of the Transvaal, O Man Mountain. Their leader, Kruger, sent his men to steal your cattle, knowing that you would blame my people and cancel our agreement. That would let him into your kingdom to look for the *egoli* and the bright stones. He has already sent his induna, Viljoen, to see you, with promises of cattle if you let them in. I know of these things."

The king sighed. "You, too, have deceived me, Mr Lodie, with your present of guns whose bullets do not fire straight or far."

Rhodes was well rehearsed for this accusation. He had no intention of revealing how he had taken the guns from Barnato, who had intended to cheat the king in the first place.

"It looks that way, but it was I who was cheated when I bought the guns. There was but one box of shot that was correct. The remainder were for an obsolete gun. The powder had been subdued which is why the bullets do not fly far. My agent, Mr van Zyl, an expert with guns, brought them to you without knowing this. He realised the problem only when he was teaching you how to shoot. His decision was not to disappoint you or embarrass me, so he went ahead, but he had every intention of correcting the error as soon as possible. I have now brought with me the correct bullets and full-strength powder. I humbly apologise for the inconvenience this has caused you."

Dr Jameson kept a straight face. Lobengula looked at Rhodes sceptically. Rhodes noted that the point of the eclipse was swiftly approaching.

He said, "I speak the truth, King Lobengula, as true as it is that I can turn the day into night and back to day."

Before the king could reply, Rhodes stood abruptly and spread his arms towards the sky in a dramatic pose. He closed his eyes and babbled meaninglessly for a few seconds and then stopped. Suddenly a strong wind sprang up and the silence was broken only by the sound of leaves rustling. The birds ceased their song and darkness descended. It became cold.

The king prostrated himself on the ground and moaned. His subjects followed suit, including his witchdoctors.

Rhodes held his pose a little longer and then began babbling again as slowly the sun reappeared from the opposite side of the moon. The king rolled over and looked first at Rhodes, then at the sun through shielding fingers. He shook his head in bewilderment. He stood shakily and slumped back onto his throne. He reached for his calabash and drank copiously until it was empty.

Rhodes sat and smiled reassuringly at the king. "Fear not, Mighty Elephant. It is over. Now do you believe me?"

"I see that you speak the truth, Mr Lodie. A man who can turn day into night has no need to lie."

Rhodes produced Grievous' photographs. He showed the first to the king. "Here is Mr van Zyl, who brought you the guns. He and the others in the picture hunted down these people from the Transvaal and killed them." Pointing to Van der Berg, he continued, "That man is the only survivor and is now our prisoner. Your cattle should have been returned to you by now."

The king, fortified by the beer, was more composed and had regained some of his dignity. "It is true. My cattle have been returned to my induna, Gungunyana." A sly grin creased his face. "You may wish to learn, Mr Lodie, that I already know the truth of this matter."

Rhodes, for once, looked bemused. "I do not understand, O Wise One."

"Hah, you do not know everything, Mr Lodie. You may be able to darken the sun, but I have a thousand eyes and ears. One of my warriors, a man named Nyati, saw the killing of Doctor Jimmy's polisa at the river and he was watching at the village of the ancients when your man Van Zyl took his revenge."

It took a few moments for Rhodes to digest this news. Then he smiled. "You are indeed an all-knowing and mighty king, Lobengula. I salute you."

"I, too, have misjudged you, Mr Lodie. You have caught and punished those who would steal my cattle and kill my people to cause bad blood between us. Because of this, I will continue to honour the agreement that gives your people the right to dig for the *egoli.*" He paused and began to giggle. "But, I think from now on we should talk about royalties."

Rhodes sighed. "Yes, I agree to that, but for now please accept my gift to you of two hundred cattle to add to your royal herds. They will arrive soon. Now let there be peace between us."

The previous tension had dissipated and everyone was smiling. Rhodes felt that he had carried the day. He turned to Jameson and

Moffat and said softly, "I was beginning to think we were not going to make it."

Jameson said, "I think you've missed your vocation in life. You could audition and win a major part in a stage production in London."

"Amen to that," chuckled Moffat.

"I think that concludes our business here, gentlemen," Rhodes declared. "We should be moving on."

"I'm afraid not, Cecil," said Jameson. "We won't get away from here until that smelly pot has done a few rounds. To refuse would insult the king and undo everything your play acting has achieved."

"I was forgetting. I hate that dreadful brew."

It was an hour before they were permitted to take their leave of the king and Rhodes did so with promises to return as soon as he could.

That evening, sitting around the fire, Rhodes turned to his companions. "I would like to think that today's agreement puts an end to the problems of my relations with the Ndebele people and my ambition to colonise this territory, but I fear that will not be the case. The road ahead contains many obstacles before that can happen. Today we have merely circumvented one of them."

CHAPTER TWENTY-THREE

Grievous' story, together with a picture of Captain Pierce, his chewed Sam Brown, Viljoen, the Boer general, and the captured member of the commando, Van der Berg, took up the whole of the front page of The Times. It was sensational and the editor, James Robertson, ordered another twenty thousand copies printed and they too quickly sold out.

Lord Salisbury sat with his Colonial Secretary in his office. The Times was on his desk. "It seems, Knuttie, that Cecil Rhodes was right all along. This leaves me with egg on my face for not giving him the benefit of the doubt. Now Robertson is making a full English breakfast of it in his editorial."

"Well," replied Knutsford, "Rhodes did agree to compromise on the Battle of Chua story in Mozambique. That saved the King of Portugal and his army a lot of embarrassment and said much for your reputation for diplomacy. He probably thought to himself, 'When I needed a friend or two, the same people I obliged turned their backs on me and chose instead to believe that ugly pipe-smoking Dutchman'. Now it seems that Robertson concurs."

"Now you're rubbing salt in it, Knuttie."

"You can't win them all, Prime Minister."

"True. I'd better be composing a suitable press statement instead of sitting here nattering to you."

Paul Kruger was also sitting in his office with General Viljoen for company. On his desk was a copy of The Argus. Like The Times, the front page was dedicated to the general's perfidious and murderous attempt to annexe Lobengula's kingdom for the Transvaal. There were even the same photographs.

President Kruger cleared his throat. "With regard to your future, General, I'm sorry to say that, for your own good as well as in the interests of the Transvaal, you are going to have to disappear, and quickly, before the press finds you. I know of a remote place where you and your wife can live out your days in peace. Naturally, you will not want for anything. I'm sorry, but this is the price for failure. When you leave here, someone will guide you to this place. We will arrange for your wife to follow in due course. There's no evidence linking this disaster to me, but the British will work it out in the end. I, of course, will deny all knowledge of the affair."

"I have failed you, Oom Paul, and for that I am sorry. Your plan was feasible and it should have worked. Perhaps it was not all in vain. Rhodes still has to convince Lobengula."

"That remains to be seen, but we live in hope," said Kruger.

The two men shook hands one last time and Kruger walked his old friend to the door.

In Nyanyadzi, runners of Beira Grass had been planted two months previously over an area half the size of a football pitch beneath the shade of the *mopani* trees. It had been watered liberally and had grown into a thick green carpet on which tables were laid out in a rectangle. Bunting made from the fallen pods of trees, painted brightly and spiked with guinea fowl feathers were strung between the trees. Off to one side was a pit of hot coals over which an ox was being basted and turned. Alongside was another pit with a cluster of three legged pots containing a variety of stews and curries made of bush meat and wild fowl. Others contained vegetables. Then there was an array of sweet dishes to complete the feast.

Neither had the black work force been forgotten on this day. They would not go hungry or thirsty.

Further back were the wagons and tents of the guests. Behind them, on the second ridge, stood the three newly-built houses overlooking the Nyanyadzi River, the vast plain, and finally the blue mountains in the distance. It was indeed a fitting venue for six people to exchange their marriage vows.

Grievous had been given the task of landscaping the area. He had built a jetty ten yards out from the river bank, complete with safety railings from which hung woven baskets containing a selection of wild shrubs and plants, while the decking was strewn with delicate bush flowers.

Here, a smiling Dr Leander Starr Jameson stood with a prayer book under his arm, facing three nervous grooms – Van Zyl, Wood-Gush, Grieve – waiting expectantly for the arrival of their respective brides. The guests looked on from the bank.

Pat had been puzzled by muted laughter as the three grooms filed past the congregation to make their way onto the jetty. Dr Jim tapped his shoulder and asked him to turn round. Even more puzzled, Pat obliged. Dr Jim reached down and unpinned something from the tails of his coat. The muted laughter from the onlookers became a roar as the doctor handed Pat a sheet of paper on which was printed, 'CHEATS AT BOK-BOK'. At last Brian had his revenge.

There was the sound of many African drums, joined by a chorus of harmony, male and female. The three women appeared, all radiant as only brides can be on their wedding day. They were in white in contrast to the surrounding scenery. Behind them walked a young black boy, dressed like the grooms.

As the procession passed, a lady guest was heard to say to her neighbour, "I wonder who that little chap is?"

Her friend replied, "Why, that's Siyakonza's son!"

"Who's Siyakonza?"

The man smiled. "It's a long story, my dear. Remind me later and I'll tell you."

Printed in Great Britain
by Amazon